BLUE STAR TATTOO

A RANGER SAM BURRACK WESTERN ADVENTURE

BLUE STAR TATTOO

RALPH COTTON

WHEELER PUBLISHING
A part of Gale, Cengage Learning

GALE
CENGAGE Learning·

Farmington Hills, Mich • San Francisco • New York • Waterville, Maine
Meriden, Conn • Mason, Ohio • Chicago

GALE
CENGAGE Learning

LIBRARY OF CONGRESS CATALOGING-IN-PUBLICATION DATA

Names: Cotton, Ralph W., author.
Title: Blue star tattoo / by Ralph Cotton.
Description: Large print edition. | Waterville, Maine : Wheeler Publishing, 2017. | Series: Wheeler Publishing large print western | Series: A Ranger Sam Burrack western adventure
Identifiers: LCCN 2016043640| ISBN 9781410494092 (softcover) | ISBN 1410494098 (softcover)
Subjects: LCSH: Large type books. | GSAFD: Western stories.
Classification: LCC PS3553.O766 B59 2017 | DDC 813/.54—dc23
LC record available at https://lccn.loc.gov/2016043640

Published in 2017 by arrangement with Ralph Cotton

Printed in the United States of America
3 4 5 6 7   21 20 19 18 17

For Mary Lynn . . . of course

PART I

CHAPTER 1

His Christian name was Sam Burrack, but hardly anybody knew it. For years he'd been known simply as the Ranger, and he liked it that way. Most criminals he hunted could be a little thick-witted at times, and should someone come tell them that a man named Sam Burrack stood outside requesting their presence in the middle of some dusty street, they might scratch their heads and wonder why. But on the other hand, should someone come tell them that out in that same dusty street the Ranger stood waiting for them . . . well, they seemed to get the picture right away.

Being known as the Ranger got rid of a lot of unnecessary introductions, he thought, taking his big pistol out of his holster, checking it, cocking it, letting it hang down his thigh. As he glanced around the dirt street, a feeling of uneasiness swept across him, but he shook it off. He wasn't sure what had caused the feeling, but he had no time to wonder about it right now. *Still, what was it? Somebody watching him . . . ?* His eyes made one more quick sweep, then he turned back to the saloon. Of course there were people watching. There were always people watching at a time like this. But this was something different. He felt eyes singling him out from somewhere — eyes that followed him for more personal reasons than mere curiosity.

At the sight of the Ranger's pistol coming up into the sunlight, townspeople along the boardwalk had hastened their pace, some of them ducking into the doors of establishments they'd had no intention of visiting in the first place. From those doorways came the sharp tinkling of bells as the doors slammed shut. And on those dusty settling doors, signs were hastily turned from Open to Closed with the flick of a nervous wrist, and swung back and forth on their thin chains.

"Oh, hell!" A voice called out from a one-horse buggy as the Ranger turned facing the saloon, forty feet away. The buggy shuddered to a halt. Both the driver and his female passenger lunged forward. The woman's hand snapped down atop her lace-trimmed hat to keep it from flying off her

head, and the driver cut a quick turn in a rise of dust and sped the rig into an alley that led nowhere but straight back to the town dump.

"Earl, for God sakes!" the woman cried out as the buggy skidded to a halt again, this time facing a pile of broken whiskey bottles, discarded furniture, and other, more dark and rancid substance of refuse. A lank red dog raised its head, a scrap of something hanging from its jaws. Flies swirled. The dog crouched on its front paws and growled in menacing warning at the buggy as the buggy horse settled, shook out its mane, and stomped the ground.

"That's him, Martha!" The driver righted himself on the buggy seat and looked back wide-eyed. "I swear it's him! It's the Ranger!"

In the street, the Ranger spread his feet at shoulder width beneath him and thumbed his dusty gray sombrero higher up on his forehead. A hot breeze licked across the tails of his riding duster. He called out toward the batwing doors of the saloon, "Curtis Roundtree . . . Billy Lee . . . Granddaddy Snake. All three of you come on out here, single file. You know the deal. I've got your names on my list." As he spoke to the saloon doors, he reached a gloved hand inside his

11

duster, took out a folded sheet of paper, shook it loose, and held it out before him, the hot breeze whipping it back and forth. There it was again, he thought, feeling eyes on him from somewhere. *From where? Behind him? Maybe. . . .* The feeling came, then passed.

From inside the saloon a voice called out, "You know what you can do with your list, Ranger!"

"You're pretty cocksure of yourself standing there in the *wide open!*" another voice called out.

"I see both your rifles in your saddle boots," the Ranger said, cutting a glance at the two sweaty horses hitched at the rail fifteen feet away. "You boys are not gunmen. I'm betting neither one of you can hit a barn door with a pistol shot. Now come on out here — it's too hot for all this foolishness."

"Come in and get us," the other voice called out. "I can part your hair any day of the week with this ole Scoffield pistol."

"Aw, come on now, Billy Lee. We both know better than that. Get out here before I change my mind and commence shooting you."

"Maybe he's right, Billy Lee," the other said in a hushed tone.

"Damn it, Curtis! Back me up here," Billy Lee hissed.

Then a third voice, this one low and calmer, called out to the Ranger, "I'm not with these men, Ranger. Don't shoot me . . . I'm coming out."

"Take it real slow. Nice and easy, Granddaddy Snake," the Ranger said. "Keep them hands high and empty."

"Okay. Here I come."

A silence passed on the empty street, and once again the Ranger felt eyes on him from somewhere. After a few seconds when no one came through the doors, the Ranger said, "Well? What's the holdup, Granddaddy?"

"Billy Lee says I cannot leave here, Ranger," Granddaddy Snake said. "He is pointing his pistol at me."

"That's right, Ranger." Billy Lee laughed. "If this old Indian comes out at all, it'll be with a bullet pushing him from behind. Right Curtis?"

"Yeah, you heard him, Ranger," said Curtis Roundtree. "Looks like you've done outfoxed yourself this time. Ole Granddaddy Snake might not have started out with us, but he'll damn sure end up that way."

"Now, Curtis, you don't mean that. You're

letting Billy Lee talk you into this." The Ranger folded his list, put it away, ran his hand down the scar on his cheek and looked around the empty street as if the answer to a puzzle lay somewhere out in the dust. "All either one of you are up for is a short stretch in jail. They feed good in Circle Wells. I often eat there myself. Don't go doing something stupid."

"There's nothing stupid to it. We're cutting our own mark here," Billy Lee said. "Ain't nobody talked nobody into nothing. Curtis and me stick together. Right, Curtis?"

"That's the truth, Ranger," Curtis Roundtree called out.

"I swear, boys." The Ranger let out a breath. "I'm really putting forth a lot of effort not to kill you both. Don't make me change my mind. At least let ole Granddaddy go. He's not up for this kind of play. Are you, Granddaddy?"

"No. I was sick half the winter. Laid up in the high country. Now I come to town to turn myself in . . . and this." He sounded disgusted.

"There — you see, boys? You've got Granddaddy upset. And me too, the longer I stand out here in the sun. You know once I start shooting, there'll be no stopping."

14

Another silence passed as the Ranger heard them whisper back and forth. Then Billy Lee called out in a calmer voice, "Okay, Ranger, we're coming on out. We meant no harm bad-mouthing you and all."

"I understand." The Ranger checked the deserted, dust-blown street again. And again the feeling swept past him, clouding his thoughts like breath on glass — there and gone.

"So, how did you say to do it?" Curtis Roundtree asked, "just pitch our pistols out first? Then come out with our hands raised?"

"Sure, that's as good a way as any," the Ranger said. "Keep it nice and slow, one at a time. We'll manage."

"I never once stole that roan horse," Billy Lee said. "I'll tell you that much right now. That horse had an unnaturally strong attachment to me for some reason. I couldn't shake loose from him. Never stole him, though."

"But all his owners said you did, Billy. Said you kept selling and restealing that horse from here to Missouri. Said it looked like you'd turned stock trader with just that one animal. If they're wrong, the judge will have to say so."

"Hell, there ain't been a judge yet seen

anything my way. I can't get a break."

"Well, maybe this time you will, huh?" The Ranger stepped to the side as one pistol lobbed over the batwing doors and then another. Both pistols landed in the dirt with a soft thud.

"Ever had a horse do you that way, Ranger?" Billy Lee asked as he stepped through the doors with his hands chest high. He stopped on the crusty boardwalk. "He followed me around like a orphan pup all summer long. My left elbow stayed wet from his nose being against it all the time — got to be plumb embarrassing, to tell the truth."

"Yeah, I had a horse like that when I was a kid," the Ranger said. "Turned out he was nearly blind. I believe he followed my scent." He spoke as he gestured Curtis Roundtree out through the doors. Curtis's big belly sagged down over his belt, and a thick mustache mantled his upper lip. "Lift your belly roll, Curtis. Let's make sure nothing's stuck up under there."

Curtis's face reddened. "There's no call to be insulting, Ranger."

"No insult intended," the Ranger said, gesturing with his pistol barrel. "Let's just take a quick look. Who knows, you might've leaned over a pistol somewhere and picked it up by mistake."

Curtis lowered his hands down around his belly, lifted it, then let it drop. "There — satisfied?" He turned an indignant gaze out across the far hills. "All us Roundtrees have been built stout and portly as far back as I can remember."

"I understand," the Ranger said, watching now as Granddaddy Snake walked out on thin bowed legs and stood beside the others. He was small next to big Curtis Roundtree. He looked frail and brittle, with a thick rag tied around his weathered forehead. Long strands of dusty gray plastered themselves across his face in the hot breeze. The Ranger eyed him. "Granddaddy? Do you still carry a pig sticker down your back?"

"Oh . . . I forgot." The old Indian turned around with his hands held high. Part of the knife handle revealed itself between the lower edge of his ragged vest and the cloth tied around his waist.

"Curtis, pluck that knife up with two fingers and pitch it over by the pistols." The Ranger offered a thin smile and shook his head. "I swear, Granddaddy. It's good to see you're still alive and kicking. The court said bring you in, but they never said what for. What did you do over at Circle Wells, anyway?"

Granddaddy Snake turned back around once Curtis had lifted the knife and pitched it to the dirt. "They accuse me of using offensive words to Stella Pierce in public, outside the Blue Horn Saloon."

"Oh?" The Ranger cocked his head slightly. "I can't imagine what words it would take to offend Wet Lip Stella Pierce."

"I know. It was only a made-up charge. But I made the mistake of eating the judge's little dog last winter and —"

"Lord!" Billy Lee cut him off, leaning forward, looking around Curtis Roundtree and down at Granddaddy Snake. "Talk about piss-poor *judgment!"*

"— and they could not think of nothing else to charge me with," Granddaddy Snake finished, tossing Billy Lee a sharp glance. "Those people do not understand the ways of a blanket Indian like me."

"He sure was partial to that little dog. I know that." The Ranger winced and pushed up the brim of his sombrero. "The judge'll go hard on you, Granddaddy. I wished I hadn't caught you, but since you're here you'll have to go back with me. Why'd you do a thing like that?"

"I did not know it was his dog," Granddaddy Snake said. "It was out on the open range . . . I was hungry. Thinking back,

18

perhaps I should have buried the bones."

"By-gawd, I'd *say so!*" Billy Lee chuckled, nudging Curtis Roundtree with his raised elbow, shaking his head. "I hope to hell we go to trial on the same day. You'll take all the sting out of my one-horse show."

"Me, too," Curtis Roundtree said. "My pole-whupping a couple of teamsters is sounding smaller by the minute."

"You're not off the hook, Curtis. The judge takes a narrow view of assault — says it tends to lead a man off in a violent direction."

Curtis Roundtree's eyes widened. "Then he ought to seen the back of my head before I grabbed up a turning pole. Whupping two liquored-up teamsters ain't no light piece of work, I'll tell ya."

"It's still assault," the Ranger said. "You'll have to make it right." The Ranger looked up the street and saw his partner, Maria, pull the jail wagon out of the alley and head toward them.

"Yeah, but Lord have mercy. . . ." Curtis Roundtree shook his head, looking down past his big belly and toeing the dirt on the boardwalk. "I'll go with my *assault charge* any day of the week compared to eating the judge's lap dog. He'll hang this poor old Injun wearing lead boots just to jerk his head off!"

Granddaddy Snake frowned. "I did not know it was someone's pet —"

"*Lord!*" Billy Lee cut in. "I can just see it. Bet you gulled that furry little sucker and peeled it down, it still yapping its fool head off."

"That's enough, Curtis, Billy Lee," the Ranger said. He looked at Granddaddy Snake. "Old customs are hard to break, ain't they, Granddaddy?"

"This is true." Granddaddy Snake sighed, and his eyes took on a faraway look. "I have never been able to grasp the ways of the white man."

"Now then, boys," the Ranger said, taking a step back. "I hate telling you this . . . but you're riding back to Circle Wells on the Misery Express."

"What are you doing driving the jail wagon, Ranger?" Billy Lee jerked his head around and saw the barred wagon coming closer, leaving a low wake of dust behind it.

"The regular driver got off to relieve himself late at night, stepped off the cliff above Jenning's Springs, and broke his neck." Dread and regret flashed through the Ranger's eyes. "So I volunteered for a while. Just to help out."

"Hell," Billy Lee offered, "if I'd known we

20

were riding in that sweat box, you *would've* had to shoot me."

"Then ain't you glad I didn't tell you right away?" The Ranger gestured them further out into the street with his pistol as the jail wagon groaned to a halt. "Come on, now, it won't be all that bad. Four days give or take." He lifted the latch and opened the squeaky barred door. "We got plenty of water, plenty of jerked meat and biscuit fix-ins."

Billy Lee chuckled, stepping up into the wagon. "Yeah, but Granddaddy here wants to know do you have any roasted hound dog, or Airedale . . . maybe a nice leg of —"

Granddaddy Snake seethed, moving toward the wagon.

"Shut up now, Billy Lee." The Ranger pushed him forward. "Don't start in causing trouble. It's too hot for it. Granddaddy eats what he wants to, I reckon." As he spoke, the Ranger cast a wary sidelong glance along the roofline. Nothing was there, yet. . . .

"Our names ain't really on that list of yours, are they, Ranger?" Curtis Roundtree asked, eyeing the Ranger. "You can tell us the truth now."

"Curtis, if your names were *really* on my list, I wouldn't be able to tell you anything along about now." The Ranger helped Granddaddy Snake into the wagon and closed the door.

"That's what I thought," Curtis said, grunting as he hoisted his weight up into the wagon. "I've always heard you'd do a man this way. They say you'll trick a feller . . . sneak up on him, do anything you have to do to get your man."

"Don't go getting bitter, Curtis," the Ranger said. "This ought to suit you a whole lot more than laying dead in the street."

Curtis rolled over on the floor, leaned back against the bars, and let out a puff of breath. Dust swirled. "I reckon we're lucky at that. Heard what you did to ole Montana Red, how you kilt him and allowed some bounty hunter to cleave his head off right out in public. And he was still alive and kicking! Heard you kilt Bent Jackson too, and even kept his horse."

"If Montana Red was still alive, he shoulda said something. I never heard him complain." The Ranger dropped the iron lock through the hasp and snapped it shut. "As far as Bent Jackson's horse, he had no more use for it. Besides, I figure he was a few horses ahead of the game by the time I stopped his clock." He stepped back from the wagon and looked at the three men. "Granddaddy? Are you doing all right in there?"

"I'm all right." The old Indian nodded and gazed out toward the distant hills. Now that the prisoners were behind bars, townsfolk began to venture forth from shadowed doorways and gathered across the dirt street.

The Ranger looked at Maria sitting in the driver's seat of the wagon. "Reckon we best get on out of here before we start drawing a crowd?"

"*Sí.*" She sat with a rifle propped against her thigh, drawing her eyes back and forth along the roofline with a troubled look on her face. "Let's go now. It is not good being out in the street this way."

The Ranger followed her gaze up along the roofline. "Oh? Something bothering you?" He asked already knowing — just wanting to hear her opinion on it. Whatever was bothering Maria was the same thing he'd felt ever since he stepped out into the dirt street, and called out the three names.

She nodded, looking down at him, and said in a quiet voice, "I think we are in someone's gun sights."

"I think you're right. I've been feeling it too." He spoke to her without a looking up or along the darkened alleyway across the street from them, or into any of the countless shadowed places where a person could be in hiding and watching them like a stalking cat. "But I haven't been able to pinpoint it."

She smiled, a stiff smile, just for the benefit of whoever was watching them. "Then why don't we get out of here and get into a better position?"

He returned the smile in the same manner. "Sounds good to me," he agreed and moved around the wagon as he put the key to the iron lock in his vest pocket.

From the window of her rented room above the barbershop, the young woman stood pulling her dress on, over her head and down, smoothing it into place along her body. She looked at the man who sat crouched at the dusty window with the rifle in his hands. "You realize that once you change your mind, that's it? I still get paid the same?"

"Keep quiet," he said, levering a round up into the rifle chamber. He'd been staring down at the street for the past fifteen minutes instead of doing what he came there to do. Okay, that didn't bother her, not as long as he understood she still got paid for her time — her time was all she was really selling here, wasn't it?

"All right." She sighed and shook out her hair, gathered it back and twisted it up off of her neck. A slight sheen of sweat dampened her dress collar. "That will be two dollars. Give it to me now."

"Keep still, whore. You'll get what's coming to you."

She cocked her head to one side, looking at him. He was a young man, yet he had the look of hard traveling and bad whiskey about him. Barely out of his teens, she thought, watching him bowed over the rifle, wiping a shirtsleeve across the front sight. He carried a roll of money in his shirt pocket, and a low-slung holster with a .45 Colt strapped down on his right hip. She'd seen the look of dark intent grow more determined on his face for the past few minutes, and now, moving over closer to him, she said, "Look, this has gone far enough. It's one thing to think about something like this . . . but don't *believe* for one second I'll allow you to shoot him from here. This is *my* room. I still have to *work* in this town."

"I'm warning you." He swung the rifle barrel toward her, his hands tight around the stock, his finger inside the trigger guard.

She froze spreading her hands, then took

a cautious step back. "Take it easy, cowboy. You don't want to do something like this. I don't know what's bothering you, but this is —"

"Keep your mouth shut and stay back." His words sliced toward her. "Don't ever call me *cowboy.* Do I look like a damn cowboy to you?"

It wasn't really a question, and she wasn't about to answer. "Okay! Okay . . ." She stepped back more, frightened now. What if he really did this? Where did it put her? What would the town do to her, being a part of something like this? Or, would it matter what the town thought or did? Would this man let her live, her being a witness? She bit her lower lip, staring at him as he turned and slowly, soundlessly, raised the dusty window an inch, then another. She had to do something! But what?

He raised up enough to slip the rifle barrel out and let it rest in his hand on the windowsill. Down on the street he watched the Ranger start back and around the wagon. One shot, he thought. He was calm, ready for it. Not a hard shot for him, not from up here. They weren't expecting a thing. He lowered his cheek to the rifle stock and settled, letting the Ranger get all the way around the wagon and up onto the seat.

Maybe once he saw the first round slice through the Ranger's head, he would go on and take out the woman too. No problem. They both had it coming, didn't they . . . ?

"Keep looking straight ahead," the Ranger said to Maria. As he settled onto the wooden wagon seat, he slipped his big pistol up out of his holster, cocking. "Something's going on up over the barbershop — the window just opened a little."

"Let me know what you want," Maria said, the reins in her gloved hands, poised.

"I will." The Ranger turned his face to her, smiling, but at the same time not watching her at all. His eyes searched peripherally up above the barbershop and caught the dark glint of the rifle barrel reaching out beneath the raised window. "Go!" he shouted, raising up all at once with his pistol as Maria slapped the reins to the horses' backs.

At the last second, when the Ranger pulled the trigger, he saw the rifle barrel swing up at a ridiculous angle, a blaze of fire streaking out, sending the shot high above the town. Inside the small, hot room, the woman had leaped forward at the instant the young man pulled the trigger. Now she lay atop his arched back, pounding him with her small fists until he managed to throw her off, struggling to lever another round into his rifle chamber. A spray of glass blasted across the room as the Ranger's pistol shot whined his head. *Damn it!* He ducked, then sprang up quick into the shattered window, taking aim at the spot where the wagon had sat only a second ago. Only now the wagon was rumbling away, the three faces of the prisoners pressed against the bars looking back and up at him. Townsfolk scattered like rabbits searching for their holes. In the street, all that remained was the Ranger, standing in the drift of bellowing dust, the open bore of the big pistol still trained on the window.

Before the young man could even flinch or ready himself for it, the Ranger's pistol exploded. The bullet hit him high in his right shoulder, spinning him a half turn on his way backward onto the unmade bed. Behind him the whore screamed. Then she fell upon him even as a spray of his blood stung her face. With a chipped porcelain wash pan drawn back, she swung full circle at arm's length, leaving a ribbon of wash water trailing behind, catching his jaw on its way with the low, pulsing ring of a muted church bell. "You crazy son of a — !" Her hand came back in another wide circle, the heavy wash pan catching the other side of his jaw on its return. *"— bitch!"*

He struggled to keep his consciousness, and did for a moment, even though his thoughts were jumbled, like pebbles bouncing down a steep sloop toward a dark canyon below. Raising the pistol from his holster, he saw not one whore but rather three or four images of her, all of them swirling before him, saying something. They all spoke to him through a shimmering veil.

He had no idea which one to shoot at. All of them were wavering back and forth, the wash pan hovering at shoulder height. But he pulled the trigger and collapsed. And even in doing so, his free hand managed to fall to his throat instinctively, gathering his bandanna up across the small tattoo that showed beneath his sweaty beard stubble. *Damn . . . what have I done?* he asked himself.

CHAPTER 2

The Ranger had already run around the side of the barbershop and started up the wooden stairs when he heard the second pistol shot. He slowed and continued upward, his back against the clapboard wall, his pistol raised, ready. But when he'd reached the top of the stairs and heard no further shots, or noise of any kind, he swung around, kicked the wooden door open and fanned the pistol back and forth. Then he slumped for a second in the doorway, pushed up the brim of the gray sombrero, and let out a breath.

A fly had swept in through the broken window and buzzed in a lazy circle around the face of the young man sprawled unconscious across the blood-soaked bed. The shot from the young man's pistol had picked the woman up and hurled her backward. She sat sideways, slumped dead atop an oak dresser, her face pitched back against the

30

large dusty mirror, which was streaked with her blood. The Ranger noted the battered wash pan still clutched in her right hand as he stepped over to the bed, took the pistol from the young man's hand, and shoved it down in his belt. He moved closer to the woman. He looked at her, then at the bed, then across the room at the shattered window.

"You saved my life, didn't you, child?" He whispered the words to the dead girl, reaching out with his gloved hand, pulling the edge of her dress down to cover her naked thigh. Her glazed, blank eyes stared upward. Her mouth hung open and askew, her rouge-red cheek pressed sidelong against her own reflection — the whore and her image cheek to cheek in dark silent waltz, like an advertising poster for some macabre, ribald theater.

"Sam?" He heard Maria say his name as she ascended the stairs and stepped inside the room. "This one is alive." But the Ranger didn't answer right away. He saw Maria's reflection step into the mirror, behind him, off to the side, and he pressed a gloved hand to the dead girl's cheek for just a second, then took a step back and turned to face the bed. Maria stood with her rifle out across her arm. She poked the tip of the barrel against the man's ribs, not hard, but just enough to cause him to stir with a slight groan.

"So he is." The Ranger reached down, took the young man by his hair, and shook his head back and forth until the man let out a longer moan and batted his eyes. Wet blood circled his shoulder wound. "Let's get him patched him up and healthy," the Ranger said. "He'll hang for this. I want him wide awake . . . not missing a single minute of it."

The sound of heavy footsteps came up the wooden stairs. Maria turned her rifle toward the man in the black linen suit as he rushed into the room and came to a quick halt. His black necktie swung up onto one shoulder and stayed there. "Whooa!" His eyes flew wide open at the sight of the rifle pointed at him. He held his hands chest high in a show of peace and gestured downward with his heavy chin toward the battered sheriff's badge on his chest. "Easy, ma'am! Sheriff Martin Petty here. Just got back and heard the shooting."

He spoke quickly, turning his eyes from Maria to the Ranger. "I know who you are . . . you're the Ranger, right?" He kept his hands up high, trembling a bit until the Ranger relaxed his gun hand and shoved the big pistol into its holster. "I've always wanted to meet you . . . heard a lot of things — that is, really *good things* — about you." He nodded toward the man on the bed, still speaking to the Ranger. "I knew that one was trouble, knew it the minute he rode in. Never should have let him stayed here. Just wish I coulda been here, been some kind of help to you —"

"Why did you, then?" The Ranger cut him off.

"Why did I what?" Sheriff Petty glanced back and forth between the two of them, Maria's rifle lowered only an inch and was still pointed at his chest.

"Why did you let him stay, if you knew he was trouble?" The Ranger pushed up the brim of his sombrero.

"Well, I — I mean. . . ." Petty shrugged his heavy shoulders, raised one nervous hand and pulled the necktie down off his shoulder. "He hadn't done anything, him or his partner . . . I couldn't just ride rough-shod over them."

"No, I suppose not," the Ranger said. "What's this boy's name?"

"He wasn't real keen on telling me," the sheriff said. "Told me everybody calls him Mac."

"Mac, huh?" The Ranger shook his head,

looking at the young man on the dirty blood-soaked mattress. "You say he has a partner? Where is he?"

The sheriff relaxed a little, seeing Maria turn the rifle away from him. She stepped over and looked down on the street through the broken window. "Oh," he said, "the other one skinned out of here. Joe the blacksmith said he came in, grabbed his horse, and got going once he saw you call them boys out of the saloon." He thumbed toward the broken window. "Joe's down there now, watching over your jail wagon. I asked him to. Figured it was the least we could do for you."

Maria looked back at him from the window, cocking her head to one side. "Where were you when this was happening?"

Sheriff Petty's big face reddened. "Ma'am, I was watching from my office window, to be honest with ya." He shrugged toward the Ranger with a pleading expression. "Only been sheriffing here a couple of months. I always heard when you're working your list, it's best to just stay out of your way. Was I wrong in doing that?"

"No. You did the right thing, Sheriff Petty," the Ranger said. "There wasn't a town sheriff here, last time I came through. If I'd known they had a new one, I would

34

have came to you first. But I wasn't working my list. We just came here to pick up three boys the judge has been holding warrants on."

"I know that now, but I didn't know it at the time," the sheriff said. He raised a hand and rounded a finger back and forth under his damp shirt collar, needing to loosen it. "Can I let my hands down?"

"Don't know why you had them raised in the first place." The Ranger smiled a thin smile and moved around beside the bed, pulled the young man up into a sitting position, then on up to his feet. Blood flowed freely from his wound. The man groaned and wobbled in place, his head down as if in prayer.

"Want to give me a hand with this one, Sheriff? We'll send the undertaker over for her."

"Sure! Of course, of course!" Sheriff Petty snapped forward, nervous, eager to help.

"Who is she anyway?" The Ranger glanced over at the dead girl as he looped the young man's arm over his shoulder.

"Oh, just some young whore, called herself Polly something or other — probably not her *real* name, though. You know how whores are."

The Ranger stopped and looked at him as

35

they started toward the door with the young man hanging between them. "Whatever her *real* name was, she saved my life, Sheriff."

Down on the street, the gathered townsfolk stepped back away from the boardwalk as the Ranger and Sheriff Petty led the wounded man toward the doctor's office, where a gray-bearded doctor stood out front with the door standing open behind him. He watched them coming and rolled up the sleeves on his wrinkled white shirt. In the jail wagon, Billy Lee and Curtis Roundtree stood holding the bars with both hands, their faces pressed forward. Granddaddy Snake still sat on the floor, his bony arms wrapped around his knees.

"That's the ticket, Ranger!" Billy Lee yelled. Then he turned a proud face to the crowd. "See that, folks? He burnt that sucker down! That's our Ranger! That's the man what took us prisoner!" He swung his grinning face back to the Ranger and added in form of a cheer, "Way to go, Ranger!"

"Shut up, Billy Lee," Maria said, parting the crowd away from the wagon. "Both of you sit down." She turned to a big man wearing a leather blacksmith apron who stood beside the wagon. "You can go now . . . thank you for your help."

"Whew, that's a load off my mind," the blacksmith replied, wiping his forehead with a thick hand. "These kind of people make me nervous."

"Oh?" Curtis Roundtree frowned at him through the bars. "I didn't make you nervous when I cleaned all your stalls and curried all the horses for you. What about that four dollars you owe me?"

"Don't worry, Curtis," the blacksmith said. "Your money'll be waiting for you."

"Waiting for me? I need it now — you see the fix I'm in." Curtis gripped the bars furiously.

"I don't have it on me right now, Curtis." The blacksmith shot a glance at Billy Lee and Curtis Roundtree, then ducked his eyes and left.

"That's right, get on out of here — you big ole chiseler!" Billy Lee said as the blacksmith moved away through the crowd, which was now drifting toward the doctor's office. Billy chuckled and turned back to Maria, pressing his face between the bars. "Looks like the Ranger popped that boy pretty good. I'll lay you five dollars to one that sucker dies on the cutting table. What do you say, ma'am? Trust my credit?"

"If she does, there's a big yellow bird gonna swing down playing a banjo," Curtis

Roundtree chuckled.

"I told you two to sit down and shut up." Maria glared at them, the rifle still in her gloved hands.

"Okay, okay! Dang!" Billy Lee raised his hands, and he and Curtis Roundtree sank to the floor. "Can't a feller just make a comment? What about my rights? Freedom of speech and all that stuff?"

"Give it a rest, Billy Lee." Maria lowered her rifle and tipped up the wide brim of her Stetson. "You could both learn some manners from Granddaddy Snake. Right, Granddaddy?" She looked at the old Indian and smiled.

"I'm all manners," Granddaddy Snake said in a low voice.

Curtis Roundtree asked in a more serious tone, "What was that second shot, ma'am, if you don't mind me asking?"

Maria answered without looking at him. "There was a young woman in the room. The man killed her."

"Oh, Lord God, please don't let it be Polly," Curtis Roundtree said, lifting his eyes skyward.

"*Sí*, her name was Polly." Maria turned to face them through the bars. "You knew her?"

"Nope," Curtis Roundtree said, "but I

would have, soon as that blacksmith paid me my money. Met a couple of cowboys on the trail up from Humbly, they said she was the best little thumper this side of —"

"That's enough." Maria cut him off. "Show some respect for the dead."

"Well, I didn't mean it to be disrespectful." Curtis scratched his dirty head.

"Only a lowdown craven coward would shoot a woman, whore or otherwise," Billy Lee said. He folded his fingers together and popped his knuckles. "Hope that sucker lives a while longer. Maybe then he'll ride back with us in this misery wagon."

"If he does, you will keep your hands to yourself." Maria glared at him.

"Why, yes, ma'am. Of course we will." Billy Lee grinned, speaking in a mock tone. "Won't we, Curtis?"

"Don't go starting trouble for us, Billy Lee," Curtis Roundtree said. Then he turned back to Maria. "Pay no mind to Billy Lee, ma'am. He just likes to blow off some. We don't want no more trouble than we've got already."

"Yeah? Says you," Billy Lee grumbled, and turned away.

In the back room of the doctor's office, the Ranger and Sheriff Petty stood back as the old doctor cut away the young man's bloody shirt and peeled it off the wounded shoulder. He started to bend over his patient, but then he stopped and looked back at the two lawmen watching him. "Why don't you both get out of here? Fix yourselves some coffee or something. This boy isn't going anywhere."

"We need to be in here with the prisoner, don't we?" Sheriff Petty looked at the Ranger for advice.

"Come on, let's fix some coffee," the Ranger motioned to Petty. As he turned the doorknob, he said to the doctor, "We'll be right outside the door if you need us for anything."

"Don't know what the hell I'd need yas for," the old doctor grumbled. "Looks like you've done plenty already." With a bloody finger he adjusted his wire-rim spectacles up on the bridge of his nose and turned back to the young man's open wound.

When the Ranger had fixed a pot of coffee on a small woodstove, he poured some for himself and Sheriff Petty and carried the cups to Petty who stood near the door to the operating room. Petty took the hot cup with both hands and blew on it, thanking the Ranger. "I swear, Ranger, I don't know if I'm cut out for this kind of work or not. Seems like there's never a point where

I can just relax for a minute and not wonder what's getting ready to happen next."

The Ranger sipped his coffee and looked Petty up and down. "Two months, huh?"

"Yep, and it's been the longest, most unpredictable two months of my whole life. First day on the job, a cowboy came riding in with two other cowboys chasing him — had a kindling hatchet stuck in his leg three inches deep. Said one of them hit him with it over a card game that happened last year! Can you believe that? I'm standing out there with a shotgun having to keep them from killing him, and he's cussing them with every breath."

The Ranger chuckled. "But you worked it out, I reckon? You're still all in one piece?"

"Yeah." Petty smiled a sheepish smile. "I can count myself lucky for that."

"Give it some time, Sheriff," the Ranger said, swirling his coffee in the cup, studying it. "It takes a little while to get the hang of law work . . . especially when you're sheriffing in a town."

Petty sipped his hot coffee and ran a hand across his sweaty forehead. "They say you won't work a town, Ranger. They say you do most of your work out in the bad-lands. . . ." Petty let his words trail off looking for an answer in the Ranger's eyes.

"It's a matter of personal preference I developed over the years, Sheriff," the Ranger said. "I do better out there hunting the ones the towns can't handle. I don't have to fool with settling disputes or making a man abide by the law. By the time a man gets his name on my list, he's long past any legal authority. He's gone beyond what decency allows. He's decided that man's law doesn't fit him and he'll have no part of it in any way." The Ranger offered a thin smile. "It makes things simple for him and me both. I don't have to wonder if a man can be rehabilitated, and he doesn't have to wonder if he wants to live or die. By the time he faces me, out there, all questions are answered. My job is to put him down."

"And you just shoot him? Just like that? No hesitation? No doubts?" Petty rubbed his chin. "I — I don't know if I could do that. Truth is, I've never even shot a man, let alone killed one."

"Doubt is what gets you killed in this business, Sheriff," the Ranger said. "If you have any *doubt* whether or not you'll put a bullet through a person, you'd best lay down the *badge* before the badge lays *you* down."

"Well . . . I like to think that if the time ever comes and I need to use my gun to save innocent people from —"

"Huh-uh." The Ranger cut him off, shaking his head. "Don't like to think what you might do. Settle it now, up here." He tapped a finger to his temple beneath the brim of his sombrero. "Know for certain what you'll do . . . because it ain't a matter of *if the time ever comes.* It'll come. A man wears a badge and carries a gun, he better recognize a killing side of himself. If he doesn't see it in himself, he'll sure see it in the man he faces. Nobody levels a gun sight at a lawman unless they mean to kill him. They are dead serious . . . you better be too."

Petty's face reddened a bit, and he sipped his coffee and turned his eyes away from the Ranger. "But surely, Ranger . . . I mean, I saw how friendly you were out there with those three men. It sounded more like you were talking to ole friends. You seemed pretty relaxed."

"Only once their guns hit the ground," the Ranger said. "Besides, these aren't the type I'm usually hunting — these are your hard-luck drifters, doing whatever they can do to get by. They're not killers. They talked a little tough at first, but you saw how they folded when I let them know they could die out there. They knew I'd kill them . . . they didn't want to die."

Sheriff Petty studied the Ranger's eyes,

seeing a dark resolve there. Something peaceful in a strange sort of way, something admirable, perhaps enviable, after all the torment this sheriff job had caused him. "If it's not too personal . . . how long did it take you to work all this out? I mean, you didn't always feel this way. How did it come about?"

The Ranger shook his head slowly, gazing down into his coffee cup. "I have no idea. It comes to you though, over time, if you're truly cut out to be a lawman. The hardest time is where you're at right now. You're just not sure of yourself yet. You haven't faced any deciding test. Once that comes you'll see whether you belong here or not."

"If I live through, it you mean."

"That's one factor," the Ranger said.

Sheriff Petty started to ask the Ranger something else, but the door behind them swung open and the doctor stood facing them with bloody hands. "You can come in now. He's starting to stir a little. Lucky for him the bullet went all the way through. Get a big-caliber bullet like that lodged in a shoulder bone, I might have had to cut out enough bone to carve a cane handle." He grinned, looking tired and drained. "I always said if you boys had to do the cutting and patching yourselves you'd be a little hesitant about pulling iron on one another."

"I pull it when it needs pulling, Doctor," the Ranger responded, stepping past him. "If I hadn't, you mighta been cutting bone out of me or my partner."

At the surgery table, the young man batted his eyes and looked up at the Ranger, who stood over him. He groaned and tried to turn his face away, but the Ranger turned his face back with a gloved hand. "Looking away isn't gonna change what you did. Why'd you do it? Who are you?" He turned the young man's face loose and looked at the bandages around his shoulder, the bands of gauze reaching over and around his neck, covering the tattoo.

"I didn't mean to kill her, Ranger. She meant nothing to me." The young man summoned the strength to glare at him, his eyes looking as hard as darts. A thin sheen of sweat glistened on his brow, plastering hair in dark curls. "I meant to kill *you.* Just you. And I *still* mean to, first chance I get."

"Then I'll just have to see you don't get a chance," the Ranger said, glaring right back at him. "What's your name, boy? I've never seen you before."

"Where's the man I was riding with?" The young man tightened his jaw, wincing a bit from the pain in his shoulder.

"I asked your name," the Ranger said, standing firm. He noted that the young man hadn't asked *where's my pal, or my partner . . . only the man I was riding with. Interesting,* the Ranger thought. "He's gone," the Ranger said, taking another approach when the young man refused to give his name. "Evidently he didn't share your views on bushwhacking me from a window?" He raised his eyebrow. "Looks like he left you to take the fall on your own. Need to pick your friends more wisely." He watched the man's eyes for a response. There was none. A hard knot, this one.

"He knew what he was doing. I didn't need no help. Didn't need it then . . . won't need it next time."

The Ranger leaned closer. "You're gonna hang, young man. Unless we meet in some great hereafter, your *next time* is swinging in the air. What's your name? Don't think your not going to tell me just because you've got a bullet hole in your shoulder. Every time I see that dead girl's face, it's all I can do not to crack a pistol barrel over your —"

"Now see here, Ranger!" The doctor stepped in, started to grab the Ranger's arm. But at the look in his eyes, he thought better of it and backed off. "This man might be just another murderer to you, to me he's

46

a *patient*! As long as he's here there'll be no —"

The Ranger cut the doctor off with a raised hand. Sheriff Petty nervously fidgeted his way to the far side of the room. "Step easy, Doc," the Ranger warned. "You rubbed me wrong when I came through the door. There's a girl laying dead because of this piece of punkwood. Looked like she died saving my life out there. I'll *have* this man's name if I have to choke it loose from him." He reached down toward the young man's throat.

"It's Mac . . . Mac McKenzie!" The young man spoke quickly, his voice weak but getting stronger, hurrying. "Everybody calls me Mac!"

"Mac McKenzie, huh?" The Ranger eased down a bit. "If that's your name, it's *mine* too." He dealt him a hard stare. "But let's go with it for the time being. Now what's your friend's name, the one who cut out on you?"

"He's no friend of mine. He's just —" Something passed across the young man's eyes. He stalled for a split second, then said. "It's uh, Andrews. Charlie Andrews."

"Oh." The Ranger nodded, not believing a word. "Spell it."

"Spell it? Hell I can't spell it. I hardly

47

knew him."

"Then spell *McKenzie,*" the Ranger said in a quick snap.

The young man stalled, looking lost.

"Never mind," the Ranger said. A pair of handcuffs flashed out of his hip pocket. He snapped one cuff around the man's right wrist and took a step back. "We'll talk after you've had some time to think about that rope squeezing around your neck. Maybe it'll help you remember some things."

"Handcuffs are hardly necessary, Ranger," the doctor said, "This boy is in no shape to try anything foolish. I demand you take those off him at once."

"He already tried something *foolish,*" the Ranger said, moving to the end of the surgery table, near the young man's feet. He reached out as he spoke, loosened the man's right boot, and yanked on it.

"For God's sake!" the doctor said, stepping toward him. "He needs rest. Leave him be. I'll do that later. You two go on . . . you're only upsetting him."

The dusty boot came off in the Ranger's hands. "Damn you," the young man groaned.

"Later?" The Ranger glared at him. Palming a two shot derringer from inside the boot, the Ranger tossed it to the startled

48

doctor. "How much later?" He took the key to the handcuffs from his vest pocket and held it up for a second. "You use your best judgment, Doc." He pitched the doctor the key. "Set him free if the spirit moves you. We'll go get something to eat, then come back and clean up whatever's left of you."

The doctor stood stunned, looking down at the key and the derringer in his hand.

"My gosh, Ranger!" Sheriff Petty said, moving closer, his breath a bit flat. "How did you know?"

The Ranger yanked off the young man's other boot and let it fall to the floor. "Like I said, Sheriff, it comes to you. It just takes time."

"But how did you know?" Petty asked again, staring at the raw dirty toe sticking out through a hole in the sock.

"I didn't," the Ranger said, a harsh, bemused expression coming into his eyes. "That's why I yanked his boot off."

CHAPTER 3

On the way across the dirt street to the jail wagon, the Ranger and Sheriff Petty saw two men carrying the dead girl away on a bloodstained canvas gurney toward the town funeral parlor. Inside the jail wagon, Curtis Roundtree and Billy Lee stood up with their battered hats held against their chests. "I say a man does something like that, he don't deserve no trail, no nothing," Billy Lee called out as the two lawmen came closer. "Hang him right here and now and be done with it. What do you say, Ranger?"

"I say sit down and keep your mouth shut, Billy Lee. You're already wearing out your welcome with me."

Billy Lee grinned. "Does that mean you're gonna ask me to leave if I ain't careful? Gonna run me away . . . I got to miss out on all this hospitality?"

The Ranger and Sheriff Petty walked past the rear of the wagon to where Maria stood with her rifle cradled in her arms. "What did you find out?" she asked.

"Nothing." The Ranger looked up and down the street. The town already getting back to normal, with only a few people still lingering along the boardwalks. "He's got something stuck in his craw. I'll just have to wait a while to find out what it is. I left him handcuffed to the surgery table." He looked at Maria and gave a wry grin. "Said his name is Mac McKenzie. Said everybody calls him Mac."

"Sure it is," Maria nodded.

"Well . . . that *is* what the other fellow called him," Sheriff Petty said. The Ranger and Maria both stared at him. He looked embarrassed and shrugged. "I'm just saying. . . ."

"Looks like we'll need to use your jail for a little while, Sheriff," the Ranger said, letting Sheriff Petty off the hook. "The territorial court pays fifty cents a day per prisoner, to cover your cost. It could be two or three days before we're able to leave. I want that boy to be in traveling shape."

"You're taking him back with you?" the sheriff asked. "You can leave him here if you want. We'll see he gets a fair trial and what's coming to him."

"If it's all the same, I'd sooner take him

with us," the Ranger said. "He's got something to tell me, but it's going to take a while coming out."

"Yes, of course, it's all the same with me. Just thought I ought to make the offer." The sheriff looked relieved. "In fact, you taking him with you is a load off my mind. We've got an empty jail right now. Putting these boys up for a few days is no problem. But I'd prefer no part in a trial and a hanging right now, if I can keep from it." He turned as he spoke, looking the prisoners over.

"Hope you've got plenty of fried chicken on hand, Sheriff," Billy Lee said, grinning. "I'm an ole Southern boy. Got to have that *fried chicken* fairly regular or else I get the weak staggers. Gravy twice a day wouldn't hurt nothing either."

The Ranger turned to Maria. "I'm going to track that other man a little ways, see where his trail's headed. Shouldn't be gone over a couple of hours. You going to be all right here?"

"*Sí,* of course." She looked at the prisoners in the wagon. Curtis and Billy Lee sat grinning at her. Granddaddy Snake sat staring off into the distance.

Sheriff Petty asked, "Do you suppose I could ride out with you, I mean, since you're not going very far? I've never tracked anybody. It might come in helpful some-time."

The Ranger looked at Maria. She nod-ded. "Take him along. I'll take care of everything here."

"I better warn you about this doctor," the Ranger said to her. "He's one of those kind that seems to think things like guns and handcuffs are unnecessary." He smiled. "So don't fly off and shoot him. He'd never let you live it down."

"I'll try not." Maria took the key from her trouser pocket and unlocked the jail wagon. "Once we get these men locked down, I'll go see about the other one. Give me the key to his handcuffs."

The Ranger brought out a key from his hip pocket. Sheriff Petty looked at it. "But, I thought . . . ?"

"I know what you thought," the Ranger grinned. "I wanted to let the good doctor see how liberal he is when the key's in his hand. But there's no way I'd give him the *right* key."

"You gave him a *key?*" Maria shot him a curious glance.

"Yep, an old one I've been carrying around. After I took a gun from our *Mr. McKenzie's* boot, I figured we'd give the doctor something to think about for a while." He grinned. "Let him do a little moral tail-chasing on himself. By now that key weighs forty pounds and getting heavier every minute. Don't worry though . . . the doctor ain't going to get near that boy now until one of us is there with him. We'll check on him before I leave."

"*Sí,* and I will sit with him after we get these three put away."

"I better warn you of something too," Billy Lee said, stepping down as Maria swung the barred door open. "I'm quite a silver-tongued devil with the ladies. If her and me ain't here when you get back, don't hold it against me, Ranger." He stretched and grinned and let out a sigh, pressing a hand to the small of his back. "It's something I have no control over . . . women just draw to me like lint to a black wool suit."

Maria shoved him forward with her rifle butt.

Nearly an hour had passed by the time they'd gotten the prisoners locked down. The Ranger had picked out a horse at the livery barn and saddled it with an old range saddle and led it back to the sheriff's office, where Petty stood beside his own big bay gelding with a rifle in his hand. "Think she'll be all right over there?" He nodded toward the doctor's office across the street.

"She's all right anywhere she goes, Sheriff," the Ranger said. "Are you going to be all right out there?"

"Sure, I'm fine. You said a couple of hours, right?"

"Right — but you never know what you might run into." The Ranger stepped up into the worn saddle and adjusted his legs and seat to it. "Are you ready?"

Sheriff Petty hesitated for a second, then caught himself and said, "Uh, yeah, sure. But you don't think we will, do you?"

"Will what?"

"Run into any trouble out there?" He nodded out into the distance, into the swirling heat. "Not that I'm afraid, just that I'd like to know what to expect."

"Wouldn't we all." The Ranger allowed a thin smile and shook his head, then turned his horse in the street and put it forward with a tap of his heels.

The horse and its shadow moved across the sand flats connected at the hooves, the rider pushing it hard, looking back now and again, as he had ever since he'd spurred the little dun out of town. This was not the kind of weather to be running a horse this hard, and Lloyd Percy knew it. But he also knew who that was he'd seen standing in the middle of the dusty street. It was the crazy Ranger everybody talked about, and he wanted no part of him. When Bobby McLawry said he was going to kill the Ranger, Lloyd tried to talk sense to him. Bobby wouldn't listen.

Then to hell with him, Lloyd Percy thought. He kept the little dun horse stretched out beneath him, white froth streaking back from the horse's mouth, until he slowed enough to round upward into the shade of rock where some of the gang waited for him. At a fork in the trail, Percy checked the tired horse down and looked all around for any sign of the others. At first he saw nothing, scanning along the higher ridge line, sunlight shining white and hot in his eyes. Then, when he did see them, he saw the four of them all at once. They sprang up to their feet as one from within the cover of rocks. The dun horse shied back a step and swung in a circle beneath him.

"Damn it, Becker," Lloyd Percy called out to one of them as he settled the nervous dun. "Can't you see it's me? Don't spook my horse! I've run him near to death getting here!"

Becker flashed a harsh smile across a mouthful of big white teeth. "Don't soil yourself, Percy. We see it's you." He moved forward, two of the others beside him, the fourth man moving off into the rocks to gather their horses. "Where's Bobby?"

"Oh man. . . ." Lloyd Percy shook his head, climbing down from the winded dun. "Bobby went nuts, is all I can tell you. He's back in town. Don't know if he's dead or alive . . . but dead is my best hunch, seeing who he was about to throw down on."

"Yeah? Who was it?" Becker squinted in the sunlight, the three of them encircling Lloyd Percy, the fourth man coming forward now out of the taller rocks with their horses in tow behind him.

"That blasted Ranger," Percy said, looking around at each of them in turn. "The one JC's always carrying on about . . . the one who killed Montana Red and Bent Jackson." He studied their eyes for a response. They all just looked at him, unimpressed.

Becker cocked his head to one side, his right hand resting down on the pistol at his hip. "And you left Bobby there? Alone? To face that killing son of a bitch?"

"What was I supposed to do . . . tip our hand? Make sure the whole town got a good look at our faces? Give everybody an idea what we're about to do? Boys, *I rob banks,* I don't stir up gunfights, especially with the likes of the Ranger. Now you've got to

57

understand that."

"It ain't *us* that's got to, it's JC," Becker said, the unpleasant smile returning to his face. "What do you suppose he's gonna do when you tell him how you left his kid brother there?" He chuckled, looking at the others for a second, then back at Lloyd Percy. "Lloyd, I hope you ain't stupid enough to think JC won't kill you over this."

"See? That's the problem with this bunch." Lloyd Percy looked worried. "Least little thing goes wrong, JC's ready to kill somebody over it. I've rode with more gangs than you've got fingers and toes, Becker. Hell, I would've rode with the James brothers except I got there late 'cause my damn watch was broke."

"We've all heard that story," Becker chuckled.

"Well, it's the truth!" Percy sweated. "I'm telling you this ain't the way men are supposed to act. Men are supposed to stick together, not fly off and blame one man for another's shortcomings! Why'd JC stick me with looking after his brother? Make me responsible, when he knows that boy's a flat-out idiot." As he spoke he looked around from one to the other, trying to gather support. "Am I right? Bud? Dewey? Stinson? Somebody say something!" He spread his hands toward them like a preacher for an alter call. They all just stared at him.

"Well, as you see, Percy," Becker said, "nobody is greatly moved by your little speech. I don't know what went on in that town, but it'll be fun listening to you explain it all to JC. Meanwhile, it'd probably be best if you let us hold onto your gun. Nervous as you are, we wouldn't want it to go off, maybe blow a hole in your foot." He grinned, his big teeth shining.

"I'll be damned." Lloyd Percy slumped, raised his pistol with a whipped look in his eyes and passed it to Hank Becker. "If I'd thought you all wouldn't listen to reason, I'd never came back. I did my job scouting out the bank. This is the thanks I get?"

"Lloyd's right," Becker said. He turned to the others. "All right, boys, let's all join in, thank Lloyd here for a job well done."

The three other men nodded and milled and thanked him under their breath. "Way to go, Lloyd," said one. "Heck of a job," said another. Then Becker leaned close to Lloyd Percy's face, grinning darkly. "There, see how much we appreciate what you done? Now get your scared-to-death ass on that horse and keep your mouth shut. If ever I meet the James boys, I'll be sure and tell ole Frank and Jesse why you was late meeting them that time."

Twenty miles back along the high trail, the Ranger and Sheriff Petty dismounted and looked out across the sand flats below. The Ranger took a pair of binoculars, wiped the lens on his shirtsleeve, and focused them down onto the long line of hoofprints leading across the sand. "I never knew this was the way to track somebody," Sheriff Petty said beside him as the Ranger scanned forward to where the trail dropped out of sight over a distant rise.

"I've been ambushed once today," the Ranger said, the binoculars still up to his eyes. "More than one ambush a day, it'll start looking like I *want* it to happen." He lowered the lens and rubbed his eyes for a second. "Besides, all we're doing is getting an idea where he's headed. For all we know he's an innocent man. Might have seen he was traveling with the wrong person and figured this was the time to go. Either way, we can see just as much from up here and make a little better time as well. There's water ahead, about seven miles past this stretch of ridges. We'll trail him that far, then head back. Sound good to you?"

"Sounds fine to me," Petty said. "I'm boiling in my own sweat, like a pig on a stick." He wiped his face and neck with a bandanna and stuffed it inside his pocket. "I don't see how you stand this heat all the time. No wonder they say. . . ." His words trailed off and he caught himself and looked away across the sand flats below.

"What? That I'm crazy?" The Ranger eyed him as he stood up and put the binoculars into their worn leather case. "You needn't be embarrassed. I've heard it said before. Who knows, maybe they're right. Maybe it's takes a certain amount of crazy to get anything done out here."

Petty stood up, too, and dusted the seat of his trousers. "I meant no offense, Ranger."

"None taken." The Ranger stepped up into the saddle and backed the horse a step.

"That just sort of slipped out," Petty said, taking up his reins and mounting his big bay gelding. "This heat must be getting to me more than I thought."

They rode on, moving at a steady pace along the high trail, taking whatever long stripes of shade came to them among tall stems of wind-sculpted rock. They didn't speak for a while until they reached a place where the higher ground ended, down in a sloop toward the sand flats. "Down there," the Ranger said, pointing with a gloved finger. Halfway down the sloop a small pool of runoff water stood on a terrace of rock half hidden by a protruding overhang.

"About time," Petty said under his breath; and they moved down, each of them keeping watch on the dark slices of shadowed cover where a man might lie in wait to kill another along this switchback trail.

"There's the story," the Ranger said, moving his horse close to the water, pointing down at the sets of hoofprints crisscrossing in the dust. His hand followed the single set of tracks that came up off a thin trail and joined the others a few yards down. "He met four riders right down there. They came here, watered their horses, and moved on, west toward the border. Can you see it, Sheriff?"

"Yep, I see it now," Petty said after a second of studying the hoofprints on the ground. His eyes followed them off and down the sloop until they disappeared from sight. "What do you figure they were doing out here? A few cowhands meeting here?"

"No, that's not likely. Always assume the worst out here, Sheriff. This is the badlands."

They both stepped down from their saddles. The Ranger lifted his canteen strap from around his saddle horn, loosened the cinch on the dun horse and led the horse to the edge of the water. "The way I see it, two men rode into your town. The others waited here for them. I figure they were sniffing out your new bank. Getting ready to make a raid on it."

"We don't have much money on hand yet," Petty said, letting his horse stand beside the Ranger's, both horses drawing deep on the pool of water while the men stooped to fill their canteens.

"They didn't know that," the Ranger said. "That's why they sent two scouts in first." He smiled, remaining patient.

"You don't figure they might have been out to kill you from the start? You're bound to have plenty of enemies, from what I hear."

"Naw, they had no idea I was coming to town, especially in a jail wagon. If they did, why send just two men? It was the bank. You can trust that."

"Then I have to worry about them coming back." He blew out a tired puff of breath. "I swear. If it ain't one thing it's another."

"They won't be hitting the bank anyways soon — not after what happened. They've got to wonder if you're onto them now. They'll steer clear of the bank for a while. Whoever's in charge can't be too happy, hearing how that boy blew the deal." The

Ranger raised his full canteen, capped it, and stood up, looking down toward the sand flats.

"What's our next move?" Petty stood up beside him. "It wouldn't do to go after them. We've got nothing to charge them on. We could be wrong anyway — chase them down and then just find out they're prospectors, cattlemen, or some such thing. They could be, you know."

"Yeah. And they *could* be Mormons, gathering here for evening prayer," the Ranger said. "But don't count on it. These boys are robbers, you can bet your badge."

Petty shrugged. "Then what do we do now?"

"Now we do the only thing we can. We go back to town. I take my prisoners on to Circle Wells, you go back to keeping the peace. It's their move now."

"See, that's the part that's so nerveracking — always waiting, always wondering."

"That's law work," the Ranger said. He nodded toward the hoofprints in the dust. "They always have the advantage of first strike. Theirs is the action; ours is the reaction. It never makes sense to me. I believe in prevention more than cure." He turned to the dun horse and dropped his canteen strap over the saddle horn. "But then, I reckon that's why a lot of folks call me crazy."

CHAPTER 4

Maria stood leaning back against the wall in the doctor's office, her rifle cradled in her arms, watching the doctor pace back and forth between her and the wounded prisoner. The doctor raised the key between his fingers and shook it back and forth. "I've a good mind to go ahead and use this. I have every right you know, for the good of my patient."

"Oh?" That's all Maria said. Then she only stared in silence. He wasn't going to open the cuffs with that key, even if he tried. Still, she let him rant, seeing how far he would go.

"Yes, absolutely! I have every right! What would you do? Shoot me? For me doing the job I'm sworn to do?" He swung an arm toward the prisoner. "Look at him. I can't even clean him up properly with his wrist cuffed to the table rail! How will he eat? He needs to be able to move his arm around to keep it from cramping up on him, for God sakes!"

"I'm feeling real stiff," the young man said, a distressed look on his face. "Getting hungry too . . . feeling weak and queasy down in my stomach from it."

"Hear that?" The doctor gestured a hand toward the young man again. "We can't wait until the Ranger and Petty return. This man needs attending right now! This is inhumane, by any standard of decency. I have a mind to write a letter to the judge in Circle Wells . . . tell him what kind of people the court has working for it. Think he'll stand still for this sort of behavior?"

Maria moved away from the wall, toward the door, and said over her shoulder, "I'm going to check on the others. I'll be right back."

"Wait! What about this poor man?"

She said as she walked out, "You have the key. Use it . . . while I'm gone."

"What?" She heard him shouting after her. "You think I won't? Well, you're wrong, little lady! I'm not afraid of this boy. This poor boy means me no harm. I'm taking this handcuff off him right now! Here I go. . . ."

She closed the door behind her and with a long sigh leaned against it for a second, shaking her head. She'd walked halfway

67

across the dirt street when two young boys came running toward her from out front of the jail. "Ma'am! You better hurry! They're killing each other in there!"

"What?" She hurried past the boys, who turned back to follow her. Townsfolk along the boardwalk shied back and watched as she hastened her steps. From the jail she heard a long, muffled scream. "You children stay back." She ran the rest of the way, threw open the door to the sheriff's office, and rushed in with her rifle cocked and ready.

"Lord, ma'am! You got to do something here," Curtis Roundtree called out to her through the bars. His face was drawn tight, frightened. He stood back to one side of the cell. In the middle of the cell floor, a ball of human limbs thrashed back and forth in a stand of swirling dust. Granddaddy Snake rolled, his long gray hair whipping about him. His thin arms and legs wrapped tight around the upper half of Billy Lee's body like a wildcat, his mouth open wide, his teeth sunk into the back of Billy Lee's head, locked there in a death grip.

Billy Lee let out another long scream. "Get him *offffff*!"

Curtis Roundtree cringed against the wall, turning his face from them. "Do something!

He's eating him alive!"

Maria hurried getting the cell key. Then she unlocked the door, and entered the cell, warning Curtis, "Stay back. Make a wrong move and I'll put a bullet in you."

"Lady! Lord God! You've got to do something!" Curtis Roundtree yelled, wide-eyed. "He's eating him like a chunk of pork. Help him. Please!"

"Turn him loose, Granddaddy." She poked the Indian in his bony back with her rifle barrel. The mass of entwined human flesh rolled away two feet, then came rolling back. Again she poked at him with the rifle barrel, this time catching the old Indian in his skinny thigh, which was clamped around Billy Lee's chest. Granddaddy Snake grunted, turned loose with his teeth, and shot her a murderous look, dark blood running down both corners of his mouth. "That's enough! Let him go, Granddaddy." She reached down with her free hand and grabbed the old Indian by his bony shoulder.

Granddaddy only growled at her, slung his shoulder away from her grip, and sank his teeth once more into the back of Billy Lee's head. Billy Lee rolled and screamed. "I said, that's *enough!*" Maria swung the rifle butt and caught a solid blow on the

Indian's knobby back as they came rolling past her feet. Granddaddy grunted, his mouth separating from Billy Lee's head. But he stayed wrapped around him like the stripe on a barber's pole.

"Help me, Curtis," she yelled over her shoulder, and together they peeled the old Indian's limbs off of Billy Lee.

Curtis yanked Granddaddy by his bony shoulders. "It's like stripping bark from an oak tree!"

The old Indian finally rolled off of Billy Lee and onto his back, looking up at Maria from the floor. Curtis Roundtree fell back against the wall, winded and sweating. "I sure hope . . . you'll mention this . . . at my trial, ma'am. This was . . . a voluntary act on my part."

"What's come over you, Granddaddy?" Maria spoke down to the old man, standing back with her rifle poised.

"He started it," Granddaddy Snake said in a quiet voice, wiping a hand across his bloody mouth as Billy Lee scrambled across the cell and dragged himself up the bars to his feet.

"Keep him away from me, you hear?" Billy Lee stepped forward now, one hand against the back of his bleeding head, his chest heaving. His other hand pointed at arm's length toward Granddaddy Snake. "He's a . . . damned cannibal, is what he is. Look at my head! Alls I did was . . . make a little remark about sheepdogs. He lost his mind!"

"He started it," Granddaddy Snake said again.

"Both of you stay put." Maria backed out the cell door. "I'll look at your head once this door is closed.

Billy Lee still gasping for breath, took a step toward Granddaddy Snake. "You got . . . the drop on me this time, old man . . . but so help me . . . if you ever make . . . another move on me . . . I swear to God . . . I'll beat you to a bloody pul—"

Granddaddy Snake let out a piercing war cry and shot forward off the floor into Billy Lee's chest. Maria saw it coming but couldn't stop it. They were back on the floor in a rolling ball, Billy Lee screaming loud and long as the old Indian sank his teeth into the same bleeding wound. "Curtis, help me," she yelled.

Once more they peeled Granddaddy Snake loose and shoved him away from Billy Lee, across the dusty floor. "That's it! He's dead!" Billy Lee screamed, pointing at the old Indian. But this time instead of stepping toward him, he moved in a wide, cautious circle around behind Maria until she backed out the door and shoved it shut. "You're dead, old man . . . and that's a fact! I'll kill you with my bare hands the next time."

"Shut up, Billy Lee," Maria said through the bars. "If you ask for it again, I won't stop it. I have too much going on right now. All three of you sit down and hush up."

"Can't you put him in another cell or something?" Billy Lee lowered a bloody hand from the back of his head and held it toward the bars. "I can't live like this, no ma'am! If he stays in here I've got to kill him." He spun toward the old Indian, a string of saliva trailing from his lips as he raged. "Do you hear me? You caught me off guard, but never again. I'm ready for you! I'm ready now . . . I'm ready, ready, ready! Try it again, *Injun*! See if you don't die!" He crouched in a fighting stance, his fists up.

"*Jesus L. Jones!*" Curtis Roundtree bellowed. He and Maria moved quick and at the same time, but too late as Granddaddy Snake sailed through the air with another war cry. . . .

When Maria and Curtis Roundtree peeled Granddaddy Snake off of Billy Lee the third time, she'd shoved Billy Lee through the barred door and moved him to the only other cell in the two-cell jail. "Here." She pitched a wet rag through the bars to him and saw the look on his face as he stood gazing around the dusty cell. Cobwebs swayed from the ceiling. Dried mouse droppings crunched beneath his boots. "Don't say a word, Billy Lee. You brought it on yourself. This will have to do until the sheriff gets back."

"Lord!" He shook his bloody head. "Talk about cruel treatment of a prisoner." He touched the wet rag to the back of his head.

"You can always go back over there with Curtis and Granddaddy," Maria said as she locked the cell door.

"No, ma'am. After him attacking me three times in a row? I'm afraid of what I'd do to him the next time. Afraid I'd lose my self-control and end up hanging for murdering him. He's lucky I didn't kill him last time."

"I understand." She stepped back, looked at both cells, and said to all three of them, "I have to keep watch on the other prisoner. I better not have any more trouble here."

"Yes, ma'am. I hope you won't forget to tell the judge all I done here today," Curtis Roundtree said. Granddaddy Snake only nodded and looked away from her.

As she turned to walk back to the doctor's office, she heard Curtis Roundtree say to

Granddaddy Snake, "You ain't mad at me, are you, old buddy? Alls I tried to do was keep the peace."

"I am not *mad* at anybody," the old Indian replied under his breath.

Halfway across the street, Joe Chancy, the blacksmith, came up to Maria, untying his leather apron and folding it. "Ma'am, I'm sorry I left earlier. I heard all that carrying-on at the jail. What can I do to lend you a hand?"

She stopped and smiled wearily. "I think I have everything settled now. But you can sit with those three prisoners for a while if you like. That would be a great help."

"I sure will," he said, heading off toward the sheriff's office. "I was supposed to be meeting with the banker, but I'll just tell him this was more important. Don't you worry about a thing."

She walked on, and inside the door of the doctor's office, she stopped and listened for a moment to the dead silence around her. Now what? She moved quietly over to one side of the door to the surgery room, pushing it open with her free hand, her other hand tight around the rifle stock.

"That's right, lady," the prisoner's voice said in low, menacing tone. "You keep coming slow and easy . . . else I'll open this buzzard's throat and throw him at your feet."

She stepped into the room and saw the terrified face of the doctor and the sharp surgery instrument pressed against his fleshy throat. The prisoner held the doctor tightly with his free arm, while his right arm was still cuffed to the rail along the surgery table. The key the Ranger had given the doctor lay on the floor. She glanced at it, then back up at the prisoner. "Real cute trick with the key," he sneered. "Now come up with the right one or this man dies!"

Maria stared at him, while thoughts and possibilities ran through her mind. "I mean right now, lady!" A thin trickle of blood ran down beneath the sharp instrument against the doctor's throat.

Maria took a deep breath, ran her finger inside the trigger guard on her rifle, leveled the weapon at them, and said, "No."

"No?" His eyes turned into dark pools of rage. "Lady, I'm not going to tell you —"

"This is a trick," she said, cutting him off. "You two came up with this. He has been wanting to uncuff you." She smiled a crafty smile. "But I'm not falling for this little play."

"Oh, my God, woman," the doctor said in a trembling voice. "This is no trick. I swear on my dead wife's grave. He's going to kill me!" The trickle of blood seemed to thicken as he spoke.

"No." She shrugged. "Sorry. I don't believe either of you," she said matter-of-factly. "You'll have to do much better than this. I'll just wait out here until you both come to your senses."

"Lady! Ma'am? Damn it! Come back here! This is not a trick. I'm going to kill him! Do you hear me? Are you nuts or something?"

"Please, mister! Don't kill me . . . it's not me doing this, it's her. I'm just a doctor, I never —"

"Shut up, sawbones!"

From the other room, Maria stood against the wall listening with bated breath, her hands growing moist with perspiration. She heard the prisoner say, "Where did she go? Did she leave? Is she a complete idiot? She thinks this is me and you playing a trick on her. How in the hell did she come to that?"

"Please! I don't know what's wrong with her," the doctor pleaded. A wet circle of urine darkened trousers. "Don't kill me. I saved your life!"

"Shut up! That wasn't no big deal. I never asked you to save nothing of mine." He raised his voice and called out across the room. "Ma'am, are you out there? I know you are! I'm not playing here. I'm going to kill him if you don't set me loose. Do you hear me, *fool*? I swear this ain't no kind of trick!"

She waited, silent, whispering a prayer to herself. If this didn't work, the doctor's death would be on her head. While a tense silence passed, she quietly took her pistol from her holster and unloaded it, dropping each round into her hand and putting it into her pocket. She knew that if all else failed, he would demand her gun from her.

After a few seconds of silence, the prisoner called out in a softer tone, "Ma'am? You are out there, right? Listen to me. I don't know why you think this is a trick, but it's not. Maybe you're just scared . . . maybe you haven't had time to think this through —"

His words stopped short. He listened to the silence and in a moment said, "Well, hell." Another silence passed. "She really has left? She's gone? Just . . . *gone*? Can you believe this? What am I supposed to do now?"

"Please, mister."

"She thinks this ain't for real. I swear to God I never seen anybody that stupid! I ought to go on and kill you just to show her I mean it!"

"But — but — if you kill me, you're still

stuck here. Please, I'm begging. Who'll take care of your wound? Don't kill me because she's too hardheaded to see what's going on!"

Another silence. Maria stood more tense, perspiration running down her temple. Her breath seemed suspended in her chest, tight and stuck there.

"Well, hell. This beats all I've ever seen," the prisoner said. "Put a blade to a man's throat, ready to kill him . . . and some stupid damn woman just walks right out the door. *Leaves!* Thinks it's all some kind of trick, a joke or something. Hell, I don't know. . . ."

In another second, Maria heard the metal instrument hit the floor. She let out a breath and slumped for a second.

"Damn it all. There, you're safe, Doctor. I give up. Go find her, tell her it's over, if she's even *at all* interested. Tell her it really was a trick if you want to . . . damn, I don't know what to say. This is a new one on me."

"I'll — I'll go tell her," the doctor said, his breath slicing in and out with each rapid beat of his heart.

"That's not necessary," Maria said, step-ping into the open door, looking at the surgical instrument lying on the floor. "I'm right here." She saw the doctor slumped back against a table along the wall, a hand to the trickle of blood on his throat. She gave them a wry smile and winked. "See? I knew it was a trick."

The prisoner stared, stunned speechless. The doctor swallowed a dry lump in his throat and coughed against the back of his trembling hand. "Lady, you don't realize how close your stupidity came to getting me killed. How in the name of heaven could you think this was some sort of ruse?"

"You are still alive, *sí*?" She stooped down to pick up the surgical instrument, walked over and laid it on the table. She leaned her rifle against the table. Both men just stared at her.

The prisoner still sat on the edge of the operating table. "Now you lay back down," she said, stepping over beside him. "You need to rest up for the ride back to Circle Wells."

She leaned in and cradled his shoulder to help him lie down. But lowering himself to the table, he saw the butt of her pistol protruding from her holster. It was his chance and he took it. He snatched the pistol with his left hand, and before Maria could make a move, he cocked it only inches from her face. "Not me, lady. I've still got some play left. Tell me *this* is a trick, and I'll put a third hole in your nose."

She took a step back and let out a long sigh. It ran through her mind that had he waited and done this instead of what he'd done with the doctor, he would now be holding a loaded gun. What irony. Instead, he'd made the play on the doctor and caused her to unload the very pistol that would have ended up in his hand. "Give me back the pistol, please. It was a gift from a friend." She held her palm out toward him, a patient expression on her face.

The prisoner gave her an unbelieving look, his knuckles white around the pistol butt. "Lady . . . listen close." He sliced each word separately. "Don't . . . start . . . acting . . . crazy again. This time, you and him . . . will . . . both . . . die. Can you understand that?"

"For God sakes, woman!" The doctor shouted. "Are you completely mad? Turn him loose. He means it!"

"No." She shrugged, walked over to the table and picked up her rifle. When she turned back to the prisoner, she smiled and studied the strange, lost look on his face.

"This pistol is not loaded, is it?" he asked her in a subdued voice.

"No." She smiled. "But this rifle is."

CHAPTER 5

Evening shadows stretched long across the dirt street by the time Sheriff Petty and the Ranger rode back in off the flatlands south of town. Maria stood up from the wooden chair on the boardwalk outside the doctor's office and stepped down to the hitch rail to greet them. They swung down from their horses, slapping dust off themselves with their hats. Sheriff Petty's black-linen suit had turned the color of scorched earth, with wide circles of sweat beneath the coat sleeves and down the back.

"It took you longer than you thought," Maria said, looking the sweaty horse over as she spoke to the Ranger.

"I know it." He ran a hand across his brow and put his sombrero on. "The heat's up worse than I've seen it in a long while. Couldn't risk pushing these horses. How're the prisoners doing?" He nodded toward the jail.

"Well. . . ." She sighed. "Granddaddy will not eat or drink. And he bit Billy Lee on his head."

"He won't eat, huh?" The Ranger pondered it for a second.

"No, he won't. But what did you find out?" Maria looked back and forth at the two of them.

"Whoever the man was, he's met up with some others out there. I think we might have interrupted a robbery in the making, coming here the way we did. I'm going to have to have a long talk with our Mr. McKenzie." The Ranger spun his reins around the hitch rail as he talked. Sheriff Petty did the same beside him.

"Good luck," Maria said. "I had some trouble with him."

"Oh? How bad?" Petty and the Ranger stepped up onto the boardwalk out of the sunlight.

"Not too bad." She shrugged. They stood at the door for a moment as she recounted what had happened at the doctor's office and at the jail.

When she'd finished, Sheriff Petty stood looking at her with a stunned expression. Then he shook his head as if to clear it and get it working again, and he said, "All that since we've been gone?"

"*Sí,* but it was not so bad. I handled it." Maria offered a tired smile.

The Ranger opened the door for them. "They always know when to pick their time."

"Oh?" Maria cocked her head slightly, stepping past him and Sheriff Petty into the doctor's office. "Things would have gone differently had you been here?"

"No . . . what I meant was only having one person here, having to guard prisoners at two locations at once."

"Then I'm glad you cleared that up," she said, smiling, giving him a skeptical look as she turned and faced him inside the office.

"Me, too," he said, returning her smile. "Now, let's hear what this boy has to say about his buddies waiting out there in the badlands."

When they entered the operating room, the doctor stood up from his chair at the long table where he sat cleaning surgery instruments with a rag and a bottle of alcohol. But Petty and the Ranger only glanced at the doctor, then swung their gaze to the prisoner. "My goodness," Sheriff Petty said in a surprised whisper, standing beside the Ranger.

The Ranger chuckled under his breath at the sight of the prisoner tied flat to the surgery table. Coils of rope encircled him from his knees to his throat. His right hand still cuffed to the rail and his left hand was now held down by a thick leather strap. "Looks like he really got to you," the Ranger said to Maria.

"I did not do this," she said. "This was the doctor's idea."

The Ranger looked at the doctor as the four of them moved over beside the prisoner. Even with the prisoner tied down, the doctor kept a cautious distance. "That's right, I did it," the doctor said, "and I'm not a damn bit ashamed of it. He came within a hairsbreadth of cutting my throat."

The Ranger looked down into the prisoner's face but spoke to the doctor. "Think maybe you could loosen this coil around his throat enough for him to raise his head and talk?"

"You want him loose, you loosen him," the doctor said. "I'm taking no responsibility for anything he does. If you ask me, you should've shot a little more to the right and saved the government the cost of a hanging. This man is unfit to live."

"Now, now, Doctor," the Ranger replied as he worked the rope loose from across Mac McKenzie's throat. "Seems I recall you saying something earlier about how we're

84

all God's creatures? Didn't you?"

"Yes I did," the doctor answered in a dry tone. "But some of us are more of a *creature* than others. This sonofabitch is a flat-out *animal*." He pointed a finger at the prisoner. "I refuse to have him on the premises. Look what he did to me!" He pointed to his throat, touching the small bandage there. "Get him out of here, I demand it."

The Ranger cocked an eye toward the doctor. "You said he shouldn't be moved for at least a week."

"Damn what I said. Move him now! I don't care if you have to hammer a spike through his ears and drag him out of here by it. If I owned a gun I would've already shot him. I want him gone! If you don't move him, I'll go *buy* myself a pistol."

The Ranger slipped a gloved hand under the prisoner's head and raised it slightly, looking down into his eyes. "You've sure managed to wear out your welcome in a hurry, young man."

"Let me tell you something, Lawdog," the young gunman hissed up at him. "I'm keeping a list of my own from here on." He nodded toward Maria, then the doctor. "Their names are on it . . . so is yours. In fact *yours* is at the top of the list." He tried to jerk his head free of the Ranger's hand and turn away from him.

"Uh-huh," the Ranger said, holding firm. "We've got some talking to do."

"Go to hell." The prisoner tried spitting up at the Ranger's face, but the Ranger covered his mouth with a gloved hand.

The doctor stepped forward and said, "Smack the cold living piss out of him, Ranger. He deserves it. Don't let him talk to you that way."

The Ranger shot Sheriff Petty a glance. Petty saw in his eyes what the Ranger wanted, and he turned to the doctor. "Come on, Doc," he said moving the man toward the door. "Why don't you and me go fix some coffee?"

The doctor resisted, trying to free his arm from Petty's grip. "I've already had seven or eight cups."

"I can tell," the sheriff said, "but let's fix some for everybody else."

With Petty and the doctor out of the room, Maria and the Ranger stood close to the prisoner. "All right," the Ranger said, "who are your friends out there and what do they have in mind?"

"I have no idea what you're talking about, Ranger." Suspicious, he flicked his gaze back and forth between Maria and the Ranger.

"You came scouting the bank, didn't you?" The Ranger stared at him with a flat expression.

"You know so much . . . why ask me?" He turned his eyes away from them.

"Suit yourself." The Ranger took a step back. "If I was you, I wouldn't go getting my hopes up, thinking those boys are going to try setting you free once we head for Circle Wells. Outlaws always tell one another they're going to stick together, but they seldom do." The Ranger watched for anything the prisoner's expression might reveal as he added, "Unless, of course you have something they want real bad. Anything like that at work here?"

"We'll just have to wait and see, won't we, Ranger," he said, shooting a piercing gaze at the Ranger. "Only time will tell."

The Ranger nodded, returning the sharp gaze. "You're right about that. Time *will* tell. I've got a feeling it'll tell us a lot between here and Circle Wells."

Lloyd Percy felt the tension all the way across the badlands into Mexico. The four other men managed to stay close around him, Becker in the lead, Bud White on one side, Dewey Toom on the other, and Stinson Carlisle bringing up the rear. He was in trouble and they all knew it. The others would answer him if he spoke directly to them, but only in short, clipped voices, with no small talk. None of these four wanted to be noted by the others as being friendly with him, not now, not after what he'd done — at least not until they saw how JC McLawry was going to react to all this.

Lloyd sweated a lot on the way to the village of Junta Cruz. The index finger of his glove stayed dark and damp from constantly running it along the inside of his wet shirt collar in a nervous gesture. All right, he'd made a mistake thinking these men might listen to reason. Now that he thought back on it, what the hell was he thinking of, coming back to meet them? He should be long gone right now.

As it turned out the Ranger hadn't been on his trail in the first place. He'd come back to them for the safety of numbers. Mistake number one, he thought. He'd also thought that maybe they were as fed up with JC McLawry as he was. That maybe they would ride off with him and form a gang of their own. Mistake number two — bad mistake. Well, nothing he could do about it now.

Where the road forked in one direction out across the flat stretch of sand toward

88

the distant mountains, and in another upward into a jagged line of ridges and rock land, they rested their horses for a few minutes and sat quiet, each man with his own thoughts on the dark possibilities awaiting Lloyd Percy in the small, dusty village ahead.

"You know this don't seem a damn bit right," he said in a final appeal to them. "Not after all we've been through together."

"Seems to me you've only been with us a short while, Percy." Becker sat with his wrists crossed on his saddle horn, appearing to enjoy this, Lloyd Percy thought, seeing the faint trace of a smile on his face. "Alls I can recall us going through together is you sitting around the fire at night talking about the Jameses, the Youngers, the Renos, and all like that. A time or two I couldn't help but think you had a notion you was better than the rest of us ole work-a-day desert outlaws." He spread his toothy white grin.

"Me? Why shoot no, Becker." Percy tried to fake a smile, but it came off nervous, stiff. A muscle in his jaw twitched beneath a sheen of sweat. "I wish you would have said something sooner. I've always been just one of the boys, far as I'm concerned." He thumbed toward Stinson Carlisle. "Hell, me and Stinson here were raiding everything from banks to whorehouses longer than I can remember. Ain't that true, Stinson?"

Stinson Carlisle spat, ran a hand across his mouth, and narrowed his eyes on Lloyd Percy. "Not together we ain't. You've implied it a couple of times . . . but unless I was lap-legged drunk and forgot, I don't think we ever done anything together."

"Well, no, maybe not *together* we didn't." He shrugged. "I just meant we've rode all the same trails. Ole boys like us go way back . . . the way we live, who we are, what we do." His eyes darted toward the others, checking, seeing if anything he said might be getting to them. "It's a sad day when men like us start turning against one another. Look around at the world." He swung an arm. "Boys, there's a day coming soon when there will be no more crime. Nobody like us to carry on. If we don't stick up for one another, you watch, one day there'll be —"

"Hush, Percy." Becker pitched him a canteen. "Here, drink some water. You've got more pouring out than you have going in. I don't want you getting lockjaw once we get to JC." He turned his horse and batted it on toward the low-standing village in the swirl of evening heat.

90

They rode on, and when they moved past the two riflemen at the edge of the village, the men nodded them on toward the cantina, then returned to their posts. The body of a young Mexican hung from the bough of a cottonwood tree near the village well, spinning back and forth slowly at the slightest touch of hot wind off the desert floor. Becker chuckled as the men behind him turned their eyes to the dead man. "Looks like JC finally got that little *señorita* he's had his tooth set on."

"Till death did they part," Dewey Toom said. "See, that's what I never understood about these people. Once they marry, that's it. They take it as serious as a dose of the fever. I call it building a fence and forgetting to put a gate in it."

"JC just busted that fence all to hell, then, I reckon," said Stinson Carlisle. Dust plumed and stirred in their wake.

Inside the cantina, JC McLawry sat at a wooden table with his face buried in the long black hair of the young woman on his lap. She sat rigid, a distant look in her tear-filled eyes. He nuzzled her neck, pressing his coarse beard stubble against her throat as he spoke to the old man in the corner with the battered accordion against his bony chest. "Play something, old man, *musica,* to cheer the *señorita* up."

"*Sí, musica, musica!*" the old man said in a rush, gathering up the accordion. His weathered hands trembled at first, then broke into a snappy tune. Three times in the past hour JC McLawry had commanded him to play, and each time, no sooner than the music started then he would demand that the old man *stop* playing. The old man noted that his straw sombrero lay empty at his bare feet. Neither the *gringo* at the table with the woman on his lap nor the others gathered along the bar putting forth any offering for his music. These *pigs*. . . . And yet he played, smiling, nodding, one dark-stained tooth visible beneath his upper lip.

JC moved his mouth to the young woman's ear, his breath hot on her skin. "Don't go brittle on me now, chicky chicky. You're the one said not as long as your husband was alive."

With his face buried in the woman's hair, JC didn't see the men step in from the dirt street until one of the men at the bar spoke above the whine of the accordion. "Well, it's about damn time. What's took you boys so long?"

"We ran into some trouble out there," Becker said, him and the other three gathered together behind Lloyd Percy. He nudged Percy forward as the men along the bar straightened with interest, tossing back their drinks and wiping their mouths, their hands falling instinctively to their pistol butts.

JC turned his eyes to them without him lifting his face from the young woman's throat. "What kind of trouble?" He stared through the shroud of glistening black hair, wisps of it clinging to his beard. He touched his tongue to one and blew it from his lips. "Where's Bobby?"

"I'll let this fool tell you all about it." Becker shoved Lloyd Percy forward. Percy stumbled and caught himself.

"Where's Bobby?" JC asked again, harsher this time, getting up from the wooden chair, pushing the woman away but catching her wrist at arm's length and holding her there, keeping her near him. On the side of his neck, the blue star tattoo stood out beneath his beard and the sheen of sweat. He stared coldly at Lloyd Percy.

"JC, I couldn't help it —" Percy swallowed hard, rubbing his nervous hands up and down on his trousers. "Bobby got loco on me! Took it in his head to kill that Ranger you're always talking about. I — I didn't know what else to do but skin it on back here and let you know about it . . . you

93

know? Figured you'd want to hear about it first thing, so we could make some plans to bust him loose. In case he's still alive?" He shrugged, nervous, his knees quaking inside his trouser legs. "I can't stand the thought of poor Bobby being in a jail cell, maybe shot all to pieces. It tears me up inside."

Listening, Becker nudged Stinson Carlisle beside him and nodded down toward Percy's trembling legs, smiling faintly, liking his fear, liking the short wet strands of hair on the back of Percy's head, and the nervous sweat that dripped from it and ran down Percy's neck. He liked the terror in Percy's voice. "Tell him what you did to help poor Bobby though, while you're all tore *up* over it."

Lloyd Percy shot a timid glance back at Becker, who bared his big teeth in a wide grin. Then he turned back to JC. "Boss, I can't make this peckerwood understand that I did the best thing . . . beating it back here quick as I could. If Bobby's alive, we've got to get him. Lord, we've just *got to!*" He shook his head.

"Yeah, well —" Becker cleared his throat. "That ain't how you were talking back there, Percy. You said you figured Bobby was dead."

"No I didn't. You misunderstood, damn

it. I said knowing who he was up against, there was good chance that the Ranger would kill him if we didn't hurry up and do something."

"Like hell you did," Becker chuckled.

"Don't tell me what I said!" Percy spun facing him, his fists clenched at his sides. Then he turned back to JC. "Listen, Boss, if I was standing wrong on this, you think I'd risk coming back here, facing you? Hell no! I'd have batted out of here. I did what any man ought to do."

JC raised his pistol from his holster and let it hang loose in his free hand, his other hand still clamped on the young woman's wrist. "So you think he's still alive, huh?"

"That's what I want to think — that's what I'm praying for, Boss. But to be honest . . . it's probably only fifty-fifty that he is. I just figured you'd want to take them odds, it being Bobby."

JC's pistol hammer cocked back loud beneath his thumb. "And there was no way you could have helped him, you say?"

Percy's eyes widened. "On my mama's grave, Boss! If I *could* have I *would* have!"

Becker, Stinson, Bud, and Dewey Toom stepped out wide from behind Lloyd Percy as JC McLawry's pistol leveled on him, seven inches from his stomach. "Nail this sucker, Boss," Becker said. "Nail him good and *hard*!"

JC felt the woman shiver and pull against his grip. She whispered a frightened prayer under her trembling breath. JC shook her. "Be still, chicky chicky." He looked back at Lloyd Percy. "If I was you I would have just rode on, Lloyd. You knew I'd kill you, didn't you?"

"Boss I — I —" He took one quick step back and froze to a jerking halt, seeing JC pull the trigger. "No . . . !"

JC's thumb clamped over the hammer, caught it right before it fired and let it down. Lloyd Percy nearly collapsed. "But see? You were wrong, Lloyd," JC said. "I've killed everybody I need to for one day." He gave the woman beside him a hungry look and pulled her against him, dropping his pistol into its holster. He buried his face in her hair again, then turned his eyes to Percy, Becker and the others.

Becker stood stunned and spread his hands. "But, Boss, what about Bobby?"

"Why don't you get a drink in your mouth, Becker, before you get me aggravated." He rooted his face against the woman's throat, then pulled back from her and wiped her hair from his lips. The men along the bar stood watching; one of them picked up a bottle of mescal and pitched it to Becker. "Talk to me about the Ranger, Lloyd," JC said, releasing the woman's wrist and wrapping his arm around her slender waist as he spoke.

"What can I tell you, Boss?" He looked around at the others, his face still stark white behind long streaks of sweat.

"Tell me what you can. Who was with him? That Maria woman, I bet. What's he riding these days? A big white horse with a black circle around one eye?"

"He wasn't riding a horse, but there was a woman with him, Boss. A real pretty woman. She was driving the jail wagon. He stood out in the middle of the stree—"

"A jail wagon?" JC cut him off. "The Misery Express? The one they use to haul men to prison?"

"Yeah, that must be the one," Percy said. "Leastwise, I saw one like it a year ago over near Humbly. They were taking men to Yuma in it, I heard."

"That's the one," JC said. "The ole *Misery Express.* I use to drive it myself back when I was a decent, law-abiding prison guard." He looked at the men along the bar and smiled while they laughed under their breath. "Of course that was before I came to my senses and helped Ernesto Caslado and his boys burn the prison down."

"I heard that was one hell of a raid," said one of the men at the bar.

"Here, here," said another, raising his bottle in salute. Now they laughed out loud and looked at one another, swilling drinks of mescal and whiskey.

Becker drank from the bottle of mescal and pitched it on to Stinson Carlisle who in turn drank and passed it along to Dewey Toom. "Boss, if you don't mind me asking," Becker said, "what about your brother, Bobby? I never thought you'd take it this way. I thought you'd want to rip right in there, see what's going on about Bobby. You've wanted to kill that ole Ranger anyway."

JC grinned. "You would think so, wouldn't you?" As he spoke he tightened his arm around the woman's waist, his hand moving down low onto the flat of her belly, his fingertips kneading her there. Her face flushed and her eyes stared far away in her shame. "But that's the one mistake everybody always makes with the Ranger," he said, his breath rushing a bit as his hand rubbed in a circle, bunching her thin cotton dress beneath it. "Everybody gets in a hurry and that always gives him the edge. Not this time, though. I learned my lesson. I know

98

how to play him."

"Then what are we going to do?" Becker felt his face redden, trying hard not to watch JC's hand at work on the young woman's stomach.

"Let me worry about it," JC said. "I've got things that need attending today. Urgent things." His hand closed on her stomach, squeezing. She winced and stared straight ahead. He took a ragged breath. "We'll head in tomorrow, find out whether or not Bobby is still alive. I've been feeling a reckoning coming with that Ranger for quite a while. This is as good a time to kill him as any. Him, and his woman too."

PART II

CHAPTER 6

Three days had passed while the Ranger and Maria waited for the young gunman to get strong enough to travel to Circle Wells. On the first day, Sheriff Petty had cleaned Billy Lee's dirty cell and rotated the prisoners. He'd put Billy Lee back in the cell with Curtis Roundtree and had Granddaddy Snake in the other cell by himself until the other prisoner arrived. That afternoon when the sheriff led Granddaddy Snake out of his cell to take him to the jake out back, Billy Lee had stood with his face against the bars and threatened the old Indian. "Hey," he'd said, as Granddaddy walked past his cell with his head lowered, "You ever lay a hand near me again, Injun, it won't be like the last. The next time I garun-damn-tee you. I'll —"

He never finished his threat, the old Indian sailed sidelong against the iron bars, ran his bony hands through them, caught

Billy Lee by one ear and a handful of hair, and slammed his forehead into the bars three times before Sheriff Petty could stop him. The bars rang and hummed as Billy Lee fell to the floor, not moving. Curtis Roundtree stood back, wide-eyed, with his mouth agape until he shook his head and said down to Billy Lee, "Lord, boy, can't you just leave things alone?"

That night, Billy Lee lay in his bunk with a fresh bandage on his forehead. He looked at Curtis Roundtree with one eye swollen shut and said, "That damned old desert rat has no idea who he's messing with here."

Curtis Roundtree shook his head. "Then you better hurry up and get him informed before he ruins you for life."

The second day the Ranger spent checking the team of horses and getting some loose oak floor planks repaired in the jail wagon. At the end of the day, while he and Maria set on the porch of the boardinghouse where they'd taken a room, they noticed a drifter ride in off the desert floor on a rough-looking buckskin, its flanks and legs full of nicks and brush scars. He wore a ragged blanket thrown around him and a sombrero with half its brim gone, looking like it had been gnawed short by hungry rats. His face and beard were the color of the dust.

Outside of the blacksmith's barn, the drifter stepped his horse wide of the jail wagon, looking it over. Then he looked around the town, up and down the dirt street, until he saw the Ranger stand up on the porch of the hotel looking back toward him. A bone-handled .45 stood resting behind the rider's belt, and his right hand fell to it and lay there as he backed the buckskin into a dark slice of shade that led off behind town and back out to the badlands. Then he disappeared.

"Who was it?" Maria asked, standing up from her wicker rocking chair to gaze out at the rise of dust with a hand shielding her eyes from the evening sun.

"If I was to guess, I'd say it's Lawrence Shaw. Hard to recognize him, but that looked like his buckskin." He sat back down in the wicker chair, crossed a boot to his knee, and set his tall sombrero on it, letting out a breath. "Yep, Fast Larry, they call him over around Cottonwood. Some say he's the fastest man alive with a six-shooter. He's the one who shot Charlie Roe so hard and fast Charlie's left boot flew off — and Roe was no slow gunman himself."

"He is still on your list, this Fast Larry?" Maria sat back down as well.

"No. He's been off my list for over a year, but he doesn't know it. If I can ever get close enough to tell him without one of us killing the other, I'll let him know. It's hard approaching a man who thinks you're out to kill him."

"What was he supposed to have done?" She pushed up the brim of her flat-crown Stetson.

"Nothing, as it turns out. He'd been charged with two counts of murder by Judge Lodge. But three miners came forward as witnesses and called the whole thing self-defense. Of course, by then Fast Larry had his knees in the wind and nobody's been able to get close to him since. I knew Fast Larry a long time ago." He stood silent for a moment. "We might have become friends . . . but he had some bad breaks dealt him."

"Too bad." Maria shook her head.

A silence passed as they enjoyed a cool gust of evening wind coming in from the north mountain range. When it had moved past them, Maria said, "We can move the prisoner from the doctor's office any time now. He is coming around quickly."

"I know it," the Ranger said. "We'll put him over in the jail come morning, give him another day, then get on back to Circle Wells."

"I think perhaps you have only left him at the doctor's this long to keep the doctor upset."

"Would I do something like that?" He gave her a wry smile. "Maybe I've left him there so the sheriff can have something to do, guarding him. Petty is a nervous man . . . worries too much."

The next morning they moved the prisoner from the doctor's office to the jail while townsfolk gathered and stared. Once the Ranger had nudged the young gunman forward, Sheriff Petty closed the iron door and locked it. "You're not going to have any trouble with this man are you, Granddaddy? You won't bite him, will you?" the Ranger asked. On the floor of Granddaddy's cell, the Ranger saw the tin plate of food sitting untouched, a circle of flies spinning above it.

"If he keeps his mouth shut, so will I," the old Indian said.

From the other cell, Billy Lee called out to the new prisoner, "You better not turn your back on that sneaking, low-down, head-biting —"

"Shut up, Billy Lee," the Ranger said. "You haven't gotten a thing you didn't ask for. Granddaddy is not the kind of man you can threaten and get by with it. The sooner you understand that, the sooner he'll quit taking chunks out of your head."

Curtis Roundtree said from the far side of the cell, "That's the same thing I've been telling him, Ranger."

"Don't you start in on me too," Billy Lee yelled at Curtis. "You don't know a damn thing about a damn thing!"

"So, Ranger . . . I expect you and your prisoners will be leaving pretty soon, huh?" Sheriff Petty asked, wiping a handkerchief across his damp forehead. "Not that I'm in any hurry. . . ."

"I understand." The Ranger smiled. "We're headed out come morning."

"I hope I've seen the last of those boys who were waiting out there for this one." He spoke in a lower tone, and nodded toward the young gunman in the cell.

"You're going to do all right, Sheriff," the Ranger said. "Never let the job get the better of you."

They both nodded, looking in at the prisoners. Then they turned and walked away from the cells, through the sheriff's office, and out into the heat and dust, where Maria met them. The three of them walked along the boardwalk toward the boardinghouse as the few remaining townsfolk dispersed before them.

There was madness in those lost, hollow eyes, Lawrence Shaw thought, looking down at his reflection in the calm, rippled surface of runoff. *Eyes of a madman, on the face of a fool. . . .* He lifted his eyes from his reflection and looked up at the morning sky for a second. *Fast Larry . . .* God, how he hated that name. He hated the name and all it conjured it up, all it implied, all it had come to stand for to himself and the rest of the world.

Hearing the name no longer brought up the image of a proud young man in shiny new boots, his hat cocked at a go-to-hell angle to match his attitude, his new bone-handled Colt resting forward on his hip in a silver-studded holster. In those days he would spin that shiny new Colt, and he would swill his beer and walk the streets of El Paso with his chest puffed out, watching people part in both directions. The world gave him far more room than he needed.

Fast Larry . . . A kid's name, he thought, a ridiculous moniker that singled him out from others for only one reason — he could kill men. He could, with the rise of a gun and the drop of a hammer, wipe fellow human beings off the face of this earth as if they had never existed. All that person might have been or hoped to be stopped short, ceasing forever before a gray drift of smoke from Fast Larry's pistol. There'd been something God-like about it in those days, yet look at him now. He'd had to scrape together the last of his pocket change just to get shoes for his horse. Then he couldn't even take a chance on getting it done.

He felt the skin on his neck turn cold, and he ran a hand across it. *Fast Larry . . .* But that young man was gone now, and in his place stood Lawrence Shaw, his hands bloody, his time coming fast. He glanced back at the reflection in the water for a second, and behind his face he saw other faces, pale, tortured visages he would some-day have to account for. They stared back, vague and ghostly, seeming to draw him toward them until he batted his eyes and looked away, shaking them out of his mind.

Yes, there was madness there . . . he saw more and more of it with each passing day. But he was powerless to stop it, and he knew that soon it would claim him and leave him somewhere to die on a burning rock, babbling his last words to some imagined old friend from his childhood, or to his long dead mother, perhaps. Either way, in the end it would be the madness that killed him . . . madness and nothing more.

Avoiding his reflection this time, he plunged his head into the water, shattering whatever rippling picture lay there; and when he raised up, he slung his hair and beard back and forth the way a dog might do to dry itself, standing up and running both hands back across his head. Four feet away, with its reins looped around a stand of rock, his buckskin raised its muzzle from the water. The horse looked at him and blew out a deep breath, then bent once more to drink.

He could have killed that Ranger yesterday. He knew it. But then what? Ride on to the next lawman and kill him, too? Then the next? And so on, until all he lived for was the sound of the next gunshot, the sight of the *NEXT MAN FALLING!* The next man *FALLING IN SOME NAMELESS DIRT STREET IN SOME DUSTY TOWN! IN SOME TOWN NOT-FIT-FOR-MUCH-MORE-THAN-A-WATER-STOP-ALONG-THE-ROAD-TO-GOD-ONLY-KNOWS-WHERE?*

Easy now . . . He caught himself ranting and checked himself down.

There it was again, he thought, the same madness, but in its other form . . . that raging voice inside him that lived deep down in a dark silence until something stirred it and sent it boiling to the surface.

He calmed himself and tried again to clear his mind from all thought except that of the morning breeze and the coming heat of the day. All right, he needed to keep busy. He lifted the worn bone-handled .45 from his belt and sat down on a rock, and laying the gun on his lap to look at it. Okay, he would clean it. He would clean it and check it and put it away and, then what? He would ride on . . . somewhere out there today he would take on some snake meat or berries, or a young elk up in the high passes this evening if he was lucky. Everything involving his sustenance required killing, he thought. Death was all that kept him alive. He would eat and ride on, then sleep and ride some more. He would sit down again on a rock somewhere, and once more clean the pistol, then check it, and spin the cylinder and put it away. . . .

Land and sky would rise and fall before him and at the end of the day he would be somewhere, anywhere. Perhaps he would be on Mexican land, perhaps American — it had all come to look the same to him. Whatever border was there slipped past his eyes and the buckskin's hooves unaware, until they came upon someone or something from a distance, and the sight or shape or color of it at last told him where they were.

He shook his head and cleared it, and looking around, realized that he had cleaned and checked the pistol and put it away, and had already ridden out on the buckskin a mile or more before he knew it. It was getting worse, he thought. How much longer would it be before he went blank and wandered aimlessly for days at a time? Or — even worse — had he already done that and just didn't realize it?

Coming around a turn in the trail that led down onto a lower terrace of flatland, Lawrence Shaw didn't see the Mexican on the paint horse until he heard the click of a shotgun hammer and turned to one side to see the man smiling at him from the shadow of a tall rock crevice. Shaw stopped the buckskin and sat slumped with his hands across the worn-down saddle horn. He stared with a blank expression until the Mexican shifted a bit, anxious in his saddle, and said, "It is wise to raise your hands when someone points a scattergun at you, *hombre.*"

Lawrence Shaw heard the words, but their meaning was lost to him as his mind tried to sort them, to catch up to them, arrange them into some kind of working order. Until he could do so, all he could hear was a jumble of words that might as well have been spoken in a foreign language. But the Mexican gave him no time to catch before he spoke again. "Do not think I won't kill you, *hombre.*"

He caught the last part of what the Mexican said, and the rest was coming to him, along with what he could see from the man's expression and the handful of cocked shotgun. "Wait," Shaw heard himself say, his own voice sounding strange to him. "It's been . . . a long time." He stared at the man but still did not raise his hands. When the sound of horses' hooves came behind him down the sloping trail, he turned slightly and saw the other riders move down and form a cautious half circle around him.

"You're looking a little puny, Sanchez," JC McLawry said to the Mexican, stepping his horse forward of the others, his arm around the young woman seated on his lap. The woman looked away as Shaw's eyes met hers. JC continued, "Why is this man alive when you clearly told him to raise his hands and he didn't do it?"

The Mexican stared at Shaw, bemused, as he said to JC, "I was just about to kill him when you rode down. I think I do it now."

He braced his hands on the shotgun.

"No, wait," JC said, as the men in a half circle around Shaw shied away from the coming blast. "I know you, don't I?" JC stared at Shaw.

"I . . . don't think so," Shaw said, struggling with his words.

"Yeah, sure I do." JC adjusted the woman's position and sidled his horse a few feet closer to Lawrence Shaw's buckskin. The buckskin pinned its ears back and blew a threatening breath toward JC's big roan. The big roan shied. "You're the one they call Fast Larry. The gunslinger, Lawrence Shaw, right?"

A murmur went through the other men. Shaw looked around at them in turn, then back to JC McLawry. But he didn't acknowledge JC's question. Instead he said, "What do . . . you want?"

JC noticed the stall in this ragged drifter's voice, and he cocked his head slightly. "You've been out here a long time, haven't you? You can barely understand what I'm saying."

"I — Yes . . . it's been . . . a long time." Shaw breathed deep and felt his mind clearing, his words starting to come easier now.

"Hear that, boys? Fast Larry Shaw." JC grinned, staring at Shaw as he spoke.

"Sanchez was about to get himself killed by the fastest gun handler alive." He chuckled, looking at the bone-handled .45 shoved down in Shaw's spent leather belt. "Except he doesn't look all that spry today. Looks like he's lost his holster somewhere."

"He was not about to kill me," Sanchez said, his face reddening. "I was about to kill him. I think maybe he is not this Fast Larry as you say. I think he is a bummer, is what I think."

"No, you're wrong, Sanchez," JC said, his mouth sneering against the woman's neck as he spoke. "I recognize that buckskin stallion. I was there when Fast Larry shot Whispering Deak Robinson down in the street at Wakely. Deak was fast as a rattlesnake . . . this man shot him before ole Deak ever cleared the top of his holster."

Shaw barely heard JC as he spoke. In his mind he pictured Whispering Deak, his face half blown off, his right boot scraping back and forth in the dirt, seeking purchase on a world fast fleeting from him. "I'm . . . leaving now," Shaw said. He backed his horse a step and had started to turn it on the trail when the men drew closer.

"Whoa now," JC said. "It's impolite to just turn and leave. I'm not through talking with you yet. Where you headed? What business have you got out here?" As JC spoke, he grinned and nuzzled the woman's cheek. "I can't have you out here getting in my way. I've got some important things going on. Maybe you better tag along with us a little while."

"I . . . don't think so," Shaw said, feeling JC press him.

"Then maybe you better think again. I'm out to take a sucker down. I don't want nobody tipping him off — firing a shot or something."

"Your business is . . . your business." Shaw raised his head enough to let JC get a good look at his eyes. "I'm hunting food."

JC looked over at the Mexican with the cocked shotgun. Ordinarily he would have already told Sanchez to blow a hole through this sucker. But not today. He had to think the way the Ranger thought, do things the way the Ranger did things, work things around to his advantage.

"Hunting food?" JC smiled, making it look friendly this time. "Why didn't you say so? We've got food — fresh water, mescal and whiskey too, if you're a drinking man." He shrugged. "I'd consider it an honor if you'd join us." *Yeah, you loco wild-eyed lunatic. Come on, do what I say.* "We're all *amigos* out here in the badlands." He swung

117

an arm, taking in all the swirl of heat and dust and blinding sunlight.

"Well, I suppose —" Shaw raised his hand and scratched his dusty beard.

"Sure, come join us," JC said. He nodded at Sanchez. "Lower the shotgun, *amigo*. This man is one of us."

Chapter 7

Lawrence Shaw held the tin coffee cup with both hands and sipped fresh water from it. His eyes moved back and forth across the top of the cup, watching JC McLawry and his men closely. Now and then he looked over at the woman huddled on the blanket in a thin slice of rock shade. Her arms were wrapped around herself as if by some strange twist of elements she suffered a chill here in this crushing desert heat. A few feet from Lawrence Shaw, JC stood up, took a bag of tobacco from his shirt pocket, and tossed it near Shaw's feet.

"How long since you've put a smoke together for yourself?" JC asked him.

"Too long," Shaw replied, his voice coming back now with use, with hearing other voices. He picked up the bag, tore off a rolling paper, rolled himself a smoke and struck a match JC handed him, drawing deep and blowing out a long stream of blue smoke. "I went into a town yesterday . . . to get my buckskin shod." His voice stalled for a second, then found itself and went on. "Needed some goods . . . some cartridges, some coffee. But I ran into a badlands Ranger . . . who has been after me. I had to leave."

"Yeah? The Ranger, huh?" JC smiled. The others sat looking at Lawrence Shaw the way they might look at a man with a third arm grown out of his chest. "Believe it or not, that's the very person we're waiting for out here. Figure he'll be by here most anytime, pulling the Misery Express back to Circle Wells. So, he's been dogging you too?"

Lawrence Shaw nodded. "He was. I suppose he still is. They say he never lets up off a man once he gets him on his list."

"Yep," JC nodded. "That's the same thing I've heard." He looked around at the others — Percy lowering his eyes as JC's gaze moved across him. Then JC turned back to Lawrence Shaw. "Let me ask you something, Fast Larry. Do you believe in divine providence?" JC leaned close, a solemn expression on his face.

"I don't believe in anything," Shaw said in a flat tone.

"Oh . . . well, it doesn't matter that you

do." JC straightened a bit and grinned. "I believe in it enough for both of us. I think that every step a man takes leads him closer to the next thing he has to do in life. Can't argue that, can you?"

Shaw only stared.

"I thought not," JC went on. "See. . . ." He tapped a finger to his head. "I know that it was more than just coincidence that we ran into each other out here. I believe it was meant to be. There's something that brought us together. And we'll be together until we do whatever it is we were supposed to do."

Shaw sipped his water, his eyes on JC yet seeming to be at some distant place. "And what's that?"

JC spread his hands. "You tell me. Here's a Ranger dogging you? The same Ranger that dogged me the past two years? Now he's got my kid brother prisoner?" Again he leaned closer. "Something's at work here, Fast Larry. Can't you see it? Can't you feel it? I mean what are the odds on us meeting like this . . . you, the fastest gun alive. Wandering around out here like a damn ghost. With no purpose." He thumbed himself on the chest. "And me, a man of direction — a leader of men." He swung his arm, taking in the scraggly gathering of outlaws on the ground. "Hellfire! Running into me is about the best thing that could have happened to you — to both of us, for that matter. I'm offering you something here."

Shaw closed his eyes for a second, and when he opened them he shook his head slowly and said, "I don't want . . . to kill anybody. Not ever again."

"Not going to kill any— ?" JC stopped short and stared at him for a moment. *This might take a little time.* "Lord, Fast Larry! Listen to you! It's a little late in the game for you to decide you're too good to *kill* anybody." He shook his head, laughing out loud, turning to the others, then back to Shaw. His laughter wound down to a chuckle, then to a sigh. "All right. I know you're not thinking straight right now. You take it easy for a spell. We'll see how you feel later on."

"I'll feel the same," Shaw said. "You . . . want me to leave?" He looked around and started to stand up.

"Take it easy, Fast Larry." JC held a hand out toward him. "Get you some food working in your belly — rest up. Clear some of this desert out of your head. Nobody's hurrying you."

Shaw eased back down, wrapped his hands around the tin cup, and looked down into it as though it were a deep well. JC turned, gestured the other men away with a nod, and walked over to the edge of the cliff to look down onto the flatland.

"Boss," Sanchez said, as the men gathered around JC, "why you no let me shoot this *loco* sucker? Why we fooling around with him? He is an imbecile, no?" He spread his hands.

"Maybe, maybe not," JC said. "Didn't you hear anything I told him, about us running into each other out here for a reason?"

"Awww, come on, Boss," Sanchez threw back his head, chuckling. "I hear you tell him, but I know that you are, how you say, *pushing his leg,* eh?" Sanchez nudged an elbow into Becker, standing beside him.

Becker give a toothy smile. "Yeah, that's what I kinda figured too, Boss . . . that you were just" — he shot Sanchez a correcting glance — "*pulling* his leg a little." Sanchez looked embarrassed.

JC breathed deep and let it out slowly, considering something for a second as he gazed down on the flatland. "Yeah, I was, at first anyway." He spat and turned to Becker and the others. "But the more I talked, the more I started thinking about it. Maybe I was right . . . what *are* the chances of us running into one another out here?"

The men looked at one another, bemused. "Well, whup me with a burnt skillet," Becker said, grinning, his big teeth seeming to take over his entire face. "Boss! For crying out loud! Don't tell me you started believing your own line. That's what happened to ole Lloyd Percy here, and look at the shape *he's* in."

"What *shape* am I in?" Percy tried to look confident, but his expression appeared a bit shaky. No one answered him.

"Forget it," JC said. He nodded at Stinson. "You, take Dewey and a couple others with you. Ride back and fan the trail down there. When you see the Misery Express, skin on back here and let me know. Whatever you do, don't let that Ranger see you. He's got eyes like a damn hawk."

"All right, Boss," Stinson said.

JC turned to the others as Stinson, Dewey Toom and two others walked back to their horses. "Becker and Percy, stay here with me. The rest of you spread forward a few miles, make sure we got no army patrols out there anywhere. I want to know about anything that lifts its head in these badlands."

"Boss, I don't mind riding the trail." Lloyd Percy tried to offer a slight smile, but it came out tight and nervous. He sweated.

"I always like to do my part."

Becker grinned. Leaning in toward Lloyd Percy's ear as if to plant a deadly kiss, he whispered, "Wipe your forehead, Lloyd. You've done plenty."

JC just looked at them, then turned, facing the woman on the blanket and Lawrence Shaw on the ground with his cup of water clasped in both hands. The two of them sat twenty yards away in the wavering heat. Near them, the men gathered their reins, mounted, and rode away. And when they were gone, Lawrence Shaw studied the cup before his face and without turning to the woman, he asked her in a low voice, "Who are you?"

She sat slumped with her head down, her glistening black hair hanging forward, shielding her face. Without raising her head, she answered, "I am nobody."

A silence passed as Lawrence Shaw gazed across the rim of his cup and watched JC McLawry and Becker turn and walk along the edge of the cliff and look out across the wide sandy basin below. "So am I," Shaw said after a while. He finished the water with a long swallow and sat staring at the empty cup in his hands.

The morning they left town, Sheriff Petty

stood holding the door to the jail wagon open while the prisoners, their hands cuffed in front of them, filed one at a time out of his office and down off the boardwalk. Maria stood to one side with her rifle. The Ranger walked behind the last one, the young gunman, who looked all around the dusty street as if to find among the townsfolk a familiar face who would come to free him. "It's not going to happen, young man," the Ranger said as if reading his thoughts. He nudged him forward. "So put it out of your mind and enjoy the ride."

When the last of the four prisoners were inside and seated on the wagon floor, the young gunman and Granddaddy Snake on one side, Billy Lee and Curtis Roundtree on the other, Sheriff Petty swung the door shut and the Ranger padlocked it. Straight across from Granddaddy Snake, Billy Lee stretched his cuffed hands out, pointed a finger at the old Indian and shook it. "I'll tell you one thing, Ranger," Billy Lee raged, "this old dog-eating cannibal will be lucky if he makes it out of here alive! He has wronged me in ways that *cannot* be made right — he's got to die for it!"

"Pipe down, Billy Lee," the Ranger said. "If you can't ride in the same wagon, I'll have to make you walk along behind it. Do you want that?"

"*Me?* Why would it be me having to walk? He's the one caused all the trouble! Look at my head! My face!"

The old Indian bared his teeth at Billy Lee with a low growl, then gazed out into the distant swirl of dust and heat. Billy Lee jerked his hands back. "There! Ranger? Did you see that? He's making threatening faces at me. Damn it! Why don't nobody take my side in this?"

"He's telling the truth this time, Ranger," Curtis Roundtree said. "I saw it myself. I'm not just saying because Billy's my friend. This is putting me on a bad spot here, the way these two are carrying on."

"You'll be fine, Curtis," Maria said, walking past him to step up onto the wagon.

"I can't say I'm sorry to see you leave," Petty said to the Ranger, shaking his head. "This is the most nerve-racking bunch I've ever seen."

"They'll settle down once we get under way." The Ranger tightened his sombrero down on his forehead. "This heat will melt all the starch out of them."

Sheriff Petty followed him as the Ranger walked around the wagon and stepped up onto the passenger side, lifting the shotgun from under the seat and checking it, then laying it across his knee. "Hope you're right about them robbers going on away," Petty said. He ran a hand along his jaw, a concerned look on his face.

"I wouldn't worry about it." The Ranger adjusted himself on the wagon seat. "Forewarned is forearmed."

Petty smiled and lifted the brim of his hat. "I've never quite understood what that means, or how it helps. But I'll have everybody here keeping a closer eye on any stranger that comes through from now on."

"That's always a good idea." The Ranger touched the brim of his sombrero, Maria slapped the reins and pulled the wagon forward. Petty and a few townsfolk stood watching as dust rose up in their wake.

The Ranger and Maria rode forward on the wagon through the stillness of morning. By noon, when they pulled off the trail into the sparse shade of a cottonwood tree at the edge of a thin stream of water, the four prisoners had drifted to sleep in the slow, monotonous pitch of the wagon and the pressing blanket of heat. They stirred at the feel of the wagon settling to a stop beneath them and looked at the Ranger through bleary eyes as he climbed down with three canteens in his hands. "Guess we'll be eating a little something here, won't we?" Curtis Roundtree stood up and held on to the bars with his cuffed hands.

"Don't worry. Curtis, we haven't forgot about you." The Ranger walked down to the stream, uncapped the canteens, laid them facing upstream in the shallow trickle of water, and let them fill as he gazed up along the distant ridges a mile away. He scanned the ridgeline, taking his time, and had just started to look back down when a flash of sunlight caught his eye. He swung toward it, but it was gone now. He was still looking for it when Maria came up beside him from beyond the cottonwood tree, buttoning her denim trousers. "Did you see it?" he asked, without taking his eyes off the ridgeline.

"I saw it," she said, her rifle in her hand, her eyes moving along with his. "But what was it? A rifle, perhaps?"

He didn't answer. After a moment, he stooped to retrieve the canteens, looping them over his shoulder. "Whatever it was, it's either gone . . . or else it's hiding. It's out of range, anyway." He turned away from her. "Wait here while I take the prisoners to relieve themselves."

"Be careful," she replied, still looking off into the distance with wary eyes.

"What's that, Ranger?" Curtis Roundtree

leaned against the bars and took one of the canteens the Ranger passed to him.

"What was what, Curtis?"

"Come on now, Ranger. I saw something up there. Saw it plain as day. So did you." He nodded down toward Maria. "She saw it too. Look how she's acting."

"Don't worry about it, Curtis. It could've been any number of things." As the Ranger spoke to Curtis Roundtree, he noticed that the young gunman's eyes seem to perk up a bit.

"Yeah? Name one, Ranger." Billy Lee sat fanning himself with his hat brim.

Granddaddy Snake only stared at the Ranger, but his eyes said that he also seen the flash of light up there, and that he knew as surely as the Ranger and these others knew — there was only one thing that could have caused it.

From high up among the ridges and scrub brush and boulders, Rance Plum, the bounty hunter, turned to his partner, Jack the Spider, and said in an exasperated whisper, "Now you've done it, you *bungling* fool. They've spotted us!"

Jack the Spider flared, staring at Rance Plum through his one good eye, his other eye covered by a black patch. "Don't call me a fool, you pompous son of a —" He drew back the binoculars in his hand, ready to crack Plum across the face.

Plum shielded his face with his forearm. "That's it, let them see it again! In case they didn't get a good look before!" Spittle flew from Plum's lips, flecks of it glistening on his pencil-thin mustache.

Jack the Spider lowered the binoculars and let out a tense breath. "I'm warning you, Plum. No more name-calling. So what if they did see it? It's just the Ranger. Him and his woman."

"That's not the point, *dear Mister Spider!*" Plum raised his voice in a sarcastic tone. "You had no idea who it might have been when you flashed those binoculars — bright enough to signal a ship at sea, I might add! We are supposed to be professionals, sir, *pro-fess-ionals!* Can you even *spell* the word?"

"Never mind what I *can* or can't spell." Jack the Spider spat and looked out and down through the hot air with his naked eye. He turned to Rance Plum. "Since they know somebody's up here, we might just as well go down and let them see it's us. Don't you think?"

Plum stared at him for a second, then said with a tight smile, "Why certainly. We're such good friends, the Ranger and I. And I've so wanted to see him . . . perhaps *reminisce* about old times."

"You don't have to act like a turd about it." Jack the Spider spat again and looked away.

"A *turd*?" Rance Plum shook his head, disgusted. "A *turd* indeed." He moved back from the edge of the rock cliff and stood up, dusting off his knees. "I suppose that's the type of crude verbiage I should expect from you."

"Why don't you pull your thumb out of it and wipe it on your shirtsleeve, Plum?" Jack the Spider moved back also and stood up beside him. "We've got no problem with him on this one. We're working for the Mexican government. Let's go down and show ourselves. Who knows, those prisoners might be some of the boys we're looking for."

"Oh, my, yes. And if they are, then what? Simply ask him to turn them over to us?" Plum turned to his horse and unspun its reins from the pinyon tree. "It must be *fascinating,* that world you live in, Mister Spider."

"Well, I'm going down whether you go or not." Jack the Spider unhitched his horse and drew it to him. "It's better than getting him spooked, thinking maybe we're following him or something. Don't forget, he once broke a board over my head."

"How could I ever forget." Rance Plum climbed into his saddle and turned his horse on the thin path. "We will go down there. But may I suggest we wait and go down tonight right after dark. If anybody else is roaming around up here, it's better that they do not see us. Can you understand that?"

Jack the Spider looked embarrassed. "I was going to suggest the same thing."

"But *of course* you were . . . dear Mister Spider." Rance Plum turned his horse in a huff, tweaked his mustache with his thumb and finger, and moved off along the winding trail.

CHAPTER 8

Throughout the rest of the day, as they traveled on in the cumbersome jail wagon, Maria and the Ranger kept a close watch on the ridges to their right. At dusk they made a camp in a dry wash surrounded by mesquite brush and gnarled scrub cedars. When the prisoners had been fed and watered, the Ranger called Maria to the side and said in quiet voice, "I'll be moving out as soon as it's good and dark. Once I'm out there toward the ridges, stoke the fire up a little more than usual and keep out of sight."

She nodded. "Will you be taking one of the horses?"

"No. I want to stay afoot." He nodded toward the wagon. "I don't want them to see me leaving on a horse. Besides, it's not that far. I'll stay within a hundred yards and circle behind whoever comes down from the ridges."

"Be careful," she said.

"I will. I don't sense any trouble. But we're going to be ready just in case."

From the wagon ten yards away, Billy Lee stood up and rattled the bars and called out, "Hey, are you talking about us over there? I don't think it's wise, leaving me and this old Injun in the same wagon over night. I might lose control and kill him. You best let me sleep out there on the ground. I won't make a run for it, I promise."

"You'll be all right where you're at, Billy Lee," the Ranger called over to him. "Get settled down now, and get yourself some sleep."

"Sleep?" He rattled the bars. "That's all we've done all day is sleep . . . this blasted heat. Now it's getting cold. We're going to need some blankets here."

"I have some blankets for you," Maria said. "I'll bring them as soon as you pipe down."

Billy Lee called out. "Hey, we could freeze out here without blankets to—"

"Why don't you sit down and quit bellyaching?" The young gunman cut him off. "You're starting to really get on my nerves."

"Oh?" Billy Lee turned facing him with a dark grin. "Well, now, look who's decided to get his two cents in, here at the end of the day."

The young gunman looked up at him from across the wagon floor where he sat leaned back against the bars beside Grand-daddy Snake. His right arm was in a sling, the bandage around his chest and neck browned by road dust. "That's right," he said to Billy Lee. "I'm sick of your mouth. Don't think I won't come up off this floor and rip your tongue out. You're not fooling with an old Indian here."

Granddaddy Snake shot the young gun-man a sharp stare.

"That's some mighty cock-proud talk for a man with a hole in his chest," Billy Lee said. "If you wasn't such a piss-poor shot in the first place, we wouldn't be stuck in this blasted wagon, now would we?" He leaned slightly toward him. "So don't start making a bunch of threats you ain't up to keep-ing . . . big, bad gunman."

On the floor beside Billy Lee, Curtis Roundtree scooted away a couple of feet. "Boys, I swear, this ain't the time nor the place for this kind of stuff. We got a long ride ahead of us. We best all get along."

The young gunman glared from one to the other, seeming to run something through his mind. After a second he let out a breath, nodded toward Curtis Roundtree and said to Billy Lee, "This fat boy is right.

We've got no reason to be at odds. We need to get together if we plan on getting out of here."

"Who you calling *fat boy*?" Curtis Round-tree huffed.

"He's calling *you* fat boy. Now hush," Billy Lee said to Curtis. Billy Lee slid down the bars and sat staring at the young gun-man, focusing his full attention on him. "What're you talking about? There's no way we're going to get out of here. If you're planning on a break-out, you just as well forget it."

The young gunman looked past him through the bars for a moment. As Maria and the Ranger moved farther away, to where the horses stood hobbled in the dry wash, he said in a guarded voice, "I don't have to make any plans. I've got somebody making the plans for me. I'm getting out." He raised his cuffed hands and thumped himself on his bandaged chest. "The question is, are you boys ready to get out too. Because if you are, you need to decide pretty quick. Once it happens, I'm not sticking around to help somebody who won't do their part."

"Yeah?" Billy Lee looked at Curtis, then back to the young gunman. "What part are you talking about? I'm not going up against the Ranger, if that's what you've got in mind. I'd sooner you stick a rattlesnake in my pocket."

"Huh-uh, me neither. I want no part of the Ranger." Curtis Roundtree shook his big head.

Granddaddy Snake just stared. He hadn't eaten the strips of jerky the Ranger passed out among them earlier. But now he put a piece in his mouth and chewed it slowly, not swallowing it.

"I'm not talking about going up against the Ranger. That'll be taken care of. What we'll need to do when the time comes is make sure you're not caught off guard. We'll need to get the keys to these cuffs, this wagon door — things like that. I don't want the three of you running in circles and falling all over one another. If you want out of here, you'll need to pay attention to what I tell you. Can you do that?" His eyes moved from one to the other, questioning them. Granddaddy Snake only stared off into the distance, still chewing the piece of jerky.

"Whew, I don't know," Curtis Roundtree said, running his cuffed hands across his broad forehead. "I'm only looking at a little bit of jail time — maybe a couple of months is all."

"Are you kidding?" The young gunman

stared at him. "I heard what you did, beating those men up. How do you know one of them didn't die? Nobody would tell you about it until you get back to Circle Wells. Then they might spring it on you, then and it'll be too late. You go down for the hangman, just like me. Think about it."

"I hate to say it, Curtis, but he might be right," Billy Lee said. "Does it make sense, the Ranger coming all this way to get you just for busting a couple of teamsters in the head?"

"But he said the judge takes a dim view of assault." Curtis looked worried.

"There, you see what I'm saying?" The young gunman leaned forward a bit. "That right there ought to tell you something."

"Well . . . that's him," Billy Lee said. "I'm a different story, though. I sold a horse a few times. They won't do much to me. At worst I'll get a year. I can do a year in jail standing on my head."

"But that won't be in the *jail,* with somebody bringing you hot meals from the hash house," the young gunman said. "We're talking about prison. Have you ever done hard time? Have you heard about the new territorial prison? How tough it is there? I've seen the way this old Indian can handle you. What do you suppose those seasoned convicts will do to you? Who knows, you might even run into one or two you skinned on a horse deal. That should be real interesting."

Billy Lee considered it. He started to say something more, but Curtis Roundtree hushed him as Maria came walking back to the wagon. She climbed up into the wagon, raised the wagon seat and took out four folded blankets. The four prisoners watched her come around to the side of the wagon. "Here, each of you take one. Shake it out good. When you are finished with them, stack them in the front of the wagon."

"Ha, I don't stack blankets," Billy Lee said. He snatched a blanket from her and wadded it up in his hands.

"Where's the Ranger?" Curtis Roundtree asked, looking around in the grainy darkness.

"He has gone into the bushes," she said, offering nothing more.

"One of these threadbare old rags won't be enough to keep anybody from freezing." Billy Lee looked at the blanket in his hands. He threw it to the front of the wagon. "I need another one."

Granddaddy Snake looked at the crumpled-up blanket Billy Lee had thrown. He smiled to himself, looking from the blanket to the wall of bars, feeling the shadow of an idea taking shape in his mind.

"That one is all you get," Maria said to Billy Lee, turning to walk back over to the low fire, where she picked up broken twigs and mesquite brush and laid them into the flames.

"See?" The young gunman said in a whisper to Billy Lee. "That's the kind of treatment you can look forward to for the next few years. That is, if somebody don't bash your brains out or run a piece of steel through your gizzard. You better give this some serious thought. Come morning, if you say you're in with me, that's fine. If not, don't come up changing your mind at the last minute. It'll be too late. There's some things that has to be done before my buddies get here. I'm going to need some help."

"What kind of things?" Billy Lee and Curtis Roundtree looked at him.

"Never mind *what* things until I hear you say you're with me on this," the young gunman replied. "You just do some thinking and let me know."

"I'll — I'll think about it." Billy Lee looked at Curtis Roundtree as he spoke.

"Me too," Curtis Roundtree said, nodding. "This ain't the kind of decision a man ought to make on the spur of the moment.

What do you say, Granddaddy?"

Granddaddy Snake watched the three of them turn to him, but he didn't even change his expression. He spit the chewed-up piece of beef jerky into the palms of his hands, rubbed his hands together, and ran his wet, greasy fingers through his tangled hair.

"Lord have mercy," Curtis Roundtree said. "That's downright disgusting."

"See? —" Billy Lee winced and shook his head. "You can't count on this old fool for nothing."

"What's he charged with anyway?" the young gunman asked, staring at Granddaddy Snake.

"He et the judge's lapdog," Billy Lee said.

The young gunman looked bemused. "You're kidding."

"Naw-sir, it's the truth." Billy Lee chuckled under his breath. "He et it plumb down to the nubs . . . ears, eyeballs, and all, I reckon."

"Whoa," the young gunman whispered, "that *is* disgusting."

Granddaddy Snake turned his face from them and rubbed his greasy hands across his forehead, back across his ears, and gazed out through the darkness, upward at the black shadow of the distant ridgeline. He sat as silent as stone.

■ ■ ■ ■

A hundred yards out, the Ranger lay in the cooling sand between a short rock spur and a cholla cactus while night settled thick and dark onto the sprawling land. A quarter slice of moon glowed in the upper dome of starlight, and about him the land drew and tightened like the belly of a cooling woodstove. The first sound to catch his attention was the brush of paw and nail across a facing of flat rock. He lay silent and watched the low black outline of a coyote move closer, then stop a few yards away and crouch, blinking shining red eyes at him. *Good cover. . . .*

The animal had not found him by sight but rather had sorted him out by scent — something whoever had been flanking them all day from the ridgelines could not do. The Ranger lay still and watched another pair of red eyes appear up out of the land and move closer in. Now the two coyotes sat staring, black against the shadowing glow of starlight until behind them, either another scent or perhaps a sound too faint for the Ranger's ears unsettled them and sent them scurrying away.

In a moment he heard the low hushed

sound of hooves on sand, and he measured the slow rhythm in his mind. Two horses, he decided. Then, listening closer, he caught the third, off-rhythm, sound. A pack mule, he thought. Two riders and their pack mule, in no hurry, yet moving with caution toward the glow of the campfire. He readied himself with his rifle in hand and lay tense now until he heard the familiar voice of Jack the Spider and Rance Plum break the quiet of the land. "I can never see a thing at night like this," Jack the Spider said, making little attempt to keep his voice down.

Rance Plum let out an exasperated breath and spoke in a strained sarcastic whisper. "Oh? How strange. Do you suppose having only one good eye might have something to do with it?"

"No, it's got nothing to do with how many good eyes a person has. Some people see better at night than others." Jack the Spider's voice was still too loud against the quiet of the desert night.

Plum gestered out into the darkness. "At any rate, it's comforting to know that your oratory skills are by *no means* encumbered."

"Hunh?" Jack the Spider's voice seemed to boom out in the darkness. "What are you saying? That I'm too loud? Then you ought to listen to yourself. You whisper louder than most people can scream."

"Never mind, Mister Spider," Rance Plum hissed. "I'm certain if the Ranger is anywhere within a mile, he's heard you by now."

From his cover in the sand, the Ranger shook his head and rose up onto his knees. "You're right, Plum," the Ranger called out from ten yards away. "I heard you and smelled you."

"Jesu— !" Startled, Rance Plum sawed back hard on his reins and his horse reared up. "Whoa!" Behind Plum, the pack mule spooked at the sidelong brush of the first horse's tail and flew into a fit of bucking and braying as Jack the Spider sidled his horse out the stir of things, hearing Rance Plum crash to the sandy ground with a loud grunt.

"Shut that animal up!" Plum bellowed from the ground, his voice carrying far across the desert floor. Jack the Spider reached out from his saddle, caught the mule's lead rope and yanked on it, trying to settle the animal. But the mule would have none of it. It kicked and honked and brayed until the Ranger stepped in, caught it by its bridle, and steadied it down with a gloved hand across its muzzle.

"My goodness, Plum." The Ranger settled the mule, then reached a hand down to

Plum. "If I'd known you spooked that easy, I wouldn't have said anything."

Plum pushed the Ranger's hand aside and scrambled to his feet on his own, slapping sand off himself with his hat. "I wasn't spooked, sir. I was simply caught unaware. We're on a manhunt. I would appreciate a little quiet!"

"Then you can start by lowering your voice," the Ranger said. "I caught a glimpse of you two up in the ridges earlier. If you act like that most times, I expect this manhunt isn't going as well as you'd like for it to." He looked back and forth between Plum and Jack the Spider in the darkness, a slight smile on his face.

"We were doing well enough," Plum said in a haughty tone. "We happen to be hand-picked by the Mexican government to track down a dangerous gang of outlaws."

"Handpicked, huh?" The Ranger handed Plum the mule's bridle, then took the reins to Plum's horse and pitched them to him.

Jack the Spider climbed down from his saddle and said as he neared Plum and the Ranger, "What he means is they couldn't find anybody else who can work this side of the border, so they hired us."

"It's honest work," Plum said, tilting his chin upward, talking to the Ranger in the darkness. "And it might surprise you to know that this gang we're hunting is led by none other than JC McLawry. How does that pique your interest?"

"McLawry. . . ." The Ranger said in a almost hushed tone. "The man with the blue star tattoo. It's been over a year since he dropped out of sight. I figured he must've gone over into Old Mex. Also figured it wouldn't be long until he wore out his welcome there."

"You're assumptions are correct on both counts," Plum said. "He and his gang do as they please. When the *federales* get too hot on their heels, they slip back here and lay low for a while. He even has his younger brother riding with him from what we've heard. We saw that you have some prisoners in the Misery Express. I hope you won't mind if we look them over . . . see if any of them might belong to JC's gang?"

"You're welcome to look them over," the Ranger said. "But you won't find any of these boys worth fooling with." Even as he spoke, he pictured the young gunman — Mac McKenzie — and tried to recall any resemblance to JC McLawry. "I've got a horse grifter, a brawler, old Granddaddy Snake and a cowboy named Mac McKenzie who got drunk and shot a young woman."

"But you don't mind if we take a look —
for our own satisfaction?" Plum moved to
the side of his horse and took down a
canteen. He uncapped it and took a swallow.

"Help yourself. You realize if I had one of
JC's men, I wouldn't turn him over to you
for bounty."

"That's the same thing I told him,
Ranger," Jack the Spider said.

Plum only tossed a gaze upwards into the
darkness, capped his canteen, and led his
horse forward, then he and Jack the Spider
walked along beside the Ranger back toward
the glow of the distant campfire.

While the Ranger, Rance Plum, and Jack
the Spider moved away in the darkness, a
hundred yards farther back, the four outlaws
from JC's gang sat atop their horses, looking forward into the night toward the faint
sound of voices where moments before
they'd heard the braying mule.

"What do you think, Stinson?" Dewey
Toom asked. Then he looked past Stinson
in the darkness to the other two men, a
stout young Texan named Barrows and an
older outlaw called Whitey. Before Stinson
Carlisle or anybody else could answer,
Dewey Toom continued, "I don't know what
the rest of yas are thinking, but if we get

tangled up out here and end up with a couple of bounty hunters on our trail, JC ain't going to be real happy. I can tell yas that right now."

"Ease down, Dewey," Stinson said in a quiet voice. "I didn't say for sure those men are bounty hunters, I just said they looked like a couple of man hunters I saw back in El Paso a time or two. Don't get nervous and soil yourself over it."

A low ripple of laughter moved across the men. After a slight pause, Stinson added, "Whoever they are, if we hadn't followed them down out of the ridges, we'd never caught sight of the jail wagon. We can thank them for that."

Dewey Toom stirred restless on his saddle. "Well, now that we've spotted it, the best thing we can do is get on back to JC and let him know. I have no ambition at all toward mixing it up with that Ranger . . . especially out here in the badlands."

Stinson Carlisle shook his lowered head. "You mean with four of us here, you're still afraid? You oughtn't admit it in the presence of men. We might think you're built different than the rest of us."

Dewey Toom's face swelled red. "Any time you think you can —"

"Awww, shut up, Dewey." Stinson brushed

his words aside, then said, "We're going to wait here till morning, see if those other two ride on or not. If they do ride on, I'm going down there and getting Bobby McLawry. To hell with all this fooling around. I can see a blue star in this. There'll be four of us against two of them — one of them's a woman. I can't ride back and face JC with that kind of information. I'd be ashamed." He glanced at the other two men on his right. "What about you, Whitey . . . Barrows?"

"Yeah, it looks puny all right," Whitey said under his breath.

"But that's what JC asked us to do," Dewey Toom said. "He knows that Ranger better than the rest of us."

"Call it to suit yourself, Dewey," Stinson said. "But as soon as the time feels right, I'm making a move on that Ranger." He spat and ran a hand across his mouth as if to close the subject to any further discussion. Then he turned his horse quietly in the night, the others following behind him single file beneath the sliver of the quarter moon and the hazy silver glow of starlight. In moments they disappeared into the darkness. The two coyotes came out onto the trail, sniffing the ground and looking at one another. Blinking red eyes, they spun in a silent flurry of fur and tail and were gone like wisps of smoke.

CHAPTER 9

At the outer edge of the campfire light, Maria stepped from the shadows and joined the Ranger as he, Rance Plum, and Jack the Spider came down into the dry wash. When they had poured themselves a tin cup of hot coffee, they moved alongside the jail wagon and looked in on the prisoners. The Ranger noted that the young gunman lay wrapped in his blanket in the dark front corner of the wagon. It appeared he was pretending to be asleep, the Ranger thought.

Rance Plum's eyes moved back and forth across Billy Lee, Curtis Roundtree, and the old Indian. "Hello, Granddaddy," he said. "The Ranger told me what happened with the judge's dog — most unfortunate." Plum smiled beneath his thin mustache. Granddaddy Snake grunted and leaned back with his blanket wrapped around him, his wrinkled face and tangled hair looking moist and oily beneath a sheen of jerky grease.

"Obviously these three are not a part of the gang we're looking for," Plum said to the Ranger. "What about the chap rolled up in the corner?" He gestured his tin cup toward the young gunman.

"Not a chance," the Ranger said. "He'd been drunk in town for a few days, him and another fellow. You can look him over in the morning if you like. He's getting over a bullet wound. I hate to wake him."

"Right you are," said Plum, looking away from the young gunman and back to Billy Lee and Curtis, who stood against the bars, their blankets draped across their shoulders. "I daresay, the men we're hunting are a whole different class of outlaw than this rabble."

"Hey, you flatheaded fool!" Billy Lee kicked a boot through the bars toward Rance Plum. "Who are you calling *rabble*? Open this door for two minutes and I'll rabble your fine feathered arse!"

"Indeed?" Plum fumed, stepped forward with his hand on his pistol butt.

"Take it easy, Plum." The Ranger moved between Rance Plum and the jail wagon. "You know how prisoners like to let off steam on their way to court."

Jack the Spider chuckled and looked closely at Plum. "I never noticed before, but your head is a little bit flat on one side."

Plum cursed under his breath.

"Hey! What are you laughing at, idiot?" Billy Lee stared at Jack the Spider and shook the iron bars. "You look like something that ought be led on a string and poked along with a sharp stick. You dead-eyed, lap-legged son of —"

Jack the Spider hurled himself at the jail wagon, but Rance Plum and the Ranger caught him midair. "Let me go! I'll rip his damn head off!" He struggled until Plum and the Ranger carried him away from the wagon and set him down near the campfire.

"Both of you should know better than this," the Ranger said to them, brushing spilled coffee off the front of his shirt. "You act like this is your first time being around jailbirds."

Rance Plum ran a hand across his forehead. "It's been a long, hot day, Ranger."

"Yes it has." The Ranger and Maria motioned the two bounty hunters toward the campfire, the flames now lower and licking sideways, sparks racing down the dry wash on a desert wind. "Rest yourselves for a spell. We'll take turns standing guard tonight, in case these men you're hunting happen to be out there."

"I have to admit, Ranger," Rance Plum

154

said, seating himself on the ground, "I thought you'd be more than *mildly interested,* hearing that we're hunting JC McLawry."

The Ranger smiled in the flickering glow of firelight. "He's just one more hard case in a world of many, as far as I'm concerned. I hope you get him — but I've no interest in him, unless he happens along in front of my gun sights."

"Oh?" Rance Plum gave him a skeptical look. "Do I sense that perhaps you've gone a bit off your game since last I've seen you, Ranger? Is this what it has come down to for you? Teamstering a jail wagon? Gathering up bummers and grifters?"

The Ranger saw the low smoldering in Maria's dark eyes as she flashed them at Rance Plum. But before she could say anything, the Ranger cut in. "It's a job that needed doing, Plum, and I was the only man available to do it." He shrugged. "I'll leave JC and his boys to you two. I've come to realize that I can't catch them all."

Rance Plum and Jack the Spider looked at one another, stunned by the Ranger's words and attitude. The Ranger turned to Maria and said, "Why don't we take the first watch? Let these two get some rest?"

"*Sí,*" Maria said, wondering herself what

155

the Ranger was up to. She picked up her rifle and moved off with him toward the dark shadows along the edge of the dry wash.

In the jail wagon a few feet behind Plum and Jack the Spider, Billy Lee and Curtis Roundtree sat watching until they saw the bounty hunters lower their heads and doze. Then Billy Lee scooted across the floor to where the young gunman lay wrapped in his blanket. "How'd we do?" Billy asked in a whisper. "Did we keep their attention away from you or what?"

Without moving, the young gunman whispered, "Yeah, you did good, real good. Keep doing what I say and we'll be out of this Misery Express in no time at all."

Granddaddy Snake raised his head from his knees, looked at them for a second, then lowered his head and adjusted his blanket around his bony shoulders.

After Rance Plum and Jack the Spider had finished eating and bedded down outside the circle of firelight, the Ranger and Maria stayed up on watch together until deep into the night. The three prisoners were fast asleep, wrapped in their blankets on the floor of the wagon. In the dark hours of morning Maria shook Plum and the Spider by their shoulders and awakened them to stand watch. Then she and the Ranger moved away with their blankets and rifles under their arms.

"Look at those jail rats," Jack the Spider said under his breath, nodding toward the sleeping prisoners. He grumbled as he poured two cups of strong leftover coffee for Rance Plum and himself. "They get to sleep while we sit up half the night. I can't see the Ranger getting stuck with a job like this. This is the kind of task that should go to a new man. He must've got on somebody's bad side back in Circle Wells."

"No, Jack," Rance Plum said, sipping his coffee and blinking sleep from his eyes. He kept his voice low. "From all I know about him, I wouldn't be surprised to learn that he actually volunteered to do it."

"Then he must be as crazy as everybody says he is," said Jack the Spider.

"Indeed." Plum glanced to where the Ranger and Maria had bedded down in front of the wagon. He added, "During the years he and I rangered together, I saw him do some most peculiar things." Plum looked around at the jail wagon, then back to Jack the Spider. "You can see where it's gotten him in life. A saddle for a pillow, sleeping on the hard ground."

"I can't see that we're doing any better,"

said Jack the Spider. "We sleep on the same ground." He dusted a hand across his trouser leg.

"But there is quite a difference," Plum said. "We're businessmen — professionals. He works for pocket change. At the end of this hunt you and I will be smoking a fine cigar, sipping wine in a plush hotel of our choosing. He will still be sleeping on the hard, dusty ground, awaiting the next miserable job handed down to him."

"Yeah," The Spider smiled. "Since you put it that way." He sipped the strong coffee and gazed out across the shadowy desert floor.

At dawn, the Ranger and Maria were up. They fed and watered the prisoners and hitched the team to the wagon while Plum and the Spider saddled and prepared their horses for the day's ride. The Ranger noticed that the young gunman did not stand up with the other three prisoners and stare at Plum through the bars, nor had he faced Plum and Jack the Spider as the Ranger had taken the prisoners two at a time out into the mesquite brush to relieve themselves.

"I trust our paths shall cross again, Ranger," Rance Plum said when he'd shoved his rifle down into his saddle scabbard and stepped up into his stirrup. "Until such time, I wish you well with your Misery Express endeavor." He smiled, backed his horse and tipped his high-crowned hat toward Maria. "We thank you for your hospitality."

"Watch your backside, Plum," the Ranger said. "You too, Mister Spider." He and Maria watched the two bounty hunters turn their horses and ride off, stirring a low rise of dust. When they were more than a hundred yards away, the Ranger turned to the wagon, saying to Maria beside him, "Now, let's see if our Mister *Mac MaKenzie* is who I think he is."

He swung the barred door open and stepped up inside the wagon as Maria stood back, holding her rifle. "Make room, boys, let me through," the Ranger said. Billy Lee and Curtis Roundtree stepped to the side. Granddaddy Snake pitched his blanket on the pile of blankets at the front of the wagon and sank down on the floor, wrapping his bony arms around his knees. "What do you want, Ranger?" The young gunman pressed back against the front wall of the wagon, stepping onto the pile of blankets.

The Ranger stared at him from two feet away. "You're JC McLawry's kid brother, aren't you?"

"Never heard of him," the young gunman said. He glared in defiance.

"Lower the sling down from your neck," the Ranger said, reaching out toward him.

The young gunman jerked his head to one side, moving away from the Ranger. "Go to hell —"

The Ranger snatched him forward, cutting his words short, and jerked the sling down an inch. The blue star tattoo stood out bright against the prisoner's beard stubble. "It figures," the Ranger said, shoving him back. "You've managed to keep your neck hidden all this time."

"What of it?" He sneered at the Ranger and cast a glance at Billy Lee and Curtis Roundtree. "Yeah, JC's my brother. I'm Bobby McLawry. JC will be coming for me soon enough. I'll settle with you — we both will. You're going to see a lot of blue star tattoos before this is over."

"That's what this was all about. Now I see why you took a shot at me." He let out a breath. "That poor girl died because of some crazy vengeance you wanted to collect for your brother. Why? So you could show him you're as tough as he is."

"I don't have to show JC a thing. He knows I'm as tough as he is. Step down in the dirt and give me a gun . . . then you'll

160

know it too."

The Ranger shook his head and moved back toward the barred door. "Boy, you have no idea how simple that would be." He backed out, closed the door and locked it.

"What's the matter, Ranger," Bobby McLawry said, grasping the bars and shaking them. "Have you ran short of nerve all of a sudden?" The Ranger ignored him.

Billy Lee and Curtis Roundtree had been silent, watching. Now Billy Lee called out through the bars, "What's the deal here, Ranger? What about Curtis and me? Are we going to be in the midst of a bad situation if his brother comes to spring him free? You can't just let us sit here and get shot at, can ya?" He directed a knowing smile at Bobby McLawry and winked as the Ranger turned away from them.

Curtis Roundtree watched Billy Lee with a troubled look on his face. He didn't see anything funny about it, and he wasn't at all interested in getting involved up with a gang of outlaws, especially not the type of outlaws who prowled these badlands back and forth across the border. Curtis whispered to Billy Lee, "Maybe we ought to sit tight here and keep our noses out of this. Not make things worse for ourselves."

161

Billy Lee whispered in reply, "Stick with me, Curtis. We'll be fine. Once we're out of this Misery Express, we'll be free to go our own way." He shot Bobby McLawry a glance. "All we got to do is side with you until we're out of here, right?"

"That's right," Bobby McLawry said. "My brother's coming. You can count on it. Just do like I tell you, you'll be free as birds."

Maria stepped in beside the Ranger as he walked forward and started to climb up into the driver's seat. "Maybe we should head back . . . leave this one in town and wait for the judge to make his rounds."

"And leave Sheriff Petty to face JC McLawry and his gang alone?" The Ranger replied to her as he settled on the seat and unwrapped the reins from around the long wooden brake handle. "JC will leave that town in ashes." Maria stepped up and sat down beside him, looking out across the desert toward the thin line of sunlight glistening in the east. "Besides," the Ranger added, running his hands along the reins smoothing them out, "JC already knows everything by now. He's out here some-where. He'll cut off any move we make back toward town. Plum and the Spider are on his trail. If he comes after us, let's hope they're not far behind him."

"What help will they be?" Maria looked off in the direction the two bounty hunters had taken toward a stretch of hills.

"Any help is better than no help at all." The Ranger slapped the reins and sent the horses forward. "I know a little about JC McLawry. He's a coward, a sneak, and a back shooter. It wouldn't matter if we had his brother prisoner or not. JC would never face me straight up toe to toe. But if knows he's got a chance to catch me at a disadvantage, he's going to take a run at me. His first move will be to try catching us by surprise — hit us quick before we can fight back. Let's just be ready for it."

A silence passed, then Maria asked in a low voice, "It has been a while since you've seen JC McLawry. How do you know he has not changed? Maybe you do not know how he thinks now."

"Oh, I'm sure he's changed some," the Ranger said. "He's gotten smarter, meaner, bolder even. But a man is what he's born with inside. That doesn't change. He might have some hard core killers riding with him. He might have become a hard-core killer himself. Deep down inside, though, he's the same sneaking coward he always was. He's just carrying it around in a different package." The wagon rolled forward ahead of a

163

low wake of dust.

A mile ahead, where the trail dipped into a long land crevice, Stinson Carlisle pushed himself back away from the edge of sandy soil and stood up, dusting his hands on his trouser legs. He looked at the others and grinned. "Boys, we'd be fools to pass this up. Their riding right into our laps."

"I think we ought to do like JC said." Dewey Toom looked at the others for support but saw none, then lowered his eyes and fidgeted with the two sets of reins in his hands.

Stinson Carlisle snatched a set of reins from Dewey Toom's hand and pulled his horse forward. "Then you stay back and get caught up on your knitting. I'm getting Bobby out of that wagon and taking the Ranger's head to JC on the end of a stick." He looked around at the others. "Anybody else ain't got the guts for it is welcome to cut out of here."

"I didn't say I wouldn't help you," Dewey Toom said, looking embarrassed. "I'm only saying it ain't a good idea —"

"We know what you're saying!" Stinson cut him off. "Lord knows we ought to. You've said it enough all damn night. Now pile your dirty ass into your saddle and act like you're supposed to act before I whip you like a dog."

Dewey Toom bristled. "One damned minute! Nobody whips me like I'm a dog —"

Barrows, the young Texan, stepped between them and picked up his horse's reins. "Boys, if we're gonna kill 'em, let's get to doing it. If not, I'd just as soon ride somewhere, get a bottle of whiskey and forget about it. What about you, Whitey?"

The older outlaw rubbed a hand along his white beard and grinned, showing his stained and broken teeth. "Drinking or killing, makes no difference to me. Either way, I don't want to stand out here and fry in my own sweat thinking about it."

Stinson Carlisle settled and let his hand fall away from his holster, stepping back from Dewey Toom, but still keeping his eyes on him. "Let's go then," he said. "I ain't never killed a Ranger before . . . it might be fun." He put his foot into his stirrup and swung up onto his horse.

CHAPTER 10

On the floor of the wagon, the prisoners swayed back and forth with each turn of the wheels on the hard, rocky trail. The wagon wound steadily downward alongside a wide dry wash that ran six feet deep, like the cut of some drunken surgeon across the belly of the land. With his good hand, Bobby McLawry reached up and grasped the bars to steady himself. Then he blotted sweat and grit from his forehead and said to Billy Lee and Curtis Roundtree in a whisper, "There's a spare key they keep back up under the driver's seat in case of emergencies. All we've got to do is get our hands on it."

Curtis Roundtree cocked his head in curiosity. "Now how do you know all this?"

"Because my brother used to drive this damned thing back and forth to the old prison before it burnt to the ground."

Billy Lee leaned forward a bit. "You mean

he worked for the law?"

"That's right . . . until he wised up."
Bobby McLawry looked back and forth
between the two of them. "Now he's got his
own gang, the Blue Stars." Bobby raised his
bandanna and showed them the tattoo on
his neck, tapping a finger against it. "You
don't get one of these babies unless you've
proved yourself worthy of it. My brother's
the one who set up the big prison break. He
helped Ernesto Caslado escape. He
would've made a fortune on the deal if it
hadn't been for that Ranger. Now, all we've
got to do is get that key —"

"But Ernesto Caslado ended up dead,"
Curtis Roundtree said, cutting him off.
"And after the way you said the Ranger did
you with that little key trick back in town,
I'd think you'd have learned your lesson by
now."

Bobby McLawry glared at Curtis. "Listen
to me, fat boy," he hissed. "None of that
means nothing. Once my brother and his
gang make their move, you're either with
me or against me. I'm getting out of here.
You either go along with it or we can leave
you laying dead on the ground. That's as
clear as I can say it."

Before Curtis could answer, Billy Lee cut
in. "Come on, Curtis. Once his brother kills

167

these fools, what are you going to do, sit here and wait until some other lawman comes and finds you?"

Curtis Roundtree's eyes moved over to Granddaddy Snake, who sat in silence watching them. "What about you, Granddaddy? Are you going along with this or not?"

"This is white man's business, not mine," Granddaddy Snake said. "You do what white men do. I will do what I do."

"Now, what's that supposed to mean?" Curtis asked, agitated.

"Forget him," Billy Lee said. "Can't you see he's rabbit-ass nuts? That's the only reason I ain't killed him already. Let him go his own way. Look at him . . . greasier than a damn pig. Won't even feed himself. I always heard an Injun goes loco behind bars. Reckon it just hit him quicker than most."

Granddaddy Snake looked away, out through the bars, and closed his eyes. A fly circled his greased forehead.

A silence passed, then Billy Lee shook his head. "Okay, how do we get the key from under the seat?"

"Our only chance is when they take us out to the bushes," Bobby McLawry said. "My brother, JC, is smart. He'll watch and wait until the Ranger and the woman are busy attending to us. Then he'll make his move. Whoever is out in the bushes then will have to get to the key while all the shooting's going on. We'll have to move quick —"

He stopped short when the sound of a rifle shot exploded from the low hills to the right of the wagon. The four prisoners spilled forward as the wagon braked to a halt. Another shot rang out. This time the bullet pinged off of the bars and raised a splintered gash in the wooden floor. "God Almighty! They're gonna kill us!" Billy Lee screamed. The four of them scrambled farther toward the front end of the wagon as a shot whistled through one side of the bars and ricocheted off the other. The horses reared and tried to bolt at the sound of the rifle fire.

"I thought you said your brother would wait!" Curtis Roundtree yelled from his position flat on the floor, spit flying from his trembling lips."

Granddaddy Snake rolled into a ball against the front wall of the wagon. Above him, Maria's rifle barked. Then she jumped down from the wagon and took cover beside it. The Ranger wrestled with the reins, lay-ing all of his weight on them, setting the brake handle with his free hand, struggling with the spooked horses. A shot splintered the wagon seat close to his thigh. He wrapped the reins tight around the bottom of the brake handle, made two half hitches in them, grabbed his rifle, and jumped down. He hurried forward, caught one of the frightened horses by its bridle and held it back, trying to settle it.

"You men stay flat in there," he called through the bars, raising his rifle and levering a round into the chamber as he spoke. He took aim on the two riders charging from the front as more rifle fire kicked up the dirt on their right side. "Get over here, Maria, quick! They're hitting us from two directions." The team horses whinnied and strained forward. But the brake held. The tight reins and harnesses creaked against the horses' pull. On the other side of the wagon, Maria dropped down and scurried beneath it, coming up beside the Ranger as shots thumped into the ground at her heels. Another shot zinged along the steel wagon frame. "Let us out of here, Ranger!" Billy Lee screamed, flat on his belly, shaking the bars with both hands.

"Take out the two in front before they shoot the horses," Maria called out to the Ranger, moving to the rear of the wagon.

"I'll keep the others busy." She took aim around the rear of the wagon and fired toward the flash of shots fifty yards away in the cover of rocky ground.

The Ranger raised his weapon and aimed again, stepping out from beside the horse team. His shot snatched one of the riders out of his saddle and sent him rolling sideways in a spray of dust, his arms flapping in the dirt like blades on a broken windmill. The other rider veered away and pounded into a retreat as the Ranger levered another round. Through the cover of swirling dust, the Ranger's shot found him, but caught him high in the right shoulder. The rider flew sideways out of his saddle and disappeared.

"Two down," the Ranger yelled back to Maria. "I'm turning these horses out of the line of fire." He leaped back up into the wagon, freed the reins, and dropped the brake handle. Shots rang out, but this time they stopped when Maria fired back, the bullets flinging up chunks of rock and dirt in the riflemen's faces.

"Damn it," Barrows cried out, scooting back in the sand to rub a knuckle into his eye. "That bitch sure cuts a straight piece of iron!"

Whitey rolled away on his side, brushing

chips of shattered rock from his hat brim. "Stinson's deader than hell out there. I saw him go down. Saw Dewey crawl off into some brush. He's hit — probably dead too by now."

Barrows crawled over beside Whitey and saw the streak of blood down the side of his throat. "You're clipped, old man."

Whitey touched his gloved fingers to his throat. "A rock chip hit me is all. I'm all right. Thought Stinson said they'd shoot them horses first thing riding in."

"Yeah, well, Stinson Carlisle said a lot of things." Barrows checked his rifle, shaking his head. "But he won't say no more. We should have listened to Dewey, I reckon. Now we're stuck with what we've got here."

Whitey raised up slightly and looked out toward the wagon, then dropped flat as a shot from Maria's rifle whistled overhead. "It ain't natural, a woman handling a gun that way."

"Any chance at their horse?" Barrows handed him a dusty bandanna and watched him mop up the blood from the cut on the side of his throat.

"Naw, they've turned the damned wagon on us now," Whitey said. "Got the horses out of sight. They're holed up good and sound."

"Damn it. There's no telling how long this'll take. I wanted to ride somewhere and get some whiskey . . . maybe some cold beer to thin it down."

"It's a long ride to town from here," Whitey said, examining the spot of blood on the bandanna.

"So? I was riding anyway."

Whitey gazed off for a second. "JC is really going to be pissed about all this, ain't he."

"Oh yes, I would say so. This ain't at all what he told us to do out here." Barrows sucked a tooth and tipped his hat brim up high on his forehead.

A silence passed, then Whitey said, "Are you all that keen on getting a blue star tattooed on your neck?"

"It ain't the most important thing in my life," Barrows said. "I never cared much for tattoos of any kind. Makes it awful easy to identify a man, I always thought." He paused and slapped a sand flea from his face. "Knew an ole boy in Waco once, had the word 'mother' tattooed down his pecker."

"You're kidding. What was that suppose to mean?"

"I don't know what he meant by it — he was strange anyway. But it never got him very far in life, that big ole tattoo. By his

173

own admission, he ran out of room for the R, so it ended up just being 'm-o-t-h-e.' "

Barrows chuckled and slapped another flea off his cheek. "He shoulda planned it better, I reckon. Ain't that the damnedest thing?"

"Could have been worse," Whitey said. "He could've run out of room for the e. Then it would just say *'m-o-t-h.'* Get it? 'Moth'?"

Barrows frowned. "No I don't. Turns out, they hung that poor boy in El Paso for deeds I wouldn't care to describe." He sucked air through his teeth. "Damn, I still miss that place — Texas."

"Texas, huh?"

"Yep, born and raised there. I'm what you'd call a Panhandle low-heeler."

"Got any friends left there?"

"One or two, if they ain't been hung."

"Any good banks to rob there?"

"There must be — everybody robs them."

Another silence passed. "Well?" Whitey wadded up the bandanna and lay staring at him.

"Well, what?"

"You said something about wanting a drink?"

Barrows grinned. "I *hear* ya."

"Think we can crawl back to our horses

without her shooting our heads off?"

Barrows's grin widened. He scooted back an inch. "Hell, you just watch us."

When the drift of the fleeing riders' dust stood on the west horizon, the Ranger unhitched one of the team horses from the wagon and rode it bareback out to where the body of Stinson Carlisle lay in a tangle of dried mesquite brush. On his way back to the wagon, he'd followed a blood trail in the sand and found Dewey Toom cowering behind a deadfall of juniper with his left hand clamped to his right shoulder. "I'm — I'm bleeding pretty bad here, I want you to know," Dewey Toom said, his face pale beneath a coating of dust. "None of this was my idea, if that means anything to you. I told them we had no business doing it. I came from good God-fearing folks — my mama was a churchgoer her whole damn life."

"There's nothing like a good upbringing, I reckon." The Ranger showed a trace of a smile. With his pistol barrel, he gestured the outlaw out of the juniper brush. "Lift that pistol from your holster and see how far you can chuck it with two fingers."

Dewey Toom turned loose of his wounded shoulder, lifted the pistol with his bloody thumb and finger, and lobbed it six feet away. "How's that?" he asked, eager to oblige. "It's true what I said about my mama."

"That's fine. Now let's take a walk back to the wagon, see if we can keep you from bleeding dry on us."

"Yes, sir." Dewey Toom staggered along in the sand with his hand clamped tight to the bleeding wound.

At the wagon, Billy Lee stood up and held the bars with both hands, seeing the Ranger atop the team horse, following the wounded outlaw as he wove like a drunkard along the trail. "I wish you'd look at the mess coming here," Billy Lee blurted out. Maria trotted forward to meet the Ranger on the trail. "If that's what your brother's gang looks like . . . you've got bigger problems than you realize. Not only couldn't he fight, hell, he couldn't even *run away*!" On the floor, Granddaddy Snake looked up for a second, then lowered his head, spit a piece of chewed-up beef jerky into his palms and rubbed them together. Flies swirled.

"Keep your voice down," Bobby McLawry said to Billy Lee, jumping up beside him. "You want to tip them off what we're up to?"

"They can't hear me. Besides, what the

hell's the big secret now?" Billy Lee swatted a fly that droned near his face. "I think it's easy to tell your big brother *JC* is trying to break you out of jail." He leaned nearer to Bobby McLawry. "Of course, it didn't go near as *smooooth* as you seemed to think it would."

"See what I was saying, Billy Lee," said Curtis Roundtree, sitting on the floor, fanning himself with his hat. "We're better off going along with things here — keep out of this big-time outlaw stuff."

"Big-time outlaw?" Billy Lee chuckled. "If I'd known this was all it took, I'd turned big time years ago. I'm just a two-bit horse grifter, but damned if I couldn't make a better stand than that. Bang, bang, it was over and done! That Ranger and the woman just powdered your brother's cheese, the way I saw it." He pointed off toward the wake of dust left in the distance when Whitey and Barrows had fled west. "Now *those two* out there seem to have the *getaway* part worked down to a fine art. But other than that, I can't see where much happened. Nothing to our benefit anyways — we're still stuck in this Misery Express, same as before."

A hush fell over the group as the sound of rifle fire echoed from the low hills on the western horizon. The Ranger looked up from where he had seated Dewey Toom on the ground. Maria had cut away Dewey Toom's bloody shirtsleeve to tend to his wound. She looked up in question at the Ranger as the prisoners turned toward the sound of the shots. "Looks like they ran straight into Plum and the Spider," the Ranger said. He said to Dewey Toom. "You're the lucky one of the bunch, as it turns out."

"Yes, sir," Dewey Toom said, swallowing a dry knot in his throat.

In the wagon, Billy Lee turned to Bobby McLawry. "Well, I take it back. They didn't have the *getaway* part worked down after all."

"You son of a —" Bobby swung at him with his good hand, but he was off balance with his right arm in the sling. The punch caught Billy Lee on the chin but didn't have enough strength behind it to take him down. Billy Lee threw both arms around Bobby McLawry and the two fell rolling on the floor.

"Ranger!" Curtis Roundtree bellowed, reaching down to separate the two men. Granddaddy Snake hugged his bony knees closer to his chest to give them more room, but otherwise only sat there, watching them pound on each other from a few inches away.

"Hold it, boys! That's enough!" The Ranger swung the door open and jumped inside, grabbing Billy Lee by his shoulders and throwing him off of Bobby McLawry. "Stay there," he demanded, pointing toward Billy Lee. Billy Lee sank back against the wall, his breath heaving in his chest. Curtis Roundtree grabbed Bobby McLawry from behind as the young man came up from the floor, the sling from his right arm dangling down his side.

"Stop it, dang it," Curtis Roundtree said, holding Bobby McLawry back in a bear hug. "It's over now. Let it go!" On the floor, Granddaddy Snake looked up at them, sighed, and ran his greased palms back through his hair.

"I won't have it, Billy Lee," the Ranger said. "There's too much going on to have to deal with your mouth all the time." He stepped back, between the prisoners and the open door.

Billy Lee settled a bit and paced back and forth, rubbing his chin. "I'll kill this big-talking idiot if you leave me near him. I swear I will, Ranger. When I do it'll be on your head —" Before he'd completely gotten his words out, he lunged at Bobby

McLawry. This time, the Ranger brought his pistol up from his holster and cracked Billy Lee behind the ear with the long barrel. The blow was enough to stun Billy Lee but not enough to knock him out.

"Oh, Lord. . . ." Billy Lee staggered back, his hand going to the rising knot behind his ear. His other hand went out, palm down as if to steady an unstable world. "I'm . . . sorry, Ranger. I don't know what came over me." He sobbed quietly under his breath. "I just can't stand it anymore. Look at this — out here in this God-forsaken desert, in this steel oven on wheels. It's driving me crazy!"

As Billy Lee staggered in place he gestured down at Granddaddy Snake, who was still rubbing jerky grease on his bony shoulders beneath a droning circle of flies. "And here's this old buzzard, stinking to high heaven — drawing flies from as far away as Kansas!" He stopped in front of Granddaddy Snake and drew back a boot. "I ought to kick his damn face in!"

"Hold it!" The Ranger saw the old Indian ready himself, like a rattlesnake ready to make a strike. But the Ranger stepped in between them and shoved Billy Lee back a step. "You get out of here, Billy Lee," he demanded. "Go on. Walk around the wagon a time or two. Get yourself calmed down before Granddaddy takes another chunk out of your head."

Billy Lee looked at the Ranger and hesitated before stepping down through the barred door. "I . . . can't promise I won't make a run for it, Ranger. Don't know if I trust myself that far."

"You're not going anywhere, Billy Lee. You're not that stupid. Get on out of here. Go cool off." The Ranger gave him a shove.

As Billy Lee stepped down and staggered off around the side of the wagon, the Ranger turned to Bobby McLawry and helped him raise the sling back up around his shoulder. "How many more men does JC have riding with him?"

Bobby McLawry stood rigid, facing him with a cold stare. "You know where you can go, Ranger."

"Wherever I go, you can bet I'm taking you with me." He shoved him back against the bars.

"Nothing suits me more, Ranger." Bobby McLawry spread a nasty grin. "I set out to kill you, and I will, one way or another. You can't offer me a thing. Either JC gets me out or we all die out here together. Now chew on that and tell me what it tastes like."

From a few yards away, Dewey Toom had heard the conversation, and he called out,

"There's nine men left, Ranger, ten counting a newcomer. A fellow named Lawrence Shaw just threw in with us. They say he's the fastest —"

"Suit your mouth, Dewey!" Bobby yelled out through the bars. "You never was nothing but a yellow cowardly bastard! I'll watch you die with your guts hanging out!" He swung his eyes from Dewey Toom to Maria. "You too, lady!"

"Easy, boy." The Ranger jerked him back, faced him. "You're right. I've got nothing to offer you. You'll hang in Circle Wells, or you die out here. All you're running on now is deep-down meanness, with nothing to lose. So I won't ask you another thing." He raised the big pistol, cocked it, and lifted Bobby's chin on the tip of the barrel. "You've got your heart set on seeing somebody die? Then watch this." A muscle twitched in his tight jaw, his finger pulled tight across the trigger. On the floor, Granddaddy Snake shied to one side and raised a hand to shield his face from bone fragments. Curtis Roundtree stood breathless, ash white.

Outside the wagon, Maria stood back slowly from attending the wounded outlaw and called out the Ranger's name in a hushed tone. But the Ranger didn't seem to hear her. "Sam . . . ?" She said his name

182

again, low, calmly. This time the Ranger seemed to hear her. He shivered for a second. Then his breath came out long as he checked himself down. "Remember this, boy. If it comes down to a bloody end, you won't have the satisfaction of watching me or her die. I won't give you that. Neither my badge nor my oath demands it of me. I'll lay them both in the dirt and call what I do to you flat-out murder." He lowered the big pistol an inch, stepped back, uncocked it, then stepped back and out the barred door.

Billy Lee stood beside the door with his hands chest high, studying the strange expression on the Ranger's face. "Go on and shoot him, Ranger," he said in a quiet tone. "It'd make this trip easier on everybody."

"Shut up, Billy Lee." The Ranger took him by the shoulder, shoved him up into the wagon, and swung the door shut.

"See how that went?" Billy Lee spread his hands, grinning at the others. "Just my luck — gone two minutes and missed the whole damn show."

CHAPTER 11

"Lawrence Shaw, you said?" The Ranger handed the wounded outlaw a canteen of water and looked down at him while Maria finished bandaging his shoulder. "When did Fast Larry throw in with JC and his bunch?"

"Just yesterday," Dewey Toom said. He swilled tepid water from the canteen, poured a dribble into his cupped hand and rubbed it on his face. "I'm sore as a boil here — weak as a kitten, too. But that's normal, ain't it?" He looked worried. "I mean, being weak? After losing so much blood?" He glanced at Maria, then back to the Ranger. "Anybody feels that way, don't they, after being shot?"

"You're going to live," the Ranger said. "Now what about Lawrence Shaw joining the gang? I always knew him to be a loner."

"Well, that may be true. I can't say he's actually thrown in with us — or *them,* I should say, now that I'm what you call out

184

of the business. We ran into him out on the badlands. Poor bummer don't even have shoes on his horse."

"Is that a fact?" The Ranger made note of it.

"Yep. JC more or less pressed him into staying with us. Lawrence Shaw's got a reputation as a fast gun, you know." He raised his brow and nodded. "Yeah, that's the thing that got JC excited. Fast guns don't come along so often in this line of work. Usually what you get out here is a bunch of big talkers, fellows too lazy to work and too dumb to uncoil a rope with both hands —"

"I know pickin's are slim among the outlaw profession," the Ranger said, cutting him off. He glanced at Maria, then asked Dewey Toom, "What about the other men? How loyal are they to JC McLawry?"

Dewey Toom shrugged his good shoulder. "You know how it goes. You stick with a man while he's on top — or if you're afraid of him. Other than that, nobody owes nobody nothing. JC's a mean sumbitch. That's why I've stuck with him so long. Afraid to leave, you might say. Besides, Whitey and Barrows cut out and look what happened to them." He nodded toward the distant hills, then looked back and forth from Maria to the Ranger. "Is my telling you all this gonna help me some? Get me a stroke or two up under the judge's robe?"

"Watch your language," the Ranger scolded.

Real sorry, ma'am." Dewey Toom ducked his head, embarrassed. "I hope it does help me some, though. You wouldn't believe what a terrible childhood I had. The fact is, just yesterday I'd decided to turn my life over to Jesus — you know, start living right? Be a better person? Get out of this whole outlaw business? But then, this had to happen."

"If you tell all that to the judge," the Ranger said, "I'm sure it couldn't hurt you any."

In the wagon, watching and listening through the bars, Bobby McLawry said to the others in a low voice, "Listen to that egg-sucking dog. I should've shot him a long time ago. But that's okay, JC will kill him real slow and painful once we get out of here."

Billy Lee smiled, looked first at Curtis Roundtree, then at Bobby McLawry. "Don't let this send you into another frenzy, but I really don't have a lot of faith in your brother's jail-breaking abilities. I believe I could put together a tougher gang out of any saloon west of Abilene."

"You don't know squat." Bobby McLawry spat and looked away. "You and your mouth! Just wait. You've blown any chance of being in on this. When JC springs me, I'll be sure and take care of you before I leave."

"Now that really hurts my feelings," Billy Lee said, grinning now, shooting a wink at Curtis Roundtree, Curtis looking concerned, curious about whatever it was Billy Lee was up to.

"Piss on your feelings." Bobby sat looking away from him.

"Well, then. If that's the way you feel about it" — Billy Lee's voice dropped to a low whisper as he darted a glance out at Maria and the Ranger — "I'll just take my *key* and go home." He lifted his loose shirttail an inch and exposed the top of the brass key shoved down in his waistband. Then he dropped his shirttail, smoothed it down, and sat grinning, gazing out toward the Ranger and Maria as the two of them lifted the wounded outlaw to his feet and led him toward the wagon.

"I'll be damned," Bobby whispered under his breath in disbelief. Curtis's mouthed gaped open, but Granddaddy Snake just sat staring, the flies stirring atop his head.

"Um-hmm, and well you should be," Billy Lee said to Bobby McLawry. Now it was

Billy Lee's turn to stare off through the bars. "See . . . while all your big-time *outlaw* talk was going on, this ole horse grifter was the only one knew how to put something together and get the job done." He gloated, raising his chin a bit. "Yep, I just reached up under that seat and there it was, shining like a beacon in the night."

"Quick, give it to me, before they get over here," Bobby said.

"Naw, let's not get in no hurry. You might lose it, the way things are going for you." Billy Lee grinned. "Besides, we might need to talk a little bit first. I'm curious just what kind of money a man might make for him- self, riding with a *big-time* bank-robbing gang like your brother's."

Bobby narrowed his gaze on Billy Lee as the Ranger and Maria brought the wounded prisoner closer to the wagon door. "Are you serious?" he asked.

"Do I look like I'm joking?" Billy Lee's expression turned somber. "From what I've seen, I could make a better hand at it than these other saddle tramps he's got riding for him."

"Maybe I've been wrong about you," Bobby McLawry said. "Maybe you've got more than just a big mouth." He glanced around as the Ranger reached out and unlocked the barred door. "We'll talk later," he whispered.

Dewey Toom stepped up into the wagon hesitantly. The Ranger nudged him forward. "Don't worry. Anybody gives you any trouble, I'll crack their head for them. Find you a spot and sit down. The rest of you men — one at a time. Let's go, relieve yourselves and get ready for a hard ride this afternoon. You can thank the McLawrys for any inconvenience from here on."

Granddaddy Snake stood up on spindly legs and moved to the door first. When he stepped down and the Ranger locked the door, Maria backed off a few feet and stood watch on the other prisoners while the old Indian padded barefoot off toward a low stand of scrub cedar. Billy Lee cocked his head, eyeing the Ranger and Granddaddy Snake as they moved out of sight. "For a man who doesn't eat or drink, he sure is quick to spill his innards."

Maria only looked in at Billy Lee, then turned away when he made a lewd face at her and laughed under his breath. Then he turned to the wounded prisoner and started in on him. "Now you, you blank-faced, warp-eyed turd. Just look at yourself. What in the blue living hell are you supposed to be? If you had any man about you at all, you'd have blown your brains out in the sand. You dirty sock full of dog sh—"

"Lord, Billy Lee!" Curtis Roundtree interrupted him in a pleading voice. "Don't you ever let up? You're wearing me plumb out. We've known one another a long time, but I swear I'm on the verge of killing you!" He squeezed his big hands into fists and opened and closed them in his frustration.

"Yeah, well . . ." Billy Lee let out a breath and slumped back against the bars. "What else is there to do in here? Sure can't count flowers on the wallpaper."

By the time the Ranger brought Granddaddy Snake back and took Bobby McLawry off behind the scrub cedar, Curtis had settled his nerves and moved over beside Billy Lee. "Sorry I yelled at you."

"Don't worry about it," Billy Lee said.

Curtis Leaned closer and whispered, "I hope you know what you're doing, wanting to throw in with a bunch like the McLawrys. Once you get on that road, there's no turning back."

"Ha, did you see any turning back from the road we were already on? There ain't never been any turning back that I've ever known of. I ain't looking forward to going to jail. What about you?"

"No, I'm not. But heck, we pull our time,

then we're out before you know it."

"Then what? Go back to horse grifting and bar room brawling, same as before?"

Curtis shrugged his big shoulders. "Well . . . yes, until we get a break in our luck. That's what we do, ain't it?"

"Hell, Curtis. There ain't any lucky breaks coming to us." Billy Lee glanced out at Maria, saw she was looking away, then turned back to him. "I'm doing some serious thinking. Only reason we ain't done more in life is because we ain't tried to. Admit it — we never thought of ourselves as being bold enough to do like JC or Bobby. We've been scared to take the chance — afraid we couldn't handle it."

"You're talking stupid," Curtis said.

"Stupid? Maybe. But what have these rootin'-tootin' outlaws done so far that we couldn't do? All they've done is get themselves shot all to hell. If they had any sense, they wouldn't be fooling around with this Ranger, they'd be off robbing a bank somewhere. That what I would do if I was them."

"That's just it, Billy Lee, we *ain't* them. We never was."

Billy Lee grinned. "That's about to all change." He patted his waist. "If this JC McLawry really comes along at the right time, I'm out of here with him. Don't forget, I'm the one managed to do what Bobby was only talking about doing. I slicked the Ranger into letting me out. I did that . . . nobody else."

"Don't go getting too cocky," Curtis warned him. A quick glance through the bars showed him that the Ranger was leading Bobby McLawry back to the wagon. "We're a long ways from planning any kind of future here."

"I'm not cocky. But I've seen the light. Give me a shot at robbing banks with these idiots for awhile. I'll get on that horse and ride it till it stops." He grinned and sat back against the bars, feeling good, folding his hands across the key in his waist. "What are you looking at, you old fart?" He chuckled, gazing across the wagon at Granddaddy Snake. The old Indian bared his crooked teeth at him and growled low, his hair hanging in greasy strands down his weathered face. Billy Lee growled right back at him, chuckling. He leaned forward and said in a whisper, "I'm onto your game, Injun." He pointed a finger and winked, his whisper dropping lower, just between the two of them. "You think you can make yourself skinny enough and greasy enough to slip through these bars."

Granddaddy Snake's eyes widened a bit

in surprise. Then he caught himself and let out a deep sigh. "Are you going to tell on me?"

"Me? Naw. Why would I do a thing like that?" He grinned and winked again. But as soon as the Ranger led Bobby McLawry back to the wagon and watched him step up inside, Billy Lee called out, "Hey, Ranger, guess what this old bag of bones has in mind. He thinks he can go right through these bars with all that jerky grease on him. Can you believe tha— ?"

Granddaddy Snake shot forward with a loud war cry, his hand going around Billy Lee's throat and choking off his words.

In a narrow clearing in the low hills, Rance Plum stood over the dying outlaw, looking down at him as he reloaded his rifle and levered a round up into the chamber. He cocked his head in curiosity and said with a thin smile, "If you don't hurry up and die, I will have to finish you off, you understand."

Whitey glared up at him, his gloved hands pressed against the dark arterial blood rising through his fingers with each beat of his heart. "I'm doing the best I can. You can leave. I ain't going nowhere."

"Ordinarily that would be fine," Plum said, "except we have to show proof to the *federales.*"

"So you're hauling me all the way to Mexico." He spoke in a labored breath.

"Well, not all of you," Plum said. "Just your head. They want to see a blue star tattoo."

"But, I never earned one."

"Oh, well." Plum tossed it off with the wave of a hand. "We have some ink and pens at our disposal. That shan't be a problem."

"Figures," Whitey winced. "I never could . . . make up my mind which side of the border I liked best. Now I'll . . . end up both places. Damn Bobby McLawry. He caused . . . all this. Getting himself arrested . . . killing a whore."

Plum's thin smile turned smug as he tossed a glance at Jack the Spider, then looked back at the dying outlaw. "So, my suspicions were correct. That is one of JC's men in the Ranger's Misery Express." He tweaked his mustache. "JC's brother, in fact. What a nice matched set of heads they'll make."

"Don't feel so proud of yourself," Jack the Spider said. "Alls we've got so far is this old buzzard bait." He gestured at Whitey. "The other one's well over the hills by now — gone to tip off JC, is my guess. Once JC

194

knows we're on him, it could get real bloody out here."

"Poor Mister Spider," Plum said, shaking his head. "Do you ever have a positive thought about anything? Life must look terribly bleak and hopeless to you."

"I'm just saying, we could get ourselves in a bad spot here if we ain't careful." Jack the Spider squinted at Plum with his one good eye.

On the ground, old Whitey interrupted them. "Suppose I could get a drink of water before I die?"

"Not a chance," said Rance Plum. "In fact, if you aren't dead in about two minutes, I propose we go on and start cutting. Get your head in a bag and get out of here. I think you're just being stubborn about it."

"No . . . I'm not," Whitey said, his breath failing him more and more. "It's not something . . . I have any control over."

"Says you," Plum huffed. He turned and looked out across the peak of the low hills in the direction the other outlaw had taken. "The longer you lie there gurgling and heaving, the more time we lose getting on your partner's trail." He spun toward Jack the Spider and added, "Go fetch the hatchet from your saddlebags, Mister Spider. We've tarried long enough."

"For God sakes!" Old Whitey pleaded.

Jack the Spider spat and ran a hand across his lips. "I think we ought to go down and see if the Ranger needs any help. It's best we work together on this before it gets out of control."

"Nonsense," Plum said. "We're going after the outlaws." He raised his rifle and let it rest back over his shoulder.

Two miles ahead on the winding rocky trail, JC McLawry led the party of men up onto a crest of sandy soil and brought them to a halt at the bend of a switchback. They'd heard the distant gunfire earlier and hastened their pace toward it. Now they stopped and sat quietly, listening to the sound of a lone rider pushing hard on the trail, coming headlong at them.

"You men fan out. Get ready," JC said over his shoulder. The woman sat in his lap, her dark hair lifting back into his face on a gust of hot wind. Beside him, Lawrence Shaw sat slumped in his ragged saddle, seeing the lost expression on the woman's face as he moved his eyes across her, then gazed ahead. The woman caught Shaw's fleeting glance and looked away in shame, JC's hand kneaded her stomach down low through her thin dress.

"Why does she let him do that to her?"

Lawrence Shaw mumbled to himself under his breath, as if no one was around, or as if he was speaking to some unseen entity in the vast dusty badlands.

"Huh? What did you say?" JC looked at him.

"Nothing," Shaw said. He drew his ragged blanket around himself, even in the fierce desert heat. "Just thinking out loud."

"Oh. . . ." JC dismissed it, giving Shaw a curious stare. Then he turned in his saddle and said to the men as he drew his pistol without cocking it, "Whoever's coming is moving fast. Don't fire any shots if you can keep from it. We've got men out there somewhere."

When the rider came into sight, they saw it was Barrows, lying low in his saddle with his wounded right arm hanging limp at his side. "Yiii!" he cried out, startled at seeing JC and the men blocking his trail. His horse whinnied in a shrill voice as Barrows reined back hard, sliding the animal down onto its haunches and sidewise to keep from running into them. "Lord, JC! I'm glad it's you. I was afraid I lost you all along the trail."

"I can see why you might think so, since you left the trail we were on." JC gave him a cold stare, his thumb poised over the hammer of his pistol. The other men tightened

197

their ranks around Barrows. "This trail goes south," JC added. "We only rode up here to get a better look toward the shooting."

"South?" Barrows looked around, feigning surprise. "Well, I must have gotten confused — the gunfire and all. Look at me. I took a bullet." He spoke quickly. "Stinson's dead, Dewey too, I guess."

"Too bad." JC reached out and snapped his fingers at Barrows. "Now give me your gun."

"My gun?" Barrows looked shocked. "For crying out loud, JC," he said in weak protest. Yet even as he spoke, he lifted his pistol from his holster and pitched it to JC McLawry. "Whitey and me came beating it back to tell you what we learned as fast as we could. But we got ambushed. A couple of gunmen hit us coming up into the hills."

JC shoved the pistol down into his waistband and stared at him with a blank expression. "But loyal *amigo* that you are, you struggled on . . . bringing me the news."

"Well, yeah. You know me, steady as a rock." Barrows tried to shrug, his wounded arm stifling him. "I was coming to tell you! We saw the jail wagon. Bobby's in it, sure enough.

"And let me guess —" JC said, "the four of you decided to go ahead and bust Bobby out . . . instead of doing like I told you to?"

"It was Stinson's idea. He thought it would get him a tattoo," Barrows said, a worried look on his face. "Dewey tried to talk him out of it, me and Whitey too. Stinson wouldn't listen."

"So now there's little doubt the Ranger knows we're out here. Not much of a chance we'll catch him by surprise, eh?" JC give a strange, dark grin and he said to the others. "You men listen close here. You'll learn a lot about what never to do if you plan on staying alive and riding with me."

"Hold on now, JC," Barrows said, his face turning more pale and worried. "It wasn't me that disobeyed your orders." His horse danced back and forth in place, and Barrows felt the world draw close and harsh around him.

"Oh?" JC chuckled, lifting the woman from his lap. "Then you must have had a mouse in your pocket. Climb down off that horse."

"Jesus, JC." Barrows voice whined. But he wound his reins around his saddle horn and began to dismount.

"Here, hold her for me, Fast Larry." JC passed the woman from his saddle to Lawrence Shaw, tossing her as if she were a bundle of rags.

Lawrence Shaw did not want the woman near him — he did not want anybody this close to him — yet he caught her instinctively rather than to see her fall to the ground. She landed on his lap as light as a puff of air, and his arms circled her, then released her. She rocked back against him and he trembled at the feel of her so close, her hair brushing across his own face for an instant as she settled. "I can't," he said beneath his breath. He sat there bewildered, his arms around her but careful in how they touched her, like a man cupping a delicate bird in his hands.

JC stepped down from his horse at the same second Barrow's boots touched the ground. Barrows spoke as he turned to him. "JC, you've got to listen to reason —"

JC's right hand snatched him and closed around his throat, raising him up onto his toes. Barrows's hands clamped around JC's wrist, struggling to loosen the grip, his eyes widening, his face already turning a shade of blue. "You men listen up," JC called out to the others as they sat atop their horses, watching Barrows struggle. JC held him at arm's length as if on display, "I realize our young friend from Texas can't speak right now. But I know if he could, he'd tell everybody here about the importance of sticking to a plan — of following orders!" He turned his face to Barrows for a second, then back to the others. "He's made some terrible mistakes in his life . . . but I always believe a man can change, don't you?"

The men nodded, watching JC shake Barrows back and forth, the man's face having turn a strange shade of purple now, his eyes looking watery, and more and more distant.

As JC spoke, the woman on Lawrence Shaw's lap looked away from the terrible scene playing itself out on the sandy ground. Shaw felt her shiver, and he ventured his face close to her ear just long enough to whisper, "Don't be afraid. I won't hurt you."

"I know," she whispered in reply.

CHAPTER 12

The jail wagon moved on along the base of the low hills. At noon, the Ranger reined in the team of horses into the sparse shade of a lone cottonwood tree that clung root-bare to the sandy earth. As the wagon rocked to a halt, the prisoners stirred, stretched and stood up, looking upward to the rocky hillside. Bobby McLawry smiled, blotting sweat from his forehead. "I figure tonight JC will make his move," he said to Billy Lee in a low voice. "This is the only trail to Circle Wells from here. The Ranger is a sitting duck beneath these hills, and there ain't a thing he can do about it." He stared at Billy Lee. "I think it's time you give me the key for safekeeping."

"It's safe enough where it's at," Billy Lee replied. "I haven't lost nothing yet."

"You were damn lucky that old Indian didn't tell the Ranger, after you blowing the whistle on him the way you did."

Billy Lee spread a smug grin. "I'm just a real lucky guy." He rubbed a hand on his throat where Granddaddy Snake's fingernails had left long red scratches when the Ranger pried him loose. Billy Lee pointed at the old Indian on the wagon floor and said, "I ain't forgot what you did to my head . . . but as tough goes, you've got plenty of sand in your craw, old man. More then this bunch of jake-house rats. I'll give you that. I almost hate having to kill you, old man."

Granddaddy Snake stared up at him with a blank expression. At the rear of the wagon, Dewey Toom sat slumped back against the bars with his hat down over his eyes. Beside Granddaddy Snake, Curtis Roundtree studied Billy Lee's face for a second, not liking this new attitude that had come over Billy Lee since he'd managed to steal the key. Billy Lee was getting full of himself, he thought, and while Curtis had seen it happen before, he'd never seen it happen in this manner. Billy Lee was seriously considering himself an outlaw of the same caliber as the McLawrys. Curtis Roundtree shook his head and looked away as the barred door swung open with a metal-on-metal sound.

"Granddaddy, come on out here," the

Ranger said. "I want to have a little talk with you."

"Hey, what about us," Billy Lee protested. "We need some cooling out same as he does."

"And you'll get it, if you settle down and keep your mouth shut for a few minutes," the Ranger said, swinging the door shut and locking it as Granddaddy stepped down with a grunt. Maria stood back with her rifle in her hands, alternating her gaze between the prisoners in the wagon and the rocky hills above them.

On the other side of the cottonwood tree, Granddaddy Snake sank down on his thin haunches and wrapped his arms around his knobby knees. The Ranger stooped down facing him and tipped up the brim of his dusty sombrero. "Tell me the truth, Granddaddy. Were you really thinking you could grease yourself down enough to slip through the bars?"

"The truth. . . ." The old Indian weighed his words for a second, then said with a sigh, "All right, then. I meant to escape. The jerky grease played into my plan."

"It was a foolish plan," the Ranger said. "You've starved yourself down for nothing. You can't get through those bars no matter how much grease you smear on yourself.

All you would manage to do is get your head stuck . . . maybe choke yourself to death."

The old Indian nodded, brushed a bony hand at a fly circling his ear, then sat silent.

"I don't like taking you in for what you did, Granddaddy." The Ranger took off his sombrero and ran a shirtsleeve back over his sweat-dampened hair. "I told you before, I wish I hadn't ran into you back in town. But I did . . . so I've got to carry out my job. As long as you're in my custody I have to treat you like any other prisoner. Do you understand what I'll have to do if I catch you making a break?"

Granddaddy nodded. "You will shoot me."

"If I had to," the Ranger said. "Don't make me do that. I've got a bad situation with the McLawrys. There's too much on my mind to have to worry about you getting away. I need your help to get this wagon to Circle Wells."

"You ask help from a man you take to jail?" Granddaddy Snake offered a thin smile at the irony of it.

"That's right." The Ranger stood and let out a long breath. "I want your word that as long as you're in my custody you won't go trying something stupid, like slipping through the bars."

Granddaddy Snake stared straight ahead for a second, then said in a resolved tone, "Okay, you have my word. I will not slip through the bars . . . as long as I am in *your* custody."

The Ranger cocked his head slightly. "You're not answering me in some tricky manner are you?"

"No. I say what I mean. You have my word."

"Good enough," the Ranger said. "Go ahead and attend yourself."

Granddaddy Snake stood and turned away, and when he'd finished relieving himself he turned back to face the Ranger. "I know you are in a tight spot with these outlaws, Ranger . . . so now I must do something I do not like to do. I must tell you about Billy Lee." Granddaddy Snake winced, having trouble saying it.

"If it's about him having the key, Granddaddy, you needn't say another word." The Ranger leaned a bit closer when he saw the surprised look on the Indian's face. He lowered his voice. "Do you think I'd be foolish enough to leave the real key under the wagon seat, knowing Bobby McLawry's brother used to drive this rig? I figured as long as Bobby and Billy Lee think they've got a surefire way out of here, it'll keep them from trying something else . . . something that might work."

Granddaddy Snake chuckled under his breath. But then a realization came into his eyes, and he stopped. "If you knew about them having the key, I think you also knew why I was using the jerky grease?"

"Let's get back to the wagon," the Ranger said without answering him.

The old Indian stepped forward, and on the way back to the wagon he said over his shoulder, "You are right, Ranger. Trying to slip through the bars was a foolish idea."

"Yes it was," the Ranger said, walking along behind him.

"Can I tell you a secret?" Granddaddy Snake stopped and turned facing him.

The Ranger nodded. "Is it about the judge's dog?"

Once again Granddaddy Snake looked surprised. "Yes. Do you already know?"

The Ranger smiled. "I know you didn't eat it. I figured whatever else you did with it is your business . . . since you're willing to go to jail over it."

"I gave it to one of my granddaughters. She lives with my people in the buttes north of Bentonville. The little dog wanted to be free, I could tell by the look in its eyes. It wore a leather collar with a bell on it." He touched a weathered hand to his throat. "A bell that rang with every step it took. Do you understand?"

"Yes, I think so," the Ranger said. "But it belonged to the judge."

"So I took the collar and bell from its neck and threw them among the bones of a small coyote." He spoke on with no regard to the Ranger's words. "Now the little dog can live as it should, to come and go as it pleases. It no longer spends its life on a fat man's lap."

"But still, Granddaddy, you had no right —"

"I have never understood what the white man calls *rights,* except that they are passed around like favor beads from one hand to another . . . always handed *down,* always from a stronger hand to a weaker hand. *Rights* have not yet worked their way down to me . . . so I am not yet bound by them." He shrugged. "Because of that, the little dog goes free, even if I must go to jail for eating him. Will you keep my secret, Ranger?"

"I have so far, haven't I?"

"Yes. As it turns out, so far you have."

Walking on to the wagon, the Ranger looked up along the hill line. "Besides, if JC and his boys have their way about it, nobody's secrets or rights will matter. I think we'll be hearing from them most any time now."

At the wagon, the old Indian stepped inside and took his place on the floor across from Billy Lee. Bobby McLawry and Billy Lee sat staring intently at Granddaddy Snake. When the Ranger had taken Dewey Toom over to the cottonwood tree, Bobby McLawry leaned forward and said to the old Indian, "You told him, didn't you? I knew you would."

Granddaddy Snake had to keep himself from smiling. "I told him nothing, you have my word."

"Your word? Why you lying old son of a —"

"Easy, Bobby." Billy Lee placed a hand on Bobby's shoulder and pulled him back. "He didn't say nothing. I can tell by the look on his face."

Bobby leaned back, but shrugged his shoulder from beneath Billy Lee's hand. "Keep your hands to yourself."

Billy Lee drew his hand away in an exaggerated manner, looked at Curtis Roundtree, and winked. "Just trying to keep peace," he said. "Us ole outlaws need to stick together."

Curtis Roundtree gave him a cautioning frown, seeing Billy Lee grow more and more confident in himself. Billy Lee's taking charge now, Curtis Roundtree thought as he watched him, wishing this fool could see what he was doing to himself. "Keep still in there," Maria said through the bars, moving a bit closer as Billy Lee and Bobby McLawry both settled back into place.

"Well, yes, ma'am," Billy Lee grinned. "I was just explaining the importance of *harmonious relationship* to my two cellmates here. It seems that incarceration is beginning to take a toll on Mister McLawry's nerves." He laughed and pulled his hat brim down over his eyes.

"What's the trouble?" the Ranger asked, following close behind Dewey Toom as the two of them came back to the wagon.

"Nothing," Maria replied. "It's only Billy Lee, running his mouth again."

"What am I going to do with you, Billy?" the Ranger asked in a matter-of-fact tone, helping Dewey Toom up into the wagon.

Billy Lee shrugged, crossed his arms, and kept his face hidden beneath his hat. "I'll leave, if you ask me nicely."

Curtis Roundtree stood up, dusting his trouser seat, and stepped out the door. On the way to the cottonwood tree he said over his shoulder to the Ranger, "Talk straight with me. How much jail time you figure I'm apt to get for whupping those two teamsters?"

The Ranger considered it as they stopped behind the tree and Curtis turned away and unbuttoned his fly. "It's hard to say, Curtis. But I can't see you getting over a month or two, providing they were both back on their feet pretty quick with no permanent damage."

"What about Billy Lee?" Curtis finished relieving himself and hiked up his trousers and fastened his fly. "Horse theft is a serious offense."

"It would be," the Ranger said, "if he'd left a man afoot, out in the wilderness. But this was horse theft from a barn, or a hitching post most likely. I'd say he could get as much as a year — two at the most. They've got this good-behavior thing going now. If he'd keep his nose clean he'd save himself six months or more."

"Good behavior, huh?" Curtis turned to him. "Think they'd give me some of that? I can behave as well as the next so long as there ain't no whiskey around."

"We'll see, Curtis." The Ranger studied the big man's eyes for a second. "Why are you asking me all this?"

Curtis hesitated, then said, "Because I'm worried about Billy. He's getting some crazy notions . . . starting to think he's some kind of desperado or something. He ain't acting like himself."

"Lots of men get that way when they're facing jail time," the Ranger said, gesturing him back toward the wagon. "They get afraid of what's waiting for them, figure they need to take on a tough attitude. He'll settle down some once the door slams shut behind him. If he don't, somebody will knock some sense into him."

"That's what I'm afraid of," Curtis said, walking in front of him. "I hate to see his big mouth get him hurt, if you know what I mean."

"I know what you mean. But that's up to him. You can't pull his time for him. Every man has to pull his own. Billy Lee is no tough guy . . . if he goes in thinking he is, he'll soon learn different." They walked on, and before they reached the wagon, the Ranger asked, "Anything else you want to say, Curtis?"

Curtis stopped and turned to him. "Just that I've got no hard feelings toward you for bringing me in." He waited for a second, then added, "And I want you to know that I ain't no part of anything that might happen out here — I mean, I ain't trying to get away. I've got jail time coming, and I ain't trying to duck out of it. I'd hate getting shot for something somebody else does. Do you understand what I'm saying?"

"I hear you, Curtis." The Ranger nudged him forward. "I appreciate you telling me."

On a clearing near the top of the hills, Lloyd Percy turned to JC McLawry who stood beside him looking down at the slim, winding trail on the desert floor. "Boss," Percy asked. "If you don't mind me asking . . . what's to keep the Ranger from turning off the trail long enough to get out from under us?"

JC cut his eyes to Percy. Behind them, twenty yards away, the other men sat among the rocks in twos and threes, sipping water from their canteens. "Look at that land down there, Percy," JC said. "How far do you think a wagon would make it across the rocks? If they didn't break a wheel, they'd sink it to its axle in the sand." He pointed to the stretch of rolling dunes, then let his hand drop to his side. "He has to come this way. And he knows I'll be waiting."

"Yep, you're right, Boss," Percy said. He'd been feeling better and better about things. JC hadn't brought up the fact that he'd ran out on Bobby. If there was any hard feelings, Percy couldn't detect them. He'd watched JC choke Barrows to death and toss his body off the edge of a cliff. Since JC had made no move against him yet, Percy decided maybe it was all forgotten, especially now that Stinson was dead and couldn't keep reminding JC about it. "I sure can't wait to get a piece of that Ranger."

"That's the spirit," JC said, raising a hand, patting Percy on the shoulder. "I like a man who goes at his work with enthusiasm."

"You know me, Boss. I'm Johnny-on-the-spot."

"Yeah, I like that. . . ." JC turned and walked back to the others, to where Lawrence Shaw sat close to the young woman. Lloyd Percy followed a few feet behind. "See, Percy?" JC looked down at the woman and Shaw. "Fast Larry is becoming a real Johnny-on-the-spot himself, when it comes to looking after my chicky chicky for me." He passed a glance over the others, a flat smile coming to his lips. Then he said to Shaw, "Are you making sure these hairy-legged peckerwoods keep their distance from her? You can't trust none of them around anything that has a warm bottom on it."

"You got that right, Boss," said a voice among the men.

The woman looked away in shame. Laughter rippled across the men. But Lawrence Shaw only looked up at JC with a flat expression. "When can I be moving on?"

"Moving on?" JC feigned a look of astonishment. "Now, Fast Larry, you know as well as I do, none of us could keep you here against your will — a fast gun like you. You're free to do as you please."

"Then I'll take my leave," Shaw said, starting to rise to his feet.

JC raised a hand, halting him. "Of course without you here, I don't know what these men might do to my chicky chicky while I'm not looking."

Shaw sank back to the ground. JC leaned close to him, reaching over to the woman and rubbing her hair. "These boys know I tire of things easily. First thing you know, I'll look away and forget all about her . . . think what they'll do if I don't have somebody to watch over her for me."

"I'll stay a while longer," Shaw said in a near whisper.

"I thought you would." JC nodded. "I got to admit I'm a little disappointed in you, Fast Larry. I figured by now, you'd be all thrown in with me . . . wanting to kill that Ranger, maybe going on across the border with us, kick up a little sand. Hell, you're what you might call a *hero* among me and

215

the boys here. Why don't you relax a little . . . be one of us? There's plenty of work for you."

"I ride alone," Shaw said.

"I know . . . and that's a damn shame." JC looked off, shook his head, then turned back to him. "I was telling Percy earlier. Said, a gunman like you, hell, if you ever got your bark on, got in a killing mood, there wouldn't be a man here could handle you. That's right, isn't it?"

"I quit killing," Shaw said, feeling the goad in JC's words.

JC dismissed his words with a toss of a hand. "Sure, you told me so . . . and I respect that. But just out of curiosity, suppose we all decide to throw down on you at once. How many of us do you think you'd drop before we got you?"

"I quit killing," Shaw said again, though his mind starting to work instinctively now the way he'd felt it work too many times in the past, his eyes taking the men in peripherally, sizing them up, checking their position. These things he did without so much as a flicker of doubt — a master of his trade, going about the business of death. "So there's no point in supposing it." His voice had become steady now, since he'd used it more in the past day than he had in perhaps three months or more.

"Whooa now, Fast Larry." JC chuckled, keeping it light, but noticing something in Shaw's eyes he hadn't seen before. "Don't take it the wrong way. We're just passing time here, waiting on the Misery Express. No harm it that, is there? Come on, tell us for the sake of conversation. There's ten of us here. How many of us would end up dead on the ground?"

Lawrence Shaw had been here before, too many times to recall, a man letting his curiosity get out front of him, wondering, calling it a harmless question, but deep inside wanting to know what it would feel like to have such a fast draw . . . what it would be like to kill him.

"How many, Fast Larry?" JC straightened a bit, his hand closer to his pistol than it had been a few seconds before. Yes, the question was eating this man up, Lawrence Shaw thought. He turned his head now, slow and deliberate, looking from one face to the next, then settling back up at JC McLawry.

"Be honest now," JC grinned. "How many of us would die, facing Fast Larry Shaw?"

A tense silence set in. Only the brush of a hot wind stirred, its breath nipping at the edges of dusty bandannas and hat brims as the men stared at Lawrence Shaw through eyes of cold stone. "Every one of you," Shaw said in a voice as cool and resolved as the updraft from an open grave. And in the silence that followed, he reached up slowly with his left hand, took his ragged hat from his head and laid it on the ground beside him.

Even the wind seemed to stop and hold its breath. Lawrence Shaw knew from experience that this was a dark, ugly game; and he knew too well that the next person who moved or spoke would be the loser. How much that person lost depended on how far that person would go to win. His cold eyes stayed fixed on JC McLawry. McLawry had asked for this, and if he let his hand drift so much as an inch toward his gun, he would die. If he spoke the next word to call it off, he would still be alive, but he'd lose the game. If he did neither, he was a coward. Lawrence Shaw held his gaze, wondering if JC McLawry knew these things — about the game or about himself.

"Amigos." Sanchez spoke first, in a shaky voice, trying to offer a nervous smile. "We were only playing here. Look at us now . . . all *serious* . . . all, *hey,* I gonna shoot you, you make a move. What is this?" He moved slowly forward toward JC, spreading his

raised hands, letting Shaw see he had no intention of reaching for his pistol. "We are all *amigos,* eh?"

"*Sí, amigos,*" Shaw said to Sanchez without taking his eyes off JC. The game was over. Shaw knew it. JC McLawry was a coward down deep. Shaw saw it clearly, whether these others could see it or not. He let his stare linger a few seconds longer than was necessary now, making sure JC got a belly-ful of it.

"That's right, Sanchez," JC said at length, a bead of sweat running like a teardrop beneath his left eye. "It was all in fun." He settled and took a careful step back, shrugging, raising his arms and crossing them over his chest — making it clear to Shaw he wanted no part of him but at the same time not looking submissive to the men. "Fast Larry knows that, don't you?"

Lawrence Shaw picked up his hat from the ground and took his time dusting it before placing it on his head. "I never doubted it for a second," he said, letting JC see the meaning in his eyes. JC looked away. Beside Shaw, the woman had been watching, tense and frightened. Now she kept herself from swooning, calming herself by brushing her windswept hair from her face.

"We all need to get a little rest," JC said

to the others. "We got a busy night ahead of us."

The men nodded, standing to dust off their pants. They moved away, looking back at Lawrence Shaw, seeing him in a new light, knowing that beneath the submissive, washed-out manner of this man there was still something to fear. Sanchez motioned for Lloyd Percy to come help him with the horses, and the two of them moved away while JC still stood near Shaw and the woman. When the men were farther away, JC said to Shaw in a calm voice, "All of us? Now, how would you have managed that?"

"You don't want to know," Shaw said, his voice still flat, yet with a menacing tone to it, his eyes fixed like cold, polished steel on JC McLawry's.

JC chuckled, but it didn't sound authentic. "All right, Fast Larry. We'll talk about it later." He reached down and took the woman by the shoulder to raise her to her feet. "Come on, chicky chicky, let's find us a shady spot for a few minutes. Don't want you burning up out here."

But before she could rise, Lawrence Shaw's left hand came out, caught JC's wrist and held it in a firm grip. "Go find yourself some shade, McLawry. She's with me now."

CHAPTER 13

The drift of dust from the wagon had now moved deeper along the trail beneath them. Sanchez and JC McLawry sat on their horses atop a ridge, apart from the other men by a few yards. They looked down at the long evening shadows cast by stands of rock and brush. Sanchez let his eyes follow the winding trail past them a few hundred yards to where it turned and wove its way east toward Circle Wells. Sanchez said, "If the wagon could have made it to the trail across open country, we could not have gotten close enough to his big rifle to stop him."

"He knows that, Sanchez." JC smiled. "Believe me, he's known that for a while. He knows we're here."

"What must he be thinking, eh?" Sanchez spat to one side. "To see that he only has this short distance to go . . . but knowing we will not let him past us. It is eating him up, I bet."

"Naw, not him, *amigo,*" JC replied. "He never lets things eat him up. Right about now, he has the vision of a mule wearing blinders. All he sees is straight ahead. All he's thinking about is getting there." JC tapped a finger to his temple. "I know how he thinks. I learned it the hard way. Don't forget, he tracked me across this badlands. You learn a lot about a man when he's dogging you."

"This is true, Boss." Sanchez hesitated for a second, then added, "But during that time, did he not also learn things about you?"

JC turned his horse sideways to him. "What are you getting at?"

"Nothing, Boss." Sanchez shrugged in submission. "I only ask the question. I see how your mind is always at work, and I say to myself, someday perhaps I will learn to think like you do."

"Don't count of it," JC said, settling himself. "I didn't get where I'm at over-night. When you lead a group of men, you have to stay one step ahead of everybody. Every move I make is like a well-planned move on a chessboard. If you think that's easy, give it a try sometime."

"No, not me. I see you do things and I

ask myself why. Then later I see the out-come, and I can only stand back, amazed by it." He grinned, doing a good job buttering up the boss, he thought. "Like a while ago when you gave the woman to this Fast Larry? I say to myself, why does JC do this? But later I realize . . . you do this to make sure he stays with us, eh?"

"That's right." JC felt his face redden a bit. He knew none of the others had heard the last few words between him and Lawrence Shaw. His best move was to let the men think he'd finished with the woman and passed her on to Shaw. "I know the man's a little desert-crazy right now, but think what he'll be worth to us once he gets his head clear and gets back onto his game." JC grinned, liking the way he'd said it. "The man just needs some direction. I'm giving it to him."

The truth was, JC wished to God he'd never taken in Lawrence Shaw. What had he been thinking? He'd pressured Shaw into coming with him at a time when the man's mind didn't seem to be clicking just right. But now that Shaw was coming around, starting to show some signs of life, JC felt more and more like he'd coaxed a mad dog into his meathouse.

"I know," said Sanchez. "It is a wise thing

you do, getting him to side with us. Some men would be afraid that a big gunman like Shaw would take over their gang — but not you, Boss." Sanchez spread a crafty grin. "You saw through him . . . him and his crazy boast that he could kill all nine of us, with only six bullets in his gun. That is impossible, eh?"

"Yeah," JC said, "that's impossible." But even as he smiled saying it, he knew what Shaw had meant. Shaw might've been bluffing about killing all nine of them, yet it was JC's eyes that he was staring into when he'd said it. JC had gotten the message.

"I am glad you say so, Boss," Sanchez went on, "because if Shaw could kill all nine of us, and he himself is hiding from the Ranger, it has to make me wonder if going after the Ranger is such a good idea." He saw the dark glare in JC's eyes and added quickly, "But you know what you are doing. Forgive me for being such a fool."

"Get back there and get the men ready," JC said in a clipped tone. "The wagon will reach the end of the hills about the time it gets good and dark. The Ranger will try to make a run for it these last few hundred yards. It's his only chance."

"Sí, Boss, good thinking." Sanchez kneed his horse around and started back toward the others. *Who was JC trying to fool?* Sanchez had seen the chink in JC's armor, the way Shaw had put him on the spot and held him there, JC afraid to even open his mouth or twitch a muscle. Now that he'd seen that much about JC McLawry, Sanchez realized some other things too.

Thinking back, Sanchez could not recall a time when JC had ever put himself out front in harm's way. Maybe he wasn't as tough as he'd led all of these men to think he was. Sanchez could lead a gang himself, he'd always thought. How hard could it be? He saw the way JC did it. JC kept the men divided into two groups, the ones like Dewey Toom, Stinson, Barrows and a couple of others. They were bums, expendable. That's why JC had sent them out to scout the Ranger for him. If the Ranger killed them, so what? Then there was the other group — these men before him. They were the serious, hard core killers, JC's elite.

"All right, *amigos,*" Sanchez said to them as he rode up. "We get ready now. At dark we hit the wagon." The men nodded and milled in place atop their horses. See? How hard was that? These men followed his orders because those orders came from JC McLawry. But they were used to Sanchez giving JC's orders for him now that Bobby wasn't here. He could do this, Sanchez thought, looking to one side, away from the men to where Shaw and the woman sat atop the big buckskin. The woman sat behind Shaw with her arms around his waist. Sanchez felt like thanking Shaw for having shown him so much in so little time. He wondered if any of these other men had seen it too . . . seen that, deep down, their boss was a coward.

"What about me, Sanchez," Lloyd Percy asked, sitting amid the men as they kept a close circle around him. "Did JC say anything about me?" His face looked tightly drawn behind a sheen of nervous sweat. For awhile Percy had thought everything was all right between him and JC. But now as the time to attack grew nearer, the men had seemed to turn cold and quiet toward him once more, as if they knew his number would soon be up.

"No, he said nothing about you." Sanchez smiled, but it didn't seem genuine to Lloyd Percy. "Don't worry, *amigo.* I will put in a good word for you when the time comes."

Low laughter rippled through the group. Percy turned all around, looking at them. Their eyes revealed nothing. "What about those two gunmen who killed Barrows? Shouldn't I ride back and make sure they're not dogging our trail?"

"JC says he knows who they are. They are two bounty hunters who follow the Ranger. They are like coyotes who stay back and take the leftovers." Sanchez's smile turned genuine now. "Be careful that you do not become a leftover, Percy." More harsh laughter stirred among the men.

Sanchez heeled his horse over to Lawrence Shaw and spoke in a lowered voice. "Just between you and me, Fast Larry, when the fight starts, take the woman and leave. There is no reason for you to stay here. I do this as a favor to you, to show you that we are not enemies, *sí?*"

"I don't need your favor," Shaw said, his voice calm, resolved, the way it had sounded earlier when Sanchez had seen he was ready for whatever move JC McLawry might make. "I'll leave when I please. For now, I might just stick around and watch the show."

"Oh? To watch us kill the Ranger?"

"He's not an easy kill," Shaw said.

"Neither are we." Sanchez jutted his chin a bit.

"We'll see." Shaw offered a trace of a knowing smile. "I get the idea you boys think he's gonna run like a whipped hound these last few hundred yards."

"What is his choice?" Sanchez shrugged.

"We'll see," Shaw said again. Behind him on the buckskin, the woman stared at Lorio Sanchez through dark, caged eyes.

Sanchez turned back to Lawrence Shaw. "JC has done much for you, Fast Larry. He took you in . . . he gave you the woman. I would think you should be —"

"He gave me nothing," Shaw said before he could finish. "I took her from him."

Sanchez smiled, hearing Shaw confirm what he'd already suspicioned. "Do not take JC lightly. He will not step back and give up what is his. Maybe he was tired of the woman, but it would be foolish for you to think there is anything more for you here. It is best you go."

"Or what?" Shaw kept his flat stare on Sanchez. "I offered you blue star boys nine-to-one odds and couldn't get a taker. I'll leave when I'm good and ready."

Sanchez turned his horse in a huff and slapped a quirt to its rump. The horse shot forward to where the other men waited. When he was out of hearing distance, the woman leaned forward and said in Shaw's ear, "But you told me we would leave here."

"I know. And I meant it," he said, watching the men gather into a tighter group with Sanchez in their midst. "But I saw no reason to let Sanchez know our plans." He eyed JC McLawry as JC rode past them and took charge of the men.

"Percy, come on out front," JC called out to the group of men. They parted their horses enough to let Lloyd Percy come forward. He looked more worried than ever, sweat streaming down his cheeks. "I got a special job for you." JC stepped his horse forward, close to Percy.

"Sure, Boss, anything." Percy watched JC move his horse slowly around him, eyeing him up and down. "I told you, I'm bent on killing that Ranger, just as much as you are."

"That's good, Percy, because I'm giving you a chance to earn your star tonight. Since you're so set on making things right for Bobby . . . I'm going to let you lead this whole show."

"You don't mean — ?" Percy looked around at the men in the falling darkness.

"I sure do, Percy. "You want in on this action so bad, I wouldn't dream of denying you the chance." He backed his horse and waved Percy forward. "Get on out front there, lead us down. Once we get this thing going I've got a special task for you. You're going to be the one who springs Bobby out of that jail wagon."

"Me?" His face turned pasty white. "Boss,

I'd love to . . . you know I would. But the fact is, damn it, I can't hardly see a thing after dark. It's a condition that's afflicted my whole family." He raised a finger to his eye. "We've all got this little —"

"Lead, damn you!" The sound of JC's pistol cocking sent Percy forward at a brisk trot toward the edge of the hills. JC turned to the others and grinned. "Never let it be said that I wouldn't give a man a second chance. Now the rest of you listen up. The Ranger will be moving, coming toward us on the trail. Keep your ears open for the sound of that wagon."

"What if he's holed up and decided to make a fight of it?" one man asked.

"He's moving," JC snapped. "You can count on it. The Ranger wants no part of me in a straight-out gun battle. He'll want to get out on the flatlands and get some room between us." JC glared at him until the man shrank back in his saddle. "Any other questions?" he called out.

At dark, when the prisoners were fed and watered, they watched through the bars as Maria and the Ranger checked their rifles and pistols and deadened the few glowing embers from the evening campfire. The team of horses remained hitched to the wagon, their reins secured and hobble ropes circling their forelegs. From the wagon Billy Lee called out, "Hey, Ranger. Don't you think it would be best if you made a run for it from here."

"Keep quiet, Billy Lee," Maria said.

Billy Lee grinned, teasing them. "Nobody would ever know. We won't tell a soul. It wouldn't mean you're scared. It would just mean maybe you had forgotten and left something in Circle Wells, and wanted to hurry back there and get it." He snickered and nodded at the other prisoners. Curtis Roundtree and Granddaddy Snake didn't join in his amusement. Bobby McLawry and Dewey Toom both sat close to the bars, a serious look on their faces.

"Leave them alone, Billy Lee," Curtis Roundtree snapped at him. "Besides, I thought you were all set to join up with the Blue Star Gang? How would you manage to do it if we made a run for the flatland?"

"Oh, you bet I'm all set to join the Blue Stars, Curtis. I'm just having some fun here." He looked around at the others. "I swear, this is the dullest bunch I've ever seen. I'll be glad when the gang gets here . . . it'll liven things up some."

In the dark, Maria and the Ranger made their way to cover behind a short rock spill at the edge of the trail. "JC will be expecting us to make a run for it because that is the wise thing to do," Maria whispered.

"The one thing we don't want to do is what JC expects us to do. He considers himself a real thinker. It throws him in a spin when things don't go the way he predicts — especially if he's been telling his men about it. We'll keep our heads down and clip a couple of them out of their saddles the first move they make. That'll give them something to think about before making their next move on us."

"What about this Lawrence Shaw?" Maria looked at him in the darkness, a sliver of a pale moon shining above them.

"He's the wild card in this hand," the Ranger said. "I can't figure him with JC McLawry. I don't know what to expect from him. We'll have to wait and see."

Maria started to speak, but the click of a hoof against rock somewhere up the dark hillside caused her to fall silent and listen intently. After a second, the Ranger whispered close to her ear. "It's them. I'll make my way a few feet up the hillside with this big rifle. You sit tight here. Don't fire until I start the ball rolling."

"Be careful, Sam," she whispered, but he had already turned and crouched and moved away quietly.

At the wagon, the prisoners settled down and listened to the slight sounds of man and horse coming down carefully from above them. Bobby McLawry was whispering now in order to keep track of the sounds growing closer. "Here it comes, boys. Just like I said it would. Now you're going to see some heavy gunplay. Then I'll be out of this stinking Misery Express."

"Me, too, don't forget," Billy Lee whispered.

"Yeah, you too." Bobby crouched against the bars, listening. For a moment the sound of hooves grew louder, closer, then suddenly it stopped and blended into the silence of the night. Granddaddy Snake reached over, took a dusty blanket from the pile at the front of the wagon, and wrapped himself in it, and closed his eyes.

CHAPTER 14

They moved as quiet as cats down the rocky slope of the hill, Lloyd Percy ahead of the others by only a few yards. They stopped now and then and listened, but there was no sound of the wagon on the dark trail below. "What's the chances JC missed his call on this one?" one man whispered to another. "Maybe the Ranger managed to get past us before dark."

Before the other man could answer, Sanchez hissed behind them in a harsh tone. "No talking. Move ahead." They nudged their horses forward and down to the trail.

Ahead of them on the trail, Maria had taken her position quickly, lying flat between a tangle of dry brush on her left and a pile of loose rock on her right. She had been listening so intently to the sound of hooves moving down through the darkness that she'd ignored the slight rustle of brush as she'd raised her rifle out before her. Now as the hooves moved closer, she heard the rustling sound again. As she'd turned slightly closer toward it, the low hum of snake's rattle called out in warning. She froze, every fiber of her being focused on the few inches between her left thigh and the menacing sound.

Any second the fight would commence, the air would fill with bullets. Across from her the Ranger would be targeted by the flash of his rifle muzzle. When JC's men fired on him, her job was to give him cover. He would fire, then move. But he couldn't move without her help. They would cut him to pieces. Beside her the rattle of the snake diminished, but only for a second. When it started again, it sounded bolder, more deliberate. Had she moved away at the first warning, there would have been nothing to fear. But with the horses coming closer, she couldn't risk changing positions. Not now. Her thumb lay across the rifle hammer, waiting. Yet she knew what the sudden sound of her rifle would cause the snake to do. Knowing it caused cold sweat to bead on her brow.

A few yards ahead of her, the horses stopped, one of them nickering at the sound of the rattlesnake. "Quiet that horse," a voice called out in a harsh whisper.

"I hear a snake," Percy cried out, wrestling with his horse's reins to settle it.

"Shut up, damn you!" the voice warned. But it was too late. The Ranger had aimed in loosely on the sound of the horses. Then when Percy's voice cried out, it was all the target he needed. His first shot split the hushed quiet, and Percy's horse flew from beneath him. Warm blood sprayed from the horse's shoulder into the faces of the other riders as Percy spilled forward and rolled away into the dirt. The Ranger fired again, this time into the thrashing sound of man and horse on the dark trail. A rider screamed and flew out of his saddle before the flash of the Ranger's rifle was gone.

In what seemed only the flicker of a second, the men returned fire on the Ranger's muzzle flash. He hit the ground, dirt and pieces of rock kicking up around him. It was time Maria gave him cover . . . afforded him those few precious seconds he needed to roll away in the darkness and reposition himself. Where was she? A bullet nipped at his shirtsleeve.

She'd wanted to use those first seconds to try and roll away from the sound of the rattler, but it wasn't going to happen. Things had started too fast. Sam was pinned now. He needed cover. Near her thigh the snake give one last threatening blast with its rattle. She bit her lip and fired as the fangs struck deep into her leg. She recocked and swung the rifle butt around to her side. It hit something solid, and she felt it give way. Even with the sound of rifle fire, she heard the snake tumble back through the dried brush. Then she thrust the rifle forward and fired again.

There she is, the Ranger thought, and just in time. Raising up enough to get off another round, he rolled away as he recocked the rifle. Maria was at work now, her rifle repeating shot after shot into the melee until he'd stopped ten feet away, aimed and returned cover for her. By now the men had singled out her position, and it was time for her to go. Her leg throbbed as if having been struck by a steel hammer. She managed to move, but only a few feet. Across from her the Ranger's rifle fire found another of the outlaws and slammed him backward off his frightened horse.

Lloyd Percy had found his footing and staggered forward along the trial as the man cried out from within the streaks of fire behind him. Percy ran blind, stumbling, panting. Ahead of him in the wagon, Bobby McLawry heard the sound of pounding boots and called out, "Over here! Hey! Over here, it's me, Bobby!" He pressed against the bars, both arms out reaching forward in the black night. Beside him Billy Lee and Curtis Roundtree sat hunkered down, watching the rifles blink on and off like angry fireflies. Billy Lee griped the key in his moist palm. From the time the Ranger had fired his first shot, Billy Lee had been trying to reach out with the key and get it into the lock. But so far, with bullets flying all around them, he hadn't been able to do it.

Percy cut left toward the sound of Bobby's voice and stopped only when he'd ran headlong into the side of the wagon. Bobby's hands caught him and yanked him close to the bars. "Who is it?"

"It's me, Percy! JC sent me to spring you!" He pulled away from Bobby's hands. "Let me go, Bobby! There's a key under the seat!"

"Damn it, Percy!" Bobby shouted. "Here's the key! Get us out. We can't reach it into the lock from in here!" He snatched the key from Billy Lee's sweaty hand and passed it through the bars to Lloyd Percy. "Hurry up, man!"

"I'm trying," Percy said, wincing at the exploding rifles behind him. He stepped around in the dark and fumbled with the lock. "Damn it!" He shoved the key into the lock and tried to turn it. It wouldn't budge. "It won't open!"

"The hell it won't, Percy! Hurry up!"

"I dropped it!" Percy squatted and felt around on the ground for it. "I can't see nothing!"

"Damn you, Percy!"

"Wait, here it is." Percy stood up near the bars with the key in his trembling hand. From behind the cover of a boulder, the Ranger heard Bobby McLawry's voice and realized someone had made it to the wagon. He raised and fired a wild shot toward the sound of their voices. The shot hit the ground wide of Lloyd Percy by ten feet, but that was too close for Percy's comfort. "Lord, Bobby! I've got to get away from here." Percy slung the key in through the bars and lunged away from the wagon. "Sorry." He ran stumbling in the darkness. "I'll be back, though. Just sit tight."

"What the hell was that all about?" Billy Lee yelled at Bobby from two feet away as he searched the wagon floor and found the key. "Am I gonna have to do it all?" Rifle fire raged.

"Give me that key!" Bobby made a swipe at the key, but Billy Lee hugged it to his chest.

"Like hell I will. So far I ain't gained a thing dealing with you. Get out of me way!" He shoved his way past Bobby McLawry and reached out once more through the bars for the lock on the back of the wagon.

The gunfire lulled for a second as the Ranger reloaded and moved down closer to the trail. He crept along the trail toward the wagon, taking slow, deliberate steps in the loose dirt and gravelly surface. Sanchez took advantage of the few seconds of quiet and moved back along the ground in a crouch, along the line of men who'd dropped down from their horses and taken position on the ground. "Percy got through," he whispered, moving past the black figures in the darkness. "Who is hit?"

They were only five yards farther up the trail than where they'd been when the Ranger opened fire on them, two horses were down, one dead and the other thrashing wildly in the dirt. "Where is JC?" He looked around, cursing the darkness. "JC? Where are you? We must pull back into the rocks."

"Right here, Sanchez," JC whispered, a bit farther back from the others. "Did you say Percy got through?"

"*Sí*, I heard his voice, and Bobby's. The wagon is up there somewhere. Maybe they got away, eh?"

"Maybe. But we won't pull back until I know for sure." JC inched forward a few feet until he came to Sanchez's shadowed figure within the inky darkness. "You heard where they are, Sanchez. Make your way there and find out what's going on. We'll keep you covered."

Sanchez ran it through his mind quickly, not wanting to say no and look afraid, but at the same time not wanting to get into the Ranger's deadly sights. "We should both go, Boss," he said. "That way, when one of us gets shot down, the other can make it through, eh?"

A silence passed, then JC whispered, "I've got a better idea. You men watch for the Ranger's rifle flash." JC raised up slightly and called out through the darkness, "Bobby, are you still there?" He ducked back down, listening, expecting the sound of rifle fire to follow the sound of Bobby's voice. Yet neither Bobby nor the Ranger's rifle replied. "Bobby! If you're there, tell me something."

At the first sound of JC's voice, Bobby McLawry had pressed his face between the bars, ready to call out to his brother. But at that second, the Ranger had reached up with a gloved hand and clamped it over his mouth. At the same time he jammed the tip of his warm rifle barrel beneath Bobby's chin. "He can't answer right now, JC," the Ranger called out. "He's got a cocked rifle ready to take his face off."

"Damn it," one of the men said. "He was laid up here waiting for us all along. We rode right into —"

"Shut your mouth," JC hissed. He paused for a moment then called out, "Ranger . . . we're not leaving without him. You can die right here, or you can set him free. There's nowhere you can run to."

"Suits me," the Ranger replied, "I had nothing planned for the evening. Now get your guts up, JC . . . come on in and collect what's left of him. That's why I waited here for you."

JC ran a hand across his sweaty forehead, needing time to think. What was the Ranger doing here? Why hadn't he made a run for the flatland. It made no sense. Nobody in their right mind would have squared off this way, two rifles facing this many gunmen! "You're bluffing, Ranger. You won't kill a prisoner in cold blood. I know better! It goes against your code as a lawman!"

"You've been reading too many nickel novels, JC. You either pull your dogs back by the time I count three, or the next flash you see will be young Bobby's brains going skyward. *One . . . !*"

"We'll kill you anyway, Ranger . . . you won't win a thing killing Bobby," JC bellowed.

"It's not about winning anything to me. Besides, I'm old enough to die, JC," the Ranger called out. *"Two . . . !"*

"This is crazy, Ranger! You've lost your min—"

"Better tell your brother Bobby good-bye, JC," the Ranger cut him off. *"Thre— !"*

"Wait! Hold it!" JC McLawry cried out, standing halfway to his feet. "Don't shoot him! We're pulling back!"

"Best hurry, then. I hate cocking this rifle for nothing. Let me hear all of you moving up that hillside nice and clear, or I won't even count to three this next time. I'll just drop the hammer on him."

"We're going — right now!" JC's voice sounded rattled. "Give us a second, for God sakes!" He spun to the men in the darkness, shouting, "You heard him, damn it! Get your horses up that hill . . . make it quick! Sanchez, get my horse. It's back there behind the rocks."

"Easy, Boss, I'll get him for you."

Sanchez moved back, stumbling over the men as they hurriedly crept away, grumbling under their breaths. A gang member named Bryce, who was wanted for murder up in Wind River country, grabbed Sanchez by his forearm and leaned in close to him, saying, "What's got into the boss? We could rush that Ranger and get this done."

"It is his brother, you fool." Sanchez shoved Bryce's hand off his arm and moved away in the darkness.

"Hmmph," Bryce said to an ex-convict nearby named Thompson, as they both crept over to their horses. "JC ain't acted right since we took in that saddle tramp gunman, if you ask me. I think Fast Larry Shaw has screwed his head up."

"I'm thinking you're right," Thompson said. "Where is that gunman, anyway?"

"I don't know." Bryce found his horse's reins and clinked into his saddle. "I think he disappeared, along with the woman."

"Good riddance, then." They both mounted and kicked their horses up the rocky hillside. "If things don't take a change here pretty quick, I might just disappear myself. I'm a bank robber. This kind of malarky ain't making me a dime."

At the top of the hill, where the thin moonlight was not blocked by the sloping land, the men gathered and looked down onto the pitch-black landscape. The horses milled and blew, catching their breaths, the men resting forward in the saddles, watching the shadowed figure of JC McLawry as he dismounted and stood slumped, with his reins hanging from his hand. "All right," he said, panting. "If this is the way he wants to play it, we'll keep him pinned and starve him out."

The men slid dubious glances at one another. Sanchez stepped down and stood beside JC. "Boss, I think he will not be there in the morning. I think he is planning to cut out of there right now, while we are unsettled."

"Unsettled! Do I look unsettled to you?" JC ranted at him.

"It is only what I think, Boss." Sanchez shrank back from him.

"*Thinking* is my job." JC thumbed himself on the chest. "Now get the hell away and let me do it."

"Yes, of course, Boss." Sanchez stepped back and stood silent.

"I'm thinking Sanchez is right, JC," said Bryce. "What stopped him from already moving that wagon out toward the flatlands while we were busy coming up the hill? We wouldn't have heard him."

JC spun around to face the men. "Who said that, huh? Was that you, Martin? Get out of here, you son of a —"

"It wasn't me, Boss," said a voice among the shadows. "I'm over here, keeping my mouth shut."

JC calmed himself and let out a long breath. "Everybody listen, and listen good. He's still got my brother . . . and we've just lost some good men down there. I know how that crazy Ranger thinks. He might've thrown me off for a minute, taking position instead of hightailing it for the flats. But nobody in their right mind would have done that. Now he's trapped until he begs us to take Bobby off his hands. Anybody got any better ideas?"

He glared at them in the darkness.

CHAPTER 15

At the wagon, Billy Lee stood with his face pressed to the bars and looked up, toward the spot where the sound of horses had faded only moments earlier. "Is that it? They just left? What kind of gang are we talking about here, Bobby? Are you sure your brother really wants to bust you out? He's not holding some ole grudge against you from back in childhood, is he?"

"He'll be back." Bobby McLawry sounded disheartened, to say the least. When the Ranger had turned him loose and crept off into the darkness toward Maria's position, Bobby had slumped down to the floor and said nothing for the next few minutes. Now as he spoke, he stood up beside Billy Lee and gazed upward with him.

From the floor of the wagon, Dewey Toom said in a quiet voice, "JC ain't licked yet. He's gathering his second wind. I just wish he'd sent somebody besides that dewberry

Lloyd Percy to get us out of here."

"Oh . . . ?" Billy Lee and Bobby both turned to the sound of Dewey Toom's voice. The man had hardly spoken a word since the Ranger took him prisoner. Billy Lee grinned. "Speaking of dewberries, now we hear from a real expert on the subject. Did we ask you a damn thing, you brownnosing, gutless punk?"

Dewey Toom, his strength coming back to him, stood up in the darkness. "Yeah, I tried to get on the Ranger's good side. Can you blame me? I'd kiss his arse plumb up to his elbows if it got me a better deal." He stood close enough to the two men for them to see his face as if through a black veil. "JC will understand what I've done. That's the only person's opinion I'm concerned about. The rest of you can suck horse-wind for all I care."

"We'll see about that, Dewey." Bobby's voice had a tinge of threat to it.

A few yards forward, in the center of the trail, the Ranger moved closer toward Maria's position. "Maria?" he whispered. "Are you all right?" He heard her thrash lightly against the tangle of brush. She hadn't changed positions since the fight started.

"No, Sam. . . ."

"You're hit?" He moved quicker toward

her. "How bad?"

"No . . . I'm snakebit. My leg is numb."

"Oh, no." He found her and sank down to her, his hand out, feeling the bandanna she'd wrapped around her thigh to stay the flow of venom. "Let's get you up to the wagon. I'll light a lantern!"

Even as her arm went up around his neck and he lifted her, she said in a pained voice, "No, you cannot risk a light down here."

"I have to." He cradled her in his arms and stumbled back along the dark, rocky trail. "I need to see how to cut in and bleed the bite."

"I — I have already made the cut, Sam. Just get the poison out."

"My God, woman. . . ." He lowered her onto the rough ground and ran his hand down from her hip until he felt the circle of warm blood. "Why didn't you — ?" His stopped, unsure of how to finish.

"Why didn't I what, Sam? I did what I needed to do. Hurry, now. I feel it moving through me."

His mouth found the open wound. His lips tasted the sweat and blood and felt the hot, swollen flesh against his lips. He drew a mouthful and spat, and drew again. "Tighten the tourniquet," she said, her voice sounding weaker. He tightened the bandanna with his free hand as he continued to draw mouthful after mouthful of poisoned blood from her thigh and spit it to the ground.

From the wagon, Billy Lee, hearing the slight commotion on the trail, whispered to Bobby McLawry beside him. "What the hell are they doing out there? Is she shot?"

"I don't know, just listen," Bobby said, his eyes pinned to the darkness. Curtis Roundtree got up from the floor in curiosity.

Granddaddy Snake only raised his face toward the sound of the Ranger's and Maria's muffled voices. He nodded to himself and settled back down. "We will be leaving here soon," he said under his breath. "The desert has dealt itself a hand."

"What does that mean, fool?" Billy Lee spoke back to Granddaddy Snake over his shoulder.

"It means that each of us must now make a decision on our destiny."

"Yeah, right, okay," Billy Lee said, tossing aside the old Indian's words. "Now go back to sleep, or wherever the hell it is you go."

The prisoners milled restlessly in place, listening. Then they moved back from the bars as the Ranger's footsteps approached and stopped at the side of the wagon. They stood in silence, feeling his presence seek them out in the greater darkness. Then they listened closely as his footsteps led off to the front of the wagon, and even closer as they heard the uncoupling of the team of horses. "What's he doing?" Billy Lee whispered to no one in particular.

In a moment the Ranger had walked back to the side of the wagon. They heard one of the team horses blow out a breath and stomp a powerful hoof on the ground beside him. Billy Lee started to speak, but before he got a word out, the Ranger said in a low and serious tone, "Anybody raises their voice, I'll start emptying this rifle on all of you." He paused for a second, then continued. "There's been a change of plans. Bobby McLawry . . . I'm letting you go, for now." The prisoners stood stunned by his words, except for Granddaddy Snake, who only raised his head and nodded. "Curtis, Granddaddy, Dewey, Billy Lee," the Ranger added. "Make up your minds right now if you want to go or stay. You've got about five seconds. Anybody goes in with me, I promise to put a word in to the judge for you."

"It's a trick," Bobby McLawry whispered. "Everybody stay where you are."

But Granddaddy Snake had already stood up and stepped to the back of the wagon. He gathered his blanket around himself and tucked it in at his waist, holding it in place. "It is not a trick." He rattled the barred wagon door. "Let me out of here, Ranger. I'm going with you."

"All right, Granddaddy." The Ranger stepped around and unlocked the door. "What about the rest of you? Curtis? Billy Lee?"

Dewey Toom cut in. "There's no need in asking me, Ranger. If this is on the level, I'm sticking with Bobby." His tone of voice turned a bit harsh. "I never believed in man volunteering for incarceration."

"Suit yourself, Dewey. What about it, Billy Lee?"

"If it's all the same with you, Ranger, I believe I might just stick here and see what develops." Billy Lee sounded cagey. "Even with you putting a good word for me . . . I'd still have to pull some time."

"Hope you know what you're doing," the Ranger said. "Curtis, let me know something."

"I — that is —" Curtis looked around in the blind darkness, wishing he could see Billy Lee's face. He swallowed a nervous tightness in his throat. "Aw, hell, Billy Lee, I'm going with the Ranger. Don't hold it against me, okay?" Before Billy Lee could comment, Curtis hurried out through the open door behind Granddaddy Snake.

"I think we ought to talk about it some first, Curtis," Billy Lee called out to him as the door swung shut.

"Billy Lee, there's nothing more to say about it. I already know what you're looking for. Our ideas ain't the same anymore." Curtis Roundtree stood around beside Granddaddy Snake while the Ranger left for a moment. "I'd rather pull my time and get done with it. You'd be wise to do the same." As he spoke, the Ranger came walking back through the darkness with Maria in his arms.

"Not me, Curtis. I'm off the hook and I'm staying off it," Billy Lee said. "If you're stupid enough to do this to yourself after him giving you a choice . . . I can't stop you. I hope we meet up again somewhere down the way."

"Me, too. Good luck, Billy Lee." Curtis spoke to the darker spot in the wagon where Billy Lee stood. "You're going to need it."

"Listen to this coward," Bobby McLawry sneered. "We'll be living high while you and that old Indian sweat it out on a rock pile."

"I hope you do, for Billy Lee's sake," Curtis said. Beside him the Ranger stepped up and handed him the hackamore reins he'd made quickly from a length of rope. "Curtis, you and Granddaddy take this horse. Follow the sound of my horse's hooves. We're going to be moving fast across some bad ground. Keep up with me." He turned and mounted the other horse, swinging up behind Maria, who sat slumped forward almost against the horse's mane. The poison was fast at work. She shivered and convulsed, and murmured half-conscious under her breath. The Ranger cradled her back against his chest. "Hang on, Maria. You're going to make it."

"What's wrong with her?" Billy Lee asked from the wagon. "Is she wounded?"

"Never mind," the Ranger said, restless, eager to get under way. "Just remember that until you know for sure I'm out of rifle range, you keep your mouths shut. I hear anybody call out to JC, I'll aim in on their voice and pick their eyes out." He hesitated for a second longer. "Billy Lee . . . are you sure you want to stay here? These are big horses. We'll make room for you."

"Don't worry about me, Ranger. I'll go where the wind takes me."

"The key is laying on the driver's seat," the Ranger said. He wondered for an instant if he should tell Billy Lee that the key he was hiding was not the real key. But with Bobby McLawry listening, maybe it was best not to mention it. Billy Lee would have to figure out his own way with the McLawrys. The Ranger had given him a choice. There was nothing more he could do. "*Adios,* until we meet again," he said and he put the horse forward with a tap of his heels.

With the fading of the horses' hooves into the black night, the three remaining prisoners stood silent for a few minutes, until at length Bobby McLawry chuckled and said, "This is the damndest thing I've ever seen. He's gone! We're free!" His voice got a bit louder as he spoke.

"Easy does it, Bobby." Billy Lee patted his shoulder. "We've got it going our way. Let's keep still for a while longer. Then we can shout to high heaven."

"Yeah, you're right. Go ahead though, see if you can reach out with that key and get us out of here."

"Why? It didn't reach before. My arm hasn't grown any." Billy Lee leaned against the bars and raised a foot behind himself for support. "He told you, there's another key on the driver's seat. Just relax until your brother gets here."

Bobby sounded excited all of a sudden. "But if I was out right now, I could catch up and put a bullet in his back. If I had a gun. If I had a horse."

"Bobby. . . ." Billy Lee tipped his hat down over his forehead and let out a long breath. "Don't make me sorry we're going to be riding together. I'm looking forward to getting rich working with you boys." A full ten minutes passed as the prisoners stood in silence, listening for any lingering sound of the horses' hooves. Finally Bobby McLawry broke the silence, saying, "All right boys, here goes." He cupped his hands and called out JC's name into the darkness. He stopped and waited for a few seconds, then called out again, this time louder.

Atop the hill, JC McLawry turned and called out to Sanchez, who sat amid the other men gathered around the licking flames of a campfire. "Sanchez, come here, quick."

"Better hurry, Sanchez," one of the men said beside him, taunting him. "Boss might be reading that Ranger's mind again." The men chuckled to themselves as Sanchez stood to answer the summons.

"*Sí*, Boss, what is it?" He stopped beside JC and looked down into the black-shadowed canyon.

"You tell me, Sanchez. I think I heard horses a few minutes ago. Just now I thought I heard a voice call out."

"Oh . . . ?" Sanchez just looked at him for a second. "Then perhaps I was right? Perhaps the Ranger has taken off to the flatlands?"

"No." JC shook his head. "It's something else. I don't know what." Sanchez had started to speak, but JC heard the voice again and held up a hand, stopping him. "Listen . . . hear it? Right down there?"

Sanchez stood silent, then cocked his head toward JC with a surprised expression, hearing what he thought to be Bobby McLawry's voice echo up faintly from the darkness. "Boss? I hear it, too." Behind them the other men stood up and stared in curiosity. From the darkness came the voice once more, this time more audible, the echo sounding stronger across the rocky, sloping land.

"It's Bobby, boys," JC called to the others. "He's calling us down there. Let's go!"

"But, Boss, this could be a trick, no?" Sanchez nearly grabbed his arm, but then thought better of it and stopped himself. "Maybe the Ranger is making him call out to us, eh? He will draw us into a trap."

"Bobby would let the Ranger cut his tongue out before he'd lead me into a trap." JC shot Sanchez a hard stare, then turned to the other men. "All of you, grab some

257

saddle. We're heading down."

Bobby McLawry, Billy Lee, and Dewey Toom stood against the bars listening to JC and his men move down and stop a few yards away along the trail. Dewey Toom asked Billy Lee in a sharp tone, "Why so quiet all of a sudden, bigmouth? Got any more wisecracks you want to make to me? Come on, give me some of that lip now." Dewey Toom grinned in the darkness. He sounded like a different man now that his freedom drew close at hand.

"Tell me something in there, Bobby," JC called out.

"It's all right, JC," Bobby replied. "The Ranger's gone. Don't ask me why, but him, his woman, and a couple of others lit out of here on the team horses more than half an hour ago."

After a moment of silent, JC called out, "Are you sure everything's jake here, Bobby?"

"Yeah, it's fine, JC." Bobby laughed. "You don't have to be so quiet. Hell, you can ride in beating a drum far as I care. I tell you he's gone!"

"Somebody strike a torch," JC said to the men. In a moment the circling glow of a flame flickered above the riders as they moved their horses closer, riding three abreast, with JC in the lead. "Bobby, this beats anything I've seen yet out of that crazy fool." At the wagon, two men hurried down from their horses and climbed on the wagon as JC got down from his horse and said to Sanchez, "Get back there and shoot the lock off the contraption."

"Wait, Boss, there's no need to," one of the men called out from the wagon seat. "The Ranger was considerate enough to leave us a key!"

"We've already got a key here," Billy Lee said. But the men atop the wagon paid no attention to him. They just laughed and jumped down and headed back to the lock on the rear door.

From a stand of bushes alongside the trail, a rustling sound stilled their laughter, and almost as one, the men's pistols came up from the holsters and cocked.

"Jesus! Don't shoot! It's me, Percy!" Lloyd Percy stood up in the outer glow of the torchlight and moved closer, his hands chest high, a frightened look on his face. "I've been hiding in there, waiting for a chance to come back and spring these boys."

JC glared at him. "How come you didn't do it the first time, like you were supposed to?"

"I couldn't, Boss, I swear. I tried, using that key they gave me. But the damn thing won't fit!" He breathed a nervous breath and stilled himself. "I saw the whole thing. I was plumb queer the way the Ranger just came back here and let everybody free. I never seen nothing like it."

"What was wrong with the key?" JC looked back and forth between Bobby McLawry and Percy as the door swung open, then drifted shut on its own power after the three prisoners hurried out of the jail wagon.

"Not a damn thing was wrong with it," Bobby said, shoving Percy backward. "Give me a gun, JC. I'm killing this yellow dog."

"Easy, Bobby," Dewey Toom said. "I never liked him, but I've got to say he might have been right. I heard him working that key like hell. It wouldn't budge." He stepped in closer to JC, while Billy Lee stood back watching, trying to get a feel for how to play things with these men.

"Where'd the key come from?" JC asked, trying to sort this out in his mind. "Is it the spare they keep under the seat?"

"That's right," Billy Lee said, stepping forward now. "I snuck it out and hid it while everybody else was too busy talking about it to do anything."

"Who are you, boy?" JC looked him up and down, an air of contempt coming over him. "Did anybody ask for your two cents?"

Billy Lee felt the urge to shy back, but he forced himself to stand firm, looking JC right in the eye. "My two cents was at work when everybody else's nickels and dimes weren't doing a thing."

"It's true, JC," Bobby said. "He got the key. He did his part, just like I told him to. I told him he was one of us now, if it's all the same with you and the rest."

"So what, he got the key," Lloyd Percy cut in. "If he got the wrong key, what good was it?"

"It's the right key," Billy Lee said, keeping his voice calm and collected. "You just couldn't keep your nerves in place long enough to use it." He cut a glance to JC, adding, "From what I've seen of your boys, you could use some good help for a change." Dewey Toom and Lloyd Percy bristled at his remark.

"Yeah?" JC grinned in the flicker of torchlight. "It's hard for me to imagine the Ranger leaving the real key under the seat. He's a real careful sort."

Dewey Toom cut in. "That's for sure, especially after what Bobby said happened with the handcuff key back in town."

"What happened, Bobby?" JC turned to his brother.

Bobby looked embarrassed, then told him the story. When he'd finished, JC chuckled and turned back to Billy Lee. "So you want to be a Blue Star, huh?" Before Billy Lee could answer, JC went on, saying, "Would you bet your life that's the real key?"

Billy Lee shrugged, keeping himself looking calm, but he felt the blood in his head begin to race a bit. What if he was wrong? He shot a glance at the barred door and saw the tongue of trip lock resting not quite shut behind the latch plate. "I'm serious about wanting to ride with you, make myself some money without bending my back for it." He grinned and took the key from under his dirty shirt. "Sure, let's give it a try."

Before anybody realized what he was about to do, he turned, partially keeping the lock out of sight, shoved the key into the lock and pretended to turn it sideways. Then he swung the door open, stepped back and shot a wicked grin at Lloyd Percy. "Like I said, nerves makes all the difference in the world."

"Jesus, Boss!" Lloyd Percy turned a sickly color. "It didn't fit. I tried, so help me, I tried hard!"

"Not hard enough, though, Percy." JC

cocked his pistol. "I'm through with you —"

"Boss, I swear to God!" JC let the hammer fall. A belch of fire hit Percy from so close, it ignited his shirt and flipped him backward. Billy Lee's eyes widened at the sight. But he kept himself in check, seeing the others watch the killing with no more than a detached interest. Percy hit the ground stone dead. JC turned and continued talking as if nothing had happened. "Why do you suppose the Ranger did this, Bobby?"

"I'm not sure, JC. Something was wrong with the woman. Maybe she was shot. They wasted no time getting out of here. We might catch up to them out there."

"Naw. We don't want to get in his rifle sights on the flatlands. We've won here. Let's gather up and clear out." He turned to the men. "Somebody give Bobby a pistol — give his buddy one, too."

Billy Lee felt himself relax a bit. He was in. He'd made a play with the key and it had worked. But then Dewey Toom eyed him and said to JC, "Boss, if you don't mind me saying so, I don't think that door was shut tight enough to be locked when he tried the key."

"You don't, huh?" JC gave Dewey Toom

an impatient stare, then turned facing Billy Lee. "Want to try it again?"

Billy Lee felt his stomach turn sour. He gave Dewey Toom a bored glance and shook his head. "Hell, why not?" He slammed the barred door shut, and this time shook it to make sure it was locked. Then he paused as if an idea had just come to him. "I'll tell you what . . . let's make it more interesting this time." He nodded toward Percy's body on the ground. "I know what I'll get if I'm wrong." He showed Dewey Toom a wide, cruel grin. "What does this peckerwood get if I'm right?"

JC chuckled, seeing the expression on Dewey Toom's face turn worried. Low laughter stirred among the men. "Sounds good to me. What do you say, Dewey?" JC eyed him closely.

"Hell, Boss. . . ." A nerve twitched in Dewey Toom's jaw. "I just don't want to see us get taken in by this wise-mouth horse grifter."

"Then let's do it." Billy Lee cut in, reaching out with the key toward the door lock. "I'm backing my words. Will you back yours?"

Dewey Toom raised a hand. "Wait now . . . let me think —"

"Think?" Billy Lee jammed the key into

the lock. "What is there to think about? You've either got the guts or you don't. Say the word, and let's settle up."

"Boss, this ain't right, him pushing me like this." Dewey Toom sounded shaky.

JC looked back and forth between the two of them, considering it. He looked at Percy's body on the ground and thought about the other two men lying dead back in the darkness. "Naw," he said finally. "Put it away. I've lost too many men already."

Billy Lee hesitated with the key in the lock, his hand ready to turn it. He'd taken his game this far. He was playing it for all it was worth, his stomach ready to heave but his eyes and hands as steady as surgeon's. "Are you sure? All it takes is one quick turn." He passed a cool gaze to Dewey Toom, seeing the sheen of sweat on the man's face.

"I said no." JC raised his voice a bit. "Are you going to have a problem following orders?"

"Sorry, Boss," Billy Lee said, feeling his stomach unwind now as he removed the key from the lock. "Just didn't want to get off on the wrong foot with you." He drew back and threw the key far out over the edge of the trail while the others looked on. It resounded with a ring of brass against rock, then fell silent. "Out of sight, out of mind," he added, dusting his hands together.

JC McLawry just stared at him for a second with a curious expression. "Bobby," he said to his brother without taking his eyes off of Billy Lee, "you stick close with your friend here. Make sure he learns what's expected of him." JC grinned at Billy Lee. "Who knows. He might be wearing a tattoo before long."

"Come on, Billy Lee," Bobby said in a quiet voice. "Let's round up Percy's horse. We've got a long ways to go."

In the darkness out on the flatlands, Curtis Roundtree looked back at the sound of the gunshot. "Lord, I hope that wasn't Billy Lee getting his head shot off."

Granddaddy Snake, sitting behind him on the horse, glanced back as well, then turned forward. "Come on, keep up with the Ranger. Billy Lee made his choice. Now he must go where that road takes him." The old Indian tapped his bony heels to the horse's sides, Curtis Roundtree still looking back as the horse picked up its pace. "He is now a part of the Blue Star brand."

"It's not a *brand,* Granddaddy. It's a skin tattoo." Curtis Roundtree turned forward to the night and the sound of the Ranger's horse, up ahead and moving fast.

CHAPTER 16

Lawrence Shaw and the woman sat quiet atop the big buckskin amid a long spill of loose rock, listening to the voices of JC and his gang, watching them move about in the circle of torchlight. When the men had left, Lawrence Shaw heeled his horse forward in the darkness while a silver reef of morning glowed in the eastern sky. But before they arrived at the abandoned jail wagon, they heard the sound of other horses moving down the sloop. Once more Shaw drew the big buckskin off to the side and waited and watched as Rance Plum and Jack the Spider slid their horses the last few yards down onto the trail.

In the first gray light of dawn, Plum spotted the body of one of the Blue Star Gang lying limp in the dirt. He stopped his horse and stepped down beside it. "Here's one, Mister Spider," he called out, leaning down and lifting the bandanna on the dead man's neck. "Luckily this one already has his tattoo."

"I've got another one here," Jack the Spider called back to Plum from a few feet ahead. "Looks like there's one more up by the wagon."

"God bless these dear outlaws." Plum pulled the long knife from his boot and spread his arm in a beaming smile, posturing there in the grainy morning light. "They simply leave their dead lying where they fall. Not at all civilized . . . yet oh so convenient!" He turned a full circle, smiling around at the desolate land.

"This one will have to be tattooed," Jack the Spider said, disgruntled, as he lifted Percy's damp bandanna and saw nothing but grimy sweat marks across his throat. "He could at least have washed himself sometime in the past week." He looked down at Percy's dead hollow, dead eyes. "Yeah, you, you stinking polecat."

Percy's mouth hung open, his face sideways on the dirt in a spill of blood. "So, Plum," Jack the Spider called out to his partner while reaching out with a dirty boot toe, and kicking Percy's mouth shut. "What say you do the tattooing this time? I did the last one."

From their hidden position, Lawrence

Shaw and the woman watched as Rance Plum stood with one boot planted firmly on the first dead man's shoulder and lifted the severed head by its hair with one final, wrenching snap. "But you do such a fine job, Mister Spider. I was never that artistic." Plum slung the head once to shed it of blood, then looked over at Jack the Spider with the head hanging from one gloved hand and the knife from his other.

"Then I ought to get paid more than you," Jack the Spider said. He dragged Percy over beside the other body on the ground and stood with one boot propped on Percy's chest. "Unless you want to do all the cutting, and I do all the art work."

"Let's not quibble, Jack," Plum said, smiling, leading his horse over to Jack the Spider, the head still swinging from his hand. "There's plenty of work for both of us."

At the two bodies on the ground, Plum halted his horse, took the burlap sack from his saddle horn and dropped it in the dirt. The head of the outlaw already in the bag rolled a half turn sideways and stopped. Flies stirred and buzzed. "I daresay, if we can stick close behind the Ranger we'll soon have this piece of work settled." Plum raised a gloved finger for emphasis. "And mind you, thus far we haven't had to do a thing but bide our time and ride in once the shooting has stopped."

"All right, Plum. This is one time you might have the right idea." The Spider grinned, taking Lloyd Percy by his dirty hair and raising his head a bit as Plum bent down with the bloody knife.

While the two men went about their gruesome work, Lawrence Shaw nudged his big buckskin forward as quietly as a drift of smoke. Feeling the woman tighten her hold around his waist, he reached back with his free hand and patted her leg gently to reassure her, then let his hand rest on his thigh near the butt of his pistol.

"You know, Mister Spider," Plum spoke as he took the bottle of India ink from his duster pocket and uncorked it, "if we were less honorable men, we could keep this Blue Star bounty going for a long time." He looked at the bottle of ink and smiled. "After all, do the *federales* really know how many members there are in this gang? We could simply work our way across the badlands, ink in one hand and a good hatchet in the other. For all the *federales* know, we could . . ."

Plum's words trailed off as he sensed the presence close behind them and turned slowly, looking up at Lawrence Shaw. The big buckskin blew out a breath. Jack the Spider turned suddenly as well, taken by surprise, his hand already reaching for his pistol. "That would be a bad mistake," Shaw said, staring down at the Spider. Then with no further regard for the man or the threat of his pistol, Shaw turned his gaze to Rance Plum, nodding at the knife in his hand. "Bounty hunters, huh?"

"Well, then. . . ." Plum tried to offer a shaky smile. He stood completely off guard, his gun hand holding the bloody knife. "To whom do I have the honor of —"

"Lawrence Shaw." Shaw cut him off and stepped his horse quarterwise for a better look at the grisly handiwork on the ground.

"Fast Larry?" Plum swallowed hard, his eyes following Shaw as he settled the buckskin and turned his eyes from the bodies on the ground back to the knife in Plum's hand. "But I thought you must be dead by now, sir."

"I'm not yet. Nobody calls me Fast Larry anymore," Shaw said. As he spoke, Plum noticed that his voice was dull — no life to it. "You're trailing the Ranger like vultures? Picking up pieces of the Blue Stars?"

"Well, yes, I suppose you could put it that way, loosely. Although I prefer to say we are working in a low-profile manner." Plum managed to slip a sideways glance toward Jack the Spider. The Spider stood tense. Plum could see he was considering his chances, ready at any second to go for the pistol at his fingertips. Plum could also see that Lawrence Shaw seemed not at all concerned by Jack's rigid manner.

"My associate, Mister Spider, and I are contracted by the Mexican government to bring these men in . . . dead, of course, for all intents and purposes." Plum made another attempt at a smile, this one working a little better now that the surprise had worn off a bit.

"When will you be seeing the Ranger?" Shaw backed his horse a step, swept a glance across Jack the Spider, then fixed his gaze back on Plum.

"Well, that's hard to say." Plum tilted his head to one side. "We will be heading across the border today. Mustn't let this merchandise go to spoil. We may well see him on our return."

"Is there any bounty left on me?" Shaw asked bluntly, once more casting a glance at the head on the ground.

"None that I'm aware of, sir," Plum said. "And even if there is, let me assure you . . .

we have plenty of business with the Mexicans."

Shaw nodded. "Tell the Ranger, I'm tired of hiding out here. Tell him, if he comes after me again . . . I'll have no choice but to kill him."

"Comes after you? Mister Shaw, I think you are mistaken. I don't believe the Ranger is —"

"Will you tell him?" Shaw stared at him.

"Well, yes, of course." Plum shrugged, nodding and turning to Jack the Spider. "Won't we do that, Mister Spider? Certainly we will. First thing when he run into him."

Jack the Spider still hadn't moved an inch or flickered his eye. Plum could only hope the Spider wasn't about to do something stupid. "Good." Shaw backed the buckskin a step, then turned it and nudged it forward along the trail.

Plum and the Spider looked at one another with bewildered expressions. "I could put one in his back," the Spider whispered, "if it wasn't for the woman being there. There could still be a little bounty money for him somewhere."

"No, no, let's not get greedy," Plum said, his voice low as the big buckskin moved out of sight around a turn in the trail. The woman had looked back at them through veiled eyes as Plum feigned a parting smile. Now he let go of a tense breath and shook his head. "Besides, Mister Spider, I sincerely doubt if you could get the drop on *that* man . . . even from behind."

"Says you." Jack the Spider spit and adjusted his pistol in his holster. "I'm no schoolkid when it comes to throwing down iron."

"Yes, well, even so. . . ." Plum smiled and rolled his eyes slightly upwards, skeptically. "Let's gather our heads and get them to the *federales.* We need to get back onto JC's trail before it gets too cold on us."

"Where do you suppose they're headed?" Jack the Spider leaned back down and took up the bottle of ink again.

"I haven't the slightest idea," Plum replied. "But the Ranger will be after them, you can rest assured. We'll simply follow him."

With early-morning sunlight beginning to warm up the coolness of the desert night, the woman and Lawrence Shaw had climbed down from their horse and now rested at the high edge of a switchback overlooking the long stretch of flatlands toward Circle Wells. In the far distance, a thin sheet of dust rose slantwise beneath the hooves of the Ranger's two team horses. Shaw studied the dust silently for a moment until the woman said quietly, "This Ranger . . . how do you know he is after you?"

"The Ranger has always been after me." Shaw's voice was hollow and flat, with no inflection to his words.

His reply had sounded vague, and she asked him, "Do you mean this particular lawman has always been after you — or just lawmen in general?"

He only nodded, leaving her more unsure of his meaning. She watched him, studying his eyes as they peered out, searching the desert floor. She noted to herself that this man had sounded alive and alert when she'd seen him call down JC and his entire gang. That was his natural state of being. Yet, outside of that tightly strung element of danger and death, he seemed at a loss. His thoughts, his words, his very demeanor seemed vacant and fragmented. He was a killer separated from the kill, and although weary of this path he'd chosen, he had so long been given to the taking of life that he could not focus clearly on anything else.

"The bounty hunter said the Ranger is not after you. I believe him." She watched his eyes search the desert below, unsure whether he'd even heard her words.

But at length he said without turning to her, "I can't."

"What? You can't believe what the bounty hunter said?"

"I can't believe anything," Shaw whispered.

In the distance, at the far end of the rising cloud of dust, the Ranger stopped the big team horse for the first time since they'd left the hillside trail. They were onto the flatlands now. Out here there was no chance of an ambush. But still he needed to press on to Circle Wells as fast as possible, even if it meant riding the big horse into the ground. Against his chest, Maria lay damp and shivering, her entire body swollen and taken on the faint smell of rotting eggs. He took up the canteen, uncapped it, and pressed it to her fevered lips. She tried brushing it aside with a weak hand, but he persisted. "Drink it. You have to. We'll be all day getting to town."

As she drew a small sip of water, Curtis Roundtree and Granddaddy Snake came up beside them on the other worn team horse. It was the first time they'd been this close to the Ranger and Maria in daylight, and seeing Maria's condition, Curtis said in a hushed tone, "Lord have mercy, she's snakebit."

"Yes. Now keep moving," the Ranger hissed.

Curtis's eyes widened as the Ranger turned facing him, his mouth still stained red from drawing the poison out of Maria's thigh, his eyes red-rimmed with a tortured look to them. He looked ghoulish and pale in the stark morning light, a sheen of dust covering him. "We stop for nothing until we get to Circle Wells. Nothing!"

"But — the horses." Curtis stared, transfixed by the sight of the Ranger and the terrible, harsh sound of his words.

"You heard him." Sitting close behind Curtis, Granddaddy Snake gigged his heels to the sweat-drenched horse's side. They moved forward ahead of the Ranger and Maria as the Ranger capped the canteen and shoved it down into his lap. "Is she going to make it?" Curtis asked over his shoulder in a muffled voice.

"I don't know." The old Indian looked back and saw the Ranger push the tired horse forward. "But do not make him tell you again to keep moving."

In the rising stir of dust behind him, the Ranger could have sworn for a second that he heard JC McLawry's dark laughter. But settling himself, he realized it was only a hot blast of wind rattling sand in the dead stems of a dried sourbrush. "Damn you, JC McLawry," he murmured, biting off the words in his pounding chest, goading the poor horse with his boot heels. He pictured in his mind the snake as it must have appeared, creeping forward in the dark night from its low, small world, bringing its poison forth here into the larger world while he and all other creatures supplicant to the desert night had stood contest to the task of living. "Damn you straight to hell."

He held Maria close as the big horse pounded on. He felt nothing real or solid beneath him those last long miles to Circle Wells, only the passing of precious time and the sweep of torturing sand across the surface of an unstable planet.

PART III

CHAPTER 17

The first week they'd spent in Circle Wells seemed like a blur, the Ranger thought, looking out through the dust-scalloped window of the doctor's office, down onto the street below. His eyes followed the rutted, serpentine road out of town until it stretched out of sight into the flatlands, and farther yet through the wavering heat into the distant image of the craggy hill line. The road lay empty except for a grimy one-horse buggy that moved along toward town from a hundred yards out. In his mind's eye, the Ranger pictured Maria, Curtis Roundtree, the old Indian and himself the way they must have looked that first hot evening when they rode into town, bareback on failing horses, looking to the townsfolk perhaps like four vanquished spirits from some netherworld blown into being on a cusp of angry wind.

The first three days, the Ranger had not

slept any real sleep. He'd dozed against his will, restlessly, from time to time, sitting on the footstool with his head bowed over on the edge of the feather bed where Maria lay fevered and lost in a gray swell of poison and pain. His hand did not leave hers unless by chance, and only then for a moment as she tossed and murmured, trying to right herself on the damp sheets. Then he would feel the absence of her hand in his, and even in his exhaustion he would seek it out and clasp it once again as if to will the poison out of her body and into his own veins.

More than once the doctor had urged him to go get some food, a bath, some rest. He had asked the Ranger at one point what good did he think it would do Maria if he got sick himself? But the Ranger only lifted his red-rimmed eyes and said with tired resolve, "No less good than I'm doing for her now." And only after those first three days, when Maria's fever and swelling waned a bit, did the Ranger leave the room long enough to check on the prisoners and attend to himself. That had been two days ago, and now Maria was growing stronger. He knew it. He willed it so.

He turned from the window as one of the women of the town had finished bathing Maria and dressed her in a long cotton gown, then fluffed two pillows up behind her back. "I'll be back to check on you in an hour," the woman said to Maria. Then she nodded at the Ranger and left with a bundle of damp bed linen in her arms.

"Look at you," Maria said in a weak voice, offering the Ranger a faint smile when the woman was gone. "You look as bad as I do."

"That's encouraging," he replied. He moved over beside the bed and took his seating on the footstool, reaching for her hand. He brought her hand to his cheek and held it there. "I talked to the doctor . . . he said it will be at least a couple of weeks before you're able to be out and around."

A silence lingered for a moment, then she said, "Well . . . ?"

"Well, that's all." He cupped her hand in both of his and pressed it gently, studying it, seeming to search their joined hands for something to say, or perhaps knowing what to say but faltering for the way to say it.

She saw the difficulty he was having, and to help him along she asked, "Are the prisoners doing well? Has Curtis gone before the judge yet?"

The Ranger raised his eyes to hers. "You're not going to believe this." He shook his head with a wry tight smile. "The judge let him go."

"You are right," she said, "That is hard to believe."

"I know, but it's the truth. The two teamsters who were supposed to testify against him didn't show up for court. So, after all the trouble getting him here, Curtis is now a free man. I've got a feeling the same thing would have happened to Billy Lee had he came with us."

"You did what you could, Sam. You made Billy Lee the same offer you made the others. You could not force it on him under the circumstances."

"Yes, but still —"

"No — do not think about it. He made the choice, not you."

The Ranger let out a breath. "I hate to see him headed where he's headed."

"That is out of your hands." She dismissed the subject of Billy Lee. "What about Granddaddy Snake?"

The Ranger shrugged. "We won't know anything until tomorrow. The judge wants to try his case separately. I tried talking sense to the judge, but I don't think he listened. At most Granddaddy will get a few weeks in jail for using profane language to Wet Lips Stella. But no white man would even be facing such a charge. Granddaddy doesn't deserve this. The sheriff won't even let him stay in a jail cell — say he smells too bad. He's sleeping in the other jail wagon over in the livery barn. I argued with the sheriff, but it didn't help. I still wish I'd never ran into that old Indian. I feel responsible."

"Maybe he will slip through the bars the way he had planned to do before," Maria said with a weak smile.

"I wish he could, to be honest with you. I feel like taking him a bucket of grease and telling him to give it his best shot."

"But you cannot, of course."

"Right, I can't." He brooded for a second.

She lifted her hand and ran it along the scar on his cheek. "You feel responsible for Granddaddy going to jail, you feel responsible for Billy Lee making a bad decision, and you blame yourself for me getting snakebit. I think you are taking too much onto yourself."

"Well — it's a fact, if you hadn't been out there backing my play, you wouldn't be laying where you're laying right now."

"*Sí,* this is true. But the same could be said if I had never been born. You do not control snakes in the desert. There is too much desert, and there are too many snakes." She let her hand drop back down to his.

"I never should have drove that blasted Misery Express. It's not my type of law work. I need a horse under me and nobody but myself to worry about." As soon as he said it, he realized his mistake and tried to correct it. "What I mean is —"

"What you mean is, you're ready to ride out and find the McLawrys and you don't know how to tell me that I must stay behind."

His voice softened. "Maria, there is nobody I trust more than you . . . nobody I respect more than you. But I've got to go on without you this time. I know how JC McLawry thinks. He's been laying low across the border, knowing I had his name on my list. He's been afraid to try anything. But now he'll feel bold, thinking he's won something. We'll be hearing from him and his gang most any time now."

"Then go," she said. She glanced away from him for a second, then added, looking back into his eyes. "But make sure you go for the right reason."

"I've thought it out, Maria. It is for the right reason."

"Oh? It is not because he has forced us to leave the Misery Express abandoned and flee for our lives? That would be for pride."

"No," he shook his head. "It's not a matter of pride. I've gotten past that."

"It is not because you have had to let a murderer go free in order to save my life?"

He thought about it for a second. "No. At first I thought it might be. But that would be for vengeance. That would be a mistake."

"Good, you *have* thought these things out. Then you do go for the right reason." She smiled and squeezed his hand.

"Yes, the right reason. All those other things might be a part of it . . . I can't deny it. But once I cut through all of that, it comes down to the face of the dead girl and its reflection in the mirror."

"The dead and the image of the dead." She nodded and let her hand slip from his.

"Yes." His hand drifted idly across the badge on his chest. "This thing still has *me* pinned to *it*. It sees what I see. I have go with it. When all else is either justified or beyond justification . . . it's still her face that tells me I have to go. I've never let a killer go free in my life. I can't do it now. You understand, don't you?"

"I would not have been with you all this time if I did not understand."

"Thanks," he whispered to the back of her hand. Reaching down to the floor beside her bed, he swept up his dusty sombrero and stood, resting the flat of his fingertips to her forehead for only a second. "I'll keep it short."

"Yes. And I will be waiting here when you return." She sighed and looked away as he turned and walked out the door.

When he left her room, the Ranger headed straight for the livery barn where he'd left his white Spanish barb horse while he'd driven the Misery Express across the desert. As he walked back toward his horse's stall, he caught a glimpse of Curtis Roundtree pitching hay down from a loft. Seeing the Ranger, Curtis ducked his face back out of the light. But the Ranger had already seen him clearly, and he called up to him, "Curtis, you don't have to hide from me. I did my job bringing you here, now it's over as far as I'm concerned."

Curtis stuck his big head forward from the hayloft and replied, "Are you sure, Ranger?"

"Yep, I'm sure. Come on down here. I need to pay Black-eye's feed bill and get a sack of grain for the road." As he spoke, the Ranger swung open the stall door and stepped inside. The big white horse with a black circle around one eye saw him and lifted its muzzle, sniffing him and shaking its mane. "Easy, Black-eye." The Ranger rubbed the horse's muzzle and moved him to one side, looking him over.

"I'm glad you feel that way, Ranger," Curtis Roundtree said, a bit out of breath, as he approached the stall door carrying the Ranger's saddle and bridle. "If you wanted to hold hard feelings, I couldn't blame you none, the woman getting snakebit and all. How is she?"

"She's doing better, Curtis," the Ranger said, turning to take the saddle and drop it atop a rail. He shook out the saddle blanket, looked it over, and smoothed it onto the horse's back. "I don't hold what happened out there against you. That would be foolish, wouldn't it?" He lifted the saddle and chucked it across the horse's back, running his hand beneath it before reaching down to couple the cinch. "I just wish none of us had to go through it, since it turned out the way it did." He turned to Curtis. "How long are you planning on staying here?"

"Not long. I don't like stable work. But I'm strapped for money right now and this will get me back on my feet." He motioned back into the darkness at the rear of the barn. "I wish there was something I could do for the old Indian. It ain't right, them keeping him here."

"Yeah, I know." The Ranger finished with

his horse, led it out into the center bay of the barn, hitched it, and walked back to the jail wagon, where he saw gray strands of the old Indian's hair hanging through the bars. "Granddaddy, are you asleep in there?"

Granddaddy leaned his head forward from against the bars. "In here I am never asleep . . . never awake, either." He stared at the Ranger. "Am I still in your custody?"

"No, Granddaddy. If you were you wouldn't be out here in the barn, I can tell you that."

"I don't mind." Granddaddy looked all around. "Whose custody am I in now?"

"You're in the sheriff's custody, Granddaddy. Why?"

"It doesn't matter," Granddaddy Snake shrugged. "I like to know who to complain to about it being cold here at night. I need more blankets." He gestured toward the pile of blankets at the front of the wagon. "At night I spread them out to make myself a pallet, but I need more blankets to cover me."

"I'll see what I can do, Granddaddy," the Ranger said. "I'm sorry this is turning out bad for you. The judge really has it in for you over that dog. Think it's about time you told him the truth?"

"No," the old Indian said firmly. "You did

not tell him, did you? You gave me your word."

"I didn't tell him . . . but I feel like it. You're going to have a hard few weeks with these people. The sheriff doesn't like Indians, as it turns out."

"Not many sheriffs do." Granddaddy Snake picked a piece of straw from his hair and flipped it away. "But now that I am no longer in your custody, maybe I will not stay here much longer. I may decide —"

The Ranger raised a hand toward him, stopping him before the old Indian said any more. "Granddaddy, you do realize that any plans I hear of a man ready to escape jail, it's my duty to report it?"

"Oh . . . no, I did not know that." He shook his head. "There are still so many things I do not understand about your people. I suppose I will be a dumb blanket Indian for the rest of my days."

The Ranger weighed his next words carefully, then he said, "Well, remember this, Granddaddy — should I happen to see you out on the badlands, I'll just assume you've been set free, unless you're foolish enough to tell me otherwise. So watch what you say to me. I am a lawman, you have to understand."

"How is the woman?" the old Indian

asked him, changing the subject. "I was afraid for her."

The Ranger looked back and forth between Granddaddy Snake and Curtis Roundtree as Curtis stepped up beside him eager to hear as well. "She's going to be all right. She's still weak, but coming around."

"And now you are going back out on the badlands to find the McLawrys." Granddaddy Snake let out a long breath.

"It's my job, Granddaddy. I won't rest until Bobby McLawry is set right for killing the girl."

"And his brother, JC, will not rest until you are set right for wrongs he feels you have done him in the past." Granddaddy Snake looked down, contemplating the situation for a moment. Then he raised his face back to the Ranger again. "The badlands will be a dangerous place to be until these things are settled." He smiled a crafty smile. "I was going to grease down some more and slip through the bars. But now I think it is better I stay here for a while longer."

The Ranger winced. "I asked you not to tell me anything like that." His wince turned to a smile. "Now I'll have to mention it to the sheriff."

"Too bad," Granddaddy Snake said. "Me and my big mouth. But you must do what you must do. . . ."

The Ranger nodded and looked the dusty jail wagon over and smiled. "Take care of yourself, Granddaddy."

"You do the same, Ranger."

CHAPTER 18

The Ranger waited until the evening shadows stretched long and dark across the streets of Circle Wells before leading his white barb out of the livery coral and to the hitch post out front of the mercantile store on Front Street. Before going into the store, he walked the few yards down the boardwalk and into the telegraph office. "Have you gotten responses from all the towns you sent the warning to?" he asked the old clerk who sat hunched over a battered oak desk.

"All but two of them, Ranger," the clerk answered in a gravelly voice. "Got no reply from Wakely or Bentonville. Wakely has been having line trouble for a long time. But I can't figure out what's wrong at Bentonville." He scratched his head up under the brim of his visor. "We should have heard back from them today."

"Wakely and Bentonville, huh?" The Ranger considered it, placing the location of the towns in his mind. The town of Wakely lay thirty miles southeast of Bentonville, right on the trail from the badlands. "If you should happen to hear anything from Bentonville, tell Sheriff Petty I'm on my way."

The old clerk looked at him through tired eyes. "You don't think Bentonville is having trouble with that bunch you're warning everybody about, do you?"

"I'd almost bet on it," the Ranger said. He adjusted the brim of his sombrero, left the office, and walked back to the mercantile store, where he took on a quarter of dried elk shank, airtight tins of beans, a two-pound bag of Duttwieler's tea, and enough ammunition and gun oil for a long ride if need be. As he came out of the store with his supplies in his arms, he saw the young deputy, Clyde Sublet, taking a wooden bowl of hash toward the livery barn. "Evening, Ranger," the deputy called out. "Got to get that old Indian fed . . . if he'll eat anything, that is."

The Ranger only nodded and went about the business of packing his supplies into his saddlebags. But no sooner had Clyde Sublet entered the livery barn, than he came running back out and down the middle of the street toward the Ranger, shouting in a frenzy, "He's gone! He's broke out of the jail wagon! Ranger! The old Indian's gone!"

The Ranger smiled a thin smile to himself and finished tightening the straps of his saddlebags as Clyde slid to a halt beside him. Then he turned to Clyde, seeing the wide-eyed look on his face. "Escaped? How, Deputy? He was there a while ago. I talked to him myself."

"I know! He was there when I took him some extra blankets like you asked me to! But he's gone now! Lord, what am I gonna do? The sheriff's out at the Maslen spread! He's gonna throw a fit! You've got to help me, Ranger!"

"Calm down, Clyde." The Ranger placed a hand on his shoulder, settling him. "He's no longer my prisoner, and I've got to be getting out of here. You'll handle it all right. How did he get out?"

"He —" The deputy caught his breath and shook his head. "He slipped out through the bars, Ranger! I never seen nothing like it."

"Neither have I, Clyde. Are you sure about this?"

"Yeah, I'm sure! The bars are greasy! You can see where he slid right through them."

"Where's Curtis Roundtree?"

"I didn't see him nowhere. Do you think

he was in on it?"

"I doubt it," the Ranger said.

Inside the barn, Granddaddy Snake crawled out from beneath the rumpled pile of blankets that lay in the front of the wagon. He'd smiled and listened to the deputy run down the street yelling. A moment before, Clyde the deputy had stepped all the way in through the open barred door and stood stunned for a second, looking back and forth at the empty wagon until he spotted the grease-smeared bars. Then the realization struck him. He had let out a short whine and dropped the bowl of hash to the floor. He dashed out of the barn, leaving the door to the jail wagon wide open behind him, just the way the old Indian had wanted him to do.

Now Granddaddy Snake climbed out of the jail wagon, peeped out through a crack in the barn wall, and chuckled under his breath. What kind of fool would think a person could slip through these bars? He shook his head and slipped out the back door of the barn, off into a stand of mesquite and juniper, letting the shadows of evening surround him.

A handful of townsfolk had gathered on the street at the sound of the deputy's voice. At the head of the gathering, the judge stepped forward, his bushy eyebrows seeming to bristle toward Clyde Sublet. "He's what? Escaped? So help me, deputy, if that old Indian isn't caught and back in that wagon tonight, I'll have you and the sheriff both rode out of this town on a rail!"

While the judge ranted, the Ranger finished preparing his supplies, and checked the white barb over one last time. He'd raised a boot to his stirrup and started to swing up to his saddle when the judge turned to him. "And where do you think you're going, Ranger?"

"My business here is finished, Your Honor. "I'm headed out."

"You can't leave while a dangerous prisoner is running loose! I won't hear of it."

"Dangerous?" The Ranger took his boot out of the stirrup and turned to face the judge. "He's charged with the use of profanity. What are you afraid of, that he'll go on a spree? Run about the streets shouting cusswords?"

Muffled laughter erupted in the crowd, but it halted abruptly when the judge swung toward them, his face reddening. Then he turned back to the Ranger. "Any man on the run is potentially dangerous! You can't leave here until he is apprehended. That is an order!"

"Judge," the Ranger let out a breath and pushed up the brim of his sombrero. "I'm not under your authority now that the prisoner detail is finished. If you have a problem with me, feel free to take it up with the captain back at the ranger station. While you're at it, be sure to mention what Granddaddy Snake is charged with — they'll get a kick out of it." His eyes narrowed on the judge's. "If you want to really explain what the problem is here, let them know that you suspect the Indian of eating your dog. They'll appreciate the fact that you're willing to spend money and man-hours on a personal vendetta while a gang of bank robbers is on the prowl."

"How dare you, sir!" the judge exploded. But even as he raged for the sake of the onlookers, the Ranger saw him pull back a step, relenting. "You haven't heard the last of this! I'm filing a complaint on you. I promise you that!"

"Then get it filed." The Ranger swung up into his saddle. "Meanwhile, instead of sending this man off to chase down Granddaddy, you'd be wise to send him out to the army fort and have them detail you a company of troops to help you here."

The judge looked concerned. "But . . . these men you're after. They aren't coming in this direction, are they?"

"I don't think so. But it wouldn't hurt to be prepared." He tipped his sombrero, backed his white barb and said to it under his breath as he headed it toward the edge of town and the distant dark shadows of the looming hill line, "Come on, Black-eye, take us up."

At the edge of the encroaching desert, he stopped long enough to draw a sip of water from his canteen. He swished it around and spat the taste of the town out of his mouth. And for the next three days he rode southwest, resting only when the horse needed rest. He put his concern for Maria out of his mind and thought of nothing but the trail and the badlands, and the men he would soon encounter. He took food and water only when the horse needed food and water; and when he'd come upon the empty jail wagon and saw the swarm of red ants still lifting grains of sand from the black bloodstains on the ground, carrying them away like souvenirs from a great battlefield, he looked at the Misery Express only in passing. Then he struck out wide and high, onto the craggy rock trail, even though the week old hoofprints led off onto the lower winding road.

■ ■ ■ ■

Near the fire, Bobby McLawry and Billy Lee sat sipping from one of the bottles of whiskey they'd brought with them on their way out of Wakely two days before. A lot had happened for Billy Lee in the past week. He'd proved himself to JC and the others at Wakely, and he now bore a star tattoo on his neck to show for it. In his pocket he now carried nearly two thousand crisp new dollars — more money than he could remember ever having at one time in his entire life. This was bank money, free and easy. All he'd had to do was stand out front at the hitch rail and hold the horses for the rest of the men. A piece of cake. . . .

He raised the bottle of whiskey and took a long drink. True, he'd killed a man in Wakely, but it wasn't his fault. He shrugged and took another drink. His hands trembled slightly, for in his mind's eye he could see the face of the man when the bullet tore through his chest. But the man's scream was dulled a bit now by the warm glow of whiskey — and Billy Lee reminded himself that the man had asked for it, running out in the street like that, coming up behind JC with a raised shotgun. If Billy Lee hadn't fired, JC McLawry would be dead right now. He tossed back another drink and passed the bottle on to Bobby McLawry.

Bobby looked at the strange expression on Billy Lee's face as he took the bottle and swirled its contents before throwing back a shot. "Something bothering you, Billy Lee? You look pale. You ain't been your wise-mouthing self the past day or two."

"Me? Hell no. Nothing's bothering me." Billy Lee grinned, touching a hand to the tender spot on his neck where the fresh tat-too stood red, puffed, and swollen. "I was just wondering how long before we dip ourselves up another load of money."

Bobby McLawry tossed back his drink and let out a low whiskey hiss. "Ain't you glad our paths crossed when they did? Just think of all that penny-ante horse grifting you was doing, and all the while these nice big banks were sitting out here just begging to be robbed."

"Yeah . . . ," Billy Lee said. "This is so easy, I can't imagine why everybody doesn't do it."

"What? You mean they don't?" Bobby laughed and poked the bottle back into Billy Lee's hand.

Billy Lee laughed with him, took another sip, and put his fingertips to his sore neck.

He gazed into the low flames of the campfire and wondered for just a second how Curtis Roundtree had made out in court, if he'd even been to court yet. What would ole Curtis think if he could see him now — two thousand dollars, all his own. In his whiskey glow he could just see the look on Curtis's face, hear him saying, *Lord, Billy Lee, two thousand dollars!* Billy Lee smiled to himself nodding, his head, feeling good and tipsy. But then he saw Curtis's face again. *You mean you kilt a man? Shot him down? All he was trying to do was keep you from robbing the —*

"Enough of that hooey," Billy Lee murmured aloud in his drunken haze. Pushing Curtis's face out of his mind, he threw back another drink, nearly finishing off the warm red rye.

"Hey! Take it easy, Billy Lee," Bobby chuckled. "We're supposed to be sharing that bottle."

"Oh. . . ." Billy Lee glanced sideways at him, then thrust the bottle toward him. "Here, you keep it. I got enough money to ride out of here and buy all the whiskey I want."

"Easy now," Bobby whispered. "JC don't like hearing that kind of talk. Nobody can leave here on their own. It's the way we do things. Wherever we go, we stick together." He leaned closer. "It keeps anybody from getting any ideas about breaking off on their own."

"What's the good in having money then, if we can't come and go as we please and spend it?"

"We can . . . only not by ourselves. There's always two or three of us goes together. That's why JC asked me to stick close to you." He finished off the bottle and pitched it to the ground. "From now on it's you and me, buddy. That's all right with you, ain't it?"

Billy Lee shrugged. "Sure, why not?" But as he thought about it, the idea of him and Bobby always together didn't feel right. He was used to him and Curtis being together all the time, but that was different. They were friends by choice, not because one had to keep an eye on the other. He looked around at his new companions. They lay sprawled around the campfire. The ones already turned in for the night had their pistols tucked beneath their saddles or their dusty blankets, only inches from their hands. Sleeping with a loaded gun was something else that would take some getting used to.

JC moved around from the other side of

the campfire and stooped down close to the two of them. "I want to let you know before I tell the others — we're not going back across the border for a while." He grinned. "Now that I've sent that Ranger off with his tail between his legs, we're gonna move around these badlands. Robbing all these new banks will be like picking a cherry tree."

His tail between his legs? That wasn't at all the way Billy Lee had seen it. It looked to him like the Ranger had sent the whole gang packing, not knowing what to do next. But Billy Lee only shrugged and nodded. It wasn't his place to say anything.

JC looked back and forth between Billy Lee and Bobby. "How's that sound to yas?"

"You already know how it sounds to me, JC," Bobby said. "I'm sick of robbing all those ragged-ass Mexican banks . . . living on goat meat and peppers all the time. This is more my style." He raised his pistol from his lap and twirled it on his finger, grinning a wet whiskey grin. "God bless America."

"I thought so." JC turned to Billy Lee and slapped his knee. "So, ole buddy, how do you like riding with the Blue Stars, now that you've got yourself a taste of it?" Before Billy Lee could answer, JC added, "You know you earned your star quicker than anybody has yet, except maybe Bobby here.

Nothing like keeping the boss from catching a bullet to get a man advanced, eh?"

"He earned it, that's for sure," Bobby said, reaching over and slapping Billy Lee on the back.

"It got my attention," JC said. "I brought in a few like Barrows, Stinson, and old Whitey, thinking they would make the grade. They were nothing but a disappointment." He squeezed Billy Lee's knee. "But you, the way you came in bold as brass, got yourself in the thick of it right away. I like that. You're the kind of man we need to keep this thing going, eh, Bobby?"

"I knew he'd fit right in," Bobby said with a smug expression. "I could tell by the way he talked he was itching for some action." Bobby nudged Billy Lee with his elbow. "And I was right."

"Yeah, you were." JC stood up and hooked his thumbs into his gun belt. "I'm thinking from now on a man doesn't earn his star within say, a month, we'll go ahead and shoot the sucker and leave him in the dirt. Can't waste time on a man. He's either got what it takes or he doesn't."

"So, JC, where we headed next?" Bobby asked, looking up at his older brother. "I know you sent Becker and Junebug ahead to scout something out for us."

"No, not to scout something out. It's already been scouted out. I sent him and Junebug to cut the lines into Bentonville. I can't see letting the new bank sitting there *un-robbed*, especially with that brand-new sheriff watching over it." He chuckled. "That's the last place in the world anybody would expect us right now. Not only are we gonna hit the town, we're circling wide and coming in from the opposite direction, in case anybody happens to be waiting for us." He tapped a finger on the side of his head. "See, boys, it takes some serious thinking to run a gang like this."

Billy Lee just looked at the two of them, still nodding, agreeing with every word. Then he ran a hand along the swollen tattoo on his neck. Things were going pretty good for him here, he thought. He wanted to be careful what he said. He could go along with these men for a while . . . make himself some money. But they were all fools — them and their stupid tattoos. He could see that. Billy Lee knew he was smarter than all of these idiots combined. He just had to play along with them for a while. As soon as he got what he wanted, he'd be on his way.

The fresh sore on Billy Lee's neck felt warmer than it had before, puffier too. It ached and throbbed farther down along his throat than it had earlier. When he lowered his fingertips from it and studied them in the firelight, the smear of blood looked yellowish, runny. "I'm gonna turn in for the night," he said to JC and Bobby. "Sounds like we've got a long ride come morning." He slid down onto his blanket and took his pistol from his belt and settled it under his saddle. His neck would feel better by morning, he thought, flipping the edge of his blanket over him. It just had to scab over and dry some. He wished he didn't have the damn thing, because now he'd be stuck with it the rest of his life. So what? He'd just pull his bandanna up and hide it from the rest of the world when he wanted to. The main thing for now was to leave it alone — let it harden up and heal.

CHAPTER 19

For two days Lawrence Shaw had stayed with the woman in her small village before moving on. They'd gone to her husband's fresh grave and he'd watched her place flowers there and make the sign of the cross. She'd spoken to the mound of sandy soil as if expecting it to answer. She'd introduced Lawrence Shaw to her dead husband. Shaw had felt odd standing there, his hand on the butt of his pistol, looking no different to those dead eyes beneath the earth, he thought, than the very man who had killed him. Yet she'd spoken Shaw's name down to the grave and told her dead husband how Shaw had saved her from JC McLawry. And she'd told these things to the grave as if it needed to know — as if Shaw would be around for a long time to come, as if she needed her dead husband's approval.

Early the next morning when Shaw left without saying good-bye, she come running barefoot from her hovel into the dirt street with only her thin serape drawn around her nakedness. She'd called out to him, but he didn't answer. He looked back once over his shoulder and saw her there, small and alone, a hand shielding her eyes from the early sun's glare. She and the earth itself rose and fell slightly with each clop of the buckskin's hooves, and behind her in the near distance, he'd saw the flutter of flowers on the raw mound of earth. "You will come back? Someday . . . ?"

He'd only nodded and turned and rode on. He could have stayed. Perhaps he *should* have stayed. The villagers were friendly. They'd made him feel welcome among them. But then, they'd had good reason to. The woman had told him in so many words that in this life there was little time to mourn the dead. Her husband understood these things, and she knew it would be all right with him if she cooked for Shaw and became his woman; and if men like JC and his Blue Stars should ever ride this way again, they would think twice before attacking the village — knowing Shaw was here.

After telling Shaw this, she'd stepped out of her thin cotton dress there in the shade of her hovel and offered herself to him, unashamed, placing a cupped hand on her dark breast. But he'd only turned from her and looked out the doorway toward the border, resisting all change to what he knew had to be. He'd thought of himself as a man who had long ago written the story of his life and read it many times over. He stood powerless now, able to do little more than watch the pages turn. So he rode on.

At the town of Wakely, he'd seen the aftermath of the Blue Star Gang's visit. But he'd only stood his buckskin at the edge and watched as undertaker and two towns-men carried the body from the middle of the dirt street. On the boardwalk two other men stood sweeping glass shards into a pile beneath the shattered bank window. When they glanced toward him, they stopped and whispered back and forth under their breath until finally one of them turned and ran along the boardwalk toward the sheriff's of-fice.

Shaw didn't wait for the sheriff. He'd seen enough. The Blue Stars would be heading for the next town. He knew it, and if he knew it so did the Ranger. "Hey, you? You there!" An old sheriff called out to him as he turned his buckskin on the hard dirt in a low stir of dust. "What do you want here? Huh? If you know what's good for you, you best ride on!" He wasn't going to give the

Ranger another run at him. He'd be waiting for him when the Ranger came hunting for the Blue Star Gang.

The next day, having taken a short cut through the high passes above the trail where the hoofprints of the gang led north, Shaw came down onto the flatlands seven miles out of Bentonville and headed for the town. Topping a low rise a mile along the road, he caught sight of the two men fifty yards ahead as they stood below the telegraph pole, one with a pair of wire cutters in his hands. JC's men. He slapped his boot heels against his horse's sides and shot it forward.

"Oh, no!" Becker said to Junebug, the toothy grin fading from his face at the sight of seeing Lawrence Shaw riding down on them. He dropped the wire cutters and reached for his horse's reins. "It's that warped-minded gunfighter! I'm out of here!"

"No! Stand still!" Junebug grabbed Becker's horse by its bridle. "He's a mad dog! If you run he'll nail you for sure."

"But he'll kill us!"

"Or we'll kill him. Now stand still, damn it. There's no place to run to. I've never seen this side of you before."

"What side? I never claimed to be a hero.

We can't kill him!"

"Like hell. I don't see no *can't-kill-me* sign on the son of a bitch's chest." Junebug stood his ground as the big buckskin pounded closer.

"Oh, no," Becker said again, this time whispering as Shaw slid his horse sideways to them and halted it ten feet away.

"Thought you left us the other day." Becker kept his voice calm, his hand poised near his pistol butt. "Haven't seen you around none. Figured you and the woman lit out. Ain't that what we all thought, Junebug?" Junebug only stared at him.

Becker rattled on. "I told Junebug just last night, said, '*Damn,* I sure liked that Fast Larry Shaw.' Hated seeing you leave so quick, never got time to make friends with you, but I figured we would if ever we got the chance to just sit down and talk a spell, you know, about this and that, what we both like and dislike and how important it is for men to just live in peace and learn to be like —"

"Shut up, Becker," Junebug hissed, keeping his eyes on Lawrence Shaw as Shaw surveyed the road and the cut telegraph lines, one end dangled down the pole and the longer end ran across the sandy soil. "I can tell by the way you rode in. You're going to try to shoot us, ain't you, Fast Larry?"

"Try?" Shaw still gazed off along the dusty road, his eyes following the line of poles in the direction of Bentonville. "How soon will JC and the others come this way?"

"Not soon enough, I don't reckon."

"Buy why kill us?" Becker pleaded. "There's no reason for it. We've done you no harm." Even though his voice had gone soft with fear, Becker moved his hand ever so slightly closer to his pistol butt.

"But you might've someday." Shaw seemed not to notice the movement of Becker's hand, or if he did notice it made no difference to him. "I don't need reasons."

"We ain't gonna stand here and do nothing," Junebug said. "I know you're fast. But if I'm going down, I'm damn sure taking you with me."

"And . . . ?" Shaw turned his face to them now, his eyes fixed on Junebug's.

"And what?" Junebug felt his breath growing tighter in his chest, his gun hand so tense it might cramp any second. "That's it . . . that's all I've got to say about it."

Becker took a cautious half step forward and offered in a timid voice, "I'd like to say one or two more things, if you'll give me a chance —"

"You damn coward!" Junebug sneered,

casting a nervous sidelong glance toward Becker. "After all the tough talk I've heard out of you. You're whining? Don't give him the satisfaction. Can't you see he enjoys this — watching a man grovel at his feet. It's a game to him." He leaned a bit forward and spat at Shaw's boot in the stirrup. "Let's get it done. I'll be waiting for ya in hell, Fast Larry . . . !"

In the ringing silence that followed, Lawrence Shaw sat staring out across the desert where a stir of hot wind lifted a dusty bundle of sage and rolled it streaming along a cusp of a long dune until it dropped out of sight. In the echo of the two pistol shots, a buzzard had swept upward from beneath the shade of a tall cactus into an updraft of hot air. Now it lay as if suspended against gravity and seemed to peer down at him.

Shaw replaced the two spent rounds and slid the pistol back down into his belt. *Enjoyed it . . . ? Not hardly,* he thought, looking down at the two dead men. Their guns never had the chance to clear leather. He'd never *enjoyed* it. Somehow he'd been stuck with it — cursed by it. That's what people never understood. To those who didn't know better, it might look as if he enjoyed it. He did it so well, with such ease. Fast Larry at work.

Fast Larry . . . if they only knew. He didn't

start off being fast with a gun. Nobody did. Like all men on this dark road he traveled, his skill came to him over time, out of necessity. As his reputation had grown, so had his need to become faster, deadlier, more heartless, until one day — he could not pinpoint when — Lawrence Shaw the man had disappeared, and in his place stood Fast Larry.

He squeezed his eyes shut for a moment and felt the shadow of the circling buzzard pass across his face. *A game to him?* He didn't think so. Shaw stepped the big buckskin high and sideways of the two bodies on the ground, and without another glance at them, he heeled the horse toward Bentonville. Would the Ranger come there? Did he know that was where the Blue Stars would be headed? Of course he knew. The Ranger knew everything. Lawrence Shaw shook his head and fixed his gaze on the road before him, feeling once more the pages turn in that book he'd envisioned. They all knew where this was going. They all thought alike whether they admitted it or not. Whether they even *knew* it or not. They were all lost spirits out here on this hard killing plane — the Ranger, JC McLawry, the devil and himself, Shaw thought. They drank from the same well.

They nourished and bathed in the same pool of blood.

It was dusk when Rance Plum and Jack the Spider came upon the large black mound in the road ahead of them. Off to the left of the trail, two horses milled and grazed on sparse streaks of dried grass. A few yards beyond the two horses, a small band of coyotes circled from one stand of cholla and mesquite to the next. At the sight of the two riders, they slunk down but did not back away. "My goodness, Mister Spider, what have we here?" Plum shoved the bottle of warm Mexican wine down between his thighs and gigged his horse forward the next twenty yards. Jack the Spider rode right beside him, seeing the black mound dissipate upward in a thrust of batting wings and angry calls.

"I don't know who they are." The Spider belched and spoke with a drunken slur, "but as long as they ain't kin, one neck's as good as another for our purposes."

"Indeed." Rance Plum climbed down from his saddle, taking his wine bottle in hand as his horse came to a halt. "Only in this case, your artistic prowess is not required." He reached out with his boot toe and turned Junebug's bloated face sideways.

"It appears these gentlemen are true initi-
ates. Dyed-in-the-wool Blue Stars, as it
were." He beamed, tipped his bottle of wine
down toward the corpses with a *"Salute,"*
and threw back a drink. "We're so busy, we
hardly have time to deliver the goods. God
bless that wonderful ole Ranger. I could
simply give him a wet smack on his dirty
jaw!"

"That's you, all right," said the Spider.

"What you mean, *'that's me'*?" Plum shot
him a hard, drunken stare.

"Nothing. What makes you think the
Ranger did this?" Jack the Spider looked
around the land warily with his one good
eye.

"Because by my calculations, dear Mister
Spider, while we were turning in our bounty
receipts, the Ranger had plenty of time to
get to Circle Wells and back — more than
enough time."

"I don't like this," Jack the Spider said,
still looking around, his hand on his pistol
butt. "We need to collect these heads and
not tarry here. It'll be dark in a few more
minutes. I don't want to be seen."

Behind them came the metal-on-metal
sound of a rifle cocking. As they froze in
place, the Ranger's voice called out from
twenty feet away behind a scrub juniper,

"You've already been *seen,* Spider. You're just lucky it's me with a bead on your spine." As they turned toward the voice, he stepped forward. "Do either of you ever pay attention to anything? Didn't you notice the coyotes shying back?"

Plum rolled his eyes in exasperation. "Please spare us the frontiersman lecture." He tossed the Ranger the bottle of Mexican wine. The Ranger caught it, swirled it, and took a sip. Plum cocked an eye at him. "Have you been listening to us?"

"Yep." The Ranger pitched the bottle back to him.

Plum's face reddened. "What I said about a *wet smack*? That was simply a figure of speech, I assure you." Beside him, Jack the Spider scoffed and muffled a laugh. Plum spun toward him, his eyes widening. "If you so much as imply —"

The Ranger cut his words short. "How many of JC's men did you turn in?"

Plum stalled, then said, shrugging. "To be quite honest, I lost count. Four, five, perhaps?"

"All of them with blue star tattoos, I'm sure." The Ranger spread a thin, crafty smile.

"Of course." Plum looked offended, then changed the subject. "We knew you must have run into trouble, sir. I only wish we could have been some help to you."

"You help best by staying out of the way, Plum." The Ranger gestured toward the bodies on the ground. "If it wasn't for them still wearing their heads, I would've guessed this to be your work. Since it's not, the only other person I can think of is Lawrence Shaw. Have you run into him? He was riding with JC the last I heard."

"Yes, indeed. Last week, after the smoke cleared at the Misery Express wagon." Plum rolled one of the bodies over with the toe of his boot and looked at the bullet hole in Junebug's bloody forehead. "My, that was some shot!" He looked back at the Ranger. "But Shaw didn't appear to be riding with anyone, except some young Mexican woman."

"Yeah?" The Ranger looked at the other body and saw an identical wound. The white rib cages of both were visible, evidence of where the buzzards had taken their meal. "Shaw was married to a young Mexican once. But that wouldn't be her. She died years ago. I remember it well."

"Shaw thinks you're after him, Ranger," Jack the Spider said. "I would've nailed him for you, but Plum was too scared to get out of my way."

"Ha!" Plum tossed his head back.

"I don't want him nailed, Spider. I just want him to know I'm not out to kill him. Somehow he's gotten it in his head over the past year, and I haven't been able to get close enough to convince him otherwise." The Ranger shook his head. "If Shaw's dealt himself into this thing with JC McLawry, it could get real ugly."

Plum turned back a long drink of wine and licked his lips and the fringe of his thin mustache. "I wouldn't worry if I were you. Jack and I are more than willing to ride in with you and wait for these Blue Stars . . . providing we get their heads afterward, of course."

"Thanks all the same, Plum. But that's not how I work and you know it."

Jack the Spider spat and said in a harsh tone. "Still hold yourself a cut above us, don't you, Ranger? We're not outlaws you know. Plum and I make our living the same way as you do. Only difference is we don't have pay coming every month like clockwork."

"Mister's Spider right, you know." Plum patted himself on the chest. "We hunt to eat, in a manner of speaking." He swirled the wine in the bottle. "No one hand-feeds us."

"You're drunk, Plum." The Ranger looked back along the trail in the failing light of evening. Then he looked at the dead outlaws on the ground and back at Plum. "Since these bodies are lying out here in the open, I figure JC and his boys haven't passed this way and seen them." He looked at the ground and saw no sign of a group of riders having passed by. "My guess is, JC thought he'd outsmart everybody, swing around the hills and come in Bentonville from the north."

Plum rubbed his face as if to clear it of cobwebs. "If that's the case, he might very well have already hit the town and done his worst. He could be long gone by now."

"No, I don't think so. He might have already hit town. But if he did, he's taking his time, doing a little celebrating. Sort of a welcome back to this side of the border." He smiled a thin tight smile. "So . . . you two really want to work with me on this?"

Plum looked surprised. "You really want us to?"

"Only if you'll do like I ask."

"And what might that be?" Plum and the Spider drew closer.

"I scout the town come morning. If they're there, you'll be waiting to the north, a mile out. I'm taking JC and Bobby McLawry down. When the rest scatter, they'll come your way. Be ready for them."

"Now wait a minute, Ranger," Jack the Spider said. "Is that all we're worth to you? We're still just around to clean up any strays?"

"Be quiet, Mister Spider." Plum smiled, once again liking the idea of the Ranger taking the chances and he and his partner collecting the bounty. "Isn't this exactly what we've been doing all along? Apparently my tactics have been sound thus far?"

"You're good at what you do, Plum. Why change it?" the Ranger said.

"There, you see, Mister Spider. The Ranger and I both know what we're doing. I've been correct ever since we started this little endeavor."

"He'll get himself killed, that's what." The Spider hooked a thumb in his belt and faced the Ranger, his one good eye gleaming.

"You offered to help, Spider. This is my way of taking you up on the offer." The Ranger returned his stare.

Jack the Spider considered it for a second. "Damn it, we're still playing second fiddle to you, any way you put it." He looked at Plum, then back at the Ranger. "Hell, all right. If you're crazy enough to face that many guns and Fast Larry to boot, then go ahead. Maybe somebody gives a damn. I sure don't."

"It's settled, then." The Ranger gestured toward the dark spot behind the scrub juniper. "Let's boil some tea and get the fire put out before nightfall. Tomorrow is going to be a busy day."

CHAPTER 20

Sheriff Martin Petty stood on the boardwalk outside his office and stared across the street toward the batwing doors of the saloon. At the hitch rail out front, the big damp buckskin rested with its head down, its mane plastered in wet strands against its neck. The street was unusually quiet for this time of morning. Many of the townsfolk had expected trouble of some sort every since the telegraph lines had gone dead the day before.

Two days ago, they'd received a wire from Circle Wells, a warning about a bunch of robbers called the Blue Star Gang. When the blacksmith, Joe Chaney, and the clerk from the mercantile store, Charlie Hayes, came to Sheriff Petty with the news of the ragged stranger who'd arrived early at the saloon and taken a table in a rear corner, Petty wasn't surprised. But he was worried. It showed on his face.

"I could be wrong, Sheriff," Charlie Hayes said, "but I think I recognize the man from down in Abilene when I lived there. I believe it's Fast Larry Shaw, the gunman." His eyes conveyed a sense of dread as his gaze moved across Joe Chaney and back to the sheriff. "If it is him, he's one stone-cold killer."

"I've heard of him," Sheriff Petty said in quiet voice, trying to keep his voice firm and level, not letting them see he was afraid. "But maybe he's just passing through. Maybe it has nothing to do with the lines being down. It could be a coincidence, don't you think?"

The blacksmith looked doubtful. "With all the trouble we've had lately? I wouldn't count on it."

"Yeah, maybe you're right." Sheriff Petty hesitated for a second, then walked back inside his office and returned with a short-barreled shotgun, broken down across his forearm. He stood loading both barrels with a nervous hand.

Hayes and Chaney looked at one another, then Hayes said, "My gosh, Sheriff. I wouldn't go in carrying that thing if I was you. If I'm wrong about who that is and this is all a coincidence . . . you'll scare that poor man to death." He took a step back and looked over at the saloon. "If it is Fast Larry, all that scattergun's going to do is get you killed."

Sheriff Petty snapped the shotgun barrels closed using both hands. "If it's all a mistake, I'll apologize to him," Petty said. "If it's not a mistake," he said, setting his jaw firmly, "one of you see to it a rider gets news out of here to Wakely, or to Circle Wells. Get some help here as soon as possible." He stepped down off the boardwalk and walked across the dirt street. Sunlight glinted off the polished stock of the shotgun.

"I hope he knows what he's doing," Joe Chaney said, his voice hushed and tight.

"Yeah, me too," Charlie Hayes whispered, running a hand over the few strands of hair he kept combed across his bald head. "He's been acting different ever since that Ranger and the woman came through here. Hope they didn't fill his head with some kind of nonsense. Martin Petty is no kind of gunman." He shook his head slowly, looking over at the batwing doors.

Inside the saloon, Lawrence Shaw sat with his palms flat on the tabletop, gazing to his left. Between his hands sat a tall sweating glass of water, and less than an inch from his right fingertips lay the butt of his pistol. Gus the bartender busied himself wiping shot glasses with a dingy white towel, keeping an alert eye on the stranger who'd refused any whiskey, and answered Gus's earlier attempt at polite small talk with a cold stare.

Already watching the batwing doors, Lawrence Shaw did not move his eyes as Sheriff Petty stepped inside with the shotgun in his right hand, not pointed quite at Shaw, but slightly poised and ready, his thumb across the right hammer. He stopped and let his eyes adjust to the change of light. He started to say something, but then, thinking better of it, he walked to the table — not too fast, but steadily, with deliberation, the way he thought the Ranger or any other serious lawman should. His footsteps sounded loud, intrusive even to himself, and when he stopped two feet back from the edge of the table, he suddenly found himself at a loss for words.

Shaw looked at him, then lowered his eyes to his water glass. A fly circled in, alighted, and touched a drop of water on the tabletop. "Good morning, Sheriff," Lawrence Shaw said, his voice as ominous as the final line in a funeral prayer. Before Sheriff Petty could respond, Shaw continued, "Ask me who I am . . . and what I'm doing here."

Sheriff Petty felt his soft shirt collar grow

uncomfortably tight about his throat. No coincidence here. This man was either a part of the trouble past or a promise of new trouble to come. Either way, he was trouble. Petty took a breath to calm himself, and hoping his voice wouldn't fail or betray him, he asked, "Well then, since you know the questions . . . what's the answers?"

"I'm Lawrence Shaw, just like the store clerk told you." He lifted his eyes to Petty again, not seeming interested or concerned with the shotgun in his hand. "I'm here to kill a man."

"You're — ?" Sheriff Petty's words stopped. It wasn't a chill that ran the length of his spine, but rather a hot, paralyzing stiffness that once set in, would not leave. He struggled against it, the feeling of it crushing his insides. "Who . . . who are you here to kill?" His throat turned dry, his thumb tightened on the shotgun hammer.

"It's none of your business, Sheriff." The lack of inflection in Shaw's flat voice did not change. As quick as the snap of a whip, his right hand streaked up, slapped down on the hapless fly and left it smeared on the tabletop. "Just be careful it's not you."

Okay . . . Sheriff Petty offered a stiff nod, not knowing what else to do. He stood rigid, lost and awkward.

"Now what, Sheriff?" Shaw's eyes seemed to glaze over in a layer of frost. He sat staring, as if looking deep inside Martin Petty and seeing nothing there worthy of any more conversation.

"Now? I'm . . . leaving." Petty turned woodenly and walked out through the doors like a man in a trance. Across the street he stepped up on the boardwalk, looked Joe Chaney and Charlie Hayes in the eyes and began pacing back and forth in short, halting steps.

"What happened?" Hayes asked.

"Nothing," Petty said bluntly. He bit his lower lip and kept pacing, casting furtive glances at the batwings doors.

"Something happened," Hayes persisted. "Look at you, Sheriff. You're as white as Lily's bloomers!"

"Come inside," the Sheriff said, taking Hayes by his arm. "Let's talk inside. That man is a killer. I've got a big problem here."

They moved inside the sheriff's office and Petty told them the whole story, short though it was. As he did, he began taking rifles from the rack and loading them. The two men listened, standing transfixed until he finished. "Then he just stared a hole in me and said, 'Now what?'" Petty looked up at them with finality, shoving a round into a

330

rifle. "And that was the end of it."

Charlie Hayes stood in the middle of the sheriff's office with his hands spread. "And that's it? That's all he said? You're sure?"

On the sheriff's desk now lay a loaded rifle, the shotgun, and an old derringer pistol he'd taken from a desk drawer. He was busy loading another rifle. "Yes, that's all he said. Believe me, I'm *very* sure!" the sheriff assured the two men. A long stream of sweat dripped from his chin onto the back of his hand. He wiped it on his shirt-sleeve, then patted his forehead with his sleeve. The dull stiffness still clutched at his spine.

Charlie Hayes looked at Joe Chaney with his mouth open, his hands still spread, as if pleading for more. Then he turned back to Petty. "You didn't ask him anything else after that?"

"Like what? His boot size?" Sheriff Petty glared at him, shoving ammunition into the rifle. "He made it pretty clear it was none of my business who he's here to kill." Petty's eyes widened a bit as he spoke. "Now if you really want more answers, you march yourself right across that street, go straight through the doors, and look a little to your left. You can't miss him . . . he's the only one there. Here —" He held the rifle out arm's length toward the clerk. "Take one of these with you. I've got plenty."

"Easy, Sheriff," the blacksmith said, seeing Petty start to get out of control. "We're on *your* side here, remember? Charlie's concerned for you. Right, Charlie?"

The clerk nodded. "Yes I am. For all of us. For the whole town! Fast Larry Shaw is the awfulest devil alive. He's killed men all across this country. For no reason, folks say! He just as soon put a bullet between your eyes as to look at you! I saw him blow a man's brains all over the street in Abilene. Blood and brains —"

"That's enough, Charlie. Sheriff Petty gets the point." The blacksmith saw the sheriff's face turning a sickly pallor as the clerk raved on. "We've got to settle down and figure what's next. Sheriff?"

"I don't know, Joe. I'm still new at this business." Petty swabbed his sleeve across his face again. "I wish the Ranger was here."

Joe and Charlie looked at one another. Charlie shook his head. "Even the Ranger wouldn't stand a chance against Fast Larry. You'd just be wishing him a death sentence. I'm telling you, there is nobody *nowhere* that can beat Fast Larry with a pistol. It's like something that ain't natural not even *human,* the way he handles a gun!"

332

Petty swallowed the dry knot in his throat. "He swatted a fly."

The two men gave one another a questioning glance. Joe shrugged. "A fly? So . . . ?"

"I mean, it was so fast, Joe! I didn't even see his hand move." Petty laid the loaded rifle down, picked up an empty rifle from his desk and began slamming rounds in it. "I knew right then, if he'd been reaching for his pistol instead . . . well, I wouldn't be standing here right now, that's for sure."

The blacksmith reached out a hand and clamped it down on Petty's as the sheriff fumbled with a cartridge. "Sheriff? How many guns do you plan on needing?" He gestured a glance at the desktop full of weapons. "There's already enough here to stave off the whole Apache nation."

"Jesus, I don't know. I figure I need to be doing something, not just standing around here, waiting!"

"Oh?" Joe Chaney took the rifle from Petty's hands and looked back and forth between the two men. Charlie Hayes saw a calmness move into the blacksmith's eyes. Joe added, "Let's think about that for just one second. Who in this town could Fast Larry possibly want to kill? Nobody I can think of." He cocked a brow. "Can either of you?"

They stood in silent contemplation, Charlie scratching his head carefully between thin strands of hair. "Well, when I left Abilene, a young woman's father swore he was going to. . . ." His words trailed and stopped. He waved the idea away. "Naw, forget it. It's not me." He looked at Petty. "And you haven't been sheriffing long enough to make any enemies."

"It's none of us," Joe Chaney said. "Nobody in this town has that kind of enemies. It has to be somebody else. Some stranger."

"I don't know," Petty said. "I looked into those cold eyes. The man strikes me as crazy, like he's here but he's not here — you know what I'm saying? I could see him just picking up that pistol and blowing hell out of somebody for no reason at all."

"Well, maybe." Joe Chaney seemed to be calming down more and more. "But that's only an outside possibility. But you go pushing the man — then that's a sure thing. Then there's no doubt he'd kill you, right?"

"So what are you saying, Joe? I stay here? Hide? Let him go on about his business?"

"Damn right, that's what I'm saying. If he's not after somebody here in town, what more can we ask of you? You're here to protect us, not to get yourself killed protecting some wanderer that happens alone.

What if he's waiting here for somebody? Who knows? Maybe that person won't even show up. Fast Larry will get up on his horse and leave. Does that make sense to you?"

"Well . . . if it makes sense to you two, I'm in no position to argue the point. I just want to do my job the best I can."

Charlie Hayes cut in, "Yes, and part of your duty is to stay alive, if you plan on doing your job. Joe's right. Sit this thing out. Leave Shaw alone. Charlie and I will get the word around town for everybody to stay indoors."

"But this man he's here to kill . . . what if it's some innocent person?"

"Sheriff" — Joe Chaney shook his head — "how many innocent persons have a gunman like Fast Larry Shaw looking for them? Shaw and his kind live in a whole other world than the rest of us. Believe me. Stay out of it. It's the right thing to do. We'll back you on it, right Charlie?"

"That's right! Stay here and do nothing. You've got my full support."

Granddaddy Snake had made good time making his way back to the buttes north of Bentonville where many of his people lived. He'd taken a string of four desert burros from the corral of an old goat tender he knew near Circle Wells. True, the goat tender hadn't been there when Granddaddy took the animals. But they'd been friends for years. The old Indian reminded himself that at the first opportunity, he needed to get back there and let the man know what had happened. Of course the burros were gone now, Granddaddy having turned them loose one at a time on this three-day journey upward across the steep hills.

Last night when he saw the fringe of a ragged tarpaulin batting the breeze and saw the little dog run out of the shade to meet him, Granddaddy stepped down from the last burro, took the rope from around its neck, and slapped its rump. "Go free. You said you wanted to." Then turning and stooping down, he caught the little dog as it sprang up into his arms. He ruffled the fur on its head. "You do not know the trouble you caused me. Perhaps I really should have eaten you." The dog barked and squirmed and licked Granddaddy's weathered face.

He'd spent the evening resting, telling his people about his adventure while he shared their meal of jackrabbit and rattlesnake, along with cans of corn and sweet potatoes his daughter had brought back from Bentonville. When the talk was finished and the bones of the meal lay in a heap — the little dog sniffing toward them — Granddaddy Snake slept soundly, his granddaughter sidled against him and the dog curled in a ball, its wet nose pressed into the crook of the old Indian's elbow.

Now, in the mid morning light, he stood atop a low butte with his granddaughter and the little dog beside him and watched the riders below swing off of one dusty trail and onto another, heading toward Bentonville. "Get down," he said, and as he dropped low himself, he caught his granddaughter by her shoulder and pulled her down with him. But he didn't move quick enough to keep Billy Lee from catching a glimpse of him.

"What the hell?" Billy Lee slid his horse to a halt as the other riders moved past him. He scanned the top of the low butte in the shimmer of the sun's glare.

"What's wrong, Billy Lee?" Bobby McLawry stopped beside him and looked up as well. By now the old Indian, his granddaughter, and the dog had moved back out of sight.

"It's that damned Injun," Billy Lee exclaimed. As he scanned the butte, he lifted a hand to the soreness in his neck. The flesh around the tattoo still felt hot and puffy, the pain had moved farther down now, into his shoulder, reaching for his chest.

"Naw, it can't be," Bobby McLawry chuckled. "Come on, let's keep moving. We don't want to eat everybody's dust."

"It's him, I tell you," Billy Lee insisted. "I saw him plain as day." He reached under the back of his hat brim. "That old son of a bitch. I ain't forgot what he did to my head."

"All right, but it'll keep . . . if it was him. Let's go get some money." Bobby quirted his horse forward. "I'm hoping they've got a new whore since I killed the last one."

"Yeah. . . ." Billy Lee answered him idly, still looking up at the buttes as Bobby rode forward. Then he yelled long and loud, up into the dazzling sunlight. "Hey, old Injun! You're up there, I saw you! I ain't forgotten you!"

Atop the butte, seventy or more feet up, Granddaddy Snake stood up and held an arm in the air.

"Yeah, there you are," Billy Lee said, talking low to himself now. "How the hell did you get out of jail so fast, you old buzzard?" He backed his horse a step and swung it toward the other riders, still looking as the old Indian dropped out of sight once more. "I'll catch up to you, Granddaddy!" he yelled. "My head ain't right yet because of you."

Atop the butte, the girl looked up at

Granddaddy Snake with the little dog in her arms. "What does he mean, Granddaddy? What did you do to him? What is wrong with his head?"

Granddaddy Snake gazed down at her and pushed aside a long strand of dark hair the wind had blown across her face. "I only bit him. But there was something wrong with his head long before that." The old Indian thought about all the times Billy Lee had sworn he would kill him. "He is the kind of man who makes promises he does not keep." He smiled. "Come now. I will take you back to the camp. I'm afraid I must leave again, for a short time."

She sighed. "You go back to the town?"

"No. But I will go near there for a while. Then I will come back and see you and the little dog."

They walked on across the face of the low butte. "Granddaddy, you used to tell me that none of the white people are good. Have you changed your mind?"

"No." Granddaddy Snake stared straight ahead. "None of them are good. But I've found that some are not as bad as others."

"Then, if they are not good why do you spend so much time with them?"

"I don't know." He thought about it. "I think it is because they puzzle me. Their minds are strange, and I learn many things watching them. They are always so busy, doing things. They convince themselves that what they do is right, no matter how wrong they are."

"But the Ranger you spoke of . . . he was not wrong, was he? Did he not do right by you? Did he not try to help you?"

"Yes, he did right. But when white men do right by you, you never know if it's for you or themselves that they do it. Sometimes they do right just to feel good . . . just to say, 'Look at me, see how good I am.' " His smile widened.

She looked confused. "What does it matter *why* a person does right, so long as they do it?"

"That is a good way to look at it, my little one." He reached down and put his arm across her shoulders. The little dog looked up at him and barked, whining and wagging its tail. "I try to look at things that way myself. But I am old and sometimes it is hard for me not to question things."

"Is this why the Ranger did what he did? Why he told the other white men that you were going to slip through the bars? He did this to feel good about himself?"

"Aw, that Ranger." Granddaddy Snake shook his head. "It is hard to say why that one does what he does. I think he does the right thing simply because it is all he knows how to do."

"Oh, I see," she said, and they walked on across the low butte toward the dusty tarpaulin, the wind rising in a flurry behind them, soon filling their footprints with coarse desert sand.

CHAPTER 21

The Blue Star Gang stopped a mile outside of Bentonville and drew their horses around JC McLawry. He took his time looking around at each man in turn, and when they'd settled, waiting to hear his plans, JC nodded toward two men who had been riding with him longer than most of the others, and said, "Bryce and Thompson. The two of you ride ahead, make one sweep through town, check it out, then get right back here."

"Sure, Boss," said Bryce, "I've been needing a drink anyway."

"Good," JC said, "then don't forget to bring us back a couple of bottles."

"You've got it, Boss." Bryce turned to Thompson and said with a grunt, "Let's go. Boss always knows who to send when he wants a job done right."

When they'd moved out along the trail into Bentonville, Sanchez looked at JC and asked in a matter-of-fact manner, "When they return, if all is well, we ride in shooting, eh?"

"Not this time, Sanchez." JC smiled. "This time we're going to do something a little different. I don't know about the rest of yas, but I think we need to take ourselves a break here before heading down to Old Mexico." He looked around from one to the other again, rising slightly in his saddle. "They've got that new sheriff in Bentonville. The way Bobby and Billy Lee talk, he's a bit timid. Right, boys?"

"He didn't show me much," Bobby said. Billy Lee only nodded. He hadn't spoken much since yelling up to the old Indian back along the trail. He'd noticed that talking only aggravated the pain in his swollen neck.

JC continued. "So we're go in there real quiet-like, take over the town, clean out the bank and a few businesses, and have ourselves a gay old time."

The men nodded, liking the idea. But Lorio Sanchez looked concerned. "But, Boss, what about the Ranger?"

JC tossed his head to one side in a haughty gesture. "What Ranger?"

The men laughed and held their horses in place. Sanchez looked around at them, then back to JC, forcing himself to smile. "*Sí,* what Ranger . . . ?"

Along the trail, the last mile into Bentonville, Bryce turned to Thompson, riding beside him, and asked as he slowed his horse to a walk, "You know, there's something I've always wanted to ask you but never have."

"Yeah, what's that?" Thompson slowed his horse as well, running a hand down the side of its damp neck and patting it.

"Back when you broke out of prison with JC and that bandit, Caslado? How much help was JC through all that? I mean, did he run the show?"

"No, it was Ernesto Caslado's play. JC just set the whole thing up for him. Arranged horses . . . shot a few guards." He shrugged. "Before that, JC was just your ordinary prison screw. He was always a tough son of a bitch. I always figured he was an outlaw in the making, if he ever got the chance."

"But he was tough with unarmed men," Bryce said. He gave a faint sarcastic smile. "How hard is that to do?"

Thompson brought his horse to a complete stop and looked at him. "What are you getting at, Bryce?"

Bryce stopped his horse too. "Don't hackle up, Thompson. It's just that I didn't like the way JC backed us all down from

Fast Larry Shaw, did you?"

"I never liked backing from nobody. But there's times it's the wise thing to do. We had the Ranger to worry about and all. JC did what he thought he had to do . . . for everybody's good. We still had to bust Bobby out, don't forget."

"All right, maybe so. Forget I brought it up." He heeled his horse forward. "But the fact is . . . I'm fairly sure I could have taken Fast Larry, if JC would have said the word."

"Ha." Thompson heeled his horse alongside Bryce's. "You're not the first one to think you could take Fast Larry Shaw. The ground from here to Texas is full of them."

"Still, I didn't like it. And once I got to thinking about that, I started thinking of other times JC ain't quite lived up to what I think a gang leader ought to be."

"Then you tell him about it once we get back." Thompson gazed forward. "I don't want to hear no talk about you taking over this bunch, if that's where this is headed."

"Me? Run a bunch like this?" Bryce shook his head. "But if somebody else was to take over, I wouldn't have any complaints."

"Like who?" Thompson looked over at him as they rode along.

Bryce shrugged. "Oh . . . say, Lorio Sanchez, for example, just to be throwing out a name."

Thompson stopped his horse again, this time abruptly, turning it to face Bryce. "Sanchez? Are you out of your mind? Ride for a damned Mexican?"

"JC rode for Caslado, didn't he? What's wrong with Sanchez? I notice when the going gets tight, JC depends on him quite a bit."

"But still. Hell, I won't ride for no chili-poppin', goat-eating' —" Thompson cut his words as he looked into Bryce's eyes. "Have you and him been talking about this? You have, ain't yas?"

"Let's put it this way, Thompson. Me and a few of the boys have all decided that if anything ever happened to JC . . . say he was cleaning his pistol and it accidently went off a couple times, maybe once in the liver, once in the head." He grinned. "We all agreed that if something like that ever happened, we'd rather ride for Lorio Sanchez than face the crushing uncertainty of being out of work."

"So, it ain't just you and Lorio Sanchez who's talked about it, huh?"

"Like I said, a few of us discussed it."

"Oh . . ." Thompson fell quiet for a moment. "I didn't mean no harm, what I said about chili-poppin' goat-eater, you under-

346

stand. That was just said in fun."

"No problem." Bryce smiled and stared ahead at the dusty outline of Bentonville in the near distance.

Joe Chaney stepped back from the dusty window, turned to Sheriff Petty, and said, "Nothing's changed. His horse is still there. Why don't you stop pacing, Sheriff. There's no point in wearing your boots out."

"I just don't feel right," the sheriff answered, turning and pacing back across the wooden floor. "I'm the law here. I ought to do something."

"We've been through all that. Now settle yourself down. Have a cup of coffee — a shot of whiskey if it'll make you feel better."

"I've had too much coffee already. And I don't drink whiskey while I'm on duty." He gestured at the small office. "If you can call this being on duty."

"Charlie will be in here in a minute with some food. You'll feel better after you've et something."

"Maybe," he mumbled, still pacing back and forth.

A few minutes later when the door swung open, and Charlie Hayes stepped inside with a tray of food in his hands, Sheriff Petty snapped his hand to the pistol on his hip, seeing the big face of Curtis Roundtree looming in the open doorway. "Take it easy, Sheriff," Charlie said, stepping to one side as Curtis moved forward with his big hands held chest high. "He's with me. I found him hanging around the livery barn."

"What in the blue hell are you doing out of jail?" Petty spoke to Curtis in amazement.

Curtis spoke quick, still holding his big hands up. "Don't worry, Sheriff, everything's jake. The teamsters I whupped didn't show up for court and the judge let me go. Said, don't do it again is all." Curtis took a quick breath. "And I won't, if I can keep from it. I came back here to collect the four dollars this man owes me for cleaning stables." He nodded toward Joe the blacksmith. "Then I'll be on my way . . . I don't want no trouble."

"Arrest this man, Sheriff!" Joe Chaney blurted out, pointing a rigid finger at Curtis.

"What?" Curtis looked stunned.

"That's right, arrest him!" Chaney's face took on a tight expression. "I guarantee he's wanted for something. If he didn't break jail, then it's a sure bet he got here on a stolen horse! Ask him — go on, ask him!"

Before the sheriff could ask, Curtis turned

to him, shaking his head. "That ain't so, Sheriff. You can wire Circle Wells and ask the livery owner! He lent me that ole plug roan that Billy Lee sold all over the territory. The thing is half blind! He said when I got through with it to just turn it loose. I swear to God!"

Petty spun toward Joe Chaney. "Do you owe this man money, Joe?"

"Well, he cleaned stables for me for a couple of weeks. You know how it goes. I paid for his supper a time or two, even let him sleep in —"

"Then pay him, damn it to hell," Petty barked. "I've got enough trouble here without settling your debts!"

Curtis looked at Joe Chaney with his palm laid out toward him. "Four dollars," he said.

Joe spread his hands. "I don't carry that kind of money around on me. I told you I'd pay you, and I would have if you hadn't gotten yourself thrown in jail. But right now, we've got problems here and you'll just have to wait until we get —"

"Shut up, Joe," Petty hissed, crossing the floor, his eyes watching through the dirty window as two riders moved slowly up the middle of the dirt street. "Oh, no. Here it comes."

Charlie dropped the food tray on the desk

and moved to the glass with the sheriff and Joe Chaney. "Here what comes?" Curtis Roundtree asked, but no one answered as they stood watching the two riders check out the town on the way toward the saloon.

"Maybe this is who he's been waiting for," Charlie Hayes whispered, more to himself than the others.

In the same manner, Sheriff Petty replied. "Lord, I hope so. Let them get it done. I want that man out of here."

"Get what done?" Curtis stepped up behind them, unable to see out the crowded window. "What man out of here?"

Out on the dirt street, Bryce spotted the big buckskin first and halted his horse in the middle of the street facing the saloon. "Hold it, Thompson! That's Fast Larry's horse!

Thompson turned his horse toward to the batwing doors, and backed it a step, his hand drawing his pistol from its holster and cocking it across his lap. "If you're still sure you can take Fast Larry down . . . here's your chance to do it. I'll even call him out here for you." Thompson lifted himself up slightly and pretended to call, raising a cupped hand to his cheek.

"No, Thompson! Wait! Damn you! I said I was *fairly* sure. I never said it was something

I was *completely certain* of."

"I understand," Thompson said, backing his horse farther away from the saloon. "You sort of owe it to yourself to be *completely* certain, before you give it an all-out effort." He offered a teasing smile. "Still want that drink you've been talking about?"

"I can wait," Bryce grumbled, frowning. He jerked his horse back a step.

"But what about the bottles you said you'd bring JC?" Thompson sat slumped in his saddle with his pistol still cocked across his lap.

"Go to hell, Thompson!" Bryce's face glowed red. "You think I'm afraid? Is that it? Well, I'm not!"

Thompson offered a slight shrug of one shoulder, his eyes revealing nothing, but his lips on the verge of breaking into a nasty grin.

"I'm not afraid! By hell! I'm not!"

"Then go on in. I'll hold your horse." Thompson lifted a skeptic brow.

"Go on in?" Bryce glared at him with a look full of ice picks and straight razors. "Damn right I will! I'll go in!" He spun his reins around his saddle horn. "I'm going in! You just watch."

Bryce swung down from his horse, landing heavily on his boot heels and turned to face the saloon doors. Then he jerked forward a step and stopped, his hand on his pistol butt. He bit his lip; a trickle of sweat broke free at the bridge of his nose. He took another halting step, and this time turned back and mounted his horse. "I ain't going in," he said under his breath, slumping in his saddle.

"What's the matter?" Thompson said. "I told you I'd hold your horse."

"I don't need you to hold my damned horse. Maybe we ought to keep a clear head, all of us. We don't need whiskey clouding up our minds."

"You're probably right," Thompson said. "I was just thinking the same thing."

Watching this scene from the window, Sheriff Petty stepped back, dumbstruck.

"Are they . . . leaving?" He looked at Charlie Hayes and Joe Chaney, who tracked the two riders with their eyes as they turned their horses around in the street and rode out of town at a quick trot.

"Now what?" The sheriff's face looked drawn. Joe Chaney let out a deep breath. "Now we go back to waiting." He turned to Curtis Roundtree. "You wouldn't by any chance have a gunman by the name of Fast Larry Shaw looking for you?"

"Naw-sir." Curtis shook his big head. "If I

did, I wouldn't be here, that's for sure. I heard the Ranger mention him on the way to Circle Wells. Even the Ranger seemed concerned."

"He did?" Sheriff Petty looked ill.

"Yep, he did," Curtis Roundtree said, leaning forward with his hands on his knees. He stood up and turned to the sheriff. "It's none of my business, Sheriff, but if those two men were part of the bunch I saw heading around to the north road on my way here, they'll more than likely be back." He wasn't about to mention that he'd seen Billy Lee among the riders. He owed his old pal that much. "If I was you, Sheriff, I'd be prepared. I'd make sure I had some extra weaponry loaded."

Chaney and Hayes just looked at one another. "I already have," the sheriff muttered under his breath.

Curtis Roundtree looked back at Joe Chaney. "Now, what say we stroll over to your place and get that money you owe me. I don't want to be here any longer than I have to."

Chaney struck an indignant poise with his chin tilted upwards. "How can you think of money at a time like this?"

" 'Cause I'd like to get it while I'll be around long enough to spend it."

CHAPTER 22

JC McLawry and the rest of the gang had stepped down from their horses and were now gathered in the shade of a cottonwood tree. When Thompson and Bryce rode back toward them on the north trail, JC and Lorio Sanchez were the first two to stand up and greet them as they reined up and slipped down from their saddles. "Well? How's it look in there?" JC asked Bryce. Then, seeing that both men stood empty-handed before him, he demanded, "Where's the whiskey? These boys have been sitting here licking their lips raw."

"Boss . . . ," Bryce stalled for a second, slapping dust off his chest with his hat brim, "the way things are shaping up, we both thought it best to forget about the whiskey and get on back here."

"What do you mean?" JC and Lorio Sanchez both stepped closer to them.

"Fast Larry Shaw is in there, Boss. He's

in the saloon, drunk and wild-eyed, we figured."

"So you saw him?"

"Well, no."

Thompson cut in. "But we saw his horse."

JC glared at them. "And his horse was drunk and wild-eyed?"

They looked embarrassed. "Boss, you know me," Bryce said. "I'm from the hard end of Wind River . . . not afraid of no man. I'd have walked right in there and had it out with him, win or lose. But we figured for the sake of the rest of yas we better let it go right then, see what you had to say about it."

"That's right, Boss," Thompson added. "We sat right in the street and discussed it. It was hard as hell not to just go in shooting." He looked around at all the others. "Then what would happen when we didn't come back? You boys would be riding in there blind!"

JC eased back a step, trying to think. He wished he hadn't already told everybody his plans. He could turn them around right here and head for Mexico. But he had told them. Now he couldn't change them and lose face just because Fast Larry was in town.

"Is the woman still with him?" he asked Bryce.

"We didn't see her, Boss."

"Forget it, Bryce." JC shrugged and turned to the rest of the gang, trying to look unconcerned. "Well, if Fast Larry wants to drink in Bentonville, so what?" He grinned, trying to hide his unease. "As long as he stays out of our way, we'll have no problem."

"I think we should shoot him," Sanchez said, just to rub JC a little.

"No . . . let's stick to our business," JC said in quick reply. "We go in as planned and do what we came to do. If Fast Larry gets in our way, we'll deal with him. Otherwise, forget that crazy bastard. Anyway, he might be gone by the time we get there." He certainly hoped so. Damn it! Why had he ever gotten mixed up with that gunman? JC turned and swung up onto his horse. "What are we waiting for? There's plenty of whiskey in town for the taking. Lots of other things too." He flashed a dark grin and turned his horse. "Let's get to it."

Farther back in the ranks, an Arkansan named Fred Shade turned to the man beside him as the column of riders moved forward. "He's scared, ain't he, Turk?"

Turk Watson spit. "Yeah, he's scared. JC should have put a bullet in him."

Shade turned to him. "JC is who I'm talking about, fool. He's scared of that *Fast Larry Shaw*. Can't you see it?"

"Oh . . . hell, yes. I *been* seeing it. I thought you meant Bryce. He never has showed me a thing."

"Forget Bryce. We used to eat them Wind River boys for breakfast. If he'd had any guts at all, he'd of taken Fast Larry's big pistol from him and hammered it up his ass." Shade's voice dropped to a whisper. "JC is the one bothering me. Have you talked to Sanchez any?"

"Yeah, some."

A silence passed as they moved forward onto the trail. Then Shade said, "So? What do you think?"

"I think Lorio Sanchez is a stand-up man. As a leader, he'd be miles ahead of JC McLawry. He wouldn't always lag back and put somebody else up front, is what I think."

"So you're in?" Shade looked at him.

"Are you?" Turk Watson returned his fixed gaze.

"Would I have brought it up if I wasn't?"

"I don't know," Turk said. "It's best that a man watches what he says at times like these."

"Are you in or out, Turk? Sanchez needs to know where you stand."

"Are you?"

"Shitfire!" Fred Shade spat and heeled his horse forward.

Lorio Sanchez had dropped his horse back alongside the column and said to the men, "Tighten up and ride light. We don't need all the dust." His eyes passed over Turk Watson with a questioning glance. Turk nodded slightly and looked away.

At the rear of the column, Billy Lee turned to Bobby McLawry beside him. "When you got your tattoo, how long did it take to heal up and quit hurting?"

"It took a few days to heal up good," Bobby said. "But as far as hurting, it never did."

"Not at all?"

"No." Bobby avoided his eyes. "Let's put it this way. If it hurt, I never noticed it. If I *had* noticed it, I wouldn't have *mentioned* it . . . because, well, you know how that sounds." He shrugged.

"Yeah." Billy Lee nodded. "It doesn't hurt. It's just annoying." His hand went to the swollen, tender flesh and patted it, to show it didn't hurt. The pain shot down all the way into his chest. Who was he kidding? It hurt like hell. He was worried. The damned thing felt infected to him. "Is this a good idea? Riding in there and staying a while?"

Bobby looked at him. "Sure. JC knows what he's doing," he grinned. "Who knows, we might take on a woman and fall in love for a few minutes."

"I figured we'd do better to just take the money and light out. There's lots of things that can go wrong."

"Don't let JC hear you making opinions on what we should or shouldn't do," Bobby said. His voice turned crisp. "Remember your place, Billy Lee."

"Sorry," Billy Lee murmured. *His place* . . . ? He looked ahead at the dusty backs of the other riders. They rode on steadily, bold, determined — men made of stone, he thought. The pain in his neck and chest throbbed with each beat of his pulse. Why did he ever get this *blasted* tattoo! He had news for Bobby McLawry. Once he had enough money shoved down in his pocket, to hell with these people . . . he was out of here.

The Ranger came to Bentonville from the higher ground in the east, moving slow, keeping his wake of dust low to the scorched earth. From one shadowed stand of rock or cactus or dry wash to the next, he edged his way downward, until beneath him the wavering rooflines, dirt streets, and alleyways took on clearer form within the glare of sunlight. He'd followed his hunch that JC and his Blue Stars would circle and ride into town from the north. Now, as he pulled the white Spanish barb back into the black shade of a rock crevice and watched the riders below split up into twos and threes, and spread out around Front Street, he let out a breath, realizing he'd guessed right.

"Stand easy, Black-eye," he said to the restless horse, patting its sweaty neck. "We'll do all right." He would have liked to have made it to the north edge of town before JC and his gang had, so he could have been standing there waiting for them. But since it hadn't turned out that way, this was no time to get in a hurry. Now he had to think of Sheriff Petty and rest of the innocent townsfolk, down there with a gang of gunman in their midst. If he'd had any belief in JC robbing the bank and riding on, he would wait and let it happen, then catch them on their way out to the badlands and have it out with them on the desert sand.

But if the Ranger knew anything at all about JC McLawry, he was certain the gang leader would want to take advantage of the new sheriff. JC would want to spend some time terrorizing Martin Petty and the people of Bentonville whom the sheriff had sworn to protect. He raised his Swiss rifle from the long saddle scabbard, checked it, dusted it, and laid it across his lap. Then he took out his big pistol, half-cocked it, and spun the cylinder down his sleeve.

He put the pistol back in his holster. He looked high to the north for a second, wondering if Rance Plum and Jack the Spider had gotten themselves into good position. He hoped so. Tugging his gray sombrero down level and low across his forehead, he heeled the white barb forward onto the thin downward path. "Take us in, Black-eye," he said, "we're going to have to play this one by ear."

While the Ranger moved in with caution from the east, Sheriff Petty and Charlie Hayes looked out the window at the dusty riders who moved with confidence and resolve along the dirt street. "Lord have mercy," Petty said, "Curtis was right. We're in for some bad trouble here."

"Shouldn't Joe and that *Curtis* fellow be back by now?" Charlie glanced nervously out the window toward the bank, then at the livery barn. "How long does it take to scrape up four dollars?"

"Maybe they saw this bunch and decided to lay low," Petty whispered. He'd taken up the shotgun from atop his desk and stood fidgeting with it in his damp hand. "I hope you warned everybody to stay out of sight for a while."

"Don't worry, Sheriff. I got to everybody. Mertz wasn't at the bank, but I made sure Carl the teller took all the money out of the safe and stashed it somewhere for a while."

"Where's Mertz?" Sheriff Petty sounded concerned.

"Carl didn't say. But don't worry about it. Mertz had his granddaughter with him. Odell Mertz is a banker. He won't take no chances. If he rides in and sees what's going on, he'll burn the wheels off his buggy getting out of here."

"Let's hope so." Sheriff Petty ran a nervous hand across his forehead. "I still don't feel right, holed up here like a damn prairie dog."

"It beats *dying* all to hell, though," Charlie Hayes said, crouching once more to look out through the dusty window. "Wonder what's taking Joe so long? I've got a bad feeling about that Curtis Roundtree, Sheriff. I don't trust the man."

Petty leaned down and saw Billy Lee and Bobby McLawry dismount outside the bank. "Oh, no! You might be right, Charlie! There's Curtis's partner right there. Is Curtis in on this?"

Inside the closed bank, Curtis stared at Carl the teller and said, "We're only talking about four damn dollars, mister! You mean to tell me you can't come up with —"

"You heard him, Curtis," Joe Chaney cut in. "He's hidden the money. Now let's get back to Petty's office. I'll pay you later!"

"You've been paying me late ever since I worked for you, Chaney. Today is payday, and I ain't leaving without my money!" Big Curtis took a step forward toward the teller window.

"I'm sorry, sir," Carl said in his best banker's voice, pushing his wire-rim spectacles up on the bridge of his nose with his middle finger. "There is not one thin dollar in this bank. Nor will there be until the danger has passed."

Curtis relented and shook his head. Then he looked back up at the teller with a stunned expression. "You said not one?"

"That's correct, sir — not one."

Curtis looked from one to the other of the two men. "Boys, I don't mean to butt in . . . but don't you think it might've been a good idea to leave a couple of hundred dollars here? Anybody hits a bank and gets no money at all, they're going to know you've been warned and hid it somewhere."

The teller's face turned sickly white. "Oh, my. . . ." Even as he spoke, there was a rattling at the front door.

"Boss, it's locked," Bryce called out to JC, who waited in the middle of the street. JC just glared at him.

Bobby McLawry laughed as he and Billy Lee bounded up on the boardwalk beside Bryce. "So what now, Bryce? Think we oughta give up? Leave town and call it a day?" Bobby stood back, raised a boot and slammed it against the door.

"I was getting ready to do that next," Bryce said, embarrassed.

"I know you were," Bobby grinned. The door only shook on its hinges. "Step back," he said to Billy Lee and Bryce. Then he drew his pistol, fired three rounds through the lock plate, and kicked the door wide open in a spray of splinters and a cloud of burnt powder. Behind the teller's barred window, Carl's hand raised high in the air, instinctively. Curtis Roundtree and Joe Chaney stood as if frozen in place as the three men spilled in through the door with their pistols pointed at them.

"All right, teller," Bobby McLawry called out, moving across the floor, "if I have to say why we're here, I'll figure you're too stupid to live!" His thumb cocked the hammer on his already smoking pistol. At the barred window, Bobby's free hand shot through the bars, snatched the teller by his hair, and yanked him forward, banging his head against the ornate iron, holding his face there. Carl's spectacles flew off and clattered out through the bars. Bobby stomped them, laughing, then pushed the teller backward.

"Fill it up," Bryce said, moving up beside Bobby McLawry and slapping a gunnysack down on the counter.

"Curtis, for crying out loud!" Billy Lee stood before Curtis Roundtree, looking stunned as Bobby and Bryce made their demands to the teller. "What in the world are you doing here?"

"Dang, Billy Lee, are you going to shoot me?" Curtis looked him up and down.

"Hell, you know better." Billy Lee stepped back and wagged his pistol in his hand. Joe Chaney stood silent, watching. "What are you doing out of jail so soon?"

"There's no money here," the teller said to Bobby and Bryce in a shaky voice.

"Think there will be after I shoot one of your arms off and asked again?" Bobby shoved his cocked pistol through the bars.

"Please, mister! I just followed my orders. There's no money here!"

"Here goes that arm!" Bobby aimed his pistol as the teller stood shaking with his eyes squeezed shut.

"He's telling the truth, damn it, Bobby," Curtis Roundtree shouted. "Shooting him won't do a thing for you!"

"Shooting somebody always does *something* for me." He grinned a dark grin at the teller. "Here goes that arm."

"Stop it! *You son of a bitch!*" Curtis jerked forward and took a swipe at Bobby's shoulder. Bobby and Bryce both swung their pistols around at him.

"You didn't know my mama, fat man! I'll shoot your damned head off!" Bobby shoved the pistol barrel into Curtis's big belly.

But Curtis only made a low grunt and stood firm, facing him with the look of a maddened grizzly. "Shoot me, then, you punkwood coward! You ain't got a bullet that'll kill me afore I yank your head off." Curtis's big hands clamped onto Bobby's head and lifted him up so suddenly that Bobby's trigger finger never got the chance to react. The toes of Bobby's dirty boot scraped back and forth on the wooden floor. Bryce stood staring with his mouth agape, his pistol pointed through the bars at the teller.

"No, Bobby! Don't shoot him!" Billy Lee wedged himself halfway between them. "Curtis! Put him down!"

Curtis heaved Bobby McLawry back against the counter. Bobby gasped and shook his head and pointed his pistol at Curtis, but Billy Lee stood in front of the big man, shielding him. His pistol pointed back at Bobby McLawry. "You ain't shooting Curtis, Bobby! Let's get the money!"

Bobby stood up on wobbly legs and turned the pistol on the teller. "All right, where's it at?"

Before the teller could refuse again, Joe Chaney moved forward, and blurted out, "I'll tell you where it's at. It's in a steel box, in the floor beneath the desk!"

Bobby and Bryce shot him a suspicious look. "It's the truth, I'm the blacksmith! I built the box and installed it there, for emergencies. Take it!"

"Open the door," Bobby McLawry demanded of the teller. As he talked, he moved to the end of the counter and shook the barred door with his free hand. "Open it or I'll blast it off! You want bullets flying around in there?"

The teller hurried, opened the barred

door, and stood back as Bobby and Bryce rushed through it. "Now, you little turd." Bobby cracked his pistol barrel across the teller's head and sent him to the floor, knocked cold.

As the two of them filled the gunnysack, Billy Lee turned back to Curtis Roundtree. "For God sakes, what are you doing here, Curtis?"

Curtis still seethed toward Bobby McLawry as Bobby and Bryce hefted the desk aside and fell down their knees, lifting a trapdoor. "The judge let me go, Billy Lee. I came back here to get the four dollars this man owes me." He pointed a big finger at Joe Chaney. Joe stood on his tiptoes, watching the two outlaws on the floor behind the counter as they lifted stacks of money and shoved them in the sack.

"For crying out loud, Curtis, you came all this way for four dollars?" Billy Lee shook his head and stepped back as Bobby and Bryce came from behind the counter with the sack of money.

"I had to, Billy. It's all the money I've got in the world. I was working at the stable in Circle Wells for room and board. But it wasn't going to get me nowhere."

Bobby chuckled at Curtis Roundtree and shook the bag of money in his face. "That's a sad story, fat man. But Billy Lee ain't got time to hear it. Look what we just made for two minutes' work."

Curtis only glared at him. "Hey, Curtis," Billy Lee said to his old pal, "come on with us. I'll share part of what's coming to me with you. You won't need to be scrounging for a dollar here and dollar there anymore." He tugged at Curtis's shoulder as the other two headed for the door.

Curtis took a step, but then stopped and shook Billy Lee's hand free. "I can't, Billy Lee. I'm going straight from here on. Something will turn up for me before long."

"No it won't, Curtis. Can't you see that? Nothing good is going to happen until you make it happen. Now come on!"

"Leave the fat man here," Bobby said. "Let's go!"

Joe the blacksmith flashed a quick glance over at the knocked-out teller on the floor. Then he turned to Bobby McLawry as Bobby stood at the door waiting for Billy Lee. "Hey, guys," Joe Chaney said in a guarded voice. "I told you about the money. Isn't there a little something for me? What do you say? Nobody will ever know."

Bobby looked at Bryce. "You heard him, Bryce. Give him something for his trouble."

"Sure," Bryce said, and he raised his pistol

and shot Joe Chaney twice in the chest. "How's that?" He grinned as Chaney spilled backward on the floor in a spray of blood.

"Looks fair to me," Bobby said.

"My God," Billy Lee exclaimed. Curtis started to step toward Bobby McLawry, but Billy Lee shoved him back. "Stay put here, Curtis. Don't come out there until we've left this town. There's nothing you can do for yourself or anybody else."

Bobby McLawry and Bryce had left, and Curtis said to Billy Lee through clenched teeth, "I can break that murdering little lizard in half . . . that's one thing I can do."

"Curtis, you'll never learn," Billy Lee said, pushing him back once again. "Now do like I'm telling you and stay out of this!" Outside, there came a loud cheer as Bobby and Bryce held the bag of money high in the air. Pistols fired amid the stir of restless horses, whinnying and spinning in a whirl of dust.

CHAPTER 23

JC McLawry spun his horse in the middle of the street and yelled to Thompson and Turk, "Get over to the saloon and get some whiskey. We got some celebrating to do!" Beside him Sanchez looked around at Thompson, Turk and a couple of others, each of them exchanging knowing glances with him.

"But what about Fast Larry Shaw, Boss?" Thompson called out in a pleading tone. "He's still in there."

"Don't worry about him. Tell him I said to come on out here and join us in a drink. I'm feeling generous!" He laughed, fired a shot in the air, and took the bag of money from Bryce's hand as Bryce and Bobby ran up to him. Thompson and Turk looked at one another with sick expressions on their faces and moved cautiously off toward the batwing doors. JC turned in his saddle and called out to the sheriff's office. "Come on out here, lawman! This town now belongs to the Blue Star Gang. I want to see you running out of this town like the devil is biting at your ass!"

Inside the office, hearing JC's words, Sheriff Petty picked up the shotgun from atop his desk. "That settles it, Charlie, I've got to go out there. I can't live with myself hiding this way, knowing I represent the law."

"Then you're crazy, Sheriff."

"Yeah, I'm crazy" — Petty picked up a loaded rifle and shoved it into Charlie's hands — "and you're my deputy. Come on, Charlie, let's die like men if we have to . . . not like rats."

But then the noise outside stopped as suddenly as it had started and they stopped at the window before reaching the door. "What's this?" Petty remarked, looking out at JC McLawry atop his horse, leaning down to the two men in the street. The other outlaws stood looking at one another, one of them holding a cash box under his arm that he'd taken from the barbershop.

JC stared at Thompson and Turk who had come running back from the saloon. "He said what?" JC had a bewildered look on his face.

Thompson shrugged his shoulders.

"That's it, Boss. Shaw just said there would be no drinking in town today. Said if you had a problem with it to come see him."

Sanchez and a couple of the others had overheard Thompson, and they shot glances at one another as they sat atop their horses, waiting to see how JC would handle this. JC shook his head as if to clear it. "Did you tell him he was welcome to drink with us?"

"Yep. He said some things, Boss — some things about you I don't want to repeat."

"What did he say, damn it?" JC raged down at him.

While they spoke in the street, the Ranger slipped into the town dump behind the saloon. He had seen Lawrence Shaw's horse hitched at the rail as he'd crept around from alley to alley, and as soon as he'd spotted the big buckskin, he knew his biggest problem would be Shaw. He wasn't about to face JC, the Blue Stars, and Lawrence Shaw all at the same time.

"Easy, Black-eye," he'd said to the horse, pulling it up close to the back wall and standing up in the saddle to reach the window sill above him. He'd made it to the half-opened window, slid it the rest of the way up with his elbow, and rolled inside. He took his spurs off and laid them on a feather bed, then crept out into the upstairs hall to the handrail overlooking the saloon below. Here he stayed hidden and watched the two outlaws come and go, smiling a thin smile to himself when Shaw had sent them away empty-handed.

Now that the two outlaws were gone and the street outside lay quiet for the moment, the Ranger stood up and walked sideways to the stairs leading down to the saloon, his big pistol drawn and cocked. "Lawrence Shaw," he called down in a calm voice as he stepped down the stairs slowly, keeping his eyes on Shaw. "Get your hand back away from that pistol. I'm not going to kill you."

Lawrence Shaw turned his face toward the Ranger, not seeming at all surprised by his being there. He came down the stairs slowly, one step at a time until he reached the floor.

"I know you're not, Ranger," Shaw replied. He raised up from his chair but kept his fingertips near the butt of the pistol on the tabletop. "You must have gotten my message from those two bounty hunters."

"I got it, and I'm telling you the same thing I told them. I'm not after you, Shaw. I haven't been for the past year."

"Nice try, Ranger, but I'm not buying it." Shaw's eyes fixed on him. "You should have stayed away if that was true."

"I've got a job to do, Shaw. Your path just

happened to cross the path of the men I'm looking for. But you don't have to die here."

Die here . . . ? Shaw cocked his head in a bemused response to the Ranger's words. "Neither would you have, Ranger, if you'd just left me alone. I only wanted to shoe my horse the day I came here."

"I saw you turn and leave town that day, Shaw. If I really wanted you, don't you think I would have gotten on your trail right then and settled up with you? Can't you understand that?"

Without answering, Shaw tilted his head back slightly and narrowed his cold gaze on the Ranger. The Ranger took a deep breath, let it out slowly, and answered for him. "No, you can't see it. You're too bent on killing or being killed to see anything, I reckon. Killing's all you know. So let's get on with it." His gloved hand tightened around the handle of the big pistol.

Lawrence Shaw's right hand moved so quick the Ranger didn't have a chance to raise the pistol from his side. Shaw's pistol came up cocked and aimed, and the Ranger felt his guts stiffen inside him against the coming explosion. Yet Shaw did not fire. Instead he held the pistol firm and steady and said, as if in parting, "I was through killing, Ranger. I wanted out. All you had to do was let me be."

The Ranger saw the end coming now, from the look on Shaw's face, from the dark hollowness that came into his eyes. "You're a liar, Shaw! Now shut up and get it done. I don't want to die listening to a lying coward." He saw a flash of bemused curiosity in Shaw's expression, and he added quickly, "That's right, Shaw, a *coward.* Look at the shape you're in . . . you hold a pat hand in *killing,* so you're afraid to let *living* turn over the next card in the game."

Shaw sat rigid, but the Ranger saw something stirring behind his eyes.

A wry smile came to the Ranger's face. "How long has it been since you've had to risk anything, like the rest of us do, *Fast Larry?*" The Ranger said the name with contempt. "I've faced the fastest guns in this territory, and none of them's ever got the drop on me like this. So come on, drop the hammer. You've got more running and hiding to do."

Shaw hesitated, his pistol seeming to ease a bit in his hand. The Ranger took a short step forward. "Do I need to make it any easier for you?" His gun hand moved slowly out to the side and lifted with his pistol pointed away toward the bar. He let the hammer down with his thumb. "There, how's that?" He took another step forward, the pistol coming down, hanging at his side. "Either kill me, right here, right now, or let me go out there and do my job." His voice became an indictment. "Some of us have to *face* our odds and go on with our lives."

Shaw stood up slowly, his pistol still covering the Ranger. "You talk a good game. But I don't believe you."

"I don't care if you believe me or not. One minute from now I'll either be dead or alive. I'm not afraid of being either one. What about you, Shaw? You gonna kill like a coward — or live like a man?"

Shaw stepped forward, a different look coming to his eyes, a hesitancy as his mind caught onto something that would take his instincts a moment longer to understand. Three feet from the Ranger, he stopped and stared at him. A tense silence passed, then Shaw seemed to let something uncoil inside himself. "All right, Ranger. This is your day." His thumb uncocked the pistol and let it down to his side. "I'm going with you. When this is over, I'm riding away from here a free man. I'll risk this much on you. But if you're lying, you're dead." He turned, nodding toward the door. "Let's go —"

But his words stopped short. In that split second since his eyes had left the Ranger, the Ranger's big pistol had snapped back in a high arc, the barrel slamming hard across the side of Lawrence Shaw's head. "Sorry, Shaw," the Ranger said as Shaw staggered backward and fell to the floor. "I should have told you — this is law work. I always work alone." He cocked the big pistol, raised it, and fired a round into the ceiling.

Outside on the street, the sound of the shot caused JC and his men to jerk back a step. "What the hell was that? Is Shaw shooting at us?" Men on foot ducked for cover. JC spun his horse out of line with the batwing doors.

In the saloon, Shaw groaned and rolled over on his side, his hand searching for the pistol in his belt but not finding it there. "You'll be all right, Shaw. You just have to sit this one out. You want to quit killing, it stops right here."

The Ranger shoved Shaw's pistol down into his waist and raised his hand, gesturing the bartender to come forward from where he was peeping around the corner of the bar. "Keep an eye on this man until I get back. Don't let him out of your sight until this is all over."

"Lord God, Ranger! I can't keep an eye on him!"

"Sure you can. You've got to. Bring your

scattergun out from under the bar."

As the Ranger spoke, he dragged Lawrence Shaw over to the bar, took out a pair of handcuffs, and cuffed him to the long brass footrail. "When I get finished, Shaw, you're free to leave. You've got my word. Do you understand?"

"You tricked me, Ranger." Shaw stared up at him.

"If I wanted you dead, you would be dead right now, Lawrence. Think about this while I go take care of my business out front."

Now that it was over with Shaw, the Ranger stopped for a second and felt a trembling sensation creep across his shoulders. But he stilled it, let go of a tense breath, took a bottle of whiskey from atop the bar, and headed for the batwing doors.

"All right, boys, that's it!" JC McLawry called out to his men in the street. "To hell with Fast Larry Shaw! We're not taking any guff off of the man. He wants trouble? He's got it!" What else could he do, JC thought, looking at the faces of his men, knowing they were seeing what he was really made of. He couldn't let this go any farther. "Sanchez, take Bryce, Thompson, and a couple others. I want that sucker dragged out here dead. Do you understand?"

"I understand, Boss." Sanchez stepped

down from his horse, drew his pistol, and added in a flat, firm tone. "And you are going with us, JC. If you are our leader, show us. Let us see you lead for once."

"You heard my orders, Sanchez!" JC bellowed, his face turning red. His hand went to the pistol on his hip. But something about the look on Sanchez's face and on the faces of the men gathering around him told JC not to draw the gun. "All right, then, damn it! I'll lead you! Are you going with me or not? He's only one man! Show some guts!"

Just inside the batwing doors, the Ranger lingered for a second, letting all the Blue Stars gather close and move forward. All of them were now as one, in a nice tight shooting pattern, he thought. All except Billy Lee, who still stood out in front of the bank, a scared look on his face. But the Ranger wasn't worried about Billy Lee. *Here goes,* he said to himself, and he swung open the doors and stepped out onto the edge of the boardwalk, seeing the startled looks on the outlaws' faces as he pitched the bottle of whiskey out into the dust in front of JC's horse.

"I'll drink with you, JC McLawry," he said. "But it'll be a *short* one for me . . . and a *last* one for you. . . ."

■ ■ ■ ■

Sheriff Petty had stepped out onto the boardwalk at the same moment that the Ranger pitched the bottle into the dirt. "See, Charlie, we've got some help," he whispered back over his shoulder. "Charlie?" But Charlie Hayes didn't answer. Instead, Petty heard the door behind him close and lock. His breath stopped in his chest, and he had to jerk forward a step to get it going again. His hand sweated on the stock of the shotgun. He wondered if it would just slip out of his grip and fall at his feet. Had he loaded it? Oh, no! He couldn't remember! *Surely to God* he'd loaded it! He bit his lip — hadn't he?

Across the street, past the backs of the outlaws, Petty could see the Ranger. Did the Ranger see him? Would the Ranger recognize him once the bullets flew? Petty stood frozen, too scared to turn back now even if he could. Outside the bank, Billy Lee also stood frozen, his pistol still drawn and hanging in his hand. He wanted no part of this! But what could he do now? He knew the Ranger had seen him. And he'd seen him with his pistol drawn. He didn't want that pistol in his hand. But if he dropped it now, where would that put him with JC and the Blue Stars? His neck throbbed in pain around the fresh tattoo.

"That pistol, Ranger," JC said, nodding at Shaw's pistol in the Ranger's belt, keeping his voice under control, trying to sound calm. "How'd you get it from him?"

The Ranger offered a fierce smile. "I picked it up off the floor a minute ago, JC, after I blew Shaw's brains all over the wall."

A low gasp moved across the Blue Star gunmen. JC sat staring, working it out in his mind. Shaw had sworn he'd kill the Ranger. And Shaw would never have given up his pistol. Yet, here stood the Ranger with Shaw's gun in his belt, his own big pistol hanging loose and cocked in his hand. JC's world felt small around him, and getting smaller by the second, even with his gunmen backing his play. "You're lying, Ranger."

"You think so?" The Ranger seemed not the least concerned with all the gunmen facing him. "All you've got to do is step down, get past me, and go see for yourself." JC noted to himself how much the Ranger reminded him of Fast Larry Shaw — calm, loose, crazy.

Bobby McLawry had inched a step closer to his brother and said to JC without taking his eyes off the Ranger, "Go on, take him down, JC. You always said you could in a fair fight."

"Bobby . . . shut up!" Sweat streamed down JC's face.

"That'd be the thing to do, all right," the Ranger said, keeping his eyes on JC, seeming to ignore the rest of the men. "Just you and me — one on one — I'll even give you the same chance I gave Shaw. You can make the first move."

Gave Shaw the first move . . . ? JC felt a dull aching down low in his stomach. The Ranger saw how his words were cutting deep into JC McLawry, exposing him to himself, making him face what he was right here in front of his own men. Keeping his eyes on JC McLawry, the Ranger said to the rest of the men, just to get them rattled, "Once I kill him, you boys have a choice. I'll take you back to Circle Wells, either in chains or draped across your saddles. Make up your minds before JC's body hits the street."

The Ranger stood silent now, knowing that the next one to move or make a sound would be the loser. Across the street, he saw Sheriff Petty standing on the boardwalk with the double-barrel shotgun. Those two rounds blasted from behind would be the

Ranger's advantage if he could count on Petty using it. Petty looked shaken — an untested sheriff who'd expressed his doubts to the Ranger only days before — but he was the Ranger's only hope.

A hot breeze swept along the street. The Ranger knew the silence was about to break in a hail of gunfire, but the thing that triggered it was far from what he'd expected it to be. From the alleyway leading between the bank and the livery barn, an elderly man in a black linen suit stepped into the street with a little girl beside him. In the midst of the deathlike stillness he called out in loud voice from twenty yards away, "What in the world is going on there?"

Get back, Mister Mertz! Sheriff Petty wanted to yell the words aloud, but before he could find his voice, Bobby McLawry, his nerves tingling raw and tight, spun in place, drew his pistol, and shot the man down. The little girl jumped back and screamed, her tiny hands covering her mouth as her grandfather struggled to right himself in the dust with his hand clasped against the bullet graze on his forearm.

Behind Billy Lee, from inside the bank, Curtis Roundtree heard the shot and saw what was coming next. "Dang it, Billy!" He reached out, wrapped a thick arm around

Billy Lee's neck and jerked him back inside the bank. Then the world exploded.

"Get him, men!" JC flung himself sideways out of his saddle as the Ranger's first round sliced a glancing wound along his ribs. The Ranger had to turn from JC and put his next shot through Thompson's heart as Thompson's pistol exploded toward him. Across the street, the big double-barrel bucked once in Sheriff Petty's hands, picking up a gunman and hurling him forward through the hitching rail, snapping it in half.

From the broken rail, Lawrence Shaw's big buckskin reared high, slinging half the rail still wrapped by its reins. Bobby McLawry ducked as the broken rail whistled past his head. Then he came up aiming at the Ranger. His shots would have been deadly and true had it not been for the second blast of Sheriff Petty's double-barrel hitting him and another man from behind. The other gunman took the worst of the blast, his chest spilling forward from the rest of his body and splattering in JC McLawry's face. Bobby went down with his back bloody, but came up searching for the Ranger with his raised pistol. "Damn it, boys, get him! Where is he?" He wiped gore from his eyes, looking all around.

In the bank, Curtis shoved Billy Lee to

the back door. "Get out of here! Now! While they're killing each other!"

"Lord, Curtis, what have I done?" Billy Lee's voice trembled. Tears welled in his eyes. He clung to Curtis's shirt. "I've gone and made the most god-awful mistake of my life!"

"But you're still alive, dang it! Get on out of here! Don't look back, don't stop! Don't ever stop!"

"Curtis, this ain't me! This ain't what I wanted at all!" Billy Lee stepped wide of the large circle of blood beneath Joe Chaney's body. Outside the shooting resounded; in the midst of it the little girl screamed.

"It's you now, Billy Lee! Get out of here!" He shoved him once more, then turned toward the sound of the little girl's screams and raced across the floor, out into the street, as Billy Lee snapped out of it and ran to the back door of the bank. Behind JC and Bobby McLawry, Lorio Sanchez, Bryce, and Turk had managed to back and fling themselves atop their horses, spurring them toward the north trail out of town. Curtis saw the pounding hooves headed straight for Mertz and his granddaughter.

"Noooo!" Curtis Roundtree yelled loud and, hurling himself out off the boardwalk and across the old man and the little girl as a bullet from Lorio Sanchez's pistol hit him high in the back. Curtis let out a tortured grunt, but with his big arms spread wide, he hugged both the girl and the man to his chest. "Don't you worry . . . little darling," he said, his voice straining against the pain in his wounded back. "Ole Curtis . . . won't let them . . . bullets hit you —" His words went unfinished as he slumped forward, covering her and her wounded grandfather, feeling another bullet hit him like the blow of a hammer at the base of his skull.

CHAPTER 24

In the street, JC McLawry had gone down with a bullet in his side. But he struggled forward in the dirt, his fingertip scratching toward a smoking pistol. The Ranger stood with a hand pressed to his wounded hip. He leveled his big pistol on JC's back and let the hammer fall. But the hammer only clicked on an empty chamber. Somehow in the melee, Bobby McLawry had managed to grab the reins to Lawrence Shaw's big buckskin and throw himself atop it. Now, seeing the Ranger's pistol was empty, he bolted the horse toward his wounded brother. "JC! Grab on!" His arm reached down for JC McLawry as the horse swept past him.

The Ranger struggled forward, blood pouring from his wounded hip. He dropped his empty pistol and snatched Lawrence Shaw's pistol from his waist. But his blood-slick hand couldn't get a grip on the smooth bone handles, and the pistol fell to the boardwalk and bounced down into the dirt. Bobby saw it as he lifted JC upward by his forearm. "Hurry, JC! Let's go!"

JC came up to his feet, but instead of climbing up behind his brother in the saddle, he gave a hard yank on Bobby's forearm and slung him down to the ground. "Sorry, brother!" As Bobby hit the dirt, JC stepped onto his back, using him to get atop the big buckskin. He kicked the horse's sides as the Ranger leaped forward for the pistol that had slipped from his hand.

My God, JC . . . ! Bobby caught a glimpse of his brother abandoning him, but he had no time to think about it right then. He snatched up Lawrence Shaw's bloody pistol from the dirt just as the Ranger made a reach for it. Bobby cocked it. And as the Ranger jerked to a halt, Bobby raised up with the tip of the barrel only inches from the Ranger's face. With his left hand he grabbed the Ranger by his shirt and held him at arm's length. "So long, you law-dog son of a — !"

"Don't shoot!" Sheriff Martin Petty cried out, his words emphasized by the sound of a shotgun hammer cocking as he moved closer from across the street. "Or I'll cut you in half, Bobby McLawry! So help me

God I will!"

Bobby McLawry heard the sheriff's boots step closer across the dirt, but he kept his eyes on the Ranger's. "It's decision time, Bobby," the Ranger said, his eyes and voice unwavering as the pistol barrel loomed in his face. "Pull the trigger . . . let's die together." With Bobby's hand still clutching his shirt, he took a step closer, his teeth clenched in defiance.

Bobby McLawry sweated, took half step back. "Petty, you're empty," he called over his shoulder. "I heard both shots! You haven't had time to reload! You're bluffing!"

Petty's hands trembled. He swallowed a knot in his throat and prayed his voice wouldn't betray him. "Pull the trigger and you'll find out, Bobby."

"I'm warning you, Sheriff, I won't be bluffed! I'll kill him, then you! Do you hear me? I know that shotgun's empty!"

Before Petty could answer, the Ranger took another step closer and said to Bobby in a whisper, "Pull the trigger and let's find out." He winked. *Winked . . . ?*

Bobby shoved him away from him and rubbed his sweaty hand up and down his thigh as if suddenly realizing he'd been holding something no one should touch. "You're crazy! Damn you to hell!" He leveled the pistol, his knuckles turning white as he tightened his grip on the trigger with determination. The Ranger smiled, stepping closer toward the pointed pistol barrel. "I'll kill you, Ranger! You're dead!"

But the Ranger saw his gun hand tremble. Bobby swung the pistol halfway toward Petty, then stopped and swung it back on the Ranger. He was coming apart and the Ranger saw it. "What about it, Bobby? You going to do anything with that pistol or not?"

"Damn you!" Bobby's eyes filled with tears, his voice cracked. "I want out of this!" He swung the pistol back and forth between them again. "Let me go! Let me out!"

"Can't do it, Bobby," the Ranger whispered, stepping close. His hand went palm up. "Either use the gun or give it up. That's all you get today."

"I'm warning you!" Bobby jerked back a step, leveled the pistol on the Ranger's chest once more.

"Pull the trigger, then. It's your only chance. Let Petty cut you down in the street. Get it over with. You were going to hang anyway." He shrugged. "What's the difference? Today, or a month from now? Will you trade today for another month, Bobby?"

"Shut up!" Bobby McLawry's mind swirled. He stepped back. He turned the pistol to his own head. Then he swung it toward Petty, then back toward the Ranger. "All right, then! To hell with it!" He squeezed the trigger and let the hammer fall. Then his face went chalk white as his gun also only clicked on an empty chamber. "Well, hell. . . ." His voice whined. He'd started to pull the trigger again when the blast of a shotgun echoed along the street and the impact of it nailed him to the ground and splattered blood on the Ranger's face.

Sheriff Petty stood stone still, his empty shotgun in his wet, trembling hands. Both he and the Ranger looked up at the sound of a second hammer cocking — and saw Lawrence Shaw standing on the boardwalk, a large circle of blood on his wounded shoulder, one loose handcuff hanging from his wrist, a gray curl of smoke lingering around the tip of the bartender's scatter-gun.

The Ranger's breath drew tight in his chest as Lawrence Shaw turned toward him as though in a trance and pointing the scatter-gun at his chest. "Put it down, Lawrence," the Ranger said in a level tone, seeing the glazed look in Shaw's eyes. He wondered for an instant if Shaw even heard him. "The killing's over."

He saw Shaw's hand tighten around the stock of the smoking shotgun. "It's . . . hard," Shaw said in a struggling voice.

"I know. But you've got to do it. Put it down. Put it down now and walk away. You'll be through killing for the rest of your life. That's what you want? Isn't it?"

"I — I can't," Shaw said. Once again his hand tightened on the shotgun.

Sheriff Petty called out, "Put it down, mister. Or I'll blow you to hell."

"Easy, Petty," the Ranger cautioned, raising a hand toward him as he kept his eyes on Lawrence Shaw. "He didn't mean it, Lawrence. He's just worried. But he's not going to shoot you, I promise. Now put the gun down. I saw what you did to your pistol. That little trick — putting one bullet in it and spinning it. I've been there myself, betting fate five to one that the next man you face will be the one meant to kill you."

Lawrence Shaw's cocked to one side, a strange expression coming into his cold glazed eyes. "It . . . was meant for you, Ranger. One way or the other . . . I wanted an end to it."

"But as you see, Lawrence, it wasn't meant for me to kill you. It wasn't meant for you to kill me. Fate lays still and doesn't do a thing without man's hand moving it along. We both get to live . . . for today, anyway. Put the gun down."

Shaw backed a step as the Ranger moved closer. "I mean it, Ranger. I want out."

"Then you are out, Lawrence. Put the gun down and leave it down." He gestured his bloody hand toward the carnage in the dirt street, at hollow dead and flesh and exposed bone, unloving and unfeeling no different than the blood-soaked dirt. "You don't have to live like this anymore. Don't make it end for you the way it ended for Bobby. He couldn't get out. You can." As the Ranger spoke, he limped forward with his hand pressed to his bleeding hip and stepped up onto the boardwalk.

As the Ranger reached out and gently tugged at the scattergun in Lawrence Shaw's hand, Shaw looked out across the bodies strewn about in the street, then looked back at him with a questioning gaze as the gun slipped from his hand to the Ranger's.

The Ranger let the hammer down on the scattergun and stepped down off the board-walk, picking Shaw's pistol out of the gore in the street.

A silence passed, and seeing that it was over, Sheriff Petty shook like a man with a terrible fever, bowing forward at the waist and retched a stomach full of fear and soured coffee into the dust at his feet. The Ranger pitched Shaw's pistol up to him. "JC McLawry left town on your buckskin. If you're wise, you'll stay here, let me track him down and bring your horse back."

Shaw thought about it, checking the bloody pistol in his hand. "I can't ask you to do that for me, Ranger. Besides, you're wounded. I'll get my horse back . . . then I'll put this gun down forever."

"You can always find another good reason to keep living by the gun if you want to, Shaw. But getting out starts right here, right now. Every fool wants out when they're losing." His eyes moved across the chewed-up remains of Bobby McLawry. Then he added to Lawrence Shaw in a somber voice, "Stop it here, while you've got the choice . . . while you're still alive and ahead of the game."

They sat, gathered in the back room of the old doctor's office like ragged birds cast out of the wake of some terrible passing storm. It had taken both the Ranger with his wounded hip and Lawrence Shaw with his shoulder wound to pry Curtis Roundtree's arms from around Odell Mertz and his granddaughter and bring all three of them here. Once the others were inside the doctor's office, Lawrence Shaw had picked up a roll of gauze and a small bottle of alcohol for his shoulder and left. Now, as the doctor dressed the graze on Mertz's arm, Curtis Roundtree stirred on the surgery table and lifted a languid sidelong glance to the Ranger. "Is she . . . ?"

"She's fine, Curtis," the Ranger said, adjusting himself on the wooden chair. The thick bandage on his hip was all that made it possible for him to sit. "Lay still and get some rest."

Odell Mertz peeked around the doctor's side at the sound of Curtis's voice. Beside Mertz, Carl the teller stood with a wet rag pressed to his head. "Is that man coming around?" Mertz asked. "Because if he is, I have a thing or two to say to him."

Curtis Roundtree collapsed with the pain throbbing beneath the bandage on the back of his head. "Mister . . . whatever you've got to ask me, I ain't answering. I'll explain everything to a judge and nobody else."

The Ranger smiled. "Curtis, it's the town banker. You saved him and the little girl. I don't think he wants to speak ill of you."

"Indeed not!" Mertz's eyes drew open wide. "I shudder to think what would have happened had you not come charging out in a hail of gunfire! You are a hero, sir!"

"I'm . . . no hero." Curtis struggled with his words. "I couldn't just stand there and let a child get hurt. I'm just a no-account rounder . . . but danged if I could live with myself, letting something like that happen."

Mertz looked at Curtis Roundtree for a second, then back to the Ranger. "And Carl here says this is one of the men you took prisoner here a few days back?"

"Yes, I did. But Curtis wasn't found guilty of anything. He'd gotten into a brawl with a couple of teamsters and smacked them around pretty good with a turning pole."

"Oh." Mertz thought for a second, then said to Curtis Roundtree, "Well, then, good for you, sir. I'm sure they asked for it." He looped an arm out and drew his granddaughter to his side. "See, darling, the nice man is going to be all right after all."

"Doctor?" Curtis asked, raising up on his elbows. "How bad is this wound in my back?"

"Bad enough to kill you graveyard dead if you don't lay down and shut the hell up," the doctor replied, shoving Curtis down with a firm hand. He swept past Curtis, stirring a packet of powder into a glass of water. "You're lucky that bullet at the base of your skull didn't blow your fool head off instead of ricocheting. I have never seen anything like it!"

"Us Roundtrees all have thick heads, Doctor, it's a family trait."

"Yes? Well that's certainly something to be proud of, I suppose." The doctor handed the water glass to Sheriff Petty. "Hear, drink this, maybe it'll stop you heaving your guts up." He pointed a finger. "You're the one who's going to mop up the waiting room, you know."

"I'm sorry, Doc," Sheriff Petty said. He turned to the Ranger, wiping a wet towel across his flushed face. "Ranger . . . is this normal. How long will it last?" He took a drink from the water glass and seemed to have a hard time swallowing it.

"Yeah, it's normal the first time, Sheriff. It'll stop when you quit thinking so much about it."

"I doubt I'll stop thinking about it, Ranger." Sheriff Petty looked away and forced himself to take another drink. "I don't think I'm cut out for this work."

"You did fine, Sheriff. There'd be something wrong with you if it didn't bother you some. You proved to yourself that you can handle the job."

"But . . ." Sheriff Petty turned back to him, lowering his voice so just the two of them could hear. "That was this time. I don't think I could go through something like that again."

"Yes, you will when you have to. And each time you'll ask yourself if you can ever do it again. Each time you'll say you can't . . . but you will."

Petty moved even closer, his face only inches from the Ranger's. "Is that how it is with you? Tell me the truth. Does it feel this way to you each time?"

The Ranger stood up without answering and tested the strength in his wounded hip before moving forward. "I've got to get on. JC is headed for the border if my hunch is right."

"Answer me, please," Petty said. "I heard how you told Bobby McLawry to go ahead and pull that trigger. I heard you tell Lawrence Shaw you knew he'd put one bullet in his gun and spun it. You said you'd done the same thing in the past, before facing a gunfight. Was that true?"

"It helped Shaw get his mind in order," the Ranger said. "That's all I wanted."

"But how did you know he'd done that . . . unless you'd heard of it or done it yourself?"

"I just took a guess, Sheriff, okay?" The Ranger smiled wearily and picked up his sombrero.

"No," Petty said, following him to the door. "That's not okay. That's not good enough. If you did something like that, then you'd have to be as crazy as I've heard people say you are. Tell me something here, Ranger. What does this work do to a man? I need to know!"

The Ranger opened the door and stopped with his hand on the knob. "Crazy, huh?" He considered it for a second. "Any crazier than a man making a life-or-death stand with an empty shotgun?" He watched Petty wince and take a deep breath as he continued. "Bobby was right, Sheriff. I heard both barrels fire, too. You had no time to reload. You were standing there empty-handed facing a desperate killer."

"I had no choice, Ranger. It happened so fast. He meant to gun you down. What else could I do?"

"Oh, I'm not judging you wrong, Sheriff. You saved my life doing it. All I'm saying is that crazy is in the eye of the beholder. Crazy is the version you get from the person who's never been there. The rest of us never have time to think about it." He stepped into the sunlight and looked at the blood-stain on the dirt street, where the townspeople had gathered now with brooms and rakes to put the street right once more. "Ask

Curtis Roundtree, he'll tell you the same thing." He limped off along the dirt street, a hot breeze licking at his shirt.

On his way across the street, the Ranger saw Lawrence Shaw coming toward him on the roan horse Curtis Roundtree had ridden into town on. He stopped and waited until Shaw brought the horse to a stop beside him. Then the Ranger squinted up at Shaw in the sun's glare. "Lawrence . . . ?"

"Don't worry, Ranger. I'm not going after JC McLawry." He patted the roan's neck. "If I was, do you think I'd be riding this barn plug?"

"No, I suppose not." The Ranger patted the roan's muzzle and noted that Shaw's pistol belt was not around his waist but rather looped over his left shoulder, the big pistol hanging by its trigger guard in front of his heart.

"I won't be coming back," Shaw said. "Once you finish with JC, you can keep the buckskin. I won't be needing that kind of horse from now on. It wouldn't be fair, forcing him to settle down just because I am. He'll want to keep a hoof in the game."

"I've already got that kind of horse myself," the Ranger replied, "but I'll see he ends up where he should." The Ranger dropped his hand from the roan's muzzle.

"For what it's worth, Lawrence, I'm glad you and me didn't have to kill one another."

"Me too, Ranger. You and I have lived in a different place than these others. For some reason that makes us kin."

"Yeah. . . ." The Ranger considered it. "I don't know how, but you're right, it does. They all saw us as being at a place they could never quite get to." He glanced at the dark pools of blood on the dirt street as brooms worked busily to cover them over with dust.

"Think that's what always kept us alive?" Shaw asked, but the Ranger could tell he already knew the answer. So he only shrugged. "Where are you headed, Lawrence? If you don't mind me asking."

Lawrence Shaw smiled, a tired smile but one that was free and unguarded for the first time since he could remember. "No, I don't mind you asking at all, Ranger. There's a woman down in Mexico. She asked me to stay with her . . . but it bothered me that she only wanted me around because I could protect her village." He nodded as he spoke. "Now that I've given it some thought, hell, I'm lucky she wants me around at all. So what if my reputation brings her and her people protection?"

"I understand, Lawrence." The Ranger

lowered his voice, as if excluding the rest of the world. "People like you and me have to take what's offered. There's too few good things come along in life . . . it'd be terrible to let one slip past, wouldn't it?"

Shaw's eyes narrowed a bit as he nodded. "You've been there, Ranger."

"Been there? I live there, Lawrence." The Ranger returned his smile and stepped back. "You'll still have to watch your back, you know. There are those out there would love to say they killed Fast Larry."

"I've learned to trust something, Ranger. Whatever comes will come. I just want to live for a while without thinking about it all the time."

"Then it will work itself out," the Ranger said, touching a finger to the brim of his sombrero. "Good luck, *mi amigo.*"

He stood and watched the roan move to the middle of the street and kick out into an easy gait. Then he collected his white barb from behind the saloon where the big horse stood sawing its head up and down at him and scraping a hoof in the dirt. "Easy, Black-eye, I'm coming," he said. He picked up the reins as they dangled and thrashed with each toss of the horse's head. Rubbing the horse's wet muzzle, he added, "Don't fret . . . we've still got a little work left to do."

CHAPTER 25

Granddaddy Snake stood on a high crest of rock looking down at the streaming dust as Billy Lee's horse turned off of the north trail and pounded out along a path cutting into a maze of tall jagged rock. He wanted to keep track of Billy Lee, for the time being at least. On foot, the old Indian turned and moved along the high edge, on an elk path that would take less time to reach the flatland than it would take Billy Lee on the serpentine trail below. He smiled to himself, imagining the look on Billy Lee's face when he came face-to-face with him in the middle of the road leading out toward the border.

From his lofty position, Granddaddy Snake stopped short when he saw Dewey Toom leading his limping horse along the trail, destined in the next few moments to come upon Billy Lee at a fork in the trail. Upon recognizing Dewey Toom, the old Indian squatted down against a round boulder and watched with keen interest.

When the two men's paths intersected, Granddaddy smiled to himself again. The tired horse reared up as Billy Lee yanked back hard against the reins, spun the animal down, and drew a pistol from his holster. Granddaddy Snake only shook his head, seeing Dewey Toom drop his reins, startled, and throw his hands into the air, his lips moving rapidly, but Granddaddy Snake was unable to hear his words.

"Aw-my-God, Billy Lee! Don't shoot! It's me, Dewey! I've been trying my damnedest to catch up with everybody. This blasted horse drew up lame on me! I heard shooting! What went on back there?" He nodded toward the distance in the direction of Bentonville.

"You're lying, Dewey. Take that pistol up with two fingers and pitch it to me. If your horse went lame, why didn't you tell somebody?"

"Damn it." Red-faced, without offering an explanation, Dewey Toom lowered his right hand grudgingly, lifted his pistol from his holster, and pitched it up. "Where's JC?" he asked. "Where's all the others?"

"They're all dead, as far as I know." Billy Lee kept his pistol aimed on Dewey Toom. "You chickened out, Dewey! You low cowardly —"

"Now hold on, Billy Lee." Dewey Toom kept his hands high. "All right, maybe I didn't feel just right riding in on this job, knowing that crazy gunslinger was going to be there. But if there was that much trouble in town, what are you doing out here? How come you didn't back JC and the rest?"

Billy Lee eased down and settled his horse. "It wasn't Shaw that caused all the trouble. It was the Ranger. He was there. Said he'd just killed Fast Larry Shaw and was going to kill everybody else. I'm no fool. I saw a way, and took it."

"Well then, see?" Dewey Toom relaxed, tried to offer a sheepish grin. "Maybe you and I was the only two smart ones in the bunch. You can't fault a man for not sticking around and getting himself killed, now, can ya?"

Billy Lee took a deep breath and let it out, lowering his pistol. "No, I suppose not. But it doesn't matter. I'm headed out of here, to Mexico. I'm through with the Blue Stars." His hand went to the swollen spot on his neck. "Wished I'd never got this damn thing. Now I'm stuck with it wherever I go."

"I know what you mean. I've been thinking the same thing." Dewey Toom looked all around the high walls of the rock land.

"Think you can put me up . . . until I can get somewhere and steal me a horse?"

"Why should I?" Billy Lee only stared at him.

"Because it's rough country 'twixt here and where you're going. The *federales* have a price on the head of anybody who's wearing a blue star tattoo. If you think you don't need a partner to watch your back . . . just say so and ride on." Even as he spoke, he thought of the pistol shoved down in the back of his belt. If Billy Lee rode on, Dewey Toom fully intended to drop him from behind. To hell with Billy Lee. Dewey Toom wasn't about to let this horse get away from him. His own horse really had come up lame, but only after he'd slipped away from the gang on their way to town.

Billy Lee thought about it for a second. "All right, Dewey. You've got a ride with me, until we get you a horse somewhere. But if we run into trouble and you turn tail and leave me, I swear I'll kill you if it's the last thing I ever do."

"You don't have to worry about that, Billy Lee. If I side with a man, I side him, come hell or high water."

"Yeah, I've seen how that works. So far I haven't seen anybody side with anybody when it comes to saving their own hide first." He reached a hand down to Dewey Toom and helped him up onto the horse behind him. "This is most cowardly, double-crossing bunch I've ever seen."

Dewey Toom chuckled. "You've got lots to learn about this outlaw business, if you don't mind me saying so." He settled himself behind Billy Lee, thinking about the pistol in the back of his belt. He couldn't believe Billy Lee would be foolish enough to trust him riding behind him. *Oh, well. . . .* Dewey Toom smiled to himself. But killing Billy Lee could wait for now. He might need this fool between himself and the bounty hunters if the situation came up. "Nobody owes nobody nothing out here. If you were looking for loyalty and honor, you should've joined the Mormons. We're dog-eat-dog outlaws. What did you expect?"

"I don't know, Dewey. Just shut up and watch my back. We've got to get you a horse."

Watch his back? Sure he would. "You're the boss," Billy Lee," Dewey Toom said, feeling the weight of the pistol in his belt behind him, liking the feel of it there.

Seven miles away, looking up from the north trail, Lorio Sanchez caught the flash of gun metal in the sun's glare, forty yards ahead and high up the side of sandy, rocky slope. When he drew his horse down instinctively, Bryce and Turk did the same on the trail behind him. He looked back at them as they pressed close into the shade and cover of rock crevices. "Get up here," he hissed. "Whoever is there will not see us until we go around the next turn." But the two men didn't move forward, so he dropped his horse back to them, stood down from his saddle, and stepped into the cover with them.

"Who do you suppose it is, Sanchez?" Bryce asked, looking up along the line of earth against the glistening sky.

"I do not know," Sanchez said. "But we cannot sit here all day and wonder. Both of you move forward and see who it is!"

Turk and Bryce looked at one another. "Why us two?" Turk asked. "Why not all three of us?"

"Because you need *me* back here to cover you if you come back this way in a hurry." Sanchez spoke, then gazed toward the spot where he'd seen the flash.

"If we come back? Huh-uh. You don't sound too sure, Sanchez." Turk drew back farther into the dark shade and seemed to take position there. "Maybe you better ease up and check it out yourself. Bryce and I have got *you* covered. We threw in with you because we got sick of JC always putting us out front. Now you're trying to do the same damn thing."

"If I am to lead, I must be able to give an order and have it followed." He drew his pistol and cocked it toward them. "If you do not want to obey me, then we will end it here and now!"

"Easy, Lorio!" Turk shied away from facing the big bore of the pistol. "We're just getting used to a new boss. We'll go, won't we, Bryce?"

Bryce spat. "Yeah, we're going. Come on, Turk. Let's get it checked out." They moved away from Sanchez, mounted their horses, and eased forward on the trail.

"Are you thinking what I'm thinking?" Turk asked in a whisper as they moved the horses cautiously closer to the turn in the trail ahead of them. "Why the hell do we keep letting somebody else tell us what to do? Nobody is going to look out for us like we'll look out for ourselves."

"I know it," Bryce answered, letting out a tense breath, keeping a close eye on the steep hillside. "You'd think we'd learn after all this time." He ran a nervous hand along his sweaty neck, over his blue star tattoo.

On the steep hillside, Jack the Spider lay in the sand with his rifle aimed across a deadfall of sun-bleached cedar and waited until the two riders moved closer into range below. In the dark shaded crevice, Lorio Sanchez waited and listened. A hundred yards farther back on the trail, Rance Plum lay behind a rock, guarding any chance of the outlaws' retreat. Now that the three men had ridden past him and deeper into their trap, Plum raised up into a crouch and moved closer, his rifle cocked and held across his chest.

When fire from Jack the Spider's rifle exploded above them, Bryce and Turk spun their horses and bolted back, Turk yelling, "Sanchez, get up here! We've got trouble!" But Sanchez had already heard. He leaped on his horse and kicked it out back along the trail, just in time to see Rance Plum stand up and shoot from twenty yards ahead of him. The shot caught Sanchez high in the chest, sending him backward out of his saddle.

"Sanchez! Tell us something!" Bryce screamed. He and Turk spun their horses at mid-trail in a cloud of dust until a shot from Jack the Spider caught Turk in the center of his back, lifting him out of his saddle and hurling him into Bryce. Bryce's horse reeled and pitched sideways, throwing Bryce to the ground. "Jesus! Sanchez!" Bryce yelled, jerking his pistol up from his holster. "Come get me! I'm down!"

This fool! This poor cowardly fool. Sanchez heard Bryce's plea but could not answer. He lay in the dirt with dark blood pumping out of him at each failing beat of his heart. How could any man lead such trash as this? At first he had thought he could, but he saw now that he'd been wrong. JC McLawry had formed this gang by surrounding himself with his own kind, cutthroats and braggarts, men unworthy to be called *desperados.*

Sanchez cursed JC under his breath and gazed up at the darkening sky above him. Inside his trouser pocket he felt the roll of bills he'd stashed there after the Wakely robbery; gathering all his strength, he managed to pull it out and lay it on his wounded chest. Yes, they will see what I ask of them, he thought. They will take the money, and if they are honorable men, they will not take my head. He gripped the roll of money in his bloody hand.

Honorable men. . . . He thought of the men he'd once ridden with back in Sonora — good men, who stuck together, who thought as one, and fought as one, they used to say.

"Aw, mi amigos. . . ." Lorio Sanchez whispered to those faces he saw now through a

shadowy veil, and as the faces seem to grow nearer to him, his foot twitched once, then turned rigid, then relaxed and dropped sideways to the dirt. The money on his chest fluttered in the hot wind.

"I give up!" Bryce raised his hands high and yelled out to the grainy image of the man moving toward him through the thick dust. Rance Plum's duster tails stood sideways on the wind as he moved forward with caution. "All right?" Bryce looked back and forth from one blurred figure in the dust to the other as Jack the Spider came toward him from the other direction.

"Why, certainly, sir. It's your prerogative to surrender at any time." Rance Plum chuckled, stopping six feet away and pitching the long knife to the ground at Bryce's feet. Bryce looked down at it, swallowed hard and looked back up at Rance Plum's smiling face. "But guess what happens now," Plum said, stepping closer.

The Ranger followed the shoeless hoofprints of the big buckskin JC McLawry was riding, and at the end of the day he made a camp in the higher reaches of the rock land above the north trail. JC had a good three-hour head start on him, but he would make up for it in the high passes. Rather than wait for the first gray light of dawn, the Ranger rode on early while a quarter moon still stood in the sky. Near daylight he came upon the two headless bodies of Bryce and Turk, but he only looked at them for a second before he moved on. Twenty yards farther along the trail he saw the body of Lorio Sanchez, intact save for the damage done by some predators in the passing night.

"Looks like Plum and the Spider forgot one, Black-eye," he said to the white barb, continuing on, following the shoeless buckskin that had passed this way in the night after the dust had settled. He'd seen another set of tracks, but that would be Lawrence Shaw, headed for the border.

At mid morning, with the sun scorching the land, the Ranger stopped at the crest of a rocky path and sat looking down to where the buckskin's prints disappeared into the deep maze of rock terrain. When the sound of a rifle shot from a two-mile distance drew his attention, the Ranger turned toward the echo and traced it back across rise and fall of jagged peaks until he pinpointed its origin. "All right, Black-eye, here we go." He heeled the big barb forward, staying high, keeping an eye down on the path JC had taken on the buckskin.

■ ■ ■ ■

Two miles ahead, Billy Lee sat down on the ground with his smoking rifle lying across his lap while Granddaddy Snake trotted out a few yards into a stretch of brush and dragged the young elk by its hind legs. "Why are you trusting this old fart?" Dewey Toom asked Billy Lee. "Are you forgetting what he did to your head?"

"I haven't forgot nothing. Don't worry about my head. Just keep your mouth shut, Dewey. I also ain't forgot what a weak little coward you were back when the Ranger threw you in the Misery Express. So don't go bringing up memories."

"Damn right I was weak. That's how this game is played. You do what you have to do right at that minute . . . then if that person turns his back on you at just the right time . . ." Dewey grinned. "You're ready to sink a knife in it and go on about your business. My mama didn't raise no fool. We should have put a bullet in that old Injun's eye and kept going, if you ask me."

"I didn't ask you, Dewey," Billy Lee spat at him. "You heard what he said. If he really *can* get rid of this blasted tattoo and stop the infection, I'm all for it."

"It's not infected, Billy Lee. They always look like that the first few days. That Injun just has you worried is all."

"I was already worried. I want this thing off of me."

"It'll leave a scar if he cuts it out."

"Let it. I'd rather have a scar than this any day. The *federales* aren't paying bounty for *scars.*"

Granddaddy Snake dragged the young elk up to Dewey Toom and dropped it at his feet. "Gut it, clean it, build a fire. We'll eat as soon as I finish the ceremony."

"Ceremony, huh." Dewey Toom spat and kicked a boot toe to the dead elk's stomach. "All you're doing is taking off a tattoo. Why does everything got to be a ceremony to you people, like it's a big deal or something?"

"If you have to ask," Granddaddy Snake said, "then you will never know."

"What's that supposed to mean?" Dewey Toom took a step toward him.

"Let it go, Dewey," Billy Lee said, raising up slightly, the rifle in his hand. "Now clean the damned elk like he told you to." Billy Lee settled as Dewey Toom relented. Then Billy Lee said to the old Indian, "All right, Granddaddy, let's get to it. Take this thing off me."

Dewey Toom grumbled but then stepped

back, dragging the elk with him. Maybe this was the best thing, he thought. Let these two get wrapped up in Billy Lee's tattoo, then bang! He would just jerk the pistol from beneath his drooping shirttail, put a bullet through their heads, and ride out of here. Yeah, this was going to work out pretty good.

CHAPTER 26

Lawrence Shaw could not help but look down now and then at the prints left by the big buckskin, but he was not following them. He'd meant what he said to the Ranger. He was not after JC McLawry or anyone else from now on. He loved that buckskin stallion, and the natural thing to do would be to follow those tracks and get it back. It was tempting, yet this was the very temptation that he knew he must struggle against, now and for the rest of his life. Killing JC McLawry would be the simple part.

But if the killing didn't stop now, where would it stop? There would always be the next time . . . some angry face in some dirt street, challenging him, some wrong either real or imagined in some dingy saloon. No, he thought to himself, seeing the hoofprints veer downward onto a different path in the rocks, Fast Larry's trail ended here. From this point on, Lawrence Shaw's trail began.

Beneath him, the roan lifted its muzzle toward things unseen, as if drawn to some scent adrift on a hot stir of breeze. It tugged slightly against the reins. Shaw settled it for a moment. Then he adjusted the holster belt up onto his left shoulder and let the horse beneath him have its way and lead him into the winding walls of stone.

Two hundred yards down the path the buckskin's tracks had turned onto, JC McLawry sat up on a ledge, hidden in the shadows with the rifle from the buckskin's saddle scabbard aimed and cocked. When he saw Shaw take a turn off in the other direction, he slumped and ran his dusty shirtsleeve across his sweaty face. *Good.* . . . His luck was still holding. The Ranger had been bluffing about killing Shaw. Maybe the Ranger bluffed about a lot of things.

See? That was the thing about the Ranger. He never gave you that extra second it took to figure him out. JC knew how the Ranger thought, but when the time came to deal with the man, there was always that split second of doubt, always that final unanswered question that caused a person to hesitate. It wasn't a matter of courage, as Sanchez had said, it was a matter of knowing when to make the first move, and then making it without delay. Well, he knew that now; and he'd remember it the next time their paths crossed. He spat and grinned to himself, lowering the rifle and easing back down to where he'd hitched the buckskin to a short stem of rock.

On the other stone-walled path, Lawrence Shaw sat at ease, letting the reins lay loose in his hands, the roan seeming to know its way. In his mind, he pictured the woman, and the village where she lived. Life would be good there, good and slow and peaceful. Should someone come looking for Fast Larry Shaw, to kill him? Well . . . he'd deal with that problem when and if it ever arose. For a moment he closed his eyes, imagining the woman and the cool, gentle nights that awaited him in Mexico.

But around the bend, Billy Lee jerked upward, hearing the soft click of hoof against stone. He slung Granddaddy Snake to the side and raised the rifle in his hands. Ten feet away, Dewey Toom stood over the pile of mesquite twigs he'd gathered for a fire. His hand had just gone back beneath his shirttail and lifted his pistol, ready to make his move on Billy Lee and the old Indian. When he heard the same sound and saw the rifle come up in Billy Lee's hand, he froze.

"Did you hear it?" Billy Lee whispered, getting a glimpse of the pistol partly hidden down the back of Dewey Toom's leg. Dewey Toom only shrugged, not sure what to do next. Granddaddy Snake stepped back, watching with detached interest. "Well, I heard it," Billy Lee said, his voice louder now as the roan moved into sight on the narrow trail.

At the sound of Billy Lee's voice, the roan bolted forward, Shaw rearing back in the saddle until he caught the reins taut in his hands, righting himself. He saw the three men before him, less than thirty feet away, saw the pistol in Dewey Toom's hand and the rifle in the other man's hand both raised and aimed at him. His first instinct was to reach for the pistol hanging against this chest. But it was too late.

Billy Lee's shot caught him and hurled him backward out of his saddle, slamming him face down in the dirt. Shaw raised his head, struggling for breath. With his arms spread-eagle on the ground, he made no attempt to go for his bone-handled pistol. Instead, he watched the gun come up in Dewey Toom's hand and aim toward his face, Dewey Toom moving closer, looking down at him. "It's Fast Larry! My God, you've killed Fast Larry!" And Lawrence

Shaw's head fell back to the dirt and didn't move.

"I — I didn't know who —" Billy Lee stood up with the rifle hanging from his hand. His left hand went to the wet poultice Granddaddy had pressed to the side of his neck when he'd finished scraping out the dried ink with the tip of a knife.

"Well by-gawd, you killed him bone-dead, whether you knew it or not." Dewey Toom grinned, letting the pistol hang in his hand. There were new possibilities here. He might have to wait and see what this was worth to him. "You're the man who killed Fast Larry! Do you know what that means?"

"Yeah. . . ." Billy Lee stepped to the side and pushed the roan's muzzle away from his shirtsleeve as the horse came forward to probe it. "It means we best get the hell out of here. If he found us out here, so will somebody else." The roan swung its muzzle back and nudged him again. "Get away from me, you half-blind fool!" He shoved it away, more firmly this time.

"The horse is drawn to you," Granddaddy Snake said, taking the roan's reins and pulling it gently away. "I think he loves you."

"Well, I don't love him." Billy Lee stepped back from the roan with his free hand to the wet poultice. "He's been the cause of trouble for me from here to Missouri. Hadn't been for him, I'd never gone to small-time grifting. I ought to put a bullet in his brain, get him out of his misery." He cocked the rifle.

"Wait, don't shoot him," Dewey Toom said. "We're going to need him till we get something better!"

Billy Lee turned to Dewey Toom now, seeming to notice the pistol in his hand for the first time. He swung the rifle toward him and asked, "Where'd that come from? What were you planning to do with it?"

As Billy Lee spoke, Granddaddy Snake walked over to Shaw's body on the ground. He reached out with his toe, nudged the limp right arm and shook his head. "Perhaps Dewey meant to kill you with it, Billy Lee. Perhaps Fast Larry showed up at just the right time. Now that you are the man who shot Fast Larry, you will have to get used to idiots with guns wanting to shoot holes into you." He turned toward them with a wizened grin. "You have gone from grifter, to robber, to gunslinger quicker than anyone I have ever seen."

"Shut up, Injun." Billy Lee kept a cold stare on Dewey Toom.

Dewey Toom sweated and spoke quick. "Okay, to tell the truth, I meant to shoot you, take the horse, and get out of here. You can't blame me." He spread his hands. "But look at it this way. Things have changed! We've got another horse now." He gestured toward Shaw's body on the ground. "And now that you've killed Fast Larry, you really, *really* need somebody to guard your back."

"Maybe so. But I don't *want* nobody knowing I killed him," Billy Lee said, a glancing at Lawrence Shaw's body. Dust already settling on the gunslinger's back.

"Aw, come on, Billy Lee, sure you do." Dewey Toom relaxed a bit and shoved the pistol down into his belt. "Maybe not now, but down the road you will. Think about it. There ain't one man in a million ever gets a chance to do something like you just did."

"I don't have to think about it." He swung toward Granddaddy Snake. "Give me your word, Injun, or I'll leave you face down. Swear to me you'll never tell a soul how this happened."

Granddaddy Snake smiled. "Me? Now why would I do a thing like that?"

Billy Lee saw how the old Indian was only repeating what Billy Lee had said to him back when they were both riding the Misery Express. "Don't play with me, Injun! I still ain't forgot what you did to my head."

"Oh?" Granddaddy Snake gave him a

curious look. "But you have already forgot what I did to your neck?"

"Shoot him, Billy Lee, and let's get going."

Billy Lee glared at Granddaddy Snake until the old Indian nodded. "All right, you have my word. I will tell no one how this happened."

"Come on, Dewey, you take this damned roan . . . keep his nose off my shirtsleeve." Billy Lee took up the reins to his horse, but before stepping up into the stirrup he turned to Granddaddy Snake. "I still don't understand why you met us out here."

Granddaddy Snake's faint smile withered from his face. "Then that is too bad, Billy Lee. It means you have not heard or seen or felt or *understood* anything that has happened to you. I have *always* met you here on this spot, at this time, at this bend in the trail. I always will."

"Crazy old Injun. Can't see why, but I'm gonna miss ya," Billy Lee grumbled under his breath as he mounted his horse. "Don't go eating nobody's lap dog," he called back to him, reining the horse forward.

Dewey Toom had climbed atop the roan and reined it in behind Billy Lee. Now as they moved onto the trail, he had to pull it back as it hurried closer and poked its wet nose out toward Billy Lee's forearm, its weak eyes seeking more the scent and image of the man than the man himself. "Keep the roan back from me, Dewey! Damn it! Don't make me tell you again." Something about the frail and faulty horse disturbed him. He didn't like seeing it. But he was stuck with it, the same way he was stuck with Dewey Toom . . . for the time being at least.

"You got it, Boss," Dewey Toom said, liking the turn things were taking here. Sure, he could put a bullet in Billy Lee's back anytime he felt like it. He'd seen that Billy Lee killing Shaw was nothing but a stroke of blind luck. But when and if he ever did it, he wanted it done in front of witnesses — *Dewey Toom, the man who killed Fast Billy Lee.*

They rode in silence for a few minutes, Billy Lee working things out in his mind, until finally he drew the buckskin up and turned to Dewey Toom and said, "You know, the more I think about it, the more I realize, that really was *something* I did back there, wasn't it?" He nodded back toward the bend in the trail behind them.

"You know it was, Boss," Dewey Toom replied, a shifty smile on his face, "Fast Larry coming in on you, him with his big

427

pistol ready to take you down . . . you ready for him, your rifle coming up steady as a rock. One on one. You dropped him dead, Billy Lee."

"That's how you saw it, huh?" Billy Lee studied his eyes, getting a picture of it that way himself now that he thought about it.

"Yep. I saw the whole thing, don't forget. There's few men will ever want to give you any guff. Like I said — one in a million."

"Yeah, one in a million." Billy Lee's jerked his arm back from the roan's wet muzzle and heeled the big buckskin forward. "I've been thinking, Dewey. To hell with Mexico, let's head down to Texas."

"Sounds like a winner." Dewey Toom rode the roan forward, its nose reaching out in longing toward Billy Lee, still seeking him. "You and me, Boss. I've got you covered. . . ."

No sooner than Billy Lee and Dewey Toom ridden out of sight around the bend in the trail than Granddaddy Snake reached out with his toe once again and nudged Lawrence Shaw in the ribs. "You can quit being dead now, gunslinger. They are gone."

Lawrence Shaw opened an eye, lifted his gaze to the old Indian, then rolled up onto his knees and dusted his front. "Thanks for not saying anything." He ran his right hand over the shattered bone handle on his pistol hanging down his chest. "At first I thought I really was hit — the impact of it." He spat dust from his parched lips and stood the rest of the way up. "The hardest thing I've ever done was laying there just now, doing nothing."

Granddaddy Snake reached out and touched the shattered pistol handle. "Many things went through your mind?"

"You can believe that." Shaw ran his fingers through his matted hair. "Many things, especially my death. The easiest thing would have been to turn and kill both those fools. I had a hard time not doing it."

"Then why didn't you? It would have been justified."

Shaw gave him a flat stare. "You already know why I didn't." A silence passed, then he added, "Anything can be justified. It all depends on what road you're riding. I'm sick of justifying. I just want to live and let live."

"And you heard Billy Lee ask why I met him out here? And what I told him?"

"Yep, I heard the whole thing. I understand it, whether he did or not. What he doesn't know now, he will before it's over. I don't owe him a second thought. Although I *do* owe him my life." Shaw looked around at the sheer rock walls and the thin paths leading out. "All I know is that we need a horse. Any ideas along that line?"

Granddaddy chuckled and nodded off past the steep stone walls. "A stage will run across the flatland from Wakely to Bentonville in the next couple of days. Maybe I will take it, and tell everyone how Billy Lee killed you."

"You gave him your word, old man."

"I promised him I would tell no one what *happened* out here, and I will not. Instead I will tell about how he killed Fast Larry in a blazing gun duel and how later I dragged Fast Larry's body away and buried it in the rocks. That is not what happened, but believe me, after Billy Lee thinks about it, he will want it told that way." He smiled.

"You're probably right," Shaw said. "But I can't take the stage. Now that Fast Larry's dead, I don't want him being seen."

"Then you climb up to the highest path and follow it," Granddaddy Snake said, pointing a finger upward toward a steep ridgeline. "It is hard traveling, but it will take you where you want to go."

When JC McLawry had heard the rifle shot moments ago, he'd spurred the big buckskin and sent it racing along the narrow trail,

430

ever downward, looking back over his shoulder. He had no idea who had fired the shot, but he wasn't going to stick around and find out. It might have been Shaw, it might have been the Ranger. Either way, he wasn't about to head in that direction. Not now. He would head back the way he'd come, get up in the crevices and lay low for a while. His frightened eyes searched back through the swirl of his own dust while the big buckskin pounded on.

At the bottom of the trail, he reined the horse in and turned it sideways, scanning the dust as it settled behind him. Okay, he was far enough away now. He could rest the horse, then move up into the rocks. He breathed deep, took up a canteen from the saddle horn, uncapped it, and took a mouthful of tepid water. He swished it and spat it out in a long brown stream. Then he took another drink and swallowed it. As he drank, he felt the buckskin turn beneath him, facing the middle of the trail once more. "Steady, damn you." JC jerked on the reins to pull the horse back sideways in the trail. But the horse would not budge.

JC kicked its side with his right boot as he yanked on the reins. The horse stood frozen, its head slightly lowered, not even letting out a breath. "Son of a — !" JC's words stopped. The canteen came down slowly in his left hand. In the middle of the trail less than twenty yards ahead, the Ranger stood on the ground with his feet spread shoulder width, his big pistol in his right hand hanging down his side.

The big buckskin faced the Ranger, knowing full well what was required of him when a man stood before him in this manner. He'd been taught to stand, and to stand rigid, as still as a pillar of stone. "Jesus, horse!" In a desperate attempt, JC yanked back once more on the reins, hoping to turn the buckskin and make a run for it — not that he was *afraid* to face the Ranger, *hell no*! Only, not now, not this way, not by surprise! He just wasn't ready for it.

"Step down, JC. I'm taking you back to Bentonville."

"Like hell you are!" JC kicked and tugged and sawed the reins back and forth. Nothing! He dropped the canteen, switched the reins to his left hand, and grabbed for his pistol with his right. The horse blew out a breath but stood otherwise without moving an inch. "Take one step, Ranger, and —" JC's voice stalled on him. His eyes flashed back and forth. And he would what? Damn! There was nothing to bargain with, nothing to threaten, no excuses to make. Beneath him stood a horse so well trained in the art of killing that it was useless for any purpose at this point except to face death with cold, calm deliberation. Why in God's name would anybody want a horse trained like this! He didn't know when to turn and run!

"It's over, JC," the Ranger said, stepping closer. "Why don't you pluck that pistol up easy like and pitch it away. The *horse* has more guts than you do. He knows how to stand and face a fight. He won't move until it's over. If you could've trained your men the way Shaw trained his horse, you might have had something."

"Stay back, Ranger, I'm warning you! You're not getting the edge this time! You not getting me shook . . . you're not gonna cause me to flinch! I'm not going to talk or listen, or let anything you say —"

The Ranger fired on the upswing, then let the pistol drop back down at his side. Before JC got the chance to finish what he had to say, he felt the ground catch him in the palm of its hard, rocky hand, and his breath left him. "That's the best idea you ever had, JC. But you didn't follow through on it . . . coward that you are." When JC hit the ground, the buckskin had taken one well rehearsed step to the side, giving the fallen rider one last clear aim at the person who'd shot him.

"Good job, boy," the Ranger said to the buckskin, reaching out and patting his muzzle, settling him. "But you've got nothing to work with here." He cocked the pistol down in JC McLawry's face, JC still holding the pistol in his trembling hand. Blood spilled from the center of JC's chest. "Either do it or drop it, JC. I won't ask you again." As JC lay with his breath heaving in his shattered chest, the Ranger turned partly to the big buckskin and ran a hand down its neck. "If I didn't already have one just like you I'd sure never let you go."

"Hey! Ranger! Down here . . . damn you! This . . . is not . . . over yet!" JC struggled with his words. He'd managed to get a thumb across the hammer, but couldn't get it cocked back.

"Yes it is, JC. You've been a coward all your life. Don't think anything's going to change now. Bet on the odds. Think about me getting you somewhere and getting you medical treatment." He reached out with his boot and kicked the pistol out of JC's hand.

JC slumped back in the dirt. "All right . . . get me . . . some help!" Even as JC pleaded, his thoughts went to the small derringer inside his right boot.

"See, that's more like it. You pumped your brother's head full of desperado nonsense, got him killed, got all your men killed some way or another." The Ranger leaned down and looked at the gaping chest wound. "You caused nothing but hurt to anybody who's ever came near you. Now it's time to do what any no-good poltroon does — lay still and let somebody save you."

"You don't . . . know me, Ranger. You've . . . never known how I think."

"Is that a fact? Did it ever dawn on you that I never cared one way or another how you *think*? You were never nothing more than another day's work to me, JC McLawry. I'm just glad it ain't raining." The Ranger stood up, holstered his pistol, stepped back, and made a low whistling sound over his shoulder toward a stand of rocks. "Come up, Black-eye," he called out. The white barb stepped out of its cover and trotted forward, stopping a step from the big buckskin. Both stallions blew and stamped their hooves and lowered their ears at one another. "Easy, boys." The Ranger flipped his saddlebags open, took out a small leather case and spread it open on the ground.

"That's right . . . Ranger. I'll . . . do my time. When I . . . get out, nothing's . . .

435

changed." He worked his leg up beneath him, getting his hand closer to his right boot.

"Don't start talking like that, JC. I can change my mind, leave you here to bleed to death." He held up the roll of gauze, and spun off a length of it.

"No . . . you won't, Ranger. I know . . . how you think. You've got to . . . take me back. It's your . . . duty." JC managed a stiff, painful grin. "I'll play the odds on you. It doesn't matter . . . how many I've killed . . . or will kill. They're all . . . faceless and nameless . . . to me."

The Ranger looked down into his eyes. "Are they?" He rolled the gauze back up, put it back into the leather case, closed it and stood up. He dusted his knees, turned to the saddlebags and put the case away. The white barb nosed forward a step toward the big buckskin, and the Ranger pulled it back. The big buckskin came forward, its ears back and its teeth bared. "No way, boys. No fighting among you." The Ranger stepped between them, took the buckskin by its reins and led it off a few feet, dropping the saddle from its back and the bit from its mouth. He pushed it away with his hand and slapped its rump. "Get out of here . . . go find your partner."

"Ranger . . . what about me? You can't just quit! Get me bandaged up," JC spoke up to him from the dirt, his fingertips managing to get down inside the edge of his boot well toward the derringer.

"I'm still thinking about it. After what you said, maybe I'd do better to let you lay here and finish up on your own." The Ranger stood watching the big buckskin as it raced back along the trail leading up to the high ridges. It held its muzzle skyward for a moment as if catching bearings on the hot breeze. "That's it, boy, keep probing, you'll find him. He might not *need* a horse like you anymore . . . but if you're not around, he'll miss you the rest of his life."

"Ranger . . . damn it! You can't leave me here like this." His hand found the butt of the derringer and closed around it, cocking it inside his boot.

"All right, JC." The Ranger had just started to turn and look down at JC when he heard the click of metal on metal. The shot came wild from JC's trembling hand as the Ranger ducked to the side, bringing the big pistol up into play. One shot from Ranger's pistol slammed JC back against the ground as if he'd been driven there by the blow of a sledgehammer. A gush of dark blood rose up from his chest, then his shattered heart slowly stopped beating.

The Ranger sighed and spoke down to the blank eyes staring up at the endless sky. "I knew if I just gave you a minute, you'd save everybody the trouble of fooling with you for the next few years." Then he turned away and stepped up into his saddle. "Take us home, Black-eye." He heeled the white barb and felt it dance forward high-hoofed beneath him. And when he stopped and looked back from fifty yards' distance, he noted how small JC McLawry's body looked here in this dissolute land and its hard walls of stone.

Epilogue

It would be two days before the Ranger rode back into Bentonville. When he did, a few townsfolk turned from whatever they were doing at the time, but cast no more than an idle glance at him as the big white barb cantered the last few yards sidewise down the middle of the street, shaking out its mane and tossing its head left and right. The Ranger patted its neck and settled it at the hitch rail outside the sheriff's office. When he stepped down from his stirrup and stretched, with his hand pressed to the small of his back, Curtis Roundtree called out his name. The Ranger turned and watched the big man come limping toward him on a walking cane, wearing a long leather blacksmith's apron and a sweat rag tied around his broad forehead. "Lord, Ranger, are you all right?" Curtis asked, coming to a halt and resting part of his weight on the cane.

"Well, yes, Curtis." The Ranger looked

himself up and down, curiously. "I'm fine . . . how are you?" Dried blood from his hip wound showed through the Ranger's trousers.

"Aw, I'm getting along." Curtis rubbed a thick hand across the bandage at the base of his skull, then across the bandage on his back. "But I've been worried to death, wondering if you made out okay. Worried about Billy Lee, too, to tell the truth. Did you happen to come across him? I mean — You didn't kill him or nothing, did you?"

"No, Curtis, don't worry, I didn't kill him. But he's on the run now. He won't be the same Billy Lee you've known all this time." He looked Curtis up and down. "Are you working? I mean, should you be? This soon?"

"None of us Roundtrees ever lay up for long. This ain't the worst I've ever had happen to me." He grinned. "Fact is, a lot of good things have come to me in the last couple of days. I saw a move and had to make it. Couldn't let a couple of bullet holes cause me to miss my chance."

"What's that, Curtis?"

"Whoo-ie. I hardly know where to start." He adjusted the wet sweat rag on his forehead. "Mister Mertz was so grateful for me jumping and saving him and his granddaughter, he's put me in the blacksmith business. I feel a little odd doing it, Joe Chancy being dead and all . . . and I sure didn't want nobody thinking I did what I did expecting any reward. But Mister Mertz said I'd be doing him a favor taking the lively barn over. Said he was fixin' to foreclose on it anyhow. Seems Joe wasn't real good about paying his debts — not to speak ill of the deceased."

The Ranger nodded. "Curtis, I'm happy for you. Here's your chance to make something of yourself. I wish you luck."

"Thanks. I'll make it. I ain't never had nothing good happen in my life. I ain't about to let this turn out bad. I even quit drinking — well, a beer now and then maybe. But not until the work's done." He rubbed his parched lips and looked down at the ground. "I'm sorry Billy Lee couldn't stick it out a while longer. We could've been partners. With my sweat and his brains, we'd have done fine at this."

"Well, look at it this way, Billy Lee wanted to be an outlaw, and now he is. You just wanted to get by, now you will. Everything works out one way or another."

"Ain't that the truth. Heck I've already added new business. That stage line owner came through here yesterday, said he always does his shoeing with the blacksmith over in Humbly. I picked him up by the neck and asked what was wrong with doing business here. Turns out he said there wasn't a thing wrong with having his team horses shoed here. So I had him sign a contract. Now I get all that business every other month for now on." He spread his thick hands in an innocent gesture.

The Ranger chuckled. "See, you might just have a knack for this work." He stepped up onto the boardwalk to the sheriff's office.

Curtis called out, "What about this white barb stallion? Want me to check him out?"

"Black-eye won't let you raise his hoof unless I say so, Curtis."

"Aw, that ain't true, is it? You just don't want me to, do you?"

The Ranger thought about it and smiled as he turned the dusty doorknob. "I'll bring him by later. You can shoe my horse anytime."

"Ranger?" Curtis called out to him again and the Ranger turned before opening the door. "I been wanting to ask somebody this. It's true I didn't do what I did because there might be something in it for me. But to be honest, if I had known there would be, it wouldn't been wrong, would it?"

"Curtis, keep it to yourself. You did a good thing, so don't question it. And whatever you do, don't mention it to Odell Mertz." He stepped inside the sheriff's office, closed the door behind himself, and leaned back against it for a moment.

"Well, I'll be," Sheriff Petty said, looking up from a stack of paperwork on his battered desk. He swatted a hand at a circling fly. "I didn't know if you'd come back this way or not."

"Figured you'd want to know the outcome, Sheriff."

"Sure do. I'm just now finishing up a report for the town counsel."

The Ranger remained leaning against the door. "Then you can tell them the Blue Star Gang is finished. I saw them laying in the trail. Bounty hunters got them — all except Dewey Toom. But he wasn't with the gang when they hit town. He must've wised up and left."

"You don't say . . ." Petty leaned back in his chair and took a deep breath. "What about JC McLawry?"

"He's dead. I shot him and left him where he fell."

"Shot him dead, huh?" Petty winced and shook his head.

"I shot him . . . he's dead. Say it that way

in your report."

Petty gave him a curious gaze. "Is there something you're not telling me?"

"Yep," the Ranger answered. Then he said no more.

Petty studied his eyes and nodded slowly. "I understand."

"Billy Lee is still running loose, for the time being," the Ranger added, "but he won't make it far. I don't count him as a gang member. He just got caught up in it."

"Well, then he got caught up in it pretty deep," Petty said, turning the paperwork around and shoving it over to the edge of his desk for the Ranger to see. "Granddaddy Snake came through here yesterday, saying he witnessed Billy Lee kill that crazy gunslinger, Fast Larry Shaw, in a one-on-one shootout."

"What was Granddaddy doing out there?" the Ranger asked with a puzzled look.

"Beats me. I asked him. He just said he had to see what would become of a man who keep threatening to kill him but never followed through on it. Whatever that means."

"I know what it means," the Ranger said, thinking about how Billy Lee and the old Indian had gotten along. "And he said he saw Billy Lee kill Lawrence Shaw?"

"Yep. His exact words were, he saw Billy Lee 'shoot that gunman right out of his saddle.' Can you believe that?" Petty's expression turned skeptical.

"No. . . ." the Ranger let out a breath and pushed up the brim of his grey sombrero. He thought of the big buckskin, seeing it climb upward into the hot breeze as if searching for something along the high trail leading toward the border. "I can't believe it, but I can live with it. Can you? You're the one writing the report."

"Hell, I don't know." Petty considered it and furrowed his brow as if struggling to understand things unsaid. "I haven't been at this long enough to know how the truth works every time. You said you can trust the old Indian's word, didn't you?"

"Yeah, you can trust it . . . once you figure out what he really means by it." The Ranger stepped forward, reached down with a gloved hand, turned the report around without looking at it and nudged it back across the desk. "I've been at this a lifetime, and I still don't know how the truth works every time." A tired faint smile came to his sweat-streaked face. His eyes grew distant as if seeking pieces to puzzles forever lost. "But at the end of the day if a right man lives and the world keeps turning . . . I don't ask for more than that. I've got a feeling that was all Granddaddy Snake was trying to tell you, Sheriff, in his roundabout way."

"Then I'll go with it, I reckon." Sheriff Petty picked up the pen, dipped it into the bottle of ink and righted the paper before him. He looked at the report and sighed. "I swear, I don't know yet if I'm suited to stay at this job."

The Ranger stood quietly, picturing the dead whore and her ghastly image in the shattered looking glass. He pictured the body of Bobby McLawry lying dead in the street, and his brother, JC, the way he'd left him on the dust-swept trail. Lastly, he pictured the Misery Express and imagined how it would come to look if left on the desert floor as an artifact for coming posterity. When they saw it, what questions would they ask? When they examined it, what answers would they find? Out in the street he heard a dog bark and another dog answered. Then he heard both dogs growl in warning as they drew closer to one another in the alley beside the jail. He thought about Maria, waiting for him back in Circle Wells, and of how good it would feel to get back to her and put all of this behind him.

Sheriff Petty sighed once more. "There's so damn much to law work I still don't know." When his hand moved across the bottom of the paper and left his scrawl attesting to the truth as he knew it, the Ranger only nodded and stepped back with his thumb hooked and resting in his belt atop the big pistol.

"But you're learning, Sheriff, you're learning."

ABOUT THE AUTHOR

Blue Star Tattoo, written in 2000 and published as *Misery Express,* was the fifth in the original issue, and is also fifth in the new *Ranger Sam Burrack* series of Western Classics, written by national best-selling author **Ralph Cotton.** These very popular novels are also known as the *Big Iron Series.* Ralph has achieved notable success with the publication and sales of over fifty novels; most have been or are on the *New York Times* Bestseller List.

Ralph lives on the Florida Gulf Coast with his wife Mary Lynn. He writes prodigiously and his books remain top sellers in the Western and Civil War/Western genres. Ralph enjoys painting, photography, sailing and playing guitar. His imagination is comfortable building characters and working with events in the past, but he reaches to the present and future to find the best way to present them.

The Western Classic series of novels introduces Ralph Cotton to a new generation of readers who will enjoy them for the first time, and find pleasure in re-reading them for years to come.

CPSIA information can be obtained
at www.ICGtesting.com
Printed in the USA
FFOW03n0330140617
36722FF